Murder Most Persuasive

An Eliza Darcy Mystery

JESSICA BERG

Murder Most Persuasive
Red Adept Publishing, LLC
104 Bugenfield Court
Garner, NC 27529
https://RedAdeptPublishing.com/

---

1.   http://StreetlightGraphics.com

Chapter One
Murder Comes to Lambton

Darcy, Adelaide Rose, and I have returned from spending an afternoon in Sydney Gardens, and while it has nothing on Pemberley's beauty, I find I can tolerate Bath well, knowing Sydney Gardens is nearby. My dearest daughter enjoys tottering in the green grass and has, on occasion, been the bane of several butterflies. Fortunately for them, their wings are quicker than her tiny fingers. Tomorrow, I plan on tackling the labyrinth, and I hope to take in the garden with my beloved Darcy at night, when lanterns and candles hanging from the trees illuminate the dark. A more romantic spot, I cannot imagine.
Lizzy Bennet Darcy
Bath 1814

The last of the caravan of Range Rovers and BMWs hooked a left at the end of the Pemberley estate driveway and disappeared into the bright autumn morning.

Despite having to shield her eyes from the intense sun, Eliza wrapped her blue-and-green-checked shawl tighter around her shoulders to keep the breath of the chilly morning from sliding over her skin. "Well, that went swimmingly."

"Swimmingly? That was bloody smashing." Joy Bingley brushed a tendril of blond hair from her face and rubbed her forefinger against her thumb. "With the amount of money those fancy blokes spent on their 'business retreat,' we could all go on holiday to Bora Bora."

For three seconds, Eliza entertained the idea of in-the-ocean bungalows, turquoise water, pink drinks with matching pink umbrellas, and her naked toes playing footsie with her boyfriend's naked toes. Perhaps it was longer, but she didn't need Great-Aunt Iris's grand harrumph from behind her to burst her vacation-with-Heath-Tilney bubble.

Every cent made over the weekend hosting and entertaining CEOs from some of the top Fortune 500 companies would be plinked and plunked like pennies into Pemberley's coffers, which had been depleted thanks to the embezzling schemes of Nancy Darcy, now Uncle Fitzwilliam's ex-wife. Not that breaking that bond had been too painful. Details were fuzzy, but a bottle of champagne or two was used by Eliza, Joy, and Great-Aunt Iris to celebrate the "taking out of the rubbish," as Great-Aunt Iris referred to it.

"I don't know about you two, but standing here staring at an empty driveway is doolally. I'll order tea." Great-Aunt Iris rested a papery-skinned hand on Eliza's forearm. "You did well, my dear. Very well, indeed." After a three-point turn, she waddled through the massive oak front doors, her briefcase-size purse bumping against her hip at every step. Caesar, Eliza's orange Maine coon cat, followed closely, swatting and biting at a long piece of yarn trailing from Great-Aunt Iris's purse.

All that was missing was Heath pointing out the obvious, that Great-Aunt Iris's emerald-green velour tracksuit, a new style she was "trying out," didn't quite go with her newly purchased purse the color of an orange popsicle.

Joy squeezed Eliza's hand. "Take five, and I'll make sure tea's ready. And a glass of sherry. I'm sure Uncle Fitzwilliam won't mind us taking a tipple or two. Don't take too long, though. I can't fight Great-Aunt Iris off the raspberry cream scones Cook made for breakfast for long."

Eliza waited until the double oak doors swung quietly on their hinges and clicked with surprising stealth for their size before she descended the ancient stone steps and ambled along the stone pathway that meandered throughout the redbrick-walled courtyard. Unlike when she'd first arrived in June, the climbing ivy no longer gleamed with green finery. Instead, fiery in its crimson glory, the ivy whispered and shivered against the stone with every little breeze.

She gave the lavender-ringed fountain in the middle of the courtyard a large berth. Even though months had gone by since a dead man's body had floated in its waters, Eliza couldn't bring herself to sit upon its edge and trail her fingers through its clear, cold water. Looking at it often brought on a case of goose bumps, and the crisp fall morning had already riddled her skin with the pesky things.

Her phone rang, and she smiled as Belle's name popped up on her screen. "Hey, Belle."

"How did your first fancy shindig go?" On the words "fancy" and "shindig," Belle mimicked the haughty accents she'd learned via binge-watching *Downton Abbey*.

Eliza snorted. "Better than your English accent. Seriously, though, it went well. I think I might be able to pull this off."

"Of course you can—No, Mary, the yellow roses are for the Hendersons' golden anniversary, and remember, she was very clear in her hatred of baby's breath. I don't know if someone might be allergic to it. Ask Brittany. She seems to know everything." Belle huffed. "Sorry about that. Business is booming, and I've got a girl out sick today, so we're all running around like headless chickens. How's Heath? Bet you miss him."

You have no idea. "He's in archeologist paradise and happily digging in the dirt. He'll be back soon, so that's getting me through."

A bell tinkled through the phone. "Oh, shoot. Sorry, but I gotta go. Baby's Breath Hater is here, and Mary isn't done with the order."

"Good luck." After Belle hung up, Eliza stood staring at her phone. She'd known that permanently moving to England would be hard, but at times like this, when she really needed her best friend, her decision wrenched her heart. Eliza leaned her back against the red brick of the courtyard's arching entrance and gazed at the Georgian mansion. It felt like eons ago that she'd pulled into the drive and seen the mansion for the first time.

Built like a gourmet cupcake, the honey-butter stone edifice rose three stories high until ancient Greek friezes, carved rosettes, and vertical triglyphs added texture and embellishment before being topped off with a white cornice the color of whipped cream.

Despite the massiveness of the building with its hundred glinting white-framed sash windows, which was so different from her humble apartment with a grand total of six windows in Sioux Falls, South Dakota, she had connected with the sprawling mansion. Even treading the stone steps up to the main entrance for the first time, she had known her namesake's feet had trod them as well. Then, Eliza had been little more than a stranger to the estate and its people.

But four months later, she knew the truth. Despite the pain of moving from everything she had known and loved, she had made the right choice. Pemberley was her estate, those were her people, and she would do anything to protect the estate and secure it for the next generations. Her cheeks warmed with pride, and she pressed the backs of her chilled hands against them. Great-Aunt Iris was right. Eliza had done well over the weekend. And if she had to give up every weekend for the next several years to undo Nancy's corruption, she would.

Her phone pinged with a kissy sound. *Heath!* She ripped her phone from the back pocket of her pants, ignored the dozen unread texts, and gazed at Heath's picture in the upper corner of their text exchange. Their last discussion had ended with several *x*'s and *o*'s from both, and Eliza hoped that their hugs and kisses wouldn't have to be over cell service for much longer. If her Heath's-Coming-Home-Countdown was correct, he would be home in less than forty-eight hours. She'd show him a kiss or two then.

Another *ping*.

Breaking her trance, she stopped staring at his profile picture and read his two texts:

I can't explain how much I miss you! Trust me, I've tried. My thumbs do not appreciate my efforts, so I am admitting defeat and my idiocy with the English language.

I may or may not have a surprise for you.

After the first text, Eliza's humming heart slowed to a near flat line as she read the second. She scrunched her nose and tapped out a text. *Care to elaborate?*

Heath: I thought you loved a good mystery.

Eliza: Perhaps I have changed in your two-month absence? Maybe I don't like mysteries anymore.

Heath: What! Whose sidekick will I be? This seems rather unfair. But still, I shall keep my mystery a mystery. Maybe you can figure it out before I reveal it?

Eliza: I am the master. I figure it out, you get to kiss me as much as you want when you get back, and if you figure it out, I get to kiss you as much as I want when you get back.

Heath: That, my love, is what we call a win-win situation. May the best man or woman win.

"Oi," Joy hallooed out the front entrance. "Tea's getting cold, and Great-Aunt Iris is eyeing the last of the scones and promising Caesar his fair share. Leg it."

Eliza waved her phone in the air. "Be right there."

"Quit faffing about with lover boy. Scones are on the line." Joy huffed and turned on a spiky peach-colored heel.

Gotta go, Eliza texted. *Joy's drinking again. Great-Aunt Iris is drooling over the last of the scones, and Caesar may or may not beat us all to them in the end.*

Heath: I told you not to have any adventures while I was gone. :) I want a full report when I get back. I love you!

Eliza: Love you more!

After stashing her phone in her back pocket, Eliza hustled along the pathway, took the front steps two at a time, and entered the grand foyer. The history under her feet and over her head never ceased to amaze her. Knowing the family drama and heartache that preceded her, she studied the tips of her boots barely grazing the gold filigree initials *E* and *F* inlaid in white Calacatta marble. The rest of the marble tiles marched out the length and breadth of the foyer in a geometrical pattern of white and Marquina black marble, the white inlaid with amethyst, jasper, emerald, and sapphire cabochons. When the sun shone in the rounded window atop the grand entrance door, the flooring came alive in a kaleidoscope of rainbows.

Stepping away from the intertwining initials of Elizabeth and Fitzwilliam Darcy, she passed the mahogany staircase curving its ascent from the marble tiles of the ground floor to the first floor and headed down the long hallway that ran the length and two side partitions of Pemberley. From the air, Pemberley resembled an *H* with no legs. Off the hall, carved oak doors opened up to various parlors, the dining room, breakfast room, library, ballroom, and other rooms that had names but no modern-day uses other than showing off Pemberley's knickknacks restored to their original beauty.

Whether or not one took Great-Aunt Iris's rubbish comment to heart, the stench of Nancy's presence still permeated Pemberley, and weekly, Tash, the butler, or the housekeeper, Mrs. Underhill, would haul out another black garbage bag and dump it in the dumpsters at the back gate. Eliza had done her best to rid the house of Nancy's gaudy decor and, with Uncle Fitzwilliam's permission, had dug up and dragged out the traditional Georgian and Regency furnishings, paintings, and decorations.

Eliza's stomach rumbled. Trailing her fingers along the white-paneled walls, she made her way down the hall and to the breakfast room.

***

"Finally." Joy jumped to her feet and poured steaming brown liquid from a silver teapot into a teacup painted with pink and yellow roses. After setting the last scone on a matching rose-embellished plate, she handed both to Eliza. "You might have to fight Great-Aunt Iris for it."

Great-Aunt Iris tsked, sat ramrod straight in her pink-and-gold-damask-upholstered wingback chair, and narrowed her eyes at Joy. "I'll have you know, young lady, that when I was about your age—How old are you?"

"Twenty-six." Joy slid Eliza a glance and grinned.

"When I was about your age, I was taking out Nazi soldiers left and right." She stabbed the air. "Eliza here may have a snappy brain in her head, but two to one says I could take her."

Eliza had once struggled under her aunt's weight when they had been using the tunnels for reconnaissance and her great-aunt needed a boost to spy through a peephole. Even though her aunt looked diminutive, she lacked nothing in grit and tenacity, which would probably win out over Eliza's poor excuses for biceps. She slid her left hand up her right arm, squeezed her flexed bicep, and added *go to the gym* to her to-do list.

Maybe she couldn't take Great-Aunt Iris in a fair fight, but she was quicker. She bit into the last scone, claiming it as hers.

Joy handed her and Great-Aunt Iris a small glass of sherry each. "To a smashing weekend. Cheers!"

They clinked glasses. Great-Aunt Iris downed hers in one gulp, sighed, and held it out for a refill.

Joy slid Eliza a glance and shrugged.

"While you two figure it out, I'll help myself." Great-Aunt Iris toddled to the liquor trolley, white tennis shoes squeaking on the polished hardwood floor, and poured the amber liquid to the brim. She toasted them. "A glass of sherry—"

"Or two." Joy elbowed Eliza in the ribs and earned a glare from Great-Aunt Iris.

"Now, where was I? Ah yes, a glass of sherry a day keeps the doctor away." She downed the second glass and reached for the decanter.

Joy flipped her wrist and woke up her Apple watch. "Now, Great-Aunt Iris, what would the 'dishy' Dr. Hamilton think of you getting sloshed at ten in the morning?"

With a grand harrumph, Great-Aunt Iris set the sherry glass on the trolley and waddled back to her chair, mumbling under her breath something about "young whippersnappers." Neither Eliza nor Joy asked for clarification.

The door opened, and one of the new maids, Willow, a young woman from Lambton, eased her way in and stood in the entrance, her feet fidgeting and her fingers worrying a loose bit of string on her sage-green T-shirt. Eliza, with her uncle's permission, had done away with the traditional servants' uniforms and required only clean and respectful workwear. Tash, Mrs. Underhill, and Mrs. Bankcroft still chose to wear the traditional garb of their trades, which hadn't surprised Eliza in the least.

When the girl didn't speak, Eliza smiled and waved her over. "Yes, Willow, what is it?"

Willow took a few more steps. "I was wondering, Miss Darcy—"

"Remember, it's Eliza. Just plain old Eliza."

"But Mrs. Underhill. She'll... Well, she said—"

Eliza held up a hand to stem the girl's stuttering. "I'll deal with Mrs. Underhill. She's really not that scary once you get to know her." Which wasn't true, but no need to scare the girl spitless.

Willow squinted at her as if Eliza had sprouted a second head. "If you say so."

"I do. Now, what's bothering you?"

"Have you heard the news from the village?"

Eliza shook her head. She'd ignored all the pings and beeps and rings throughout the weekend, so odds were she'd missed quite a few bits of news. "I haven't. The weekend retreat had me up to my eyeballs with events and all that jazz. Why? What have I missed?"

"Probably something juicy." Joy hid a yawn behind her hand.

Eliza pointed at Joy. "How is it that you, Miss Juicy Gossip Girl, are missing out on something?"

"You had your bigwigs, I had my book. And boy, was I on a roll. I don't stop for nothing. When I got to the part where the Marquis of Ravensbrook Abbey begins to ravish the lovely and delectable heroine—"

Great-Aunt Iris sighed, set her elbow on the chair's arm, nestled her chin in her hands, and gazed doe-eyed at Joy.

Joy shook her head. "Anyway, long story short, I turned my mobile off."

"Willow, it seems that you're in the know." Eliza leaned against her great-aunt's chair. "You have a captive audience. Do tell."

The girl's cheeks reddened, matching her flame-colored hair. "Well, there's been... someone..."

"Spit it out, girl. I'm too old to buy green bananas, and I'm certainly too old to sit here waiting for you to tell us this news of yours."

"Great-Aunt Iris," Eliza whispered, "if you scare her too much, she won't come back, and you know as well as I do that good staff are hard to come by these days." She sent the young girl, probably no more than twenty, an apologetic smile. "Go ahead. You were saying? There's been a..."

"Murder," Willow spit out. "There's been a murder."

Willow darted from the room, leaving Eliza, Joy, and Great-Aunt Iris gaping at each other.

Great-Aunt Iris broke the silence first. "She could have at least told us the name of the dead person. Or where they were found. Or why they died."

Joy whipped out her phone and scrolled. "Crikey! The murder happened on Friday night."

Eliza did the same with her phone, and sure enough, several unopened texts from the Lambton friends she'd made over the past months tantalized her with cryptic information about the murder.

Joy shook her phone. "That's the last time I turn my mobile off. I don't care who's getting into whose pants."

A sharp knock echoed through the breakfast room, and Tash opened the door. "Miss Eliza—" He smiled, transforming his craggy face into one etched with laugh lines. "Eliza, Lord Darcy would like to see you in his study."

"Thank you, Tash. I'll be right there."

He nodded regally and shut the door.

"I wonder if he straps a broomstick to his back to create his formidable posture." Joy had many theories about Tash's stoic and austere presence, but the broomstick theory was, by far, the most plausible.

"Possible."

"Yes, yes, that's all well and good, but the murder." Great-Aunt Iris fluttered her hand at Joy's phone. "What does that contraption say?"

Joy cleared her throat. "This 'contraption' says that a murder happened at the Foxed Hound Friday night, and the victim is Felix Payne."

"Who's he?" Eliza asked.

"How should I know?"

Great-Aunt Iris huffed.

Joy ignored her and typed a text. "There, the village gossip queen should know everything. In a few minutes, we'll know more than the police."

"Don't abandon your post. Curious minds want to know." Eliza tapped her temple. "I'll be right back."

"Wild horses couldn't drag me away." Joy clutched her phone to her chest.

"What about a pack of wild men?" Eliza quirked an eyebrow.

"Pfft, I'd make them fall wildly in love with me, and they'd have no choice but to fan me with palm leaves and feed me grapes." Joy wrestled an iPad and Apple pencil from her purse, which was almost the size of Great-Aunt Iris's. "In fact, that puts me to mind of a great storyline for my work in progress, the one I was talking about. A disinherited duchess who, after being on the run for two days, runs into—quite literally—the ne'er-do-well Marquis of Ravensbrook Abbey, who eventually—"

"Don't spoil it," Eliza said dryly.

"Fine. I won't tell you, but there may or may not be a ripped dress involved." She tapped the screen of her iPad. "It's going to be a bestseller."

"Aren't all your books bestsellers?"

"That's beside the point. This is going to be the best of the best of the bestsellers." She shot Eliza a pointed look. "Maybe this time, you'll actually read one of my books."

"As soon as you write a bodice-ripping mystery with Agatha Christie flair, I'll be the first to read it and give it a five-star review."

"Really?"

"Wild horses couldn't make me do otherwise."

Great-Aunt Iris pushed to her feet, her body quivering, her eyes bright. "If you don't mind, girls, I have business with your great-uncle. It's about time he got up anyway. Sleeping away the day like this is simply not done. It's unChristian, that's what it is."

Eliza shuddered at her great-aunt's business. It was no secret, courtesy of the old woman herself, that she and her husband of sixty-plus years, William Darcy, still... Eliza shut her eyes. It didn't seem possible. Shouldn't have been possible. Great-Uncle William, at the ripe old age of ninety, spent the vast majority of his day in their room and didn't even come down for meals anymore.

She shared the not-this-again look with Joy as Great-Aunt Iris toddled from the room, her white tennis shoes squeaking on the hardwood floor.

After a final eye roll, Joy snatched up her white Apple pencil and wrote across the screen.

Eliza took that as her cue, left the breakfast room, and moseyed to her uncle's study for what was surely not as horrendous or as juicy as murder.

ELIZA trailed her finger across the spines of leather books, some old enough to have seen the Battle of Waterloo. The aromas of pipe tobacco, brandy, and old books quieted her thoughts about an unknown man's murder.

Eliza had no right to investigate, and she should, as Detective Chief Inspector Wentworth had told her the last time she inserted herself into a murder investigation, keep her *nose out of police business.* She sniffed. In her room, she had a touristy constable hat proving him wrong. She also had some scars from her encounter with the killer as well, but she had no need to dwell on such negative thoughts.

Everything had settled to normal relatively quickly, as murder and embezzlement were involved. Well, as normal as could be expected after quitting her career as an English teacher, moving across the Atlantic Ocean, taking up her role as future mistress of Pemberley, and working to get the estate back on its financial feet. Add to that Heath's extended absence, and she wasn't sure she could take any more surprises.

"So, you will be in charge of everything until I get back. Tash and Mrs. Underhill will be here to assist you, but I am confident that you will do very well."

Eliza's finger paused on a leather-bound edition of *Lady Chatterley's Lover*. She swallowed, but her dry mouth allowed only a gulp of air.

Uncle Fitzwilliam chuckled. "You didn't hear a word I said, did you?"

"Yes. You are going away for the next few days for a business trip, and you'll be right back."

He scratched at his salt-and-pepper muttonchops and quirked an equally graying eyebrow. Despite the gray speckled throughout his hair, there was a youthfulness about him that had been missing when she first met him. His skin still held its summer's tan, and his hazel eyes twinkled with mischievousness, providing a glimpse of him in his younger, carefree days.

He scrunched up his face and tapped his thumb on his fingers as if working out a difficult math problem. "You are only fifty percent correct."

Following his gesture to sit in a leather wingback chair next to him, Eliza sank into its cushions and slid down, hoping that somewhere, a hole would open up and suck her in. There was a tunnel, after all, so it made sense there would be a trapdoor somewhere in the massive, rambling estate.

"So, what's the half I got wrong?"

"Let us start with what you guessed correctly. I am going away, and I will be back."

"And the wrong part?" Eliza asked.

"It won't be for a few days, it is not a business trip, and I won't be 'right' back."

"That's more than fifty percent wrong."

"I am a generous fellow." He scooted to the edge of his matching leather chair and rested his elbows on his knees. "There's only so much that technology can offer when trying to reconnect with someone. Andrew and I are discovering this truth, so I have made the decision to fly to the States and visit him. Hopefully, meeting face-to-face after all these years can help dissolve the decades of pain we have both suffered."

"Why can't my dad come over here?"

Eliza had bawled when she said goodbye to her parents the day she fulfilled her one-way ticket to England, leaving America for a life across the pond. Her mother had promised to visit soon, but her father had hemmed and hawed, claiming a busy and unknown future schedule. Eliza hadn't pressed the issue, knowing that what had sent her father running from England in the first place—*stupid Nancy*—still haunted his relationship with his brother. But that didn't stop her from rubbing her fingers over her heart in an attempt to dispel the dull ache settling in her chest.

"I think there are too many ghosts here for the first personal reconciliation. So I must go to him. Neutral ground."

"And you don't know when you'll get back?"

"I'm staying until your father and I have worked things out and things are as they were before." He rubbed his hands over his face and inhaled. His broad chest expanded, pushing the buttons on his purple-and-blue Prince of Wales checked shirt to their limits.

Eliza laid a hand over his. "I know. It's okay." She sat up straight and smoothed her hands over her dark skinny jeans, which were a little skinnier than before. *Drat all the teas and signing up to be Mrs. Bankcroft's culinary guinea pig.* "I'll keep things in shipshape and will try not to have too many raves, orgies, or parties while you're gone."

He blinked, and a cheeky grin replaced the firm line of his mouth. "If you can get one or all those over Tash's head, I'll give you my Austin Healey 3000."

Ideas of humanely gagging Tash and locking him away in the attic skittered through her head. Her uncle's sexy scarlet roadster barely made an appearance, but when it did and she was lucky enough to ride shotgun, she squealed with delight and terror as the car hugged England's curvy country roads. She never felt more alive than when zipping along, the world a blur. Unless, of course, she was in Heath's embrace. Then she felt electrified.

She played her index finger over the dimple in her chin.

"Eliza, what is it? If you are worried about the estate, please do not concern yourself. After your efforts and the splendid results of all your hard work this weekend, you have proven yourself capable of anything you put your mind to."

"I've proven that I can host a weekend getaway for a bunch of people who have more money than they know what to do with. It's the day-to-day details that have me questioning my life choices."

"Well, I have to leave in order for all your nefarious plans to come to fruition to earn the roadster." He stood up and poured her a glass of water from a crystal pitcher. "There are too many people in your corner to let you fail, and before you know it, you'll have had your fill of orgies and raves, and no doubt Mr. Tilney will make an appearance soon. Think of all the adventures you will share when I get back."

"You're right. As always. Besides, with Great-Aunt Iris at the helm, what could possibly go wrong?" She sipped the water. "Have you heard about the murder?"

"Yes. Sad business, that." He scratched at his muttonchops. "Felix Payne wasn't always the lowlife criminal he turned out to be."

"You knew him?"

"We were chums once, long ago. His father worked for mine. Felix would come over with his father almost every day during the summer, and we'd tramp around the woods and fish in the stream until it was time for him to leave."

"If you were so close once, what happened?"

"It is complicated. I'm ashamed of my actions and often wish I had done things differently." When Eliza leaned forward in her chair and tilted her head expectantly, he sighed. "I'll say this. I was a classist prig and thought it beneath me to associate with the son of one of my father's gardeners."

"Is that why you don't like to use your title?"

"One of the many reasons. But enough memory lane for one morning. I have last-minute details to work out, and I'm sure you have another 'smashing' weekend to plan."

Eliza pecked her uncle's whiskery cheek and walked to the door.

"Oh, Eliza dear, please, for my sanity, do not go sniffing around the Foxed Hound or, as Wentworth accused you of last time, sticking your nose in police business."

"Who, me?" Eliza mimicked his arched eyebrows. "Point well taken, Uncle, but I promise not to get involved. Besides, I don't even know this man. There would be no point in 'putting my nose in police business' anyway. Between keeping tabs on Great-Aunt Iris and keeping this house from imploding while you're away, I have no time for murder.

Chapter Two
Pemberley Receives a Surprise Guest

While breakfasting on delicious Sally Lunn buns and tea in Sydney Gardens with Darcy, I made a new acquaintance. Miss Anne Elliot is a delightful young woman and doted on Adelaide Rose. I believe she has two rather rambunctious nephews and seems to love and not simply tolerate children. I told Darcy that I would not be sorry to know her better. She is in town visiting her father, Sir Walter Elliot, and one of her sisters, Miss Elizabeth Elliot. According to Darcy, rumor about Bath is that Sir Walter has found himself on the rocks due to profligate spending and has let his estate to an admiral and his wife.

Lizzy Bennet Darcy

Bath 1814

Eliza closed her laptop with something close to a *bang*. The bitten-apple logo at the top glared at her. She rubbed her eyes and looked again. That had only made the glowing fruit angrier. Seeing imaginary angry, glowing fruit was a reasonable sign to go to bed.

The grandfather clock in the corner loudly ticked away the seconds, and Eliza braced for the twelve clangs about to erupt from its wooden breast. It didn't disappoint, and she wondered, as she always had from the moment she'd first heard it months ago, how it managed not to wake up the entire household. But after the clock's last note, the house remained in darkness except for the lights blazing in the sitting room, where everyone had abandoned her hours ago.

A *creak* echoed from the hallway.

Maybe it was the looming threat of having the rambling place under her charge or maybe it was the too-many caffeinated beverages to stimulate her mind to keep working a few hours ago or maybe it was the subconscious thought that a killer was still at large. Whichever "maybe" was to blame, Eliza slammed her hand over her heart, jumped to her feet, and searched the room for a hiding place impervious to ghosts.

After several moments of calculating whether she would fit under the chaise lounge or should risk shutting herself in the wardrobe—a thing she once heard was not a very bright idea—she forced herself to take a deep breath. Ghosts weren't Pemberley's thing. *Yeah, it's not ghosts, but it has a habit of murder.* Hating herself for even thinking that, she shook her head with more force than necessary, hoping to expel the bad vibes to make room for some common sense.

Ice cream. That'll do the trick.

Her new mission accepted, she ambled to the door with studied carelessness and grasped the door handle.

It turned. On its own.

Eliza squelched a squeal and doubled back into the room and knocked her knee on a decorative side table. She gasped a swear word, bent over, and grasped her throbbing knee.

The door creaked open.

Eliza wasn't sure she had any more breath in her lungs to scream or yell or send any vocal signs of distress. What she did have, though, was a china vase decorated with colorful birds of paradise. Grasping the vase's slim neck, she brought it over her head, twirled on her good leg, and tightened her arm muscles to hurl it at the intruder.

"Eliza!"

Eliza's arm stopped midmotion, and the two fingers still remaining around the expensive vase tightened to keep it from slipping from her grasp and shattering on the floor.

"Heath?"

Her heart raced, but she wasn't sure whether that was from the adrenaline pumping through her veins or the love urging her to throw herself into Heath's arms and kiss him. Either way, the man deserved to have something thrown in his face. She set the vase down gently, snatched a throw pillow from the nearest chair, and chucked it at his head.

He caught it and peeked around its lacy edging. His lips twitched. "So, my surprise worked, I see."

"You, you, you—" Eliza sprinted into his arms and squeezed him until he tapped the small of her back.

"Can't breathe."

"Sorry." She loosened her hold and kissed him until he chuckled against her lips. "Now what?"

"Can't breathe." He caressed her lips. "If I knew I'd get this reaction from you every time—"

"Don't even think about it. This is an anomaly, that's all. Besides, maybe I'm punishing you for your ungentlemanlike behavior by purposely trying to suffocate you."

"Ah, who am I to stand in the way of justice?" He held out his arms like a martyr bravely going to his demise. "Lady Justice, have your way."

And she did. Until the clock struck one and they came up for air.

Heath straightened his rumpled dress shirt. "I say, that was the most brilliant suffocating experience yet."

Eliza blew at a stray black curl dangling over her eye. "You've had others?"

"Summer camp of '02 was a harrowing time for all." He shuddered. "It's terrifying what unsupervised ten-year-old boys can get up to."

"Like *Lord of the Flies* terrifying?"

"Not that bad... Although, we did create a bonfire so large that it set a nearby cabin on fire." He reached for her hand. "At least no one died."

Eliza's fingers flexed.

"What is it?"

Eliza wiggled her hand from his, turned off the sitting room lights, and closed the door after them. The hallway, lit only by moonlight streaming in through the windows, glowed eerily. "Speaking of dead, have you heard about the murder at the Foxed Hound?"

"Murder? At the Foxed Hound? The taxi driver was talking about something, but honestly, I wasn't up for a chinwag with the old man. I heard something about a dead man and a pub, and instead of telling him to put a sock in it, I put my earbuds in. Thought that would go over better." After looping her arm in his, he headed to the staircase. "What happened?"

It didn't surprise Eliza that even on a train to Lambton, Heath hadn't heard about the murder. She'd made the mistake of trying to strike up conversations with fellow train passengers, and it wasn't done. She had found no sympathy about that from either Joy or Great-Aunt Iris, women who normally spoke over each other to get an edge on any conversation. They, too, turned mute upon entering a train car.

As Heath and Eliza walked upstairs to her room, she filled him in. "And now you know what I know."

Heath leaned his tall frame up against the doorjamb and opened her door. "Mysterious death, ex-con victim, a killer at large... So what's your game plan?"

"My game plan?"

"Yeah, you know. Where you go in, solve the murder, and rub Detective Chief Inspector Wentworth's face in it?" He reached into her room and flicked on the light switch, illuminating all the tulip-y décor. Eliza had often considered redecorating, but with the estate's depleted coffers, it would be a waste of money, and as it had been her first room upon arriving at Pemberley months earlier, the familiar décor comforted her.

Atop her bed, Caesar glared at them, his slitted eyes reflecting disdain at having his beauty sleep interrupted.

"First of all, I did not rub it in his face the last time. We actually came to a nice understanding." Eliza sat on her bed and scratched Caesar between the ears. His rumbling purrs filled the room. "There's proof right there if you need it."

Heath plucked the souvenir black constable hat off her dresser and tossed it from one hand to the other. "And secondly and thirdly?"

"I have no intentions of involving myself in a murder investigation that has nothing to do with me or Pemberley. This Felix Payne guy means nothing to me. Why get back on Wentworth's blacklist for a stranger?"

"I thought you and he had come to an 'understanding'?"

"Ooh, you're incorrigible."

"I thought that's what you loved about me." A grin foiled his attempt at a pout, and his cornflower-blue eyes twinkled.

Eliza stood and sashayed toward him, enjoying the warmth swirling in her belly as his eyes darkened. "That and other things." She nipped at his lower lip. "I missed you."

"I missed you too." He kissed her, and after a few blissful moments, he pulled away. "So, the sleuthing gang isn't going to reunite for this one?"

She walked him to her door. "You and Great-Aunt Iris can soothe each other's wounded spirits over breakfast tomorrow. Mrs. Underhill made up your usual room several days ago, so be sure to rest up for what will surely be a morning of questions."

After one last good-night kiss, Heath walked down the hall toward what had become his room when he visited. It wasn't as close as Eliza had preferred, but whenever talk circled to Heath's room being only six rooms from Eliza's, Great-Aunt Iris made noises that would make a grand dowager proud. So, six bedrooms it would be until... Eliza's body warmed. No, no sense in putting the cart before the proverbial horse, and if she ever let on that she was thinking about permanent room reassignments so soon, it wouldn't be a horse taking her for a joyride in that very cart back to Singleville. It would be an ass.

Best to keep her mind on rebuilding Pemberley's eaten-away accounts. After sinking into her tulip-adorned bed, she eyed Elizabeth Bennet Darcy's journals tucked nicely on a tabletop bookshelf she'd bought specifically for them. Since ridding the house of thieves and one murderer, Eliza had taken the books from their hiding spot and displayed them as they deserved. She'd devoured her namesake's words until she had almost memorized them. So much life had happened within those very same walls. Elizabeth and Fitzwilliam's legacy didn't deserve to crash and burn all because of Nancy's horridness. *No, come hell or high water... or handsome, incorrigible men... or murders, I will get Pemberley back on her feet.*

ELIZA shaded her eyes against the morning sun as she brought up the rear of the posse as they entered the Trusty Teapot for their habitual Wednesday-morning tea.

As Great-Aunt Iris stepped into the threshold, a hulking man darted out the door. Iris faltered and tripped backward into Eliza's chest.

"I say!" Iris harrumphed, drew herself up to her full five-foot-one-inch frame, and shook her finger at the man's back. "Say, you."

The man's long strides paused. He cocked his head.

"You." Great-Aunt Iris took a step toward him.

The man cocked his head the other way as if trying to decipher where the high-pitched command was coming from.

"What are you doing?" Eliza latched onto her great-aunt's arm.

Iris swiped away Eliza's hand. "Teaching this young man a lesson." She marched down the sidewalk, walked in front of the man, pivoted as quickly as her white tennis shoes would allow, and came toe-to-toe, forehead-to-chest with the stranger.

Heath and Joy, who had entered the tea shop before the kerfuffle, hustled to the duo and joined Eliza.

"Someone ought to box your ears. Did your mother never teach you any manners?" The question was accompanied by Great-Aunt Iris's finger to the man's sternum. "Ah, here's the man to do that boxing for me." She pointed at Heath.

Heath stared at the little old lady and the bulky man-flesh covered in tattoos. "Boxing days are over, I'm afraid, Mrs. Darcy."

Eliza grabbed her great-aunt's hand and held it. "Sorry, sir. She's normally very well behaved but not today, it seems."

"Nah, no worries. My gram was a nutter too." The man's grin revealed a gap as wide as a straw between his two front teeth.

"You... you... cheeky devil, you!" Great-Aunt Iris sputtered, wrestled her hand from Eliza's grip, and stabbed her finger in the direction of a teardrop permanently inked near the man's left eye. "And whoever gave you that is doolally."

"Again, so sorry. We'll be taking her home now." Eliza drew her great-aunt away.

"Oh no you don't. You promised me tea, and tea is what we'll have." With one last queenlike glare at the stranger, Great-Aunt Iris readjusted her purse and waddled to the teashop.

The man's bellowing laughs faded as he stalked along the sidewalk, then they ceased as he turned down an alley.

"That was... interesting." Eliza grinned as she watched her great-aunt march into the Trusty Teapot.

Heath laced his fingers through hers as they walked. "Speak for yourself. Your great- aunt relegated me to a fistfight with that bruiser. And who do you think would've won?"

Eliza paused and palpated his right bicep. Warmth oozed through her veins as his muscles hardened under her fingertips. "You, of course."

"You're delusional." He kissed her right in front of the Trusty Teapot.

A sharp rap on the window startled them. Great-Aunt Iris's breath fogged up the glass, and her beady gaze didn't relent until Heath unlatched his arms from around Eliza.

She sighed and took a step back. "You know who I'm related to, don't you? I think it might run in the family."

"Don't remind me," he whispered and placed his hand on the small of her back as they entered the teashop.

The first time Eliza had stepped into the shop months ago, she had wanted to bottle up the smell and make it into a candle. And as soon as she found out the Trusty Teapot's Wednesday special was Ethiopian spiced tea, Eliza had created a new tradition of Wednesday-morning tea in Lambton, rain or shine. The stress that had her shoulders perpetually by her ears melted off, and she slid into an empty seat across from Joy and Great-Aunt Iris.

Joy faked a punch. "Oi, that man was ready to kick your bloody arse."

Heath held up his hands. "I am informed that I would have won."

Great-Aunt Iris snorted. "Eliza's barmy."

Eliza was saved from replying as their regular server stopped at their table. "Good morning, Monica."

"Good morning, ladies." Monica smiled at Heath. "And gentleman. Back from your dig, are you, then?"

"It's a good thing I'm not MI5 or anything. The entire village of Lambton would know my business and secrets before I did."

"Speaking of secrets"—Monica's brown eyes sparkled mischievously as she squatted and rested her elbows on the white tablecloth—"did you see the man who was just in here?"

Great-Aunt Iris poked at the young woman's elbows until she removed them from the table. "Saw him? He ran over me."

"I'm sorry about that, Mrs. Darcy, but you can be glad that's all he did to you."

"Really?" The old woman's eyes rounded, and she leaned closer, placing her elbows squarely on the table.

"I've heard he recently got out of prison." Monica dropped her voice. "For murder."

"I knew he looked like a bad egg," Great-Aunt Iris said.

"What's he doing here?" Eliza eyed the tea things on the counter behind Monica. Her stomach rumbled.

"His name's Oliver Wright. Apparently, he's got some cousins in town who will tolerate him long enough to give him a bed and throw some food at him occasionally. One of them, Louie, a new bloke, works in the kitchen. Odd fellow, really. Mum says I shouldn't have much to do with him."

"At least someone listens to her elders." Great-Aunt Iris pinned Joy with a glare.

"Who? Me?" Joy clutched her clasped hands to her chest.

"Anyway..." Monica stood. "The manager gave Louie an earful for allowing Oliver in the kitchen, and you should have heard Oliver effing and blinding his way through the dining area."

"Do they think he had anything to do with the murder of Felix Payne?" Eliza asked.

"Folks around here sure think a lot of things, and most don't like the look of him. Not that I can blame them." Monica glanced at the clock on the wall. "Well, look who got to talking your ears off. Getting to be elevenses instead of breakfast."

"I'm up for either. I'm easy." Joy shrugged and studied her cuticles.

Eliza snorted.

Joy slid her a look. "It doesn't mean what your naughty American brain thinks it does."

"Or does it?" Heath grinned.

"Oh, put a sock in it. Just because my characters get all up in each other's bits doesn't mean their creator does. I have standards. I'm a lady."

Great-Aunt Iris raised an imperial eyebrow visible only due to the shaky application of a rust-colored eyebrow pencil. "Let's order tea, shall we?"

After they ordered and Monica left, Eliza tapped her fingernail on the tablecloth. "I wonder if this Oliver guy could be the killer. It'd be a stupid move on his part. He recently got out of prison. Why would he want to go back in? And he looks like he's in his late fifties. He'd be in prison the rest of his life."

"I thought you weren't putting your nose in," Joy said.

"I'm not, I'm just…"

"Putting your nose in," Heath finished for her.

"Aren't you guys curious? He's as good a suspect as any in this village, and if it's true that he just got out of prison for killing someone—which would have to have been manslaughter, or else he'd have life in prison, right?—then why is he roaming around? The police must have another suspect in mind."

"Probably skipped town. That's what I would do if I murdered someone," Great-Aunt Iris said.

"And how would you do that? You can't drive, and they'd have the train stations watched," Joy said.

"You'd drive me, of course. Although your driving is a bit wonky." Great-Aunt Iris tapped her chin and flicked her gaze from Heath to Eliza. "Changed my mind. Eliza's driving me."

"You're forgetting someone," Eliza said.

"No, you drive, Joy rides shotgun, as you call it, and Heath is our muscle to fight off the law."

Heath chuckled and proffered an imaginary hat. "It'll be my pleasure."

Great-Aunt Iris preened.

"And what about Great-Uncle William? Are you going to leave him without a word or any last testaments of love or adoration?" Just as she had that morning without so much as a by-your-leave. *Poor man is probably wandering the house, hunting for his wife.* Not an uncommon occurrence.

"I say, that does throw a spanner in the works." Great-Aunt Iris rubbed her chin. "I'll think on that. We could stash him in the boot." She clapped. "Ah, the tea has arrived."

While Eliza sipped her favorite tea and nibbled a strawberry tart, several ideas flitted through her head. *Could Heath really have kicked Teardrop Man's butt? I hope Great-Aunt Iris isn't serious about stashing her ninety-year-old husband in the trunk of a car! Why is a known ex-con, a murderer, no less, wandering the streets after a murder was committed days ago?*

ELIZA glared at Heath as he counted the poker chips in front of him. Then she glared at her nonexistent pile of chips. Then she glared at Joy, who had gone all in and lost three turns and stood over Eliza's shoulder, clucking her tongue. "I thought you were supposed to be good at this kind of thing."

"And why should I be good at this kind of thing?"

"You've gambled in Deadwood, haven't you?" Joy huffed and plopped back in her chair.

"Just because I took an old-timey picture in Deadwood once and threw a few dollars in a video lottery machine doesn't make me a high-stakes gambler like Wild Bill Hickock or Poker Alice." Eliza scooted the owed amount of lemon-flavored Jammie Dodgers over to Heath. "Here, take your cookie—biscuits and gloat somewhere else."

Heath bit into one and grinned. "I plan to do my gloating where it can best be appreciated." He flicked a crumb across the table at her.

She forced a smile and wrapped her arms around her chest as rain pelted the darkened library windows, matching her mood. She hadn't thought she would cry when she dropped off Uncle Fitzwilliam at the train station that afternoon, but she'd gone and made a fool of herself right there on the platform. Pemberley was empty without his presence, and the reality of her actually being mistress of the place and not simply playing at it swirled in her gut. The rain picked up speed and sounded like a thousand tapping fingernails begging for entrance.

"What's wrong?" Heath came to her side and rubbed the back of her neck.

"Nothing." She ignored his scoff. "Nothing major. Probably nerves about Uncle being gone and..." She waved away his concern. "I'm fine. Overemotional, I guess."

He crouched next to her. "I have a piece of news that might make you feel better. I'm chuffed about it." His eyes crinkled. "I think... I hope you will be too."

"What is it?" she prompted.

"I received a job offer. Head of field archaeology for a local archaeology research company based out of Bakewell."

"That's within twenty miles of Pemberley, right?"

He nodded, and his gaze never wavered from hers.

"But your job at the university. You worked so hard to become a professor. You'd give that up?"

"I realized my passion for archeology isn't in the classroom or some stuffy academic setting. I want to get my hands dirty. This would give me the perfect opportunity."

"And have you accepted it?" Her chest tightened.

He twirled a piece of her hair around his finger. "I, ah, wanted to consider all my options and think about some things before accepting it."

She traced the edge of his cheek with her thumb. "When do you need to give your answer?"

"In two weeks."

"Two weeks?" Her heart raced, and her mind whirled. Maybe she hadn't put the cart before the horse. *Slow down.*

His new job could mean many things besides his heart belonging to her. Perhaps, as he'd stated, he wanted to get out of academia. Maybe he really wanted to work for that company, and it happened to be in the same county as Pemberley. Eliza stilled her thoughts with a sigh. Two weeks gave them plenty of time to figure out their future. *Nah, who am I kidding? Two weeks is hardly any time.* She sought Heath's hand and squeezed.

He stood and pulled her to her feet. "So, what now?"

"I was about to ask that same thing of you."

Joy didn't bother hiding a yawn. "Heath, if you want my opinion, which I sense you don't or you would have asked me, I think you should take the job because..." She circled her hand in Eliza's direction. "And if you two are as knackered as I am, then I vote for bed. You'll see. In the morning, everything will make more sense, and you'll have plenty of time to 'chat.'" Joy hooked one-fingered air quotes and winked.

"For once, I agree with Joy." Heath hauled Eliza to her feet.

Joy scoffed and bit at a wayward cuticle. "That, my dear moppet, was always your problem."

"I struggle sometimes figuring out how you two lasted as a couple for two years," Eliza said.

"I'm as gobsmacked as you." Joy sashayed over to Heath and planted a chaste kiss on his cheek. "It was fun while it lasted, but any more would have been a bloody cock-up." Joy pointed at Eliza. "He's *your* problem now."

"Since when am I the problem?"

Three knocks echoed down the hallway and leeched through the open library door. Eliza's spine straightened, and her gaze flicked from Heath to Joy. Silence filled the room once again.

Another knock and another came until a fusillade of knocks reverberated through the house.

"Who could be at the door at this hour?" Heath asked.

Eliza shrugged and sighed. "One of us has to open the door."

"Why? Where's Tash?" Joy asked.

"I gave him the night off. Gave all the staff a night off, actually."

"Why?"

"Because I'm not a taskmaster, and with only us three and Great-Aunt Iris and Great-Uncle William, I figured I'd give them the night off to do whatever."

"Aren't you the kind mistress, but now we have to go see who it is, and as it is near midnight, it could be anybody." Joy jumped at another barrage of knocks. "Let's go together. Safety in numbers, right?"

"Or three very easy victims for a killer on the loose." Heath hooked his fingers like claws. "Bwahaha."

Eliza and Joy smacked Heath in the chest and ventured out of the library, down the hall, and to the main entrance. The double oak doors vibrated with another cascade of knocks.

Heath cracked his knuckles. "Here goes nothing." He unlocked the doors and swung one open. In fell a deluge of rain and a soaked individual.

Joy squeaked and jumped backward. Eliza, too stunned to move, could only stare at the man panting on all fours in the foyer. Heath grabbed the nearest object, an antique vase, and poised it over the stranger.

"Miss Darcy." The man lifted his head.

The russet-brown skin, dark-amber eyes, and salt-and-pepper hair could belong to only one person.

"DCI Wentworth?" Eliza gaped.

Heath set the vase back, offered the detective chief inspector a hand, and hauled him to his feet.

DCI Finn Wentworth stumbled, caught himself on the open door, and waved away Heath's support. "No, I'm fine."

"You are not fine." Eliza sat the dripping man on the stairs and closed and locked the door against the rain and any other late-night visitors. "What? How?"

Wentworth shivered in his soaking-wet khakis and a long-sleeved T-shirt emblazoned with the Manchester United logo. Eliza had seen the suit-and-tie police officer in civilian clothes often enough that the shock had worn off from the first time she'd witnessed it, but something about the dripping-wet sports fan punched her in all the feels.

"Joy, can you get a couple of towels for DCI Wentworth?" Eliza sat next to Wentworth and placed her hand between his shoulder blades.

He jerked but didn't shake off her hand as she had expected him to.

"Are you okay? No, that's a dumb question. You are most certainly not okay. What happened? Are you hurt? Sick?"

Wentworth rested his elbows on his knees and planted his face in his palms.

Joy skidded around the corner, towels flapping over her shoulder. "Here." She placed one over his shoulders, one across his lap, and one over his head. "You look awful. What's going on?"

Heath crossed his arms and shook his head. "I'm afraid, DCI Wentworth, that if you don't answer these ladies' questions, they'll kick you back into that blasted weather."

Wentworth straightened. "I'm being framed..." He swallowed. "For murder."

Chapter Three

Eliza Darcy Puts Her Nose in Police Business... Again

Miss Anne Elliot called on me this afternoon, and I had a delightful time. While most women smile and pat a child's head and then expect the child's nanny to remove them from the room, Miss Elliot sat on the sitting room floor and played with Adelaide Rose for a full quarter of an hour. Adelaide Rose was loath to leave the attentive guest, of course, and made her opinions known to the entire house. Miss Elliot refused my apologies and stated that the young are just as welcome to their opinion as the old and that the young probably have better ones after all. Yes, I like Miss Elliot very much.

Lizzy Bennet Darcy

Bath 1814

Eliza narrowed her eyes and rubbed her forehead. "Come again?"

Wentworth, his shoulders draped in a now-damp towel, echoed the gesture, but at least his teeth had stopped chattering. "I'm being framed for murder."

"Whose?" Eliza asked.

"Felix Payne's."

"But why? I don't understand," Eliza said.

Wentworth shook his head, and his visible skin prickled with goose bumps.

"Here. Let's get you dry and warm, and then we can talk." Eliza offered him her hand and, between her and Heath, hauled him to his feet.

Within fifteen minutes, Wentworth sat garbed in a pair of Uncle Fitzwilliam's sweats and a sweatshirt and bundled in an afghan. He clutched a cut-crystal whiskey glass in his right hand, stared at the copper-colored liquid, then downed two fingers' worth in one gulp.

Wordlessly, he held out the glass and jiggled it. Joy, the closest to him, bounced up and poured him another drink from the study's drink cart and poured a glass for herself.

"What?" She sank into her leather chair. "A man can't drink alone." She tapped her temple. "That's even in the Bible somewhere, so you can't judge."

Eliza sighed. "I'm not sure that's exactly how it goes."

"Close enough." Joy clinked her glass against Wentworth's stationary one. "Here's to murder happening *again*."

Wentworth scowled into his glass. "I keep replaying everything through my head, you know, and I can't make heads or tails out of any of this bloody mess."

"Sometimes it helps to talk it through, out loud." Eliza gestured to Joy and Heath. "We'll help any way we can."

She wasn't sure whether Wentworth snorted with derision or because being out in the cold rain had affected his nasal passage. Either way, she ignored him and scooted to the edge of her leather chair.

He downed the second glass of whiskey and seemed to contemplate whether getting trollied, as Joy called it, was worth it. The decision apparently made, he struggled out from the blanket and poured himself a third glass of whiskey. He walked to the window and, with some effort, closed the large curtains. "No need to advertise you have company. Especially me."

Eliza was about to shake the information from him when, his back turned to them, he snorted a derisive laugh. "You know what's bloody stupid about this whole thing?"

No one answered his apparently rhetorical question.

"I was looking forward to the next two weeks. My wife took a ladies-only holiday, my youngest is at boarding school, the gods gifted me with a free night's stay at the Foxed Hound, and I thought, like the git I am, that I would be baching it up, heating ready-made chicken tikka masala and knocking back a few bitters every night." His head jerked backward as he emptied the glass. "Was in the middle of one of those when... well, when the decision to hide and lick my wounds was made for me."

"I'm afraid you'll need to start from the beginning," Eliza said.

Wentworth's shoulders shuddered, and after several seconds, he walked to his chair and slouched unceremoniously. "The beginning? Harder to pin down than you might think, as the start to all this happened several years ago."

Joy clamped down on a yawn. "We've got nowhere to be, and your little knocking stunt put me in such a state that I won't be able to sleep anyway."

Wentworth continued as if Joy hadn't spoken. "Several years ago—feels like ages, really—there was quite a dustup over a botched investigation. The wrong people were put in prison, and most of the guilty ones escaped prosecution. Some pretty nasty business was uncovered, and as I refused to side with the corrupt officials and at times gave evidence against them, I made quite a few enemies along the way. Some of the higher-ups were able to weasel their way out of it. They blamed constables, blamed officers for not following protocol." He pinched the bridge of his nose. "Said anything, really, to keep their hands as clean as possible. Most of the debacle was swept under the rug, leaving hard feelings and distrust between...

well, everybody. To say I made a few enemies in the process would be an understatement."

"What happened next?" Eliza asked.

"The dust eventually settled, and everyone pasted on smiles and got on with police business."

"But things weren't the same, were they?" Heath asked.

"Not by a long shot. We got along to get along, but very powerful people wanted—want—my head." He brought his empty glass to his lips and frowned at it. "Needless to say, I kept my head low."

"How does this equal you falling through our door all soaking wet in the middle of the night?" Joy asked.

"I'm getting there." After blowing out a breath, he leaned forward and rested his elbows on his knees. "Last Friday night, as you know, Felix Payne was murdered at the Foxed Hound. Well, ah, I was there."

"So, you got a jump start on the investigation?" Eliza asked.

He shook his head. "I wish. No. I was there for a pint and my free night's stay, a gift for my service, according to one of the waitresses at the pub." He snorted. "That's my luck. Get a gift and then can't bloody enjoy it. Should have known better than to eat at the fish-and-chip shop next door to the pub."

Heath groaned in commiseration. "Made that mistake once. Thought death was coming for me for two days."

Wentworth wiped his hand over his mouth. "Tell me about it. I was too sick to go through the pub, so I gathered my overnight bag and snuck down the back steps, went home, and waited for death to find me in the toilet. Long story short, I left before his body was discovered in one of the upper guest rooms."

"But weren't you called in?" Eliza asked.

"Not on duty that night. Not sure I would have answered even if I was. I was too ill to move, much less answer my phone. I didn't know about Felix's murder until Saturday morning. By then, the noose was already tightening around my bloody neck." Wentworth wrapped his fingers around his neck.

Eliza echoed his motion. "How so? How could you be framed for a murder you didn't commit?"

"Say, you didn't actually commit the murder, did you?" Joy peered owlishly at Wentworth.

"Have you bloody lost the plot?" Heath's eyebrows hitched.

"One has to be sure." Joy sniffed and turned away from Heath's incredulous look.

"No, I didn't murder Felix Payne. Problem is somebody did, and very powerful people will make sure I take the fall on this one."

"But how? Why?" Eliza asked.

"There's the rub. My fingerprints are on the glass the victim drank out of and on the door handle of his room."

Before another accusation of murder could come out of Joy's mouth, Eliza asked, "But how is that possible?"

"Beats me. All I know is the evidence is damning, and no one, not even my partner, who somewhat believes I didn't do it, wants anything to do with me."

"That doesn't make sense. Why do they think you killed someone you don't even know?" Heath's forehead furrowed.

"Because I did."

SILENCE permeated the study, and the downpour of rain, which had settled into a drizzle, spattered against the windows. No one spoke.

Eliza was the first to break the silence. "You knew him?"

"Felix and I were old chums once upon a time. We ran around together, terrorized the village as boys." Wentworth shook his head. "By the time we were young teens, Felix was taking our childhood pranks and trouble-making ways to a whole new level. I could see he was on a path I didn't want to head down. He was sixteen when he did his first stint in juvie."

"Definite friendship killer," Joy mumbled into her glass.

"If only that were true. I actually kept in contact with him during his time in prison and those short periods when he was out." A humorless laugh ripped from his chest. "Thought I could be a good influence on him. Figured our childhood connection would count for something. I was a fool. A damned bloody fool."

Joy gaped at him. "This is starting to sound like one of those convoluted penny-dreadful plots."

"Joy, that's not nice," Eliza scolded.

"No." Wentworth sighed. "She's right. If only I had listened to my mum, dropped all ties with Felix, I wouldn't be in this situation. Stupid, stupid, stupid." He punctuated his words with fist punches to his left palm.

Eliza braced her hands on her knees. "And now he's murdered with your fingerprints on his glass and on the doorknob to his room. Add on you were there the night he died and your personal connection with him and, well, you have quite the situation on your hands. Surely, you can plead your innocence, right? I mean, no one in their right mind would believe you capable of murder."

"Didn't you listen?" he snapped then sagged in his chair. Rubbing his neck, he smiled apologetically. "I'm sorry. There are very powerful people, inside and outside the force, who would love nothing more than to repay me for my 'betrayal' of the police brotherhood, so to speak. Some of the evidence I gave put a few men behind bars, and some who escaped prison can't look at me without remembering what I did, including the chief constable, Jayesh Kapoor. No, Miss Darcy, they are out for blood and will snap at this fortuitous chance to get rid of me. And I'm afraid anyone I ask to help me will suffer the consequences." Wentworth's Adam's apple dipped.

"So, having been warned, would you... Uh, could you..." He tugged at the sweatshirt's collar as if it had suddenly tightened.

"Of course I will help. You can stay here." Eliza jumped to her feet and snapped her fingers. "In fact, I have the perfect place to hide you."

"Won't the staff know I'm here?"

"Nope. I gave them the night off. No one here but us three."

"You're not going to hide me in the tunnel, are you?"

"Don't be silly. Everyone, including the police, knows about the tunnel after the last debacle here at Pemberley. No. I have something even better." Eliza pulled Wentworth to his feet and crooked her finger at Heath and Joy. "I learned about this secret gem when I was de-Nancy-fying everything and putting Pemberley back to its Regency Era glory."

"A dungeon?" Heath's eyes brightened.

"No, but that would seriously be cool. Follow me. It's better if I show you." Eliza led the way out of her uncle's study, down the dark hallway, and to the base of the main staircase. "Now, how many levels does Pemberley have?"

"I sense this is a trick question," Joy whispered to the others. "Don't answer it."

"Ah, come on. How many?"

Heath ticked the numbers on his fingers as he called out the levels. "We're standing on the first floor, which you Americans would consider the ground floor, and then there is the second floor. If you count the servants' quarters below us, that would put Pemberley at three, right?"

"Wrong." Eliza smiled. "Follow me." She took the stairs two at a time and waited until Wentworth, bringing up the rear, stood next to her. "Now, we go this way."

Eliza latched onto Heath's extended hand as they walked down the long portrait gallery. The eyes of the deceased seemed to follow the small group as their footsteps scuffed along the carpeted passage. Unless specifically invited for a tour, not many people were allowed on the top floor, as it housed the bedrooms and private living spaces, which had provided Eliza's secret destination the ability to stay hidden for so long.

At the end of the gallery, a large window would, on a moonlit night, spread an eerie glow. The ebony panes served as a stark reminder of the darkness outside and the rain still pitter-pattering against the glass. Eliza pulled Heath closer.

"Brilliant. You've brought us to a dead end. Want Wentworth to camp outside on the window ledge?" Joy wrapped her arms around her middle and peered behind her.

"Oh ye of little faith." Eliza walked over to an ornately carved bookshelf that, to her, had always seemed a little out of place at the end of the gallery. Her curiosity had gotten the better of her, and in the process of touching and opening all the books, she had opened up a new world. Quite literally, as the bookshelf had swung open to reveal narrow wooden steps scarred with black scuff marks and gouges.

Repeating what she had done the first time, she placed her index finger on the top of the spine of *The Romance of the Forest* by Ann Radcliffe and flicked it toward her. An inner mechanism clicked, and the bookshelf creaked and opened on hinges.

Joy and Wentworth gaped. Heath whistled under his breath.

"What the bloody hell?" Wentworth peeked around the now-open bookcase. "What kind of place is Pemberley?"

"According to Uncle Fitzwilliam, this place is full of secrets." Eliza grinned. "He didn't even know of this place until I showed him." Eliza snagged her phone from her back pocket and switched on her flashlight. "Come on."

She ascended the narrow steps and chuckled when Joy's muffled swear words filled the space.

"Do these ever end? Are you taking us to Narnia?" Joy's breath puffed in short gasps.

"I wish. No. It only leads to, well, here." Eliza stepped onto aged hardwood flooring and splayed her flashlight's beam over the room.

ONE by one, the others finished their journey up the steps and stood next to her.

Heath snaked an arm around her waist. "What is this place?"

Eliza reached behind him, felt along the wall, and flicked a switch. A lone lightbulb stuttered to meager life and, from its place hanging in the center of the room, created a halo of light.

Exposed wood lying horizontally marched straight up the walls for four feet before taking a nearly forty-five-degree angle up to the ceiling, where it flattened out along the roof barely eight feet above the floor. Darkened timber joists resembling a large rib cage held it all together. Cobwebs hung in corners and swayed in the minuscule breeze squeezing through the one small window encircled by an age-eaten frame. Other than the cobwebs and the lone lightbulb dangling from its cord, the cramped room was empty.

Heath spread his arms out. "This room can't be more than eight feet wide." He walked heel to toe the length of the room. "And barely ten feet long."

"I didn't say it was the Ritz." Eliza crooked her finger. "But here's the best part." She pressed against a knot in one of the support beams, and an inner mechanism clicked. "Open sesame."

A four-foot-by-twelve-inch section between two timber joists creaked open.

"How on earth...?" Heath whispered.

"Blame a spider, my less-than-graceful escape attempt, and the pure luck of me trying to break my fall." Eliza grinned at her astounded audience. "Suck in your guts and watch your heads."

The door opened into the official attic, a large room as dusty and cobwebby as the hideaway niche they had come from. Trunks and boxes littered the floor, and discarded and forgotten furniture was piled up along the walls or crammed into corners.

Eliza grinned at her companions. "I think we can gather enough stuff to make Wentworth's stay as comfortable as possible."

"Why can't he stay here?" Joy asked.

"Everyone knows the attic is here. Most of the staff were helping me clear this place out or shoving things up here for storage after Nancy left. The whole time, I never expected the surprise on the other side. Anyway, no one, except for Uncle Fitzwilliam and me, knows the existence of the secret room. It's too risky." She rubbed her hands together. "All hands on deck. Let's see what we can find."

A half hour later and everyone coated with a layer of dust and cobwebs, they had furnished the tiny secret hideaway with a squeaky cot complete with a thin mattress that had seen better days, a rickety chair probably on its last leg, and a wobbly table. Eliza finished the military tucking of the sheets, fluffed a pillow, and ran a finger along the top hem of a gingham quilt Joy had stolen from a chest in one of the guest rooms, as the old blankets in the attic all smelled of mothballs. "There. You should be nice and comfy."

"I hope, Wentworth, you're not scared of ghosts," Joy said.

"Ghosts. Humph. Nothing but a bunch of codswallop, that." Wentworth gave Joy a side glance, but his shoulders slouched, and he situated his back against the wall instead of the dark abyss of the room outside the halo of light.

Brushing off her hands, Eliza gave the little hideout the once-over and nodded. "This will do for tonight. In the morning, when things are bright and we've all had a chance to think and sleep, we can reconvene."

"Um, don't you think we're missing something?" Joy shook her head at their blank stares. "A toilet. What is Wentworth supposed to do for that sort of thing?"

Eliza scrunched up her nose. "Never thought of that. Well, the main attic's staircase does lead directly to a servants' hall, which has a servants' bathroom close by. No one uses that staircase anymore, and as far as I know, Tash, Mrs. Underhill, and Mrs. B don't use it or the bathroom at all." She chewed on her lip for a second. "Wait here a sec." She squeezed into the main attic area, rummaged around, and returned with a porcelain chamber pot. "Here. To minimize the time you're spending outside the secret room, you can use this to... you know, do your business, and then at night, you can sneak to the bathroom and dump it out."

"Won't people be curious at the sound of a flushing toilet in a bathroom no one supposedly uses?" Heath asked.

"No one lives on this side of the house. Most of the east wing is closed up and only used when a lot of people are expected. We didn't even open that side this past weekend for our guests. We used the bedrooms in the west wing. I think the last time it was used was for the family reunion."

Eliza handed Wentworth the chamber pot painted with chubby naked cherubs. He took the proffered gift gingerly and peeked inside as if scared of what he would find.

"I never did understand why cherubs are always completely starkers." Joy peered at one of the angels, who seemed a little too excited about being naked. "See what I mean?"

"So, about the staff. None of them can know, right?" Heath asked.

"Right. We'll have to be very careful. Not that I don't trust the staff, but one misplaced word by one person would compromise Wentworth's safety," Eliza said.

"What about Great-Aunt Iris?" Joy asked.

Eliza shrugged and held out her hands. "What do you guys think?"

One no and two yeses echoed around the attic.

Wentworth, the lone no, gaped at Joy and Heath. "You really think Eliza's batty great-aunt can keep a secret as huge as this? There's a warrant out for my arrest! If I'm found before I can solve this, I'll... I'll... oh, bugger it!" He slouched on the cot, and it creaked under his weight. "Put a blinking neon arrow pointing at the bookshelf. Hell, show your conjuring trick to the chief. End it all."

"Don't go throwing a wobbly." Joy sat next to him on the cot. "Great-Aunt Iris is a valuable member of the team and, as far as I know, hasn't told a secret she wasn't supposed to unless, of course, you count her blabbing about Eliza's inheriting Pemberley."

"Are you trying to make me feel better? Because if you are, you're mucking it up."

"You're tetchy because of stress and exhaustion." Joy jumped to her feet. "You'll feel better in the morning and hopefully will see that we're right."

Eliza crossed her arms. "Joy's right. We're all tired, and you, Wentworth, must be at your wits' end. We'll talk again in the morning. And as for Great-Aunt Iris, she's either a part of the team, or you can find somewhere else to hide out."

"Blimey." Wentworth scratched at days-old stubble. "Knew you were trouble the first time I interviewed you."

Eliza smiled sweetly. "And look who you came running to first."

"That, Miss Darcy, is where you're wrong. You are my last resort, and as everyone thinks I consider you a nuisance and a police busybody, they won't put two and two together." He pointed at himself and then Eliza.

"A nuisance?" Eliza's face heated. "You, you—"

Heath stepped between them. "Okay, time to break it up, go to separate corners, and live to fight another day." After wrapping his arm around Eliza's waist and guiding her toward the door, he grinned ruefully at Wentworth. "If I were you, I'd sit back and enjoy the ride. Fuss too much and you might overturn the boat and find yourself up over your head."

Wentworth muttered, "Bloody bollocks" and kicked at one of the cot's legs.

Eliza bit her lip to stem her laughter and followed Heath and Joy down the stairs and back to the bookshelf. She slid it shut, and the same mechanism that had clicked open clicked closed, locking Wentworth in and everyone else out.

Joy cuddled her arms around her. "Poor Wentworth, having to sleep in the creepy little hole in the creepy attic." She eyed Eliza. "Being as lover boy here never shares your bed, can I? At least for tonight?"

"Scared of ghosts?" Eliza teased.

"Of course I am. Being British automatically signs you up for a full appreciation and respect for them. As you are only half British, I can see why you don't take them seriously."

The hair on the back of Eliza's neck still stood at attention from the attic's ambiance. Maybe she was more than half British. Definitely pushing the three-quarter mark, as she—or at least her neck hairs—most certainly believed in ghosts. "Oh, fine. If I don't let you, you'll whine about it, won't you?"

"You know me so well! Finally, someone gets me."

Heath rolled his eyes but walked the girls to Eliza's room. After Joy opened the door and stole the side of the bed farthest from it, Heath cocked an eyebrow. "Shall I sleep outside your door again?"

"Only if you wear your dancing-taco pajama pants."

"They're in the laundry. I'll have to provide my bodyguard services another night. Perhaps I could—"

Eliza stopped his rambling with a kiss. "Good night, and don't let the ghosts bite."

"Likewise." He grinned. "The only one I want nibbling you is me."

"Get out of here." She playfully shoved him in the direction of his room and waited until he entered and shut his door before entering and shutting hers. "Really?" Arms crossed, she stalked to her bed, where Sleeping Beauty lay sprawled over the entire thing and snored gently.

After grabbing her pillow and a throw from the bottom of the bed, Eliza made herself as comfortable as possible on the chaise lounge. The wind had picked up and sent raindrops pelting into the windows. With that and Joy's snoring, Eliza wasn't sure she would ever fall asleep. Not that she needed to blame the outer noise. She had enough inner turmoil clamoring around to scare any sleep away. And with a cop-on-the-run holed up in her attic, a murder to solve, a killer to find, and the ongoing effort to keep Pemberley from burning to the ground, Eliza wasn't sure she would ever sleep again.

Chapter Four
The Making of a Murder Scene

*I happened upon Miss Anne Elliot walking with her father and sister
in Sydney Gardens. July has proved a hot month, and there is little
surcease from the heat within doors. Under the shade of Sydney Gardens' trees, the heat is tolerable. I am glad, for once, that Darcy was not
with me, as I do not think he would have liked Sir Walter and Miss
Elliot. They seem like proud, unpleasant people. I laugh at myself, as I,
too, had thought Darcy proud upon first making his acquaintance, but
I soon found that his pride was in his family and his ability and rooted
in good upbringing. The Elliots' pride is noisome and seems rooted in
pretense and a false notion of their social standing. Miss Anne Elliot
thankfully does not suffer from this malady.*

Lizzy Bennet Darcy

Bath 1814

Somewhere outside Eliza's bedroom window, a bird trilled a
morning melody. A six-o'clock serenade, if Eliza's bedside clock
could be trusted.

Her head pounded from her sleepless night, and her back ached
from sleeping on the chaise lounge. Joy, still sleeping, was curled up
in the middle of the bed, one foot sticking out of the covers. Struggling to her feet, Eliza bit back a groan and, holding her breath,
stretched her back in various positions in an attempt to free several
knots that had tied themselves into tight balls during the night.

No use. She would have to walk it off.

Even though Joy deserved to be wakened, Eliza tiptoed around her room gathering clothes, slid into the en suite bathroom, and readied herself for what would surely be a bugger of a day. Before leaving the bathroom, she rifled around in the medicine cabinet for ibuprofen or Tylenol or any pain reliever but came up empty. *Perhaps Mrs. Bankcroft will have something.*

Within fifteen minutes, she was dressed in black leggings and an oversized sage-green cable-knit "jumper" Great-Aunt Iris had given her last week. Figuring she was presentable enough despite the dark circles under her eyes, Eliza snuck out of her room and tripped over Caesar.

He blinked at her and butted her shins with his head. His motor purred to life as soon as she picked him up.

"Hey, buddy. Long time no see. What have you been up to?" It hadn't taken long after settling into his new home for him to take to Great-Aunt Iris. What with the crooning, petting, and sneaked treats, she was his newfound friend and partner in crime.

He licked Eliza's nose.

"Let me guess. Mrs. B has already given you breakfast." She set him down and walked toward the staircase. He followed closely at her heels. "If you think you're getting a second breakfast, you are sadly mistaken."

Even if Eliza hadn't known the way to the kitchen, she could have followed her nose to Mrs. Bankcroft's sacred domain. The smell of sausages and caramel rolls, a treat Mrs. Bankcroft made often after she'd found out those were Eliza's favorite breakfast treats, wafted down the hall.

"You stay," Eliza ordered her cat and entered the kitchen.

Caesar, who never obeyed commands on principle, sashayed into the room and jumped on a chair next to the huge work counter laden with kitchen paraphernalia.

"Morning, Mrs. B." Eliza perched on a barstool across from the counter and rested her elbows on the wooden surface.

"Why, you look poorly, Miss Eliza." Mrs. Bankcroft paused the rolling pin long enough to give her the eye. She clicked her tongue and took to flattening out a pie crust.

"Just tired is all."

"And it's no wonder, too, what with your running around. I'm surprised you don't run your feet right off you."

Eliza rubbed circles over her temples. "Do you have anything to take away headaches, backaches... and the onset of tennis elbow?"

"Here, finish rolling this dough out and don't go putting a hole in it, you hear?"

"But... but..."

Mrs. Bankcroft waddled out of the kitchen.

"I've never rolled out dough in my life," Eliza finished to the empty room. Praying the baked-good gods would smile upon her, Eliza gingerly rolled the dough until it was as thin as she thought it should be and checked for the tiniest holes, which Mrs. Bankcroft's eagle eye would surely spot.

"Here you go, Miss Darcy." Mrs. Bankcroft waddled into the kitchen and set on the counter two dark-brown glass bottles, one labeled Lavender and the other labeled Rosemary. "Sniff these."

"You wouldn't happen to have ibuprofen or Tylenol?"

"I don't take stock in that modern voodoo." Mrs. Bankcroft patted the tops of the bottles. "This here natural remedy does as well and won't harm you in the end."

Eliza wanted to argue that many things found in nature had the habit of harming, but she bit her lip. There were some fights a girl couldn't win. "Thank you, Mrs. Bankcroft." Her tummy rumbled. "When's breakfast?" It wasn't fair that she was surrounded by the intoxicating aromas of sausage and caramel and had yet to bite into any of it. If she could only peek at the food resting snugly in the warming pans on the end of the counter... With Mrs. Bankcroft's attention directed on inspecting Eliza's rolling job, Eliza slithered down the counter and lifted one of the lids.

A spatula came down softly on her hand.

"What was that for?" Eliza pulled her hand away from the lid and furrowed her brow.

"Now, you get on out of my kitchen. It'll be breakfast before you know it."

"But—" Eliza's stomach rumbled again.

With a huff, Mrs. Bankcroft plunked some day-old scones on a plate, rustled up a pot of tea, and collected it all on a platter and returned her attention to her pie crust.

Eliza took that as her cue to leave—without a single sausage or even a bite of gooey caramel roll. As she left the kitchen, she glanced back. Caesar, who had hopped up on the stool she had vacated, chewed on a tiny piece of sausage Mrs. Bankcroft had given him. She glared at the scones on the platter. Her stomach didn't want day-old scones.

But she knew someone who probably wouldn't chuck them back at her. Although after last night's tiff, she wasn't sure if the detective chief inspector was a glass-half-empty or glass-half-full kind of guy, especially after she'd stuffed him into a creepy hole in an equally creepy attic. Assuming the main staff were back at their duties, Eliza slunk through the halls, peering behind her at every sound. Eventually, she made it to the end of the portrait gallery, flicked the leather-bound book, and slipped into the stairwell. As soon as the bookshelf clicked closed, the stairs were shuttered in darkness broken only by the meager light from the attic's few windows. With each step, she investigated the narrow treads with her toe before placing her foot down and made it to the top, surprised she and the tray hadn't tumbled down the stairs.

"Surprised you didn't go arse over teakettle down those steps." Wentworth's voice, devoid of the anger from the night before, sounded gruff and scratchy with sleep.

"Then you'd have to scrape me along with the scones and tea off the landing."

"Scones? Did you say scones? And tea?"

Eliza chuckled. "Looks like you could use it."

In the dim light the sparse attic windows afforded, Wentworth sat in the middle of the cot, still in the clothes he'd slept in. His short-cropped hair lay flat on one side and stuck straight out on the other. He must have noticed the direction of her gaze and pressed the sticky-outies down with his fingers.

She set the tray on a rickety table they had scrounged out of a back corner the night before. "Breakfast is served. Careful, though. You might chip a tooth on the scones. Could have had caramel rolls and sausages but *no*."

"There is some information that I do not need, and that is a perfect example." He hobbled to the table, grabbed a scone, and clinked it against the plate. After pouring himself a steaming cup of tea, he sat down on his cot, swirled his scone in the dark liquid, and took a bite. "Not bad."

"I'll try to do better for lunch."

Wentworth waved off her concern and paused. "What are you doing?"

Eliza moved the lavender bottle away from her nose and sniffed. "Headache. Supposedly, according to Dr. Cook, this will make it go away."

He eyed the bottle. "Willing to share?"

"There's some rosemary if you want to give that a whirl." She tossed it to him.

"Where's the rest of your posse?"

"Sleeping, I imagine. Thought I'd bring you some food and then go gather the troops."

He swallowed his last bite of scone. "Thank you."

"For a day-old scone? Don't mention it. Please."

"No. Thank you. What I'm asking you to do is making you an accessory after the fact. If they find me, they will, between the damning evidence and very powerful people who want to see me destroyed, have enough to send me away for a very, very long time. And you'd be charged with aiding and abetting a criminal."

Eliza swallowed. An oily sensation swirled in her gut. She hadn't thought that far. Hadn't really thought at all. Stashing him in Pemberley's attic had been the neighborly thing to do.

"As a matter of fact, I'll be leaving. I really shouldn't have come here." Wentworth set his cup down and stood. "Thank you."

"No." Eliza matched his stance. "You're staying."

"But—"

"No buts. You. Are. Staying." She paced the floor and rubbed her temples. "All we have to do is find someone, anyone, who can vouch for your whereabouts at the time of Felix's death."

"There is no one. Remember? My kids are out of the house. My wife's out of town. I didn't invite any mates over. I left the pub without anyone seeing. I have no alibi for the night of the murder."

ELIZA'S gut twisted, but she forced a smile. "No worries. We'll find the real killer, and then you can do a told-you-so dance to all those twits who thought you guilty of murder."

Wentworth scoffed. "Doesn't quite work that way. Without access to police files and reports, I have no way to find the killer."

"I didn't have any of those things, and I found out the killer."

"No. The killer found you. Remember? And you almost died."

Her smile deflated. "I don't like how you retell the story."

"Someone's got to keep you alive and your ego in check. Might as well be me."

Not waiting for an invitation and tired of standing, Eliza sank next to Wentworth on the cot. With a groan, it dipped dangerously close to the wood-planked floor. "Last night's a little fuzzy. So let's revisit some things, okay? You were at the Foxed Hound the night Felix was murdered?"

"Yes."

"Do you know who gave you the free night's stay?"

"No. But the waitress, Amanda, I think is her name—nice girl—wasn't surprised when I showed up. Said she had strict and secret instructions to make sure my food and drink were compensated, along with my room."

"She used the word 'secret'? That didn't seem odd to you?"

"Don't look a gift horse in the mouth, right?"

"I don't even know what that means, and I don't really care to know right now." She held up a hand to stem his explanation. "Did you see Felix?"

"Yes."

"Did you speak with him?"

"Yes. It would be rude not to."

"Did you see him leave the pub to go up to his room?"

"No. I went to my room around ten, and Felix was still in a corner booth, six pints into what was probably a ten-pint evening."

"And when did you sneak out the back?"

His russet-brown cheeks darkened to umber. "I didn't *sneak* anywhere. I didn't want to sick up the bad fish I had in front of the whole pub. Did myself and them a favor and went home via the back staircase. I don't remember the exact time but probably around ten or half past."

Eliza rubbed her forehead. The lavender oil had yet to take effect. Combined with the impending doom stalking her thoughts, her brain pounded out a vicious beat on her skull. "And your fingerprints were found on a glass in his room and on the doorknob of his room?"

He nodded. "My fingerprints were found on his glass, too, the poisoned one he drank out of."

"Poison? Yeesh! Are you sure you didn't go up to his room to catch up? Maybe you had one too many and forgot that part."

His glare had her mouth snapping shut. "I've never been in any of those rooms at the pub until that night. And I was only in *mine* for a few minutes before going down to the bar and then before I went home sick. I never went to Felix's room. Didn't even know he was staying there."

"I know you mentioned some higher-ups who wanted to see you off the force, but to frame you for murder? That seems a little bit of an overkill. Does anyone outside the police force truly hate you? Enough to see you rot in prison?"

"Who doesn't?"

Eliza raised her hand.

"You don't count."

She pointed at the stairs. "Wanna leave this lovely hideout?"

Wentworth grinned. "Not many people are lucky enough to stay in a swanky place like this."

Swanky it was, if one considered the cobwebs fluttering in the minuscule breeze allowed through the poorly insulated window to be upscale. However, it was warm-ish and hidden from the prodding eyes of the police hunting for the innocent Wentworth.

"You never answered the question." Eliza squeezed her forehead with such force she was sure she'd left indents.

"A lot of people hate me. Comes with the job, I suppose. But there is one person who wouldn't mind if I dropped over dead." Wentworth heaved to his feet and paced the breadth of the attic. His stocking feet kicked up small tufts of dust. Eliza mentally added *sweep the attic* to her growing list of to-dos. "He's actually a relative, a distant relative, mind you. I don't like claiming I share any blood with that leech, but one can't choose their relations, can they?"

Eliza thought of all the family nuts she had met months ago at the Darcy–Bennet reunion and shuddered at the thought of Margery Wickham and her sycophantic sisters. And Garrison. His disappearance still mystified family and investigators looking into his sudden falling-off-the-face-of-the-earth stunt, but Eliza would be lying if she said she missed the weasel. As Nancy Darcy's spineless stooge, he'd helped her bilk Pemberley and Uncle Fitzwilliam out of tens of thousands of pounds. The jury was still out on the total, but that was information Uncle Fitzwilliam kept to himself. Add on Garrison's disgusting propensity to want to people the earth with his cousins, and Eliza wanted to push him off the edge of the earth if he hadn't already disappeared off it already.

Eliza pursed her lips. "Every family has them, but enough to want to see a relative rot?"

"His name's Timothy Elliot, and from the moment he oozed from whatever hole he was spawned in, he's been a thorn in the Wentworth clan's side. He's a bloody wanker."

From her experience with Heath's colorful adjectives for people, especially when sharing England's narrow roads with them, Eliza understood Wentworth's contempt for this Timothy Elliot.

"That bad, huh?"

"Worse, but as you are a lady and a young one at that, I will refrain from continuing on with my thoughts of him."

"What makes you think I'm a lady?" She held an imaginary teacup to her lips, held out her pinky, and sipped pretentiously at the pretend liquid.

He smirked. "You're young, then."

She set her invisible cup down and folded her hands in her lap. "So, why does Timothy hate you?"

"How much time do you have?"

"It's not even six thirty in the morning. Joy's probably still sleeping in the middle of my bed, and Heath is more than likely making early phone calls for work. So you have at least another hour before the team assembles."

"Eons ago, probably the same time your Fitzwilliam and Elizabeth Darcy roamed the halls of this estate, my great-to-the-nth-degree grandmother, according to family legend, was involved in a love triangle."

"Oh, do tell. I adore love triangles."

He waited for a beat until she dropped her folded hands from under her chin to her lap. "Anyway, Anne Elliot was her name, and when she was a teenager, under horrible family advice, she broke off her engagement with a young naval officer, a Captain Frederick Wentworth, because he was penniless. Some years later, I think it was around eight or so, he comes back a naval big shot and very, very wealthy."

"Wait a sec. Those names sound oddly familiar somehow." Eliza snapped her fingers and screwed her face up in thought. "Bingo! Elizabeth Darcy mentions them in her journals. Didn't he still love her, and she still loved him, but they were both too stubborn to show their emotion or break first?"

"You're not wrong, but this is my family history, not yours, so belt up." His smile took the sting from the command. "Guess who shows up to send all things sixes and sevens? If you're thinking someone with the surname of Elliot, you'd be right."

"I remember reading this part. Wasn't he a jerk?"

"Yes, a right wanker, really. Now, promise not to interrupt again? If you keep that up, you'll confuse me on the convoluted family tale."

Eliza stuck her pinky finger out.

Wentworth ignored it. "Anne Elliot's father was Sir Walter Elliot, a titled man with a grand estate, Kellynch Hall, but with no money, as he'd squandered it."

"Of course he did." Eliza bit back her words and her grin. "Sorry. Won't happen again."

"Anyway, this doesn't keep a random widow—can't remember her name—from sniffing around the old geezer and insinuating herself into his life. Well, as Sir Walter never had sons, his title and estate were destined to go to his nephew, William Elliot, instead of Anne. The moment William realized, though, that this lovestruck—or should I say title-struck—widow could trap the old man in her web, marry him, and even carry his child, William acted quickly."

"I see. If Sir Walter remarried and had a son, the title and estate would never go to William."

"Exactly. And didn't I tell you not to interrupt? Never did listen, did you?"

Eliza shrugged. "You didn't pinky swear. So I'm not under any obligation to hold my side of the bargain. Now, please go on."

Wentworth's forehead scrunched, but he quirked an eyebrow and continued. "Well, to keep an eye on the romantic proceedings, William slithers into the family fold and pretends to woo Anne and almost succeeds in his dastardly plot."

"I remember reading about this in Elizabeth's diary. Do you think he loved Anne at all?" Eliza asked.

"Depends on which family lore you listen to. Luckily, Anne and Frederick Wentworth made up before William could go through with his plan, and after Sir Walter found out what his heir was up to and all the dodgy deeds he had done years before and his longtime hatred of the Elliot family, Sir Walter disinherited him."

"I didn't think they could do that. Wasn't Kellynch entailed?" Just as Pemberley had been. Although, without that stupid law that required an estate and its money to go to the firstborn son instead of daughters, her sixth-great-grandparents would have never met, and she wouldn't be sitting in a dank, secreted room with a fugitive.

"No, not all estates were entailed. And in the end, Sir Walter had a change of heart and became so dependent on his daughter, Anne, and his son-in-law, Frederick, that before he died, Sir Walter went through the legal trouble to make Anne his heir, and she became Lady Anne, Baronetess of Kellynch Hall. Hundreds of years later, the Wentworths from Anne and Frederick's branch still own Kellynch Hall."

"I didn't know you had siblings. Do you go for visits? Is it as grand as Pemberley? In what county is it? When do—"

Wentworth held up a hand and stemmed her questions. "I do. Yes. No. Somerset." His eyes crinkled. "And I own it. I am Sir Finn Wentworth, Baronet of Kellynch Hall."

ELIZA didn't care that her jaw still hung open. Wentworth deserved such a sight for, first, keeping such a secret to himself and, second, breaking it to her in such a way. *What's with people around here springing monumental news like they're telling someone they like ice cream?*

"Your face is going to get stuck like that."

She snapped her mouth shut then opened it again. "But... but... I don't understand. You have a job. Like a real job."

"I'm not one of those blokes who could ever sit around twiddling my thumbs. I have an estate manager who takes care of everything and runs Kellynch better than I ever could." Wentworth shrugged. "Comes with being the firstborn, I guess."

"So, you're really a baronet?" Eliza tilted her head and studied him.

"Yes." He sighed.

He was apparently done with that line of questioning. "So, how does Timothy fit into all of this?"

"Long story short, he believes that Kellynch Hall and the baronetcy were stolen out from under the nose of his ancestor, William, when Anne's father passed the property to her. And instead of letting things go, he has only increased his campaign to have a 'piece of the Wentworth pie,' as he calls it. I keep telling him I can't cut him out of a pie that was never his in the first place." He massaged the back of his neck. "He won't let it go. If anything, the past couple of weeks have been heating to boiling over. Nasty letters, lawyers, those types of things, all contesting a will made hundreds of years ago."

"And if you're out of the picture?"

"That's the crazy thing about this all. The estate will never be his. No matter what happens to me. It would go to my oldest child."

"What if he could overturn the will?"

"How? He's not the first to contest the will, and no one's been able to overturn it. Sir Walter Elliot was of sound mind when he made it. Timothy is so blinkered to the truth. Honestly think the man is a nutter."

"Good thing you only have to deal with him through lawyers."

Wentworth snorted. "I wish. Works at the Foxed Hound."

"You're full of surprises this morning, aren't you? I should have gathered everybody for this."

"I could do without any and all of these surprises. He was bartending Friday night. When he saw me, there was such a gleam in his eyes that I wanted to ask him if he was feverish or demon possessed. I didn't, though. Kept myself to myself, went to my room, and you know the rest."

"He mustn't have been pleased about you getting comped a room."

"I don't think he knew about it. If he had, he certainly would have said something."

Eliza snapped her fingers. "How many drinks did you have Friday night?"

He cocked an eyebrow. "Since when did you become my mum?"

"I don't care if you were so drunk you had to sleep under the table. I have a theory."

"I had two."

"And how many glasses were found in Felix's room?"

"Two." Wentworth held up two fingers.

"And both had your fingerprints on them?"

His eyes widened. "Yes. And one had my DNA."

"Is it possible for someone to wipe the spot where you drank from and get rid of the DNA?" Eliza asked.

"If they did a proper job of it."

"So, that might be an explanation of how your fingerprints popped up in a room you've never been to."

"Explains the glasses but doesn't explain them on the doorknob, both inside and outside the room."

She chewed on her bottom lip. "Well, shoot. Still, that doesn't blow the other theory out the window. We'll get to the bottom of this. I promise."

"Eliza, I really can't ask this of you. It's too dangerous."

"You didn't ask." Anticipating a challenge and perhaps an argument she couldn't win, she grabbed the tray and walked to the steps. "I'll assemble the team, and we'll come up with a game plan. I'll be back." She scampered as quickly as the steps would allow to the tune of Wentworth growling out her name much the same way her father and uncle did when they suspected she was up to trouble.

It ignited a homesickness in her—for home and for her parents—and renewed the ache in her chest for her absent uncle. Shoving her emotions into the recess where all other Midwesterners stashed theirs, she placed her ear to the back of the bookshelf in an attempt to hear whether anyone was on the other side. After hearing nothing, she pushed a lever. The shelf clicked, and instead of letting it swing open, she caught it, poked her head around, and seeing no one, slipped out and closed the bookshelf.

"That's where you've been."

Eliza slammed her hand over her heart and whirled. "Great-Aunt Iris, you scared me half to death. You need to quit sneaking up on people." She cocked her head and peered down the gallery. "Where were you anyway? I checked before coming out."

Her great-aunt grinned and pointed at Caesar, who was sitting by her feet. "Behind it when it opened. Your cat gave you away. Sitting at the bookshelf, pawing at it. Odd, I thought. So I waited."

Eliza glared at Caesar. "Traitor." He must have left the kitchen soon after getting his second breakfast and scampered after her only to be shut out before he could slip in behind her.

He licked his six-toed paw and slid it over his ear.

"You and Caesar could have been waiting for a long time."

Great-Aunt Iris tapped her purse. Knitting needles stuck menacingly out of it like a row of chevaux-de-frise, protecting it from pilferers. "We would have entertained ourselves." She let some yarn dangle, and Caesar clapped it between his front paws and bit at it. "Wouldn't we have, Caesar? Besides, I know the staircase exists. Forgot which book did the trick. Figured I'd wait until whoever went up came back down."

"How did you know about this and Uncle didn't?"

"I found it years ago, quite by accident." She waved her hand at the bookshelf.

"And you kept it a secret from everybody?"

"Of course." Great-Aunt Iris's eyes twinkled. "You never know when the need for a secret room will arise."

Eliza shook her head and wondered what went on in her great-aunt's head under all that fluffy white hair.

"Do you know anything about the room? Why it was created?" Eliza asked.

"I have no clue, but that's what makes it so intriguing." Great-Aunt Iris rubbed her hands together and grinned.

"So, no one else knows it exists besides you, me, and Uncle Fitzwilliam?"

Great-Aunt Iris screwed her face up, which compounded her wrinkles. "No." She narrowed her eyes at the tray clutched in Eliza's hands. "What do you have up there?"

Eliza swallowed and avoided her great-aunt's inquisitive gaze. "Nothing." Which was not quite a lie. She didn't have any*thing* up there.

"Don't you get smart with me, young lady. Are you harboring a criminal?"

"No... kind of... not really." She leaned down and whispered, "Can you keep a secret?"

"Of course I can, girl." Great-Aunt Iris blinked. "Well, except for that one time."

"Never mind. This is really important. Like really, really, really important. No one can know. Not even Great-Uncle William."

Great-Aunt Iris waved a dismissive hand. "He wouldn't remember it anyway. But your secret is safe with me." She shook off Eliza's hands. "Now, out with it."

Eliza gazed down the gallery to check for intruders. "Detective Chief Inspector Wentworth is being framed for a murder he didn't commit, and he's in hiding in the secret room. If he's found, he'll go to prison." She gulped. "And so will I for aiding and abetting him."

"Oh, goody." Great-Aunt Iris clapped. "I was wondering when another adventure would happen. I was getting bored."

"This isn't an adventure. This is life-and-death kind of stuff."

"Bah. When you get to be my age, death isn't as scary. Bring it on, I say."

Eliza wanted to remind her great-aunt that she was only twenty-six and wanted nothing to do with death, but as that would fall on deaf ears, she followed Iris down the gallery to gather the rest of the troops. The room's secrecy didn't feel as secret as it once had. She paused at the top of the main staircase, and while her great-aunt and Caesar descended the steps, she stood and contemplated her future as either mistress of Pemberley or Inmate 2456 of Block C.

Chapter Five
A Slight Scheduling Snafu

I admitted to Darcy over breakfast this morning that I was wrong. After looking correctly shocked and denouncing that I would ever be wrong (as every good husband does), Darcy listened attentively—or, at least, as attentively as he could with Adelaide Rose destroying the cravat Darcy's valet had worked on arduously. I had thought that Bath would be a study in boredom and dull, insipid afternoon visits and soirees that I would be forced to tolerate. I never thought I would find myself befriending a young woman in need of advice on something I quite think of myself as an expert on now that I have found it: love.
Lizzy Bennet Darcy
Bath 1814

"Blimey!"

Eliza shook her head at her cousin's fifth repetition of the word. "Can't you think of anything else to say?"

"No, I cannot, and you can't expect me to be a bloody wordsmith when I've found out our DCI is minted."

"You're not going to be weird around him now, are you?"

"Of course not." A gleam lit up Joy's eyes. "But he doesn't know that. I wonder how easy it is to make him squirm."

"With the past couple of days he's had, I'd wager that he'd do more than squirm at your attempts to tease him." Heath sauntered over from the breakfast buffet set up along the wall of the dining room.

The steam billowing from the sausages, scrambled eggs, and one caramel roll on his plate set Eliza's stomach to rumbling. It had been almost two hours since she'd smelled the breakfast fare, and the one scone Cook had thrown at her had gone to Wentworth's stomach instead of hers.

"Hold that thought." Eliza dashed to the buffet counter only to be halted by Great-Aunt Iris. Her lilac-colored tracksuit matched the lilac scent floating around her, which nearly dulled the aromas of the food in the warming pans.

"You look a picture this morning." Eliza kissed her great-aunt's proffered cheek.

"A picture of a walking lilac bush. Might as well sprout branches and put leaves in my hair." Great-Aunt Iris fluffed her permed white hair then cut in front of Eliza and grabbed a plate. "Age before beauty, and with this outfit, which I shall return directly, I need all the help I can get this morning." She waddled down the buffet, peeking into dishes and poking at several sausages before choosing one.

By the time Great-Aunt Iris had reached the fruit platter, Eliza eyed the food on her own plate and considered the propriety of eating with her fingers at the buffet. Besides her and her great-aunt and Heath and Joy, no one else was in the large room. For the sake of secrecy, she'd dismissed Willow as soon as the food was set up since she needed to reveal Wentworth's new fun facts. But still, some things were not done in Pemberley, and her proximity to her great-aunt made her an easy victim of a gnarled finger in her shoulder along with a scolding in her ear.

It didn't take long for everyone to get their food and create a tight circle at one end of the large mahogany dining room table.

"Did you know Wentworth owns an estate in the south?" Joy wagged a skewered strawberry in Great-Aunt Iris's direction.

"Of course I did."

"But... but how do you know everything?" Eliza asked.

"Simple. No one pays attention to little old ladies. Apparently, we're all old, senile, and batty." Great-Aunt Iris held up a finger. "I might be two of them, but I'm certainly not senile."

"Not yet," Joy muttered into her teacup.

Great-Aunt Iris rewarded her with a regal glare. "And, might I add, I do have excellent hearing."

"Now she reminds me." Joy set her elbows on the table. "So, what else did we miss from the tête-à-tête between you and Wentworth?" She wiggled her eyebrows. "Heath doesn't have anything to worry about, does he?"

"You betcha. I'm crazy about Wentworth. His sparkling personality is what really drives me wild."

"Joy, you're right. I do have some competition." Heath placed one hand over his heart and the other dramatically on his forehead. "What shall I ever do when Eliza Jane Darcy leaves me for DCI Finn Wentworth?"

Eliza chuckled. "I don't think it was the trouble with spandex that kept you from excelling in the theater."

"Hey now, no need to get mean." Heath winked and nudged her shoulder with his.

Great-Aunt Iris gave them all the eye. "Humph, I wonder about you young people nowadays. Back in my day—"

"You're right. As always." Joy cleared her throat. "Now, Eliza, please, no more interruptions. You heard Great-Aunt Iris." She ignored Eliza's raised eyebrow. "Continue, please."

With only a few more interruptions, mainly from her great-aunt, Eliza relayed her conversation with Wentworth and revealed all the little nuggets she'd gleaned.

"This Timothy bloke seems a right tosser," Joy said.

"Yeah, I was surprised I didn't see steam coming from Wentworth's ears when he told me about him."

"Your two-glass theory explains how two glasses with Wentworth's prints made it into a room he swore he never went into. Your great-aunt is right. You do have a snappy brain." Heath saluted Eliza with a glass of orange juice.

"But that doesn't explain how his fingerprints are on the doorknob." Eliza rubbed her temples. She could feel her headache coming in for another attack after being defeated by lavender oil.

"Who's in for a drink at the pub?" Joy asked.

Great-Aunt Iris tsked. "Really, Joy, isn't it a bit too early in the morning for a tipple? Even for you?"

"Your words hurt sometimes, Great-Aunt Iris. Really, they do." Joy sat up straighter in her chair. "You don't have to drink, but it would look conspicuous if we went to a pub and didn't order anything from a certain bartender."

Eliza craned her neck to look at the grandfather clock on the wall. "I don't think the pub is open at eight in the morning. However, we could go in for lunch, snag a bite to eat, Joy could drink for us, and maybe we can gather some intel." Her to-do list niggled at the back of her mind. "Until then, I don't know about the rest of you, but I have some work to do."

"Quite right. Your great-uncle needs his breakfast." Great-Aunt Iris's normally peachy skin rosied. "And his morning exercise." With an extra bounce to her waddle, she left the room.

"Why?" Joy whined and squeezed her eyes shut. "I think she enjoys torturing us. Maybe Great-Uncle William rides a stationary bike or something."

"I haven't seen an exercise bike in this entire place." Eliza shuddered and attempted to drown that realization by gulping the rest of her coffee.

Heath groaned. "I question my life choices sometimes, especially when I'm around you three."

"Me?" Eliza asked. "What did I do?"

"You could have bloody well let us think there was an exercise bike somewhere in this rambling place." Joy pushed away from the table. "Well, I have a love scene to write." She squirmed. "Don't want to anymore but needs must."

When the door closed behind Joy, Heath kissed Eliza. "Thought they'd never leave."

"Cousins and great-aunts can be a pain in the butt."

"Speaking of life choices, we should probably chat about my job prospects." He traced her ear with his finger.

Her skin tingled at his touch, and warmth pooled in her belly, but doubt doused it all with the icy waters of what-ifs. What if he took this job because of her and then the same dating gods who had damned her to years with Seth decided she and Heath didn't deserve happiness? She closed her eyes against the creatively evil ways they could decimate romance. *What if Wentworth's warnings come true, and I'm thrown into a jail cell?*

"Eliza?" Heath cupped her cheek. "You all right? Look, we don't need to talk about my—our—future now if you don't want to."

"It's not that." She played with a button on his dress shirt. "I would love nothing more than for you to take this new job. Knowing you're close and that if we did decide to—" Eliza bit her lip.

"Yes?" His pupils dilated.

A knock on the door preceded the entrance of the tall, slender frame of the housekeeper, Mrs. Underhill. Eliza put ten to one that no one would ever peg the woman for a housekeeper of a grand estate. Instead of looking like stereotypical housekeepers who were stout, old, and gray-haired with a clanking loop of keys hanging from their hips, Mrs. Underhill's fiery-red hair piled on top of her head, pale and freckled face, regal nose, and sharp chin defied all expectations.

"I'm sorry to interrupt, Miss Darcy, but I wanted to inquire if you added to the list for this weekend's event before I make my final order."

While Eliza had had some success with getting Tash and Mrs. Bankcroft to at least call her Miss Eliza, Mrs. Underhill, though the youngest of the main staff by twenty-plus years, refused to do so and insisted on calling her Miss Darcy. Perhaps that was the very reason she had yet to feel comfortable around the woman or have the same camaraderie that she did with Tash and Mrs. B.

"I don't believe we need anything else. Thank you, Mrs. Underhill."

As soon as the door closed, Eliza thunked her head against Heath's chest. "If she calls me Miss Darcy one more time, I'll lose it." Her stomach swirled and dropped to her feet.

"Eliza?" Heath placed his palm against her cheek. "Hey, you all right? You look as if you've seen a ghost."

"No, no, no!" Eliza paced the room and slapped her palm to her forehead. "This can't be. This is not good."

"Should I call for Joy? Tash? Eliza, please." Heath stopped her pacing and drew her into his chest. "What's wrong?"

Eliza rubbed her forehead in Heath's sternum and groaned. "Care to guess who's this weekend's guests of honor?"

Heath's beating heart was all she heard for several moments until a "bloody hell, it's a police do, isn't it?" rumbled in his chest.

All she could do was nod as the sensation of success whirled down the drain and emptied into the pit of her stomach still at her feet.

TRAFFIC zipping down Lambton's narrow streets mirrored Eliza's thoughts zigzagging through her brain. *How am I ever going to make any of this work?*

Even the eclectic architecture of the buildings failed to charm her as she, her great- aunt, Heath, and Joy made their way to the Foxed Hound. On a good day, she would stop and admire the mixture of tan stone buildings topped off with rust-colored terra-cotta shingles hugged up against whitewashed stone facades with thatched roofs. Normally, she would have appreciated the chrysanthemums spilling out of the shops' window boxes. However, that day was not a good day and far from normal. Clutching Heath's hand, she anchored herself with the fact that if her plans did burn in the fires of hell, he would visit her in prison. *Maybe. Probably.*

"Chin up," Heath whispered as they neared the Foxed Hound. "In the time I've known you, I have never seen you fail. If anyone can do this, you can."

"Ha! You've only known me for, what, four months?"

"And I'm thrilled to be changing that number daily. Imagine us sixty years from now, still having adventures." He slung his arm around her shoulder.

"Probably will end up like Great-Aunt Iris."

"Really?" He waggled his eyebrows.

She smacked his chest. "Only if you're lucky. But trust me, I've screwed up many times in my life. Many, many times. Want a list?"

He grinned. "Nope. Just want a chance to get into trouble with you."

"Here's your chance." Eliza paused at the corner of the pub. A sign painted with a tipsy-looking hound holding a pint swung in the breeze, and towering sunflowers planted in an old whiskey barrel leaned against the white stucco wall of the pub. "I'd bail if I were you."

He kissed the top of her head and gazed down at her. "Never. I once swore to be your sidekick for life, and I never break my promises."

With a thundering heart, more from Heath's smoldering look than nerves, Eliza followed her group into the pub.

She'd been in the pub only once before, with Joy, but it had been the last stop on a pub crawl that Eliza had thought she would never recover from the morning after. With the white walls bright in the light streaming through the windows, the Foxed Hound didn't seem as sketchy and, with the aroma of fish and chips tantalizing her nose, didn't smell of yesterday's spilled alcohol.

Exposed wooden beams darkened with age and hundreds of years of smoke crisscrossed the ceiling of the large main room. In the middle of the room, a large circular mahogany bar was a hive of activity. Bartenders pulled levers, mixed drinks, and plopped in lemons or cherries or olives, all under the glow of the backlit alcohol bottles shelved around a large mirror. A small army of servers carrying trays laden with glasses scurried between the bar and tables full of lunchtime patrons. Eliza joined her group at one of the abandoned tables wiped clean by a waitress.

"Which one's Timothy?" Joy jerked her head in the direction of the bar.

Eliza compared the two bartenders to see which one matched the description Wentworth had given her. "That one." She pointed at the man of medium build whose sandy hair and weathered complexion marked him as an outdoorsman.

"I hate it when the bad guys are good-looking." Joy pouted but brightened as the waitress approached.

After they ordered their lunch and drinks, Eliza put Joy to work, and her friend happily accepted her mission after promises of free drinks and the opportunity to practice her powers over men in order to further ensnare Jack Willoughby, a friend of Joy who had no clue he was going to be her husband one day. Eliza knew she should feel sorry for him, but he had earned and proven his reputation as an unrepentant flirt during Eliza's first stay at Pemberley and deserved to be the victim of Joy's machinations. It balanced the scales.

Joy, armored in skinny jeans, tan half boots, and a white tank top that might have been one size too small, sashayed up to the bar and positioned herself nearest to Timothy. Even from several tables away, Eliza knew the second Timothy caught sight of Joy's blond-bombshell looks. He slicked back his hair, ran his finger along the collar of his black polo shirt, and blinded Joy with a smile.

Great-Aunt Iris sighed and rested her cheek in her hand. "I remember the moment your great-uncle looked at me like that." Her eyes glistened with tears, but she sniffed and swiped at her eyes. "Look at me getting all soft in the head." A smile lit up her red eyes. "In fact, I've got it better than most women my age. Most of their husbands are either dead and in the grave or barely alive and dead in the bedroom department, if you know what I mean."

Eliza knew all too well, and from Heath's sigh, she figured he knew more than he wanted to. She also wanted to argue that Great-Uncle William really did seem barely alive, but apparently, the man had enough life in him when the occasion called for it.

"What do you think they're talking about?" Eliza tilted her head in an attempt to listen, but the sound of clinking, eating, and patrons chatting drowned out any sound from Joy and Timothy's conversation.

"From their body language, I'd say they're getting pretty cozy," Heath said.

He was right. Joy rested her right foot up on the bottom rungs of a barstool and cocked her left hip in the opposite direction. Every once in a while, her fingers would stray to her hair and twirl a piece. Timothy's gaze followed every swirling motion.

After a few more hair twirls, two added bonuses of Joy's lick-and-nibble-her-bottom-lip trick she often stole from one of her female protagonists, and the finale of a light touch on Timothy's arm, Joy pivoted and sashayed back to the group.

She slid into her seat and sipped a gin and tonic the waitress had delivered moments before. "That was brill! I didn't know the lip-biting thing actually worked in reality. I shall try it on Willoughby when I see him again."

"Does Willoughby have any clue of his future with you?" Eliza asked.

"Of course not. That would take all the fun out of it." She brightened as the waitress set their orders on the table. "Oh, finally. I'm starving."

After everyone had at least gotten a few bites of their food, Eliza wiped her fingers free of fish-and-chips debris. "So, what did you find out?"

Joy held up a finger, chewed, and swallowed. "Yes. Timothy Elliot is a proper prat and a gossip. Never knew men to be gossips, but there it is. I mentioned how ghastly it must be working in a pub that had a murder, and that's all it took for him to start talking. Threw poor Wentworth under the bus right away. Said it wasn't a surprise that such a hard-hearted man like him would commit a murder."

"That's harsh. I know Wentworth can be gruff and rough around the edges, but I wouldn't say he's hard-hearted." Eliza bit into a fry.

"That's not all." Joy leaned forward and motioned them all to do the same until their noses nearly touched. "Said it was probably guilt after all these years that made him take justice into his own hands."

"Justice for what?" Heath asked.

"According to Timothy, Wentworth was the sole person responsible for Felix Payne's *acquittal,* which got him off the hook for murdering a child."

WENTWORTH, still sitting on the cot where Eliza had last left him, peered owlishly at her and the rest of the gang assembled in the attic and scratched at a healthy amount of graying stubble.

Even with the afternoon sun shining outside, the tiny room's window allowed in a paltry amount of light, enough to intermittently sparkle against a floating dust mote.

Great-Aunt Iris, who had surprisingly climbed the narrow steps with less huffing and puffing than all of them combined, pursed her lips and stared down her nose at Wentworth. "Does my Fitz know that a person he associates with allowed a murderer, a child killer, to go free?"

Wentworth groaned and massaged the back of his neck. "Bloody bollocks, for the hundredth time—"

"Might I remind you, DCI Wentworth, whose secret room you are holed up in?" Great-Aunt Iris's finger wagged in his face.

Not looking the least chagrined, he continued. "For the hundredth time, Felix Payne could not, under any circumstances, have killed that poor child. Tragic, yes. Should justice be served? Absolutely. But not at the cost of an innocent man's freedom."

Great-Aunt Iris sniffed. "Innocent? That man is a hardened criminal who just got out of prison for some nefarious crime, or so I was told by Willow, who heard it from her mum."

Wentworth pinched the bridge of his nose. "Sadly, you might have a point. The Felix of recent years is a far cry from the Felix I knew as a young lad. However, ten years for manslaughter by gross negligence is hardly the same as a life sentence for the intentional killing of a child, which Felix didn't commit." He studied his hands, which trembled. "Look, drudging all this up is useless. It was twenty-five years ago."

"But what if it helps solve the current murder?" Eliza risked sitting next to the bristling detective. "What happened?"

Wentworth closed his eyes, leaned back in the cot, and thumped his head on the wall. "Felix had gotten out after a two-year stint for assault. I was at Kellynch Hall for some business matters with my estate manager, and we happened to meet up at the White Lady."

"Were you a detective then?" Joy asked.

"No. Just a gormless constable with more gusto than brains, I'm afraid."

Eliza studied the coppery lines webbed along Wentworth's russet-brown skin. She'd noticed his wrinkles before, but perhaps the lighting of the room gave the illusion they were carved deeper. Or the strain of the past few days had dug its claws in and deepened them irrevocably.

He twisted his head and met her gaze with his dark-amber eyes. "At the time, it didn't matter that I was the law and Felix was anything but. We were old mates meeting up for a drink, is all, until..."

"Until what?" Joy, who had plunked down on the dusty floor, hugged her knees to her chest.

"Until twenty-one-year-old Finn Wentworth got good and bloody trollied and committed a crime with his good old but just as stupid pal, Felix Payne."

Great-Aunt Iris harrumphed so grandly that Eliza feared the sound had leached down through the walls.

Heath grinned. "Raid an old granny's flower patch, did you?"

"You have no idea how much I wished the next morning that I had. Instead, Felix and I took Old Man Hawkins's rotting lorry for a joy drive. By the by, he looked more like a hawk than a man and just as nasty with his claws when he caught young children stealing vegetables from his veggie patch. Anyway, at the time, dead drunk, we thought it was retribution for all the times we had his nails in our necks."

"Let me guess." Heath's grin widened. "You didn't get his lorry safely back home."

"Unless you consider the bottom of the River Brue its home, then no."

Great-Aunt Iris clutched her purse to her chest and directed her spiked knitting needles at the newly revealed lawbreaker.

Raising an eyebrow but leaving his thoughts to himself, Wentworth forged on. "At the time, we barely escaped drowning, but after we crawled up the bank, we had a right laugh about it and somehow stumbled to our respective places. Thought my epically stupid mistake would go unnoticed. Felix might have had a few or most of his moral screws loose, but he could be trusted with a secret."

An awkward silence stretched on for several seconds. A *bang* resounded up through the walls and echoed in the room. They jumped.

"Staff are moving tables and such for the weekend's events," Eliza said. Still, even though the wing beneath them was mainly unoccupied, that didn't mean a stray guest couldn't wander the main corridors below. She would have to remind Wentworth and the others to be as quiet as mice, especially with the police descending upon the place the next day. Her gut twisted.

Wentworth released a shaky breath. "It wasn't until after I woke up from my drunken stupor with a mother of a hangover that I heard about the murder of a village child, Teddy Price, a young lad of ten. Ghastly it was, too, and when I heard they'd arrested Felix, I was gutted."

"What happened then?" Heath asked.

"Couldn't let my old mate get life for a crime I knew he couldn't have committed, and my alibi, well..."

"You couldn't give the exact reason why, or else you'd have been fired and prosecuted for theft," Eliza finished for him.

"That's the long and short of it. I concocted a believable alibi, swore Felix couldn't have done it, prayed the power of the uniform would add some fairy dust over my lies, and in the end, Felix was acquitted."

"I bet the parents were absolutely devastated," Joy said.

"The lad's mum never recovered. Ended up losing her mind. Started thinking every ten-year-old boy in the village was hers. Would nab them, take them home, feed them, call them Teddy, and would sob when parents or authorities, who knew exactly where the missing boys would be, retrieved them from her."

"And Teddy's father?" Joy asked.

"Was convinced Felix had done it. Swore he saw him running down the lane around the time his boy was killed. Probably did, as that would have timed perfectly with our travels home. Man damn near vaulted himself on Felix when the acquittal verdict was read. Swore he'd see him dead before he got away with killing his child."

"And you're positive that Felix couldn't have killed Teddy?" Heath asked.

Wentworth nodded. "We were too busy trying not to drown for him to have killed anybody."

Eliza's skin tingled. "And where's Teddy's father now?"

"No idea. Again, it was twenty-five years ago and happened in a different county over a hundred miles away. Why should we care where his father is?"

"Because the death of a child never quits haunting a parent, especially a parent who thinks the man who killed his kid got away with it."

Chapter Six
Of Fools and Family

I hate to speak ill of others, but I'm afraid that I have found two people more pompous than Caroline Bingley. At least Caroline has beauty and wealth—or at least, her brother's wealth— and a glimmer of intelligence to support her belief in her grandeur. Darcy met Sir Walter and Miss Elliot tonight at a ball put on by an acquaintance, and I have never seen Darcy so repulsed by two people other than Wickham. Darcy overheard Sir Walter make a snide comment about him and how wealthy untitled gentlemen were beneath his notice and should come back for an introduction when they had at least gained a knighthood.

Lizzy Bennet Darcy
Bath 1814

Friday dawned with the correct atmosphere for the dread prickling Eliza's skin. She flicked the curtain back in place, obscuring the dreary, rainy weather from her sight.

Alone with her thoughts since the early morning, when Caesar prodded her awake with his paw, Eliza paced her office. She'd made it hers, and somehow, knowing that the Oriental carpet she trod upon was one that Elizabeth Darcy's slippers had once slid across comforted her.

The first time she'd stepped foot into her predecessor's favorite room, dust covers had hidden the Georgian and Regency-era furniture. After months of rearranging and cleaning, every time she walked into the room, she still felt as if she were going back in time.

In the middle of the room, chaise lounges covered with maroon velvet created a tidy sitting area around a walnut coffee table edged with engraved miniature rosettes. A mahogany armoire was tucked in the corner. Five mahogany-and-gold-leaf mirrors hung on the walls, giving the smaller-sized room depth and light. Scattered throughout were several Regency-style rosewood étagères four shelves high, each displaying period knickknacks that Eliza had dug out from where Nancy had buried them in Pemberley's attic. Added to that collection was the matching set of gilded vases Eliza's uncle had anonymously sent to her on her twenty-first birthday. Eliza lifted one from its spot, traced the petals of a painted rose, and wondered if her namesake had done the same. According to family legend, those vases were gifted to Elizabeth Darcy on her wedding day.

Eliza set them back on the shelf and moved to the room's pièce de résistance. She had situated Elizabeth Darcy's mahogany writing desk to give her the best view of the world outside the window. The desk was simple in design, with two layers of small cubbies and drawers. Eliza traced the silver and gold filigree curlicued throughout the dark wood. It seemed odd to have her laptop on top of the hundreds-of-years-old desk, but the twenty-first century didn't run on parchment and ink.

For several minutes, she stood behind the matching chair and tried to convince herself to sit down and work. But worrisome thoughts darted around in her mind. *How am I going to keep Wentworth's presence a secret? I've literally invited the fox into the chicken coop! How can we get him out of this awful mess?* All the clues she'd gathered and gleaned over the past few days lay in a jumbled mess in her head. But the old nursery's chalkboard they'd used the first time was too out in the open for such a secret mission. She needed to write her thoughts down where they wouldn't be stumbled upon by staff or the weekend's guests.

She rubbed her temples, ambled to the sash window separated into six squares of glass, pulled the curtain back, and rested her forehead on one of them.

The stream running through the estate, usually sparkling in the sun's rays, swirled its gray, dull waters down toward Lambton. Chrysanthemums, dahlias, freesias, phlox, and zinnias currently took precedence over the roses, although a few still hung with fading glory. Soon, the gardener, Giles, would be out preparing the garden for winter's bite and giving all the winter bloomers a pep talk for their upcoming showtime.

She wished someone would give her a pep talk, but then again, perhaps she would end up kicking them in the shin for even trying to circle her little black rain cloud with silver. With something akin to a growl, she stomped to her laptop, opened it, jammed a few keys here and there, and after ensuring that everything was in order for the group's arrival at two, went in search of her posse and found them holed up in the library.

Great-Aunt Iris, perched in a high-back leather chair and knitting as if humanity would end the moment she stopped, was giving Joy the regal eagle eye. "I'll have you know, young lady, that back in my day, we did not go about waving our private affairs in public. It isn't done." She pinned Eliza, who claimed her spot next to Heath on a love seat, with the same look she'd given Joy. "Isn't that so?"

Eliza bit her tongue against the reminder that her great-aunt not only waved her very private affairs in public but dang near tooted them all through a bullhorn. "Yes." She leaned into Heath's shoulder and whispered, "What did I agree to?"

Heath chuckled and wrapped an arm around her before scooting her closer. "Your great-aunt and Joy were having a 'discussion' on whether or not Joy's dating life is up for public debate."

"Great-Aunt Iris does not care if my heart shatters into tiny pieces." Joy pouted indignantly from her seat.

The old lady in question harrumphed, her fingers never ceasing to knit the pastel rainbow wool into a tiny cap. "You whinging away over Willoughby will never solve the issue. If you want that man—and I don't see why you would, worthless chap—you must take the first step." She quit knitting for one second and pointed a needle at Joy, who had opened her mouth to retort. "Besides, all this could be for naught. Happiness in marriage is entirely by chance, I'll have you know."

Eliza gave Joy a smile in hopes it would bolster her cousin's frown. It failed.

"But you and Great-Uncle Fitzwilliam are happy, aren't you?" Eliza sat forward and rested her elbows on her knees. "I bet you were the cutest couple."

Great-Aunt Iris sniffed and patted her puffy white hair. "People often did say we looked brilliant together." She brandished her knitting needle again. "But I gave your great- uncle no choice but to love me. I let him know from the get-go what side his bread was buttered on. No matter my demands, though, it could have all fallen apart like poor Andrew and—" Her peachy complexion reddened, and she pressed her lips together until they whitened.

Eliza perked up. Even after all these months, she'd only figured out some of the mystery behind the estrangement between her father and uncle. Nancy had been involved, which didn't surprise Eliza in the least, as the detestable woman's character was known to be "beastly" if one were listening to Great-Aunt Iris and "bitchy" if one were taking Joy's opinions to heart. Her uncle hardly spoke of his ex-wife, and whenever Eliza pressed to know the particulars of it all, his eyes, normally bright, would shutter those secrets in and shut Eliza out.

"Please, I need to know. If it weren't for all this secrecy, we wouldn't be missing Uncle right now. He'd be here telling us to keep our noses out of business that isn't ours." Although with DCI Wentworth holed up two floors above them, it was their business whether they wanted it to be or not. When her great-aunt persisted in silence, which was unusual, Eliza soldiered on. "Okay, tell me where I go wrong. Nancy first got her claws into my dad, right, because Uncle Fitzwilliam was not healthy, and most people thought he'd die long before his time, right?"

Great-Aunt Iris nodded and continued knitting.

"Then, Uncle Fitzwilliam recovers from a near-death illness and regains his strength. Which, because Nancy is a... a..."

"Social-climbing tart," Joy pitched in.

"Yes, that, she breaks my dad's heart and goes in for the kill with Uncle Fitzwilliam."

Another nod.

"Did my dad really love her?"

Great-Aunt Iris sighed and laid down her knitting. "Yes, my dear, I'm afraid he did. He couldn't understand why she'd left him for Fitzwilliam. We all had our suspicions, and I knew she was messing with my nephews for their money, but nothing I said worked. It did the opposite. So I kept my opinions to myself."

"And Uncle Fitzwilliam didn't find this odd?"

"As I've said before, Nancy was the master manipulator. In the end, the boys had a blinding row, and I never saw my Fitz again for over twenty-five years."

"So a broken heart and a heated argument between them sent my dad across the ocean to never speak nor want anything to do with his family again? That seems rather melodramatic." Eliza pursed her lips and studied her great-aunt. "That's not all, is it? What is it you nor anyone else wants to tell me?"

Great-Aunt Iris, her eyes shiny with unshed tears, stuffed her knitting in her purse, hoisted herself to her feet, and paused by Eliza on her way out the door. She rested a warm, papery palm on Eliza's cheek. "Some things are better left unsaid. You may wish to unhear the very words you were eager for the moment you hear them."

"But—"

"You young people nowadays, always wanting what you shouldn't have." She tutted a few times. "Enough of this sad business. Don't we have a house full of police coming soon and their quarry stashed in our attic?"

Eliza stuffed her father and uncle's mystery to the back of her mind to dwell on later and checked the time on her phone. "T minus four hours. We must gather for one last ops meeting." She chewed on her bottom lip. "Does anyone know what we can make a temporary board out of? I don't want to use the chalkboard in the nursery. Too exposed. Especially with who'll be milling around the place soon."

Heath snapped his fingers. "Say, where did you hoard all those cardboard boxes you emptied when you redecorated the place?"

Eliza smiled. Many of their phone conversations—the ones when she was at Pemberley and he was at his dig site—had centered around the horrendous task of de-Nancying the place and giving it a new life, which constituted opening boxes upon boxes and un-earthing the antiques Nancy had hidden. Not wanting to bother breaking them down when other tasks were at hand, Eliza had simply had staff store them in one of the many unused spaces in the servants' quarters belowstairs.

"Now you're using your little gray cells, mon ami." Eliza quoted her favorite little Belgian detective and even added the mustache preening of Hercule Poirot.

Joy snorted and rolled her eyes. "Brains *and* good looks? Who would have thought?"

Heath waved away Joy's jab, and Eliza, set to meet with the senior house staff within the hour, directed Heath and Joy to fetch different items while Eliza and Great-Aunt Iris created a diversion from the arts-and-crafts hunting and gathering, which the octogenarian performed to perfection. After an Oscar-worthy "fall" down the steps and a "fainting" experience to fool even the most astute witness, Great-Aunt Iris had insisted upon an audience to make sure she didn't stop breathing. When Eliza "attempted" to call the doctor, Great-Aunt Iris, with a quickness that shocked all onlookers, hopped to her feet with a peppy "I'm feeling much better. Everything's tickety-boo" and walked away on squeaky white tennis shoes, Eliza shuffling after her.

"Have you never used tape before?"

Joy sent Eliza a withering look, attempted to flick her fingers free of the packing tape, and when the adhesive only latched onto another part of her skin, she held her hand out to Eliza. "Don't say a word."

Wentworth, eyeing them from his cot, groaned. "Bloody hell. If you two can't even figure out how to tape boxes together, how on God's green earth are you going to solve this bloody mess?"

"Should have thought about that before you came knocking on our door." Eliza smiled and turned the flattened and taped cardboard "chalkboard" around for inspection. "Ta-da!"

"It's..." Great-Aunt Iris scrunched her nose and squinted at the mess of intersecting lines and the asymmetrical shape of the makeshift board. "It's..."

"A cock-up. That's what it is." Wentworth scowled.

"Didn't sleep well?" Eliza asked sweetly.

"Not likely with all the scurrying that goes on around this place at night."

Joy squeaked and glanced around her as if an army of mice were readying an attack.

"Add on the cheerful message I got this morning, and it's no wonder I'm in such a good mood."

Eliza ignored the sarcasm dripping from the detective's words. If anyone had a reason to be acting like a petulant child, it was Wentworth. He'd all but choked on a roll and coffee when she'd informed him of their soon-to-be weekend guests. The near-choking incident was followed by a barrage of very English, very creative swear words.

"This is why we need to write down all the information we have. The more organized we are, the faster and more efficiently we can work."

Wentworth, still giving the jerry-rigged board the stink eye, crossed his arms and didn't bother volunteering to help hang the contraption. Eliza batted her eyelashes at Heath, and within five minutes, they had the cardboard tacked on the wall closest to the cot and other accoutrements Eliza had dug up for Wentworth's comfort.

"It's crooked." Great-Aunt Iris paused her knitting long enough to jut her chin in the direction of the slanted board.

Eliza slid a side glance at her great-aunt, but the little old lady had gone back to knitting. Having finished the pastel-rainbow baby hat, she had started on another project, the length of which forecast a mint-green-and-coral blanket. While Great-Aunt Iris was hardly without her knitting supplies, the increase in productivity had Eliza's forehead furrowing. If it kept her great-aunt out of trouble, Eliza wouldn't give it too much thought. She already had too much on her mind as it was.

Joy dug around in her purse and proffered six Sharpies—three red, three black. "Stole these from Fitzwilliam's study."

Eliza took a black one, plucked off the cap, and placed the tip on the cardboard. "Well?"

"Start with the victim." Wentworth nabbed a red marker and wrote *Felix Payne-46-ex-con-just released from a ten-year stint in prison.*

"How do you know his age?"

Wentworth quirked his eyebrow at Eliza. "Childhood mates, remember? We were in the same years during primary school."

"What about the crime scene?" Heath asked. "He was poisoned, right?"

Wentworth nodded and wrote down the facts of the crime scene: *Felix was found lying on the floor in the middle of his room. Two pint glasses are on the table. One had Felix's DNA and fingerprints. The other had Wentworth's DNA. Both had Wentworth's fingerprints.*

"Probably planted by Timothy." Eliza went to write Timothy's name on the cardboard, but Wentworth stilled her hand.

"You seriously think he'd commit murder and frame me for it? He has the means and opportunity, but where's the motive?"

"You said he wants the estate, has even gotten nasty about it."

"But it can't be his. Deep down, he has to know that. Probably bluffing his way, hoping to wheedle me down until I throw him some scraps."

Eliza chewed on the marker's cap. "But you did say that he was probably nuts. And crazy people do crazy, stupid things. We can't rule him out. How else does that explain the two cups you drank from being in a room you've never been in?"

Wentworth's face scrunched. "Fine. Anyone have a pencil?"

Joy dug around in her purse and came up empty-handed. Heath shook his head, then they all turned their attention to Great-Aunt Iris, who, on noticing the stares, lifted her head from her task, tsked, and after a little digging in her purse, found a pencil. Eliza was sure she would never be surprised at what her great-aunt dug from her purse and grinned at the image of her pulling out a lamp, like Mary Poppins.

Wentworth printed Timothy Elliot's name under the Suspects column. "There. Happy now?"

"Delighted." Eliza tapped the back of his hand arched against the board. "See, we can work as a team. Compromise and all that."

Wentworth stared at where her finger had poked him. "How I love compromising."

Eliza ignored his moody reply. "Do you want to write, or should I?"

Not giving her a chance to put her mark on the board, Wentworth filled in the blanks: *Timothy Elliot-30ish-bartender at the Foxed Hound-a right wanker.*

"That's not a technical police term, is it?" Eliza pointed at the insult.

"This is the least caustic term used at the station." Wentworth continued writing: *Hates me, wants me out of the picture, thinks he'll inherit Kellynch Hall.*

"Do we know what Felix was poisoned with?" Heath reworded his earlier question.

"I'm sure the reports have come back, but I am not privy to that information anymore." Wentworth's shoulders heaved.

"Isn't there anyone you can trust? Someone who can sneak you information?" Joy asked.

"Tried. Called everyone who I could think of that I could trust. Came up against wall after wall. My sergeant even seemed wary of me. Said she didn't want to get us both into trouble. Don't blame her." He snatched his phone out from under his pillow. "Decided that it might be best to turn this thing off in case they could track me or something."

"She should know she can trust you." Eliza bristled at the nameless sergeant who had turned her back on her chief.

"You'd think differently if you knew the powers that be and the games they play. There is always only one loser. And it's never them."

Turning her attention to the board, Eliza made her first mark under *Wentworth's fingerprints*: *poison?* and was about to march out the twenty-five-year-old event in which Felix was fingered for murder when an alert pinged from her phone.

"Darn it! I've got to meet up with Tash, Mrs. Underhill, Mrs. B, and Willow. Guests arrive in three hours." She gave Heath her marker, enjoying the shiver down her spine when their fingertips touched. "Wentworth, don't forget to put all the details of your past joyride and the events of that night on here. No buts. As you said when we started, the victim often holds the key to his or her own death. We need to know everything about Felix." She paused and studied Wentworth's stooped shoulders. "And as you're also a victim, we need to know everything about you as well."

At his groan, Joy offered a supportive smile. "Don't worry. Anything and everything you tell us stays here. Kind of like Vegas."

Wentworth slid a glance at Great-Aunt Iris and grunted. Even though her attention was seemingly on her knitting, her alert posture and gleaming eyes proved why she was such a powerful spying weapon.

After one final look at the board, Eliza, her gut swirling with dread, snuck back to the main part of the house.

MRS. Underhill scowled at Eliza's hurried entrance into the kitchen.

"Sorry I'm a little late." Eliza, laptop clutched under her arm like a football, skidded to a stop and attempted to regulate her breathing so as not to sound as out of shape as she was. *Add "work out" to list. Again!* "Never realize how large Pemberley is until you have to run the whole gambit." Of course, of all days to forget her laptop in her office, that was the one day she was at the highest and farthest point from it only to have to backtrack to the center.

Mrs. Underhill's frown deepened. Eliza often wondered if the formidable woman could link her ancestry to the ancient Amazonian warriors. Add an Irish ancestor to account for the red hair perpetually swathed in a bun and the spattering of freckles across her porcelain skin and the woman needn't bother with DNA testing.

"I was told this meeting would begin at eleven." She tapped her gold wristwatch.

Eliza chewed her bottom lip and sought the kinder faces of Tash, Mrs. B, and Willow. Tash gave a slight wink, Mrs. Bankcroft all but glared at the housekeeper's profile, and Willow's pale complexion and skittering gaze reminded Eliza that she wasn't alone in her fear of the housekeeper.

Eliza recalled what she'd told the young woman about being able to handle the housekeeper and questioned the truthfulness of that statement. *It isn't a crime to change one's mind.* She thought of the poster she used to hang in her classroom, one emblazoned with Ralph Waldo Emerson's famous quote: "Foolish consistency is the hobgoblin of little minds."

Not wanting to be foolish or a hobgoblin, Eliza changed her mind and smiled up at the six-foot housekeeper. Mrs. Underhill stared down her nose at Eliza, making her feel much shorter than her five foot ten inches. This was not the Uncle-Fitzwilliam's-in-the-house housekeeper who, despite being prickly and somewhat condescending, had shown a willingness to like and help Eliza. While the housekeeper did know the ins and outs of Pemberley and probably understood how to run an estate much better than Eliza ever would, the disdain vibrating off the woman made Eliza's mind whirl and consider mutiny.

Tash cleared his throat. "We must begin, I'm afraid, if all is to be in place when the guests arrive."

"Yes, sorry." Eliza's face burned, but she rallied and, after opening her laptop, handed out the paper copies of the schedule she had stashed between the keyboard and screen then walked the senior staff and Willow through the weekend's events.

One hour and several questions later, Mrs. Underhill, Tash, and Willow left the kitchen. Eliza wilted onto a barstool snugged up against the giant work counter and plunked her head in her arms.

"There, there." Mrs. Bankcroft tutted softly and situated a cup of tea by Eliza's elbow. "Have a cuppa."

Eliza, her head still in her arms, peered sideways at the painted pink roses splattered on the china. "Have anything stronger?"

"Now, now, all will be well. You'll see." She patted Eliza's arm with a plump hand and tottered about the kitchen.

Eliza sipped the chamomile tea, and soon, her nerves stopped twitching, and the warmth seeping from the cup into her hands soothed her frenzied mind. So much so that she peered into her cup, wondering if Mrs. Bankcroft hadn't put a little extra something in it.

"Miss Eliza?" Mrs. Bankcroft leaned over the counter. "I know you've got quite a lot on your plate, and I don't want to give undue concern, but I think... I'm sure that Willow is nicking things."

So much for settled nerves and silent thoughts.

"What things?"

"I have some tea that will help the frog in your throat. Want to try it?" Mrs. Bankcroft reached for Eliza's empty cup.

"No." She cleared whatever was clogging her windpipe. Clearly, it wasn't a frog, but predicting what the cook was about to list off, it was quite possibly fear. "I'm fine. What things, again?"

"Nothing of importance, really. Which is odd and why I didn't mention it until now. Plates and cups and silverware. Those types of things. Why on earth a girl like her, who has a home to go to with her own things, would want to nick 'em, I've no clue."

Eliza knew exactly where the plates, cups, and other missing kitchen paraphernalia were—stacked in the attic on a wobbly table she'd unearthed. Curse on her for not knowing that Mrs. Bankcroft took such careful inventory. *Eliza, you are a complete idiot!*

There was no need to feign guilt. She added to it by smacking her forehead. "Ah, that's my fault, I'm afraid. Willow isn't to blame. I take snacks and such into my office or my room and totally forget to bring them back. I promise to pick up after myself in the future and bring stuff back to the kitchen."

Mrs. Bankcroft cocked her head as if testing that theory. Eliza could have kicked herself. *Why, when I've been clean and responsible, suddenly have a fit of irresponsibility?*

"Stress, I'm afraid."

The cook took that explanation in stride, and for a few minutes, the only sound was the soft rustle of plastic wrap and crinkling of brown paper as Mrs. Bankcroft set to making a cold lunch of meats and cheeses.

Eliza finished her tea and hopped off the barstool. "Thanks, Mrs. B."

Mrs. Bankcroft paused her carving of a thick chunk of ham. "Lunch will be ready at half past and served in the dining room." She set her knife back on the ham. "Oh, and come to think of it, you might want to speak to Tash and Mrs. Underhill. More than kitchen stuff has grown legs and wandered off. Odd that, eh?"

Forcing a smile, Eliza waved off Mrs. Bankcroft's concern. "I'll check with them, but I'm sure it's a result of me rearranging things."

Eliza, with a sinking gut, left the kitchen to the tune of Mrs. Bankcroft's knife slicing through a hunk of meat.

Good grief. I can't even keep the staff from asking questions. How in the world am I going to hide Wentworth from a house full of nosy police officers?

After texting her posse to leave the attic like their lives depended on it and to bring the pile-up of dishes with them, Eliza settled in the dining room, where the only company she had was the thoughts of her and Wentworth's impending doom clanging in her head.

She placed her arms on the table and rested her head on them. Doom surrounded her. She might not be able to forecast the weekend's outcome, but she could get a report on the troubles clouding her family's life.

Scrolling through her recent calls and texts, she cringed when she realized the last time she'd called or texted her family. Belle's name, too, which normally made several appearances a day, was oddly absent from the list. The last time she'd spoken with Belle was Monday morning. *Feels like a lifetime ago.* But it wasn't. In four days' time, Eliza's dreams of securing Pemberley's future had morphed into a nightmare with more than a building's future on the line.

She tapped "Mom" and waited, and before she was sure she would be shuffled to voicemail, her mom answered.

"Eliza ..." Her mother's voice faltered, and a muffled sob echoed through the phone.

"Mom? What's wrong?" Eliza's skin prickled, and a chill slithered down her spine. She'd seen her mother cry only a handful of times, and all of them were at funerals. Her mother's silence had her cradling the phone closer to her ear. "Mom?"

"Oh, Eliza... It's awful." Another sob, that time unmuffled. Eliza imagined her mother, tall and proud, bent over with grief.

"Mom, is it Dad? Uncle Fitzwilliam? Is someone hurt? Are you hurt?"

Her mother sniffled. "No one's hurt... at least..." Broken breaths accompanied more sniffling. After a few moments, she cleared her throat. "Sorry about that. I just found out... But there's no sense in worrying you."

"Nuh-uh, it doesn't work that way. You have to tell me now, or I'll only think the worst."

"Eliza?" Her father's voice replaced her mother's, and he sounded weak and old.

"Dad?" Unable to keep still, Eliza paced the dining room. "Please tell me what's going on."

"I... Yes, Pam, she needs to know. It's the only way this family can heal. Eliza, I..."

"Say it, Dad. Please." Her shoulders scrunched as if preparing for a blow.

"You know about the reason I left England, right? And that Nancy and I had been an item before she and Fitzwilliam married."

"Did you and Uncle Fitzwilliam have another fight? I thought you two were reconciling."

Her father cleared his throat. "We were, and then letters showed up in the mail." His voice wavered. "Letters from England. From Nancy."

Eliza had never actually seen red before. She'd heard about it. Some of her past students had used the phrase in their creative writing assignments, but she had never experienced the sensation. Until then. And in the center of the reddish hue swimming before her was Nancy's smug, pretentious face, smirking from a jail cell. She clutched her phone until she was sure it would snap in two. She prayed it would, then it would save her from having to hear the rest of her father's story.

"Eliza, they were letters I had written her all those years ago."

"Is that all? We know you and that... witch... were together before she married Uncle. I don't understand what all the fuss is about."

"They were letters I had written *after* she married Fitz. Love letters I had written during..."

Eliza wanted to plug her ears and make nonsense noises like a child to drown out her father's voice. The sound of her father's sobs broke her heart, and tears trickled down her face.

Andrew sniffled and whispered, "Our affair. Our love affair had not stopped after she married Fitz. Don't you see? The ghosts of my past have followed me across the ocean, the one place I was safe from them... from *her*."

Eliza's heart plummeted to her stomach, and she thought she was going to be sick. "You mean you were sleeping with Nancy *after* she married Uncle Fitzwilliam, *your brother*?"

"Yes."

That simple admission stabbed her in the gut. "But I don't understand."

"I was a fool. A fool in love, and I believed her lies that she'd made a mistake and would leave Fitz for me. It only took two weeks for me to realize the snake she was and the dirty disgusting prat I had become. That's when and why I left England, thinking I could leave my past and my mistakes behind me."

"And you never told Uncle Fitzwilliam?"

"I couldn't. I knew it would hurt him beyond repair. So I picked a fight, said things I really didn't mean, and used that as my excuse for leaving my homeland... my family."

Eliza pulled the phone from her ear and stared at the glowing screen. All her life, she'd looked up to her father as a demigod, as one who'd sacrificed to save others, as a father who would move heaven and earth for his daughter, as one who loved his wife and treated her like she was his life's breath. To have the evil truth spoken from his lips, that he'd committed adultery with his sister-in-law, was a stab to the heart too powerful to overcome.

Her finger hovered over the end call button, and on the fourth repetition of her name, she pressed the red icon.

Chapter Seven
And the Oscar Goes to Great-Aunt Iris

*It seems that my dear friend Anne has an admirer. Her estranged
cousin, Mr. William Elliot, has returned to the family folds a widower
and is a charming, handsome young man looking for a new wife. It
seems as if he has taken a notion to my friend. Anne seems unaffected
by him, and I cannot say that I am displeased. There is something
about Mr. Elliot that I do not like. He reminds me of Wickham. Darcy
agrees and says that if a man such as Sir Walter and a woman such as
Miss Elizabeth Elliot dote upon him, he is a man not to be trusted.*

Lizzy Bennet Darcy

Bath 1814

B*reathe. You must breathe, Eliza Jane Darcy, or then you'll faint,
and what will Mrs. B say?*

Following her own advice, Eliza, standing in front of Pemberley's
large double-door entrance, took two breaths for good measure and
wrapped her black cardigan tightly about her to keep out the chill.
Despite the sun displaying all its glory at one in the afternoon, its
warmth was no match for the brisk autumn breeze. Even if a tropical
sun were beating down on her, it would do no good. Her father's devastating confession and the sounds of her parents' grief had chilled
her to the bone. In addition to the pain her father's past actions
had inflicted on her family, the strain it would put on her parents'
marriage now that her mother had to reconcile the past actions of
her husband, and the nearly insurmountable barrier this would in-

95

evitably put between the brothers, Nancy had somehow, from behind bars, hooked her nasty claws into Eliza's family as she had
threatened months ago. She couldn't have taken those damning letters with her to prison, so that left one option—someone in Pemberley was a spy. Her chest tightened, and she pressed her fist over her
sternum. If she could get through this weekend... If she could solve a
murder... If she could free Wentworth from suspicion... If she could
sniff out the spy... Then, maybe, she could breathe and think clearly
enough to help her family.

The first of several cars, sleek and black, turned in to the drive
and wended their way up to the front of the estate. Eliza wiped her
clammy palms on her black leggings, rearranged her soft-pink cashmere sweater, and toyed with a cameo brooch pinned above her left
breast.

Footmen she'd hired for the weekend jumped into action, and
for the next several minutes, all was a flurry of activity of people and
luggage. Eliza had meant to head count, but no one stayed in place
very long, and she gave up. Abandoning her post, Eliza put her best
lady-of-the-manor smile on her face and directed her steps toward
the man taking charge of the group.

Tall and slim, the man towered over the rest of his comrades.
Power dripped off him. Everything from his ramrod posture to his
crisp black uniform jacket to his starched white uniform collar con-
trasting against his antique-brass-colored skin had Eliza readjusting
her clothing, again as if readying for an inspection. His black peaked
hat, wrapped with the black-and-white diced band with the Derbyshire Constabulary badge dead center, sat squarely on his head.

"Hello and welcome to Pemberley." Eliza stuck her hand out.
His warm hand nearly engulfed hers. "You must be Chief Constable
Jayesh Kapoor." *The man who apparently has it out for Wentworth.*
She sucked in her cheeks slightly to keep from grinding her teeth.

"And you must be Miss Eliza Darcy." His lyrical voice didn't hearken back to his Indian ancestors but instead rang with the lilt of Ireland.

"The one and only." Eliza smiled and turned her attention to a woman who introduced herself as Amelia Cronk, the police and crime commissioner for Derbyshire.

The woman's clipped and precise Queen's English accent did not match the image of the woman Eliza had after speaking to her over the phone to finalize the weekend's events. The woman's short and stout frame nearly burst her layers of a puce-colored suit jacket and a dress shirt the color of boysenberries. Standing next to the handsome and dignified chief constable, poor Amelia looked how Eliza felt—frumpy, disheveled, and ever so ready to come apart at the slightest change in pressure.

"Welcome to Pemberley, Commissioner Cronk."

"Please, call me Amelia."

Eliza wasn't sure whether Chief Constable Kapoor snorted with derision or laughter, but Amelia's beige skin bloomed with scarlet blotches, and the blades of her once-slumped shoulders nearly touched.

"Of course. Thank you. Well, if you are all ready, let me introduce you to Pemberley." Eliza gestured for everyone to follow her and led them down the stone walkway, through the arch, past the fountain, and into the courtyard.

Someone whistled, and others whispered in what Eliza assumed was admiration of the estate's grandeur. Once they reached the main entrance, Eliza stepped to the side and greeted each person with a handshake, a smile, and a "Welcome to Pemberley." After the last and fifteenth time, Eliza brought up the rear and closed the double doors behind her.

Pemberley's weekend guests, in a mix of uniforms and civilian clothes, branched off in different directions, inspecting intricate woodwork, art, and Regency antiques displayed in the foyer. Eliza allowed them to roam for a few more minutes before speaking.

"Again, welcome, everyone, to Pemberley. I hope you will find everything to your liking, and please, if you need anything, let me know. For now, I will turn you over to the care of Tash and Mrs. Underhill." Eliza gestured to the butler and housekeeper standing almost at attention by the stairs. "In your rooms, you will find the printed itinerary, map of Pemberley, and location of the meetings and sessions scheduled by Commissioner Cronk."

Tash and Mrs. Underhill got to work, and soon, everyone dispersed from the foyer. Eliza exhaled, hoping to dislodge whatever pressed against her sternum.

"Ah, Miss Eliza. A moment of your time, please."

Eliza jumped.

"Sorry to have startled you." Chief Constable Kapoor had taken off his hat, and his hair, wavy and black without a speck of gray, belied the deep wrinkles at the corners of his eyes. He gazed down at her, his dark eyes looking into her rather than at her. When Heath did the same thing, her insides felt like the oozy chocolate inside a molten lava cake. When the chief constable did it, her gut churned.

"No worries, sir. What can I do for you?"

"Is there somewhere we can speak in private?"

Eliza led him to the library, which, in addition to the old leather chairs and thousands of books, boasted several round tables draped in black cloths. Chairs, rented from the same place as the tables, were clothed in black as well. "This should do for now. I think a meeting is set to begin in here in about thirty minutes if I remember correctly."

"Shouldn't take that long." He locked his arms behind him and walked to the window. "You have a lovely estate."

"Thank you."

"I should warn you that when the press gets wind of us being here, what with the murder in Lambton, you will have reporters at your door."

Great, that's all I need. Might as well invite a carnival and a band while I'm at it.

"I wouldn't worry about it too much, sir. We'll simply lock the entrance gate." Eliza cocked her head. "But why would your presence here draw the press?"

"Ah, now we get to the heart of the matter. Most folks won't look too kindly upon the constabulary, especially since people are already regretting voting that Amelia Cronk into office, not only for spending money for a conference in posh digs like this but that we're not spending our energy solving a local murder. The press, the feckin eejits that they are, will sniff out any story to sell copies." He drummed his fingers on a black-clothed table. "More fool them, I say, as we already know who killed Felix Payne. It's only a matter of time before he's caught."

Eliza's windpipe closed, and she barely managed an audible "Who?"

He smiled, an action that, rather than radiating humor or joy, squished his wrinkles tighter together. "I'm surprised you haven't heard the gossip, Miss Darcy."

She shrugged or at least hoped it came off as a shrug and not a twitch. Surely, twitches signaled guilt. "I've been rather busy lately."

"In that case, let me enlighten you. I think you might be familiar with him, as he was in charge of the murder investigation here a few months ago."

"Detective Chief Inspector Wentworth?" Hopefully, the chief constable would translate her squeak as one of surprise and not panic.

"Just the man." He stopped drumming his fingers and concentrated his gaze on her. "You haven't happened to have seen him since last Friday, have you?"

ELIZA had never been more grateful for Tash, as two seconds after the chief constable's question, the butler had stepped in the doorway and summoned him. After a promise to return to finish their conversation, Chief Constable Kapoor left the room.

Forcing herself to relax, she straightened book bindings and traced her finger over the embossed titles in the leather until her heart rate slowed and she could think clearly. She needed to get to Lambton. She needed to sniff out information, information unavailable due to Wentworth's fall from grace. What she needed was a distraction.

Knowing the perfect one, she relayed her plan via text to Heath and Joy. Their first mission: Gather the secret weapon. Their second mission: Release the secret weapon at the appointed time.

Until then, Eliza rearranged books, lightly dusted the wooden shelves, and thought. Not that it was doing her much good. Forcing her family's emergency to the back of her mind, she concentrated on the imminent danger. Since the beginning of the Wentworth debacle, she'd made mistake after mistake. And her planned afternoon's errand might prove to be as ridiculous. It was true that she could take the rarely used back road out of Pemberley, which was ingeniously covered by a curtain of willow branches both at the entrance and exit, but Joy's poor Range Rover would certainly receive a twig lashing, and if Chief Constable Kapoor got wind of their trip into town, Eliza wouldn't be able to play it off as a normal shopping trip. No, her trip into Lambton had to be legitimate and disclosed directly to the chief constable. No secrets, other than the large one wallowing two stories above her, could be kept from the policeman. His gaze hinted he did not suffer fools gladly—or in any other emotional state—and Eliza had no intention of being a fool. At least, not on purpose.

Heavy footsteps echoed down the hallway. Eliza texted *now* to the group chat. Seconds after Chief Constable Kapoor stepped into the library, his mouth already opening in what Eliza assumed would be the first in a line of questions, Great-Aunt Iris, resplendent in a magenta velour tracksuit and squeaky white tennis shoes, her knitting needles gripped in a fist, burst in behind him.

"Oh, do excuse me, sir. I need my niece." Great-Aunt Iris waddled past the uniformed policeman like a goose being chased by a fox and, with dramatic breathlessness, latched onto Eliza's arm. "My dear. You'll never guess."

Eliza blinked at her, and if this had been a stage performance and she the audience, she would have given her great-aunt a standing ovation. "You seem quite overcome. Here. Come sit."

Her great-aunt waved her away. "It's not me, daft girl. It's my friend Geraldine. I got word that she has received the worst sort of news and would like me to console her. Could you take me into Lambton to see her?" Great-Aunt Iris turned her batting eyelashes, battling a sheen of tears, on the chief constable. "Would you mind terribly, sir? Geraldine is one of my nearest and dearest friends since girlhood. Do you think you could spare Eliza for the afternoon?" As if on cue, a single tear slid down the old lady's leathery wrinkled cheek.

"Er ... of course, Mrs...." For the first time since arriving at Pemberley, the chief constable looked out of his element and rather boyish in his confusion.

"Oh yes, I'm sorry. With all the fuss, I never introduced you. Chief Constable Kapoor, this is my great-aunt, Mrs. Iris Darcy. Great-Aunt Iris, this is Chief Constable Jayesh Kapoor."

"It is nice to meet you, sir." Great-Aunt Iris's smile doubled. "What would this world come to if we didn't have dedicated policemen like you?"

The chief constable stammered. "Why, yes, thank you. Ah, the pleasure is all mine, of course, in making your acquaintance."

Eliza waited for the off-stage sound techs to hit the laugh track, indicating this was all a farce and the audience should play along.

Great-Aunt Iris folded her hands as if in prayer and tucked them under her chin. "Please, sir, may I steal away my niece? I'm afraid I've come to rely on her since her arrival."

"Of course, Mrs. Darcy. She's dotted all the i's and crossed all the t's so well that I'm sure the weekend would run smoothly even if she weren't here."

"Thank you, Chief Constable. I will not soon forget this kindness." Great-Aunt Iris snatched Eliza's hand and pulled her from the room. "Come, girl. We must hurry, for I'm afraid of Geraldine's tidings."

The door clicked shut on "tidings," and it took all of Eliza's willpower not to break down in a fit of giggles. From her great-aunt's reddening face, it seemed she was struggling with the same malady.

When they eventually made their way to the back of the mansion and out one of the service entrances, she and her great-aunt released their giggles.

"You should have been an actress," Eliza said after she'd controlled her breathing enough to speak.

"I say, my dear, you're not half bad yourself. Need to work on your timing perhaps a bit more, but other than that, flawless." Great-Aunt Iris patted Eliza's cheek and huffed. "I must be going barmy. Forgot my purse."

"I can go get it for you."

"The day I can't retrieve my own purse is the day you can take me out to pasture. Besides, your young man and Joy are late. Sometimes, I wonder if we'd be better off sleuthing without them."

Before Eliza could defend Heath or Joy, Great-Aunt Iris dipped inside the house and disappeared. Eliza used that time to ensure she had her cell, her purse, and her wallet then leaned against the stonework. The back of the estate, reserved for merchant and servants' entrances and a place to put the garbage cans, wasn't quite as grand as the front. Guests rarely went there, as it was an unwritten rule that no one really wanted to see the less-becoming sights of Pemberley.

Although the backside of the estate was a far cry posher than a prison cell, she knew she would end up in one if the chief constable caught even a whiff of his prey under—over—his very nose. The fact that he had even asked if she had seen Wentworth sent a skitter down her spine. *Did someone spot him coming onto the property? Did some nosy curtain twitcher with nothing better to do than look out windows see Wentworth dash down the road leading to Pemberley?*

An arm snaked around her waist. Heath drew her to his side and kissed her hair. "You all right?"

"No," she whispered and bit her lip to keep her lips from quivering. *Only a foolish woman cries in the face of adversity. What happened to me being a grown-ass woman?*

"Showing weakness doesn't mean you've failed. You know that, right?" His thumb caressed her cheek. "Besides, if you don't let me help, I'll have to put in my resignation as your sidekick. No sense in carrying dead weight around."

She mirrored his smile. "Too bad for you I like you enough that even if you were dead weight, I'd still drag you along." She tipped up on her tiptoes and kissed him. Like a long, luxurious bubble bath, it steamed away her troubled thoughts.

Something stabbed her in the side. Eliza, refusing to relinquish her hold on Heath, laid her cheek to his chest and peered at her great-aunt.

"I leave you unchaperoned for less than five minutes, and this is what I come back to?"

"Come now, Great-Aunt Iris, you were standing there for over a minute before you decided to dig your finger in Eliza's rib cage." Joy winked over the old lady's head. "Taking notes, eh?"

"Well... well..." Great-Aunt Iris blustered then flicked at least three imaginary flecks off her magenta tracksuit. "Never you mind. Let's be off."

"Who's Geraldine?" Eliza asked her great-aunt as she led the group down the flagstone walkway to the garages.

"Who?"

"The woman you used as an excuse to get me out of the house."

"Oh, that frightful woman? She was a battle-ax. Hated children. Wonder that she had any of her own. Come to think of it, I wonder how they ever came to be. Never saw a man about the place." Great-Aunt Iris hauled herself into the back seat.

Joy snorted, and Eliza hopped in the front passenger seat, met Heath's gaze in the rearview mirror, and matched his raised eyebrow with one of her own.

After fiddling with her seat belt and requesting Heath's assistance with the admonition that he keep his hands to himself in the process, Great-Aunt Iris blinked as if conjuring up the very woman. "Nasty bit of work, her. She's dead now, God rest her soul." She screwed up her face. "Of course, not sure God and that woman were on speaking terms. Anyway, all the Lambton children, including all of us country folk who ran out to play when the weather allowed, avoided her cottage as if the very devil lived in it."

"So, we're not going to console her over her grievous news." Eliza slid a glance at Joy's twitching lips.

"I wouldn't console that woman dead or alive. But as she is dead and cannot tattle on our little fib, why then, what's the harm in using her name? Serves her right for all the curses she spat our way."

"She sounds deliciously terrible. Like a storybook villain." Joy backed out of a garage stall and drove past Pemberley, almost as if making a show of them leaving. "Come to think of it, with a few minor changes, I can turn my malicious male into a wheedling and wormish woman. Geraldine seems the perfect fit."

"Does she get her just deserts in the end?" Great-Aunt Iris poked her head between the two front seats.

"Of course. She might actually meet her maker in the process of trying to mess with true love."

Apparently satisfied, Great-Aunt Iris relaxed her head against the headrest. Eliza did the same, but instead of imagining the wonderful ways in which justice would be served to an old enemy, Eliza thought about all the disastrous ways her sleuthing plan could go all sixes and sevens.

JOY zipped into a parking space along the narrow road in front of the Trusty Teapot and grinned. "We're here. Alive and well."

Eliza opened her eyes and peeled her fingers from her thighs. From the heavy breathing in the back, she assumed Heath was double-checking that his lungs worked to full capacity.

Great-Aunt Iris coughed. "If old age doesn't kill me, I know what will."

As if not hearing them or their complaints about her driving on the entire journey from Pemberley to Lambton, Joy pulled down the SUV's visor and checked her makeup in the mirror. She used her fingernail to smooth out a wrinkle in her otherwise perfectly lined lips. "Beggars cannot be choosers, you know, and instead of whinging away, we could be questioning the locals."

"Joy's right." Eliza grinned at her cousin. "Don't get used to it. Remember, we won't ask questions. We'll let the conversation go where it will naturally go, the murder, and we'll be nothing more than innocent bystanders hearing whatever information comes our way. You all have your assignments, right?"

Great-Aunt Iris tapped her temple. "Got it right here."

"You don't want to write them down or anything?" Eliza dug in her purse for some paper and a pen.

Her great-aunt waved away the offered material with an offended sniff. "I, unlike you young people nowadays, have not rotted away my brain by watching the telly for hours upon hours. That contraption will be the death of society. I'm sure of it."

Eliza wisely kept her lips sealed about the amount of useless trivia Great-Aunt Iris shared after her "telly-watching" sessions. "Right. Sorry. Joy? Heath? You good to go?"

After they assured her they had it covered, they exited the SUV and parted ways. Eliza's destination, the Trusty Teapot, was only a few steps away, which didn't give her stomach more than a few seconds to churn with anxiety. As per usual, the smells of the tea shop settled her nerves, and she sat at a back-corner table away from the large picture window.

"Miss Eliza?" Monica all but skipped to the table. "What a lovely surprise." She whispered, "Have you heard the newest gossip? It's causing quite the stir."

"Oh, really?" Faking nonchalance even while her nerves tingled with anticipation, she leaned back in her chair and fiddled with the starched white tablecloth.

Monica pulled up a chair and rested her elbows on the table. "You'll never guess who people are saying killed Felix Payne." When Eliza raised an inquisitive eyebrow and gestured with her hands for Monica to spill the information, the young woman nearly wiggled in her seat. "They're saying it's Mr. Wentworth who did it. Can you imagine? I don't believe a word of it, of course. My mum always says I can read people like books. And if anyone's a good book, it's Mr. Wentworth."

Eliza agreed but mentally added the caveat that if Wentworth were a book, there needed to be a few cracks in the book's spine and several dog-eared pages to complete the comparison.

"That nasty Oliver Wright, the one who ran over your great-aunt, came in about an hour ago. Oh, and I found out what he was in prison for. Not murder but a list longer than my arm, and he apparently beat up a cop. Anyway, he kept spouting lies about Mr. Wentworth. How the great policeman—he used finger quotes when he said that, by the way—had finally cracked and killed an innocent man. Said that was proof that no one could trust any coppers. Cussed until he was blue in the face, and after the manager threatened to call the cops, he finally left."

The tea shop's door opened, and Monica jumped to her feet. "I'll be right back. What would you like?"

Eliza ordered her usual and picked at the pilled fabric on the tablecloth until Monica, her face flushed, returned. She set down Eliza's Ethiopian spiced tea and plunked back in her chair. "Sorry about that. Anyway, where was I?"

"Oliver."

"Yes. No. What was I talking about before?"

"Wentworth being a good book."

"Thank you. My mum says that I'd leave the house without my head if it weren't sewn on." Monica rolled her eyes. "I asked her once where she thought I'd gotten that from."

"How did that go?"

"Not very well." She sighed. "But I can't believe Mr. Wentworth would poison someone."

"Poison?" Eliza's fingers stilled from the pilled-fabric picking. That was the first time she'd heard a civilian identifying the cause of death. "How do you know he was poisoned?"

Monica grinned the impetuous smile of youth. "You'd be surprised how many people don't see me as I serve them their tea. Sometimes, I think I'm invisible for all that people notice me."

"You must hear many things you shouldn't." Eliza reminded herself to never underestimate Monica or any other waitstaff, for that matter.

"If I had a quid for every time I heard something I shouldn't, I could finally pay for uni and then some instead of stashing my meager tips under my mattress."

"I shouldn't ask you to tell tales." Eliza paused and sipped her tea. "But poison is so horrid, isn't it?"

That time, Monica skipped placing her elbows on the table and leaned forward, her forearms supporting her. "Do you think the killer is a woman?"

"What makes you think that?"

"Women are notorious for poisonings. I was watching a documentary on the telly about female killers, and poison was their go-to."

Monica had a point. Reminding herself to ask Wentworth about any femmes fatales in Felix's life, Eliza mirrored Monica's posture. "I suppose people are making assumptions."

"No. At least, this wasn't just any old person. It was Dr. Hamilton. He was having tea with someone."

Eliza recalled Joy's mention of him two days ago. "I hear he's rather dishy."

"Nah. He's old. Like in his forties." Monica's nose squinched. "My mum thinks he's dishy, though. She puts makeup on to go to his surgery." Her tone made it seem as if her mother had not only put on lipstick or mascara but had also gone butt naked.

"Whether he's 'dishy' or not, as a doctor, he could diagnose poisoning pretty easily. Could be run-of-the-mill arsenic or something."

Monica's forehead furrowed . "Don't know. All I heard was poison. But isn't arsenic a bit old-fashioned? Something grandmas use?"

Eliza's failed attempt at getting the name of the poison left a sour taste in her mouth. She sipped her tea. "Whatever poison was used, it served its purpose. I'm sorry for the poor girl who found the body. What a horrible thing to come across."

"That's what I told Amanda."

"Who?"

"Amanda Fielding. My friend. She works at the pub. As a waitress. She's the one who found the body."

Eliza forced herself to sit up slowly and carelessly. "How awful. I bet she was upset."

"Upset?" Monica glanced around the tea shop and at the customer who had walked in earlier. She lowered her voice. "Cried for hours. Thought about smacking her one. You know, how they do in movies to get them to stop blubbering."

"Probably sees everything every time she closes her eyes. I can't imagine."

"That's the thing. She claims she doesn't remember anything but the body lying there in the middle of the floor, the dead man's black eyes staring at her. My mum says she's blocking out the bad stuff. That her brain is protecting her from her memories." Monica shrugged as if she believed only half of what her mother had said and stood up. "Her brain might be protecting her from her eyesight, but it's not doing the same for her nose."

"Her nose?"

"Yeah. She can't bring up any images of the room or anything, but she can't get the smell of mouse out of her nose."

"Mouse?"

"That's what she said." The shop's door opened, and several customers walked in. "I should get back to work, or the manager will give me an earful."

"Monica?"

"Yeah?"

"You will be... be careful, you know, who you're talking to about all this?"

"Of course, Miss Eliza. I'm not daft, you know." With an impetuous shake of her head and an eye roll, Monica trotted off to the new customers.

After finishing her drink, paying, and leaving a hefty tip, Eliza walked out of the tea shop—her steps leaden with dread—and into the daylight. Despite the warmer-than-normal fall temperature, she hugged her cardigan around her, which did nothing to dispel her shivers. True to her suspicions, it wasn't the temperature chilling her to the bone. It was the case and the danger hovering over Wentworth's head.

Chapter Eight
Police and Beer Gone Bad

I visited Anne today at the Elliots' rented townhouse and had the misfortune of being alone with Miss Elizabeth Elliot and her friend, Mrs. Clay, a simpering woman with nothing to recommend her. A quarter of an hour in their presence made me pine for Louisa Hurst's and Caroline Bingley's company. I feel for Anne that these two women are her companions, and from the comments Miss Elliot made about her sister, I wonder that Anne turned out as well as she did. I also gathered that Mr. Elliot's suit with Anne increased daily, and from Miss Elliot's pinched lips and sour expression, she is not at all happy about the impending nuptials. Nuptials I hope Anne is intelligent enough to not go through with.
Lizzy Bennet Darcy
Bath 1814

" I hope you gathered as much gossip as you did shopping bags."

Eliza placed her hands on her hips and eyed the pile of bags in the back of the Range Rover.

"You said to make it look natural." Joy gestured to the mountain of products. "This is natural." She shut the back door and dusted her hands together. "The more you buy, the chattier shopkeepers are."

No wonder shopkeepers rarely speak to me. Eliza hopped into the passenger seat and looked over her shoulder at Heath, who was grinning like a Cheshire cat, and Great-Aunt Iris, who quivered in her seat. "I take it you two found out something juicy."

Heath's grin grew. "You'll never guess."

"Ladies first, young man. The sooner you understand this, the better off you'll be." Great-Aunt Iris speared Heath with a regal look then turned her gaze on Eliza. "You'll never guess."

"I'm sure you sniffed out some great information, but let's wait to share anything until we're safely in the attic and can put everything on the cardboard."

This was met with groans then silence, broken only by the wild clicking of knitting needles, permeating the Range Rover all the way to Pemberley.

After helping wrangle in the bags of Joy's shopping spree through one of the back-entrance doors, Eliza dashed to her room to freshen up and found her cat waiting outside the closed door.

Caesar stared reproachfully at her with his bicolored gaze.

"I know, buddy. It was an emergency."

He must have taken her apology in stride, as he allowed her to pet between his ears twice before flouncing into her room, jumping onto her bed, and snuggling into a ball.

"Go ahead. Make yourself comfortable."

Not that Caesar needed her permission to do so. If only she could take a little catnap herself. She plopped onto the bed next to him and with one hand stroked his fur and with the other dashed off a text to her mom: *Wanted to remind you how loved you are! Let me know how things are going when you can. Tell Dad I say hi and love you.* The message blurred before her. She sniffled. At some point, she would have to talk to her father, but not right then. Not when his betrayal of Uncle Fitzwilliam burned like a brand on her heart.

After freshening her makeup, she changed into a cream-colored V-neck dress speckled with peach and baby-blue lilies, slipped into matching peach heels she knew would squeeze her toes and give her one heck of a blister, and left her room, keeping her door inched open so Caesar could go in and out as he pleased.

It was time to deal with the police force encamped downstairs. Even though most of the guests had rooms in the west wing, Kapoor and Cronk, who had paid the upcharge for suites on the second floor, could or possibly had walked by the secret bookcase several times. Eliza kneaded her fist over her heart, which pinched as if it sat at an angle.

Heath's door opened, and when he caught sight of Eliza, he smiled.

The laugh wrinkles crinkling around his eyes, the dimple in his right cheek winking at her, and his lopsided grin chased away her worries. She dashed into his arms, pressed her ear to his chest, and concentrated on the methodic beating of his heart. Slowly, her rapid heartbeat matched his relaxed one.

"What would I do without you?"

"You, my love, would do wonders and take on the world." He kissed her and, after breaking off the kiss, caressed her cheek with his thumb. "Question is, what would I do without you?"

"Probably find someone slightly less crazy and not have to deal with at least one knitting needle to the ribs daily."

"Hazards I'm willing to take on."

Rumbled voices seeped up the staircase.

"Speaking of hazards, would you like me to accompany you downstairs?" Heath asked.

"Thought you'd never ask." Eliza squeezed his hand, released it, and descended the stairs to mingle with Pemberley's guests in the dining room.

No more than five seconds after Heath left her side to get glasses of champagne, Chief Constable Kapoor stepped into her path. "And how was your great-aunt's visit?" He balanced a glass of champagne in one hand and a plate of hors d'oeuvres in the other.

Eliza, in keeping with the wine-'em-dine-'em event, gave a brilliant smile and saluted with her champagne glass. "I believe Geraldine is doing as expected. Great-Aunt Iris was quite invigorated with her visit, and of course my cousin uses any trip into Lambton to get her shopping fix." She pointed at Joy, resplendent in a scarlet wrap dress, who was currently flirting with an officer by the punch bowl.

Chief Constable Kapoor gave an indulgent smile and sipped from his glass.

"Are you and your group finding everything to your liking? Is there anything I can do to make your stay more enjoyable?"

"We are more than satisfied. Pemberley is a beautiful estate." He scanned the room. "I'm surprised to see that your uncle isn't present."

"He's away on business, I'm afraid."

"Of course. He's a very busy man, I'm sure. It was a sad business, what happened to him, but it seems as if he fell on his feet with not much damage." His gaze raked across the dining room's furnishings and decor as if guessing their worth.

Eliza pressed a finger to her right eye to stop its twitching. "Yes, we Darcys are resilient."

"Tell me, does your uncle know yet of Wentworth's fall from grace?"

Then her left eye joined her right eye's twitching but in alternative beats. It was as if her nerves were playing the bongos with her face. "As I said, his business is of a rather serious and delicate nature. We haven't been in contact with him since he left."

"Poor devil. He and Wentworth got on well, I believe. It's always tragic when one of our own takes a turn to evil." He glared at his full plate as if envisioning that his prey, stuffed and ready to devour, was lying on it. "I'll find him. Don't you worry, Miss Darcy. Until then, be vigilant about security. Wentworth couldn't have gone far, and he might, knowing your uncle was a friend, try to weasel his way onto your property."

"Our security is top-notch. I'm not worried in the slightest." Forcing herself to twist her lips into a smile, she tilted her glass toward him. "I must double-check with my staff that everything is as planned for your evening's events. Enjoy the rest of your evening, Chief Constable Kapoor, and please, don't hesitate to let me know if you need anything."

After making a show of idle chitchat with the guests, with a longer session with Commissioner Cronk, looking very plum-like in her purple dress, Eliza caught the eyes of Heath and Joy. They also made some additional rounds, smiled, and nodded, and eventually, they all met in the hallway and climbed up the staircase.

"Bloody hell, what an insufferable group. I've never fake smiled so much in my life." Joy massaged her cheeks.

Eliza couldn't help but agree, feeling herself much like a wrung-out dish towel. Her right eye still continued twitching on beats one and three, and her left eye took over on beats two and four.

Heath took her right hand in his and untangled her fisted fingers. "You can relax now."

"Can I? It's almost as if he knows. First, he asked me this afternoon if I've seen Wentworth, and now, he reminded me to beef up my security on the off chance his prey comes creeping into Pemberley. I get the sense that Kapoor hates Wentworth and wants to see an innocent man put in prison. He can't seriously think that Wentworth would commit murder, can he?"

The possibility of dealing with a hatred so intense as to willingly persecute an innocent man haunted Eliza as she gathered her great-aunt and met her posse in the secret attic.

"Why does Chief Constable Kapoor hate you? Was he one of the higher-ups you got dirt on?" Eliza crossed her arms and peered down at Wentworth.

Wentworth's eyes widened, and he clenched his lips.

Eliza sighed and sank into a wooden chair she'd stolen from one of the unused rooms. She probably shouldn't have asked that question first thing as she entered the attic, but time was of the essence. She had to know the severity of Kapoor's hatred in order to deal with it. "I'm sorry. I—" She gestured to her sleuthing posse. "*We* need to know who we're dealing with."

Growling out various phrases, which Great-Aunt Iris sniffed at, Wentworth scrubbed a hand over his face, currently sprouting a salt-and-pepper beard. "At the time of the investigation, Kapoor was not chief constable but very much on his way to achieving that office. He was—is—a ruthless man, and he was part of the good ol' boys club, but he had enough people in his back pocket and had gleaned enough dirt on all of them that after he threatened to expose all their past sins, they made sure that he was one of the guilty to go unscathed and escape a prison sentence or any consequence, as you can see." Wentworth rubbed the back of his hand across his mouth as if trying to erase a foul taste. "I know it all. He knows I know it all. But there's nothing I can do about it while the rotten ones are still in control. I thought for sure with the new commissioner, I'd finally have my chance, but it seems Kapoor has either sucked Cronk into his dealings or has enough dirt on her to keep her in check."

Eliza circled her temples with her fingers. "So, you weren't joking when you said that Kapoor wants nothing more than to get rid of you."

"Sadly, no. I'm sure he's already got a cell lined up for me."

Eliza furrowed her forehead. "Say, I've been trying to get the chemistry between Kapoor and Cronk figured out. It's clear they loathe each other, but who holds the power? It seems Kapoor does, but isn't Cronk, as police and crime commissioner, above him on the totem pole?"

"She not only outranks him, but it's her job to hold him accountable," Wentworth said.

"Well, she doesn't have a very strong hold over him. She dang near cowers when he approaches her. Let's keep those two on our radar." Eliza checked the time on her Fitbit and stepped to the makeshift crime board. "We don't have much time, so let's get started. I had a nice little conversation with Monica. Apparently, she overheard Dr. Hamilton tell someone that poison was used to kill Felix."

Wentworth straightened. "Dr. Hamilton, eh? He's an odd one. Wife raves about him. Me? I don't understand what the fuss is all about. Nothing more than a quack."

Great-Aunt Iris quirked a regal eyebrow at Wentworth. "Dr. Hamilton is an excellent man. A gentleman."

Not giving her great-aunt a chance to continue her scolding, Eliza asked, "How did he know it was poison? Was he in charge of the autopsy?"

"I wouldn't think so. He's not a pathologist. To my knowledge, he's never done an autopsy, at least not in a criminal investigation."

"And this is where I come in." Joy beamed. "I was chatting Timothy up, and one thing led to another, and we got to talking about the murder. Of course, he was quick to throw you under the bus, Wentworth, on which I had to agree. I do hope you understand."

Wentworth waved off her concern and gestured for her to get on with it.

"Yes, well, he was bartending that night and actually whinged away about not being the one to find the body. Nasty little man. Instead, some 'ridiculous excuse for a waitress,' as he put it, found it. Set to screaming the whole place down, apparently. Anyway, the 'fool girl' ran down the steps, calling for help, which the *estimable* Dr. Hamilton was all too eager to offer." She grinned at Great-Aunt Iris.

"And then what?" Eliza asked.

"That's where Timothy's story ends, I'm afraid. The hysterical waitress was shoved in his care, and he had to put up with her carrying on about the dead man's 'black eyes.'"

"Black eyes? But Felix's eyes were blue," Wentworth said.

"Aren't dilated pupils a sign of poisoning?" Heath asked.

"That's probably how Dr. Hamilton was able to guess poison without being in on the autopsy or anything," Joy added.

Eliza held up a finger to halt the conversation then wrote down Dr. Hamilton's name and under it put *at the crime scene after Felix's body was discovered, unofficially concluded poison as cause of death.*

"Monica did mention that her friend Amanda Fielding found the body. Stated that all her friend could remember was the man's black eyes and a mousy smell in the room," Eliza said.

"Mousy smell?" Heath asked.

"That's what I said, but Monica couldn't elaborate. Said that's exactly how Amanda had put it, the smell of mouse."

"That eliminates at least one poison." Wentworth scratched his chin. "If the murderer had used arsenic, she would have smelled bitter almonds or something like that."

"What poison gives off a mouselike odor?" Joy asked.

"That should be easy enough to find out." Eliza dug her phone from her purse, tapped in her search query, and after a few moments, pumped her fist. "Poison hemlock."

"Are you sure?" Wentworth asked.

"That's what Google says." Eliza double-checked the information. "Yup. Apparently, the poison in the plant, coniine, is in every part of the plant, from tip to root, and can take up to several hours to show any effects."

"So, someone could have slipped him the poison before he even went up to his room." Heath tapped his bottom lip. "Which opens up Felix's murder to anybody."

"When you spoke with Felix that night, did he seem okay to you?" Eliza asked.

Wentworth scrunched his face. "Not really. He seemed strung out, you know. Made sense, though. Not easy for an ex-con to fit back into society, especially village society. He bought me a drink, and we chatted a bit. I figured he'd already had a few. Was slurring his words and constantly wiping his mouth with the back of his hand. I told you that I thought he was already six pints in."

"But did you see him drink that much?" Great-Aunt Iris asked.

"No. But he was there before I arrived. Wouldn't put it past him to start drinking in the early afternoon."

"And how long did you guys talk?" Eliza asked.

"Not long. Said he'd had a rough day and wasn't feeling the best. Thought he might have a touch of the flu. He went off to his booth in the corner soon after that."

"And you stayed at your booth?" Eliza asked.

"Yes and no." An edge of annoyance crept into his voice. "I was seated at the bar. And I already told you that I left around ten after two drinks."

Great-Aunt Iris cleared her throat and skewered Eliza with *the look*. "If you had let me finish earlier instead of interrupting me like some petulant schoolgirl, I could have told you that Felix was acting funny before he went up to his room." When all eyes turned on her, she preened. "I needed my hair done." She pointed a knitting needle at Eliza's raised eyebrow. "Now, before you go getting your knickers in a twist, girl, I'll have you know that I did complete the snooping list you gave me, which all came to nothing, mind you. Well, except for the overheard whisperings at the grocer's, which led me to a much better clue."

Eliza pursed her lips and struggled to compute her great-aunt's ramblings. "So you got your hair done and did grocery shopping?"

Great-Aunt Iris harrumphed. "You young people nowadays never listen."

Eliza bit her lip to stop a grin. Her great-aunt would only accuse her, again, of being a "petulant schoolgirl."

"I said that a clue I overheard at the grocer's led me to see if I could squeeze in a hair appointment with my hairdresser, Gemma Fielding. Two ladies were gossiping in front of the carrots—an odd place to discuss murder—and I heard them say that Gemma was telling anyone who was willing to listen all about her daughter finding the dead body. Gemma Fielding is Amanda's mother, and I'm one of her regulars and figured she'd squeeze me in, as I'm also one of her favorites."

"And what did Gemma Fielding have to say about it all?" Wentworth asked.

"Now, apparently, after he was two or three drinks in, he complained that the beer was bad. Gave Amanda a hard time about it. Accused her of serving him swill. She was able to settle him down and gave him a free drink. Said he was unsteady on his feet but thought that was the work of the fourth pint."

Wentworth snorted. "It takes more than four pints to make—" He closed his eyes and shook his head. "It took more than four pints to make Felix go legless."

"This means that he was poisoned in the pub, not his room." Eliza pinched the bridge of her nose to stem an oncoming headache.

Wentworth puffed out his cheeks. "Which means that anyone in the pub that night could have poisoned him."

NO doubt about it. Poison was nasty and sneaky and insidious and made solving a crime much harder.

Eliza's stomach churned, and she wiped her sweaty palms over her dress. Everyone else in the attic must have felt the same as she did if their hopeless gazes pinned to the floor meant what she thought they did. She needed fresh air and a moment alone with Heath.

After ensuring the coast was clear, Eliza half dragged and half walked with Heath down the gallery. She ignored the painted faces staring at her. It was bad enough being judged inept by human eyes. There was no way she was adding to her feeling of inadequacy by paying any attention to people with powdered wigs and heaving bosoms.

"Ah, Miss Darcy, just the person I was looking for." Chief Constable Kapoor materialized out of nowhere.

Eliza fought the urge to look behind her at the bookcase, shrouded in shadow as evening settled in. Not normally welcoming darkness, she was glad for once that sunlight did not stream through the window, highlighting the bookcase's presence. More than ever, she likened the bookcase to the beating heart in Edgar Allan Poe's "The Tell-Tale Heart." Despite knowing that Kapoor wasn't aware of the bookcase, her nerves were on fire, and she could almost hear the piece thump out "Look here, look here, look here." His proximity to it, as he was housed on the second floor, made the situation dire. One misstep, and they were all done for.

"Hello, sir." Eliza glued a smile to her face and squeezed Heath's hand. "What can I do for you?" She winced. Definitely didn't sound as hospitable as a good hostess should. Trying again, she asked, "Is anything the matter?"

"No, nothing at all. Wanted to pick your brain." Kapoor motioned for her and Heath to walk with him.

Eliza gritted her teeth but fell in step with him. That time, Heath's hand squeezed hers. His jaw was clenched so tight, she feared the next thing she would hear was cracking teeth. His ears were bright red and his face pale. Someone didn't appreciate Kapoor's presence, not that she disagreed.

"What would you like to pick our brains over?" They had come to the top of the stairs, and Eliza followed Kapoor's gaze down the gallery.

"What's all on this floor?"

"Besides the bedrooms and special guest suites, private living spaces for the family, and the gallery, nothing. All the staterooms, of course, are on the main floor. Why?"

"Old houses intrigue me. Don't they you? You never know what might be hidden in secreted spaces. No priest holes, eh?"

A pang hummed through her chest. She forced a laugh and caressed Heath's arm. "I'm sure if there were such a thing, Heath would have sniffed it out. Isn't that right, dear?"

He didn't balk under Kapoor's scrutinizing gaze. "That's a problem with archaeologists. We see something old, and we want to dig it up. Eliza here has put an absolute ban on digging or even thinking about digging anywhere on the property."

"But there is a secret tunnel, correct?"

Ah, the hunt is on. Eliza was sure that if Kapoor hadn't had any restraint, he would have been rubbing his hands together and licking his chops. "You are correct about the tunnel part. As for it being a secret, well, that's been blown to smithereens after the investigation a few months ago." Before he could ask what she knew was coming next, she offered to show him the tunnel. Even gave him a flashlight before he ducked into the doorway and disappeared. As long as he was sniffing there, he couldn't put his unwanted nose anywhere else. For a while, at least.

Unfamiliar voices wafted down the hallway and through the door of Uncle Fitzwilliam's study, reminding Eliza that just because one police officer was in the tunnel, that didn't change the fact that other officers of the law openly roamed the halls of Pemberley.

The door banged open, and Commissioner Amelia Cronk stumbled in, looking even more plum-ish than she had hours ago. Eliza tilted her head. No. The dress was the same shade, then she realized the woman's face was almost as purple as her clothing.

The officer swayed over to Eliza and Heath, bringing with her the smell of brandy. "Have you seen Kapoor?"

Even though Amelia had managed to fit those four words all into the space of one, Eliza understood her enough to explain that he was indisposed.

Amelia floated forward on her tiptoes until she nearly tipped over and whispered loudly, bathing Eliza's face with brandy fumes, "If you see him, tell him I'm looking for him."

Heath set Amelia back on her flat feet. "Is it something I can help you with?"

Amelia took her dandy old time perusing Heath's body, from his head to his toes. For a second, her purple face lit up, creating an odd color arrangement of pink and red blotches. She blinked, and her face crumpled. "Sadly, no." She pitched backward, righted herself, and tripped out of the room, muttering savagely, "He can't. He wouldn't."

Not waiting for any other interruptions, Eliza grasped Heath's hands, exited her uncle's study, stopped only long enough to grab a sweater from a hook beside one of the side entrances, and escaped into the night.

Somewhere, a fox screeched. Eliza pulled her sweater tighter around her. She had enough problems on her plate without wasting any brain cells in trying to figure out the issue between Amelia and Kapoor, but she couldn't help wondering if Amelia was friend or foe. It was possible Eliza could use some leverage to gain personal information about Kapoor. Anything she had on Kapoor could prove useful later.

"I've been thinking about the hemlock. Doesn't it have a bitter, unpleasant taste?" Heath pulled her down beside him onto a wooden bench deep within the flower garden and twirled a piece of her hair around his finger. "Could that be why he complained about the beer going bad?"

"Not bad, Watson." She winked at him. "But if that was the reason, we could talk to Amanda Fielding. Maybe she remembers the exact time she gave him that drink."

"Even better, she might remember who was in the bar at the time."

Despite her heavy sweater, the evening chill slid its icy fingers around her rib cage. She pressed into Heath. "Problem is, how do we ask her such blatant questions without it getting back to Kapoor or the investigating officers that we're snooping around? That will certainly put us on their radar, a place I want to be as far away from as possible."

"I'm sure you'll think of something. You always do." Heath pulled her to him, his head lowered.

She licked her lips in anticipation. A flash of light caught her attention. She spun, and Heath's lips smacked the side of her head.

"I hate when you do that," he mumbled before attempting a second try.

Instead of curling into him, Eliza grabbed his hand and pulled him off the bench and toward one of the outbuildings. "Didn't you see that?"

"See what?"

"A light."

"The only thing I was concentrating on is now dragging me halfway across the estate in search of strange lights."

A flicker played off the glass panes of a gardening shed.

"See?" Eliza marched ahead, that time in step with Heath.

"Eliza, wait." He halted. "Don't you think we should check it out before storming in there?"

"I'm a—"

"I know. You're a grown-ass woman, but at least let me open the door with you. Share the danger."

Together, they twisted the handle and ripped the door open.

Someone screeched. A flashlight fell to the wood floor.

Heath grabbed a hoe and brandished it over his head as Eliza picked up the flashlight and swished it around until she found the perpetrator.

When she did, she nearly dropped the flashlight. "Garrison?"

Chapter Nine
Wentworth Gets an Unwelcome Roommate

Darcy and I have returned from a recital where we made the acquaintance of a certain gentleman, a Captain Frederick Wentworth. He is quite a handsome, dashing man. They barely spoke, however, and I do so wish that Mr. Elliot would leave my friend alone. Captain Wentworth is by far the better man and the best match for Anne, and from the way he studied Anne, I'm afraid he loves her to near distraction. I should know because that is how my beloved Darcy is looking at me at this very moment. I must cut this entry—
Lizzy Bennet Darcy
Bath 1814

Eliza wasn't sure of her next actions. She debated whether to smack her distant cousin over the head with a shovel—because of all the trouble and heartache he had helped Nancy wreak upon Pemberley and her family—or hug him because he was alive and not dead in a ditch somewhere. She cringed. He was the same man who had offered to extend the family line with her.

No shovel, because she was a good person, and definitely no hugs, because Garrison was most definitely not a good person.

"What in the hell are you doing?" Eliza directed the beam into his face.

He shielded his eyes. "Put that bloody thing down, crazy woman."

Next to her, Heath inhaled a sharp breath and muttered, "Not a smart move, man. Not a smart move."

"Excuse you?" Eliza took a step closer.

Garrison stepped backward into an arsenal of garden tools. He hissed a swear word, and his gaze flicked around the room in search of Eliza and Heath. It finally settled somewhere in the proximity of Heath. "You going to stand there and let her torture me like this?"

"Torture?" Heath studied his cuticles. "Not sure we share the same definition of that word, but whatever my lovely lady is currently doing, I see no need to bring it to an end."

"She's blinding me." Like a mole coming up from the depths, he squinted, his face scrunching with the effort.

Feeling only slightly sorry for the creature, Eliza lowered the beam to his chest. A royal-blue cashmere sweater replaced Garrison's bleached face. Even standing several feet away from him, Eliza recognized the quality of the material. If what she'd learned about her uncle's wardrobe held true for her slimy cousin, the sweater covering Garrison's torso could easily cost $150. Not that she wouldn't put Garrison above stealing the thing. She trailed the beam of light down his arms. The light reflected off the glass face of an impressive-looking watch. His jeans were not Walmart jeans.

Anger warmed her body and numbed her. It was quite reasonable to suppose that it was his ill-gotten pilfered gains from embezzling from her uncle that had clothed him in elegance. Money that had been entrusted into the estate's coffers to keep up Pemberley and the legacy of the Darcys for generations to come was covering the body of Garrison Wickham in finery that made him look like a royal boob.

"You look none the worse for wear." Eliza didn't attempt to hide her sarcasm—sarcasm he missed.

Garrison preened. Actually *preened*. Eliza eyed a shovel in the corner. Perhaps smacking him with it wasn't entirely off the table.

Heath ran his fingers down her arm until they wrapped around her fist. Slowly, he eased her fingers free from the ball she'd squeezed them into.

"You never answered my first question," Eliza ground out between clenched teeth.

"And what was that again?" Garrison blinded her with a slimy smile.

She growled.

Garrison's already bleached skin went translucent, and his smile slipped.

"Eliza asked you what in the hell you were doing," Heath said.

Garrison's Adam's apple dipped to the collar of his fancy-pants sweater. "I, uh, thought that perhaps the dust had settled enough for me to, you know, come back, but then I saw all the official-looking vehicles." He tapped his nose. "I can smell a cop from a mile away. Figuring I couldn't waltz in the front door to a warm welcome, I was looking for something to use to break into one of the servants' entrances."

Eliza wasn't sure whether the adjective *stupid* would cover Garrison's mentality and decided to up the stakes to something more creative.

Heath stared at him. "Are you a bloody moron?"

"No need to be mean." Garrison checked his watch. "It's getting on midnight. Do you think we could, you know, go inside and have a nightcap or something?"

Head pounding with a sudden ache, Eliza massaged her temples. "You are a fugitive from the law and an enemy to this family. What makes you think I'm going to invite you into my home, the very home you leeched off for years?"

"Can't we let bygones be bygones?"

It was Eliza's turn to hold Heath back. His muscles bunched under her staying hands.

Ignoring Garrison's pitiful huddle against the rack of gardening tools, Eliza pierced him with her gaze. "I can promise you one thing. You will never be invited into Pemberley ever again. I don't have time for you, and if you prove yourself as invisible as you've been the past few months, I won't tell Wentworth I've seen you." The second that Wentworth's name crossed her lips, Eliza regretted it.

Garrison's eyes sharpened. No longer the cowering, whining victim, he straightened and stepped closer to Eliza. "Wentworth, eh? Isn't he the copper accused of murder, the one who sent Nancy to prison and me into exile and is now supposedly on the run?" His smile didn't reach his eyes. "It pays to keep an ear on the underbelly of society. How do you suppose to tell him? You either know where he is, or you delivered an empty threat."

"And who are you going to run and tattle to? Every police officer in the area and England, for that matter, knows you for what you are, and with a warrant out for your arrest, you'd be sacrificing yourself." Eliza kept her voice even, but her insides vibrated with fury and fear. To think her weasel of a cousin would be her ultimate downfall sent bile up her throat. She swallowed. "Besides, I can tell Chief Constable Kapoor that I saw you. I'm sure he'll send a team to find you in no time. I don't need Wentworth."

"And I don't need to speak to a soul to leak the juicy morsel that Miss Eliza Darcy may or may not know the whereabouts of a murderer."

That was it. That was how she would explode, quite literally, if her heart rate and beating brain had anything to say about it.

Heath snatched Garrison's shirt collar and slammed him up against a shelf. Metal creaked and groaned. Tools and cans rattled. "I like to think I'm a reasonable bloke. Really, I do. And as I believe in second chances, I'll allow you fifteen seconds to get your bloody arse off Eliza's property."

"And in twenty, the Lambton police station will get an anonymous call." Garrison's words rattled through his strangling shirt collar, but his message was clear.

Heath let go. Garrison, clearly not anticipating such a move, fell to the floor in a heap of dust and vicious words.

"We can't stay in here the rest of our lives." Eliza planted her hands on her hips and loomed over Garrison. "What do you propose?"

"You give me a place to hide for a while, and in turn, I won't rat you or Wentworth out to the police."

"I'll say you're lying."

"Want to take that risk?"

Eliza cursed the moron at her feet and wished he'd stayed the slimy creep he'd been and not morphed into a manipulative snake. Or that he'd never come back at all.

It was so tempting to put Heath as watchdog over the wanted criminal and run and get Kapoor. Easy peasy lemon squeezy until Garrison went through with his threat. Having a sense of Kapoor's hatred for Wentworth, she knew the man would take it as gospel and probably twist some judge's arm into coming through with a search warrant.

"You're in for a nasty surprise." Eliza grinned, not caring that her smile didn't reach her eyes.

Garrison guffawed and waved away the threat.

Eliza kneeled down and got as close to his face as she dared before whispering, "Your soon-to-be roommate doesn't like you very much. When I'm not there, there's nothing I can do to protect you from him—not that I would."

His pupils dilated. "Wentworth is here? In the house? You can't put me with him. He'll know that I'm here. You can't—" His rambling stopped, and he sneered. "Although when he finds out the little secret I know, he'll be putty in my hands."

"And what secret do you know?" Eliza backed away from his oozing smile and gleaming eyes.

"I know who killed Felix Payne."

ELIZA had heard only two catfights in her life. Once was when she was five and her family had moved into a new house. A stray tom had somehow snuck in, and Eliza's cat, Jupiter, fought tooth and claw to evict the miscreant. The other had taken place in the likeliest spot: a sketchy alley behind a bar. Not that she was actually in the alley, but she didn't need to be in it to hear the chorus of fingernails-on-a-chalkboard screeching and low-in-the-throat growls.

As she stood in the attic, her arms crossed over her chest, she witnessed her third catfight, albeit with humans instead of felines. Wentworth, his forehead scrunched, eyes slit, and lips tightly sealed, stared at Garrison. Every few seconds, a growl rumbled in his chest. Garrison, sitting as far from Wentworth as possible, cowered and squeaked.

Eliza, with Heath at her side, sat in the middle of the two toms and, as her job as mediator had failed before even beginning, sought only to keep them from making too much noise. Not that mediating was ever in the cards. From the second Wentworth saw Garrison ascend the final step after Eliza, she knew that bouncer and not mediator was her job until she could get rid of Garrison—legally, of course.

"Tell me again why this... this... wanker is here." Wentworth pointed at Garrison. "He should be behind bars."

"He should be under your direct supervision. We can't trust him enough to put him anywhere else," Eliza reminded him.

"Hey, I'm sitting right here, you know. No need to talk about me as if I weren't even in the room."

"Wish you weren't." Eliza spun on him. "You were the one who thought you could traipse back in here, and for what? If you were expecting a warm welcome or anything more than a swift kick in the butt and a trip to jail, you really are delusional."

Heath laid a hand on her arm and squeezed gently. "Garrison, tell Wentworth what you told Eliza and me in the garden shed."

Garrison pursed his lips and shook his head like a petulant child. "He needs to promise not to hurt me and, when this is all done, to not arrest me."

Wentworth, fists clenched, nearly launched himself off his cot and onto Garrison. It was only Eliza's plea that had him dropping to the mattress, his body quivering. "I will make no such promise," Wentworth growled.

"But what if he knows who the real killer is?"

Wentworth sliced the air with his hand. "I don't care if he could solve every cold case ever known to man. I'm not letting a wanted felon go free to save my own skin."

"In that case"—Garrison folded his arms and slunk in his wooden chair—"I'm not helping."

From the chief inspector's livid complexion and his stoic, bull-like countenance, Eliza knew he wouldn't budge. She had no choice but to ingratiate herself with her weaselly cousin. "Garrison, if you help us by telling us everything, and if you promise to be on your best behavior, I will ensure that you are compensated."

Her cousin's arms dropped to his knees, and he thrummed his fingers against them. "How?"

"Money." The only language he understood.

"How much?"

"Depends on your behavior and usefulness." *Nothing if I can help it.*

After a few moments, Garrison steepled his fingers and rested them under his chin. "I accept, on one condition."

Eliza pictured her happy place, a place where no Garrisons existed. "And what would that be?"

"When Wentworth—"

"DCI Wentworth to you." Wentworth's scowl had even Eliza taking a step back.

Garrison's Adam's apple bobbed. "When DCI Wentworth and I leave this *lovely* place, I get to leave first and get a fifteen-minute head start."

Ignoring Wentworth's growling curses, Eliza bid Garrison down. "Ten. Any more than that and you don't get your 'consulting fee.'" Even if her cousin had thirty minutes, there was no way she would actually let him get away. Little white lies, although her mother insisted they were as evil as the big ones, had never failed Eliza before. And in cases of extreme emergency, such as the one she was embroiled in, she could even argue they were justified.

"Fine."

"Now, spill it before I change my mind and chain you permanently up here."

Apparently taking Eliza's threat as gospel, Garrison told his tale of woe, including but not limited to his flight from injustice—which garnered a massive eye roll and a "bloody bollocks" from the detective chief inspector—a few nights' stay in a dodgy hotel room that didn't have air-conditioning or Wi-Fi, and ended with him tripping, literally, into a den of thieves. "And so, my dear cousin, this put me directly in the path of Oliver Wright and his cronies."

"If you don't get to the part where you tell us who killed Felix Payne, I will..."

Wentworth didn't need to finish his threat, as Garrison's skin had turned ashen from the insinuation.

"Haven't you been listening? Oliver Wright is your guy. He's Felix's murderer."

Eliza dampened her excitement for two reasons. First, Garrison was slime living on slime and couldn't be trusted. Second, just because Oliver looked the part of a criminal didn't automatically make him guilty of the crime against Felix.

"What's your proof?" she asked.

"Proof? Have you seen the guy?" Garrison threw his hands in the air.

"Yes, but that won't add up to much in a criminal investigation." Eliza slid a glance at Wentworth, who, instead of growling, had transitioned into a palpable silence.

"He knew Felix Payne. They were partners in crime, and when everything went all sixes and sevens, it was Oliver who got caught. Felix ran, leaving his partner—ex-partner now—to take all the blame. Needless to say, Oliver was set on revenge and had only one goal after getting out. Make Felix pay." Garrison's grin set Eliza's stomach to roiling. "And guess who was the arresting officer for poor Mr. Wright?"

Eliza followed her cousin's sly glance to Wentworth.

Wentworth rolled his shoulders as if readjusting the weight of the world. "I remember that day very well and the day in court, where my testimony helped put him behind bars for a laundry list of charges, including assaulting an officer." He moved his jaw back and forth.

"It all adds up, then," Heath said. "Kill two birds with one stone, right? Kill the man who betrayed you and then frame the man who put you away for years."

More than anything, Eliza wanted to wrap up Heath's summary with a neat bow, but doubt niggled at the back of her mind. *Why would a man released from prison risk such a ghoulish crime so soon?* He could have slipped the poison into Felix's drink somehow, even though no one had mentioned Oliver's presence at the Foxed Hound. *And even if he was able to sneak in and out without being seen, how did Oliver, whom Wentworth never mentioned seeing, get ahold of the two glasses with the DCI's fingerprints and then plant them in the room?* And then there was the bigger question of Wentworth's fingerprints on the doorknob. If Oliver did do the awful deed, he certainly didn't do it alone.

DESPITE A RESTLESS night's sleep, after a full English breakfast, Eliza was invigorated and ready to tackle Amelia Cronk. Eliza had successfully evaded Kapoor's attempts to trip her into a conversation, and with the start of the first session, she was free to get down to business.

Her plan to seek the commissioner at the first break, however, evaporated the moment Amelia ran from the library midsession, bumped into Eliza in the hall, and scooted into the bathroom. The sounds leaking through the closed door had Eliza's full English breakfast swaying dangerously in her gut.

Great, that was all they needed—a bout of food poisoning. Mrs. Bankcroft would be devastated, and so would Pemberley's future weekend-getaway customers.

At the sounds of a toilet flushing, water running, gargling, and spitting, Eliza walked several feet away and pretended to rearrange some flowers. When the bathroom door opened, Eliza glanced in Amelia's direction. It didn't take much for her to turn her fake concern over the woman's well-being into the real thing. Moisture beaded on Amelia's white face. Her curls, probably dampened from splashing water onto her face, hung there limply.

"Amelia, are you okay?"

Though clearly not even close to okay, Amelia gave a shaky, wan smile. "Yes. Something didn't agree with me." She rested a hand on what her ugly outfits had hidden before: a bump. Amelia cleared her throat and pulled the oversized cardigan closely about her body. "I... uh..."

"Congratulations." Eliza's smile slipped slightly upon remembering the encounter with a drunk Amelia the night before.

Amelia's bleached face turned crimson.

Fearing the commissioner would faint on the spot, Eliza led her to Uncle Fitzwilliam's study. "Here. Sit. Would you like some water?"

The slight dipping of her curls was the only indication she had nodded. After fetching a glass of water from the breakfast room and handing it to Amelia, Eliza slid into a leather chair across from her.

"Would you like me to help you to your room? I'm sure I can make excuses for you if someone comes looking."

Amelia waved away the offer. "I'm presenting the next session."

"I'm sure Chief Constable Kapoor will understand if you can't present."

A derisive snort escaped Amelia's mouth before she could stifle it with her hand, and she kept it there so long that her skin bleached where her fingers latched into her flesh. To Eliza's surprise—and Amelia's as well by the start she gave when the tears touched her hand—the woman was crying.

"Amelia?"

The commissioner released her mouth, leaving a white handprint on her mottled face. "Stupid hormones. Forgive me."

"Please let me go talk to Kapoor. I'll see if I can—"

"No!" Amelia's left hand latched onto Eliza's arm. A diamond engagement ring winked up at her.

"I mean, no, thank you. I'll be fine. I need a moment is all."

"If you're sure."

Amelia sipped her water. "Yes. Please. You won't say anything about my condition to the others? Kapoor knows but no one else, and I'd like to keep it that way. For now."

Eliza's shoulder blades touched at the ominous tone in Amelia's words. "Your secret is safe with me." Trusting her gut, Eliza went for a dig. "I get the sense that Kapoor isn't the most understanding of men."

The first ray of hope for in-depth information died the moment Amelia's open mouth and bright eyes descended into a tight-lipped nod and curtained gaze.

"Let me know if I can make your stay here more comfortable." Thankfully, it would end Sunday morning.

Tucking the information—or at least the little bit she'd gleaned from Amelia—away for later, Eliza left the room and texted Heath and Joy to gather Great-Aunt Iris and meet her in the attic. With the police in their designated meeting rooms and the staff helping Mrs. Bankcroft clean up after breakfast, the second floor would be clear.

It wasn't until Joy reached the top of the attic steps and hissed a "bloody hell" that Eliza realized she hadn't seen Joy and therefore hadn't warned her about Garrison's presence. After hearing Great-Aunt Iris's scathing sermon to Garrison on the Wickham stain upon Pemberley, Eliza also realized she had forgotten to mention the small detail of Garrison's presence to her great-aunt.

"Hello to you, too, cousin." Garrison, displaying his stupidity for everyone, leaned toward Joy, his lips aiming for her cheek.

Surely, stopping Joy from punching Garrison's lights out deserved some sort of award, but instead of giving an acceptance speech, she placed Heath between Garrison and Joy, hoping his muscle would come in handy if Joy's restraint snapped. Then she sat Great-Aunt Iris as far away from Garrison as possible and recapped the previous night's adventures.

By the end of the tale, Great-Aunt Iris had brandished her knitting needles. Instead of knitting, they were aimed at Garrison's heart. Granted, they were several feet away from touching him, but from the militant scowl on her great-aunt's face and her ramrod spine,

Eliza wouldn't have put it past the woman to throw one like a lawn dart.

Joy, her eyes narrowed to slits, glared at Garrison. "And why should we believe a rat like you?"

"You don't believe me?" He grasped his chest as if stunned by Joy's proclamation.

"I didn't trust you before the whole embezzlement scheme. Why should I have changed my mind after? Do you really not have any idea how you tore this family apart or how close you were to destroying the very estate and your *family* you've been leeching off for years?"

He blinked at Joy as if he couldn't compute the disastrous role he had played. "Would an apology at this point really help?" He shrugged and flicked a piece of dust from his cashmere sweater, indifferent to the stares aimed at him.

Eliza clenched her fists, stemming their need to find any soft part of his body. The pain he'd suffer would be nowhere near the pain he'd inflicted on Uncle Fitzwilliam. Her family's troubles stemmed from Nancy, of course, but Garrison Wickham's willing involvement had brought her family and her ancestor's legacy to near destruction.

Joy tilted her head, sighed, and shrugged. "True to form. So glad you haven't changed, Garrison. So, what makes you so sure it was Oliver who killed Felix?"

Eliza wanted to smack the smug look off of Garrison's face but figured she would let Heath, who was clenching and unclenching his fingers, have first dibs. "Out with it," she ground out between clenched teeth.

"Oliver tossed me a few quid here and there for some surveillance on our chap over there." He nodded in Wentworth's direction.

That time, it took more than words to keep Wentworth from pummeling Garrison's face in. Heath's muscles rippled under his T-shirt, and the veins in his forearms bulged as he kept Wentworth's formidable form from splitting Garrison in two. For a split second, Eliza relished the sight of her normally laid-back, proper beau displaying his wares, but common sense prevailed.

"Cut it out. All of you. Do you want the police, who are only two floors below us, to come investigate?"

That cut through the testosterone-infused fog, and Wentworth and Garrison sat down, shoulders bunched, heads lowered slightly, gazes never wavering.

"But why do you think this little spy mission equals murder?" Eliza asked.

Garrison shrugged but never broke eye contact with Wentworth. "If Oliver wasn't planning on using Wentworth's location for anything, why did he need to know his exact whereabouts? If he wanted to frame Wentworth for murder, the copper better damn well be at the murder site. Hard to pin murder on someone if they weren't even there in the first place."

Something about his explanation didn't sit right with her, but perhaps her dislike for Garrison, which was quickly evolving into hatred, had her blinded to the truth simply because it was coming from the mouth of her lying, good-for-nothing cousin.

She needed to go back to the scene of the crime. She needed to milk all she could out of Timothy Elliot, Wentworth's familial nemesis and the Foxed Hound's bartender. Sliding a glance at Joy, who was twirling a piece of blond hair around a manicured finger, Eliza formulated the perfect plan. *It will take wit and cunning. Oh, who am I kidding? Who needs those when a cleavage-revealing top and makeup will do the trick?*

"Joy, I hope you don't have any afternoon plans."

Chapter Ten
Flirtations and Interrogations

I was correct in my assumptions concerning Captain Wentworth's adoration of Anne. According to Lady Russell, a family friend of the Elliots, Captain Wentworth had declared his love to her years ago when he was simply Mr. Wentworth and not a wealthy war hero, and she did not accept his suit. I have a strange suspicion that Lady Russell had a hand in persuading an impressionable young Anne to deny her heart for the coldness of money and societal standing. I'm afraid I do not know what to think of Lady Russell.

Lizzy Bennet Darcy

Pemberley 1814

Having successfully hidden in her office from all police officials until her stomach reminded her she'd missed lunch, Eliza snapped her laptop shut and ambled to the kitchen. To her luck, the head staff were chatting over mugs of steaming coffee, and after eating the provided plate of cold ham and cheese and checking with Tash, Mrs. Bankcroft, and Mrs. Underhill about the preparations for the afternoon sessions and arrangements, Eliza went in search of her great-aunt. Never one to accept being out of the loop, Great-Aunt Iris would certainly bristle at being left out of any snooping.

Eliza found her in her bedroom. Great-Uncle William hovered nearby, his wrinkled face drawn and haggard. His welcoming smile to Eliza barely made an indent on his lips.

Dwarfed by the high-backed chair upholstered in emerald-and-silver brocade, Great-Aunt Iris looked tiny in the chair's clutches. Her knitting needles were still, and she sat, slumped to the side, her unwavering gaze latched on the view out of the windows.

Eliza's heart stuttered in her chest, and her stomach dropped to her feet. She rushed to her great-aunt's side and latched on to the old woman's hand. "Great-Aunt Iris?"

Relief flooded through Eliza, warming her from the tips of her toes to the tips of her ears, when her great-aunt tilted her head toward her. Whatever relief she'd experienced before drained away. Great-Aunt Iris's normally bright eyes were dull and red-rimmed. The healthy pink glow which usually belied her great-aunt's age had curdled to a sickly gray more reminiscent of congealed oatmeal than peaches and cream. Her great-aunt had been the picture of health that morning. Garrison's return had probably been too much for her. "What's wrong? Are you sick?"

Instead of a grand tsk worthy of any proud dowager duchess and a hand slicing through the air to kill Eliza's stupid questions, Great-Aunt Iris weakly fanned her hand. "I am all right. Stop your fussing."

More than her great-aunt's stillness, her monotone scold worried Eliza. "You are not okay." She rested the back of her hand against her great-aunt's forehead. Warm but not feverish.

Great-Aunt Iris swatted at Eliza's hand with no more harm done than if a kitten were batting at a Burmese mountain dog. "I said leave me."

Eliza sent Great-Uncle William an entreating gaze. "How long has she been like this?"

"About an hour or so. She won't let me call for help. Says it is only a cold and to stop making a fuss over nothing."

So, the same speech she'd given Eliza. "Who do you normally call when she's sick?"

"I'm not sick. Haven't been sick a day in my life," Great-Aunt Iris mumbled and managed a stern enough glare that Eliza's fear of her great-aunt's imminent demise evaporated. She waved off Eliza's patting and readjusting and refused an extra pillow. "Stop fussing, girl." Holding her hand out to her husband, she said, "My William will look after me, won't you, my dear?"

"I won't leave your side for a moment, my love." He shuffled to the chair across from his wife and attempted to push it closer to her.

Eliza helped him rearrange it until the arms of the chairs were touching. Great-Uncle William settled in and grasped his wife's hand. Eliza's heart skipped a beat, and for a second, she got a glimpse of what the old couple before her had looked like sixty years ago. Tears pricked at the backs of her eyes, and she bit her inner cheek to keep them in check.

"Now, don't you have plans with Joy?" A coughing fit interrupted Great-Aunt Iris's scolding. "Be off with you, now, and I will want a full report when you get back. Understand?"

Eliza pressed a kiss to her great-aunt's forehead. After a reassuring nod from her great-uncle, Eliza left the room and, before closing the door, snuck a look at the couple. Great- Uncle William leaned over and pressed a kiss to his wife's lips, caressed her wrinkled cheek with his equally wrinkly and liver-spotted hand, then sat, cradling her hand in his by the large window facing the rose garden. *Will I be so lucky as to find a love to last this long and look like this decades later?*

Walking through the gallery, she gazed up at the portraits and wondered which ones had found a lasting love like her sixth-great-grandparents and her great-aunt and -uncle and which had married for money and status and lived as mere roommates under one expansive roof.

"Eliza, there you are." Heath's voice hailed her from the opposite end of the gallery near the staircase.

The answer to her question stood twenty feet away. The love be-tween her great-aunt and -uncle, the famous love between Elizabeth and Darcy, the one that broke down the walls of pride and prejudice, flashed through her mind. With something akin to ferocious hunger, she wanted that and knew exactly who she wanted it with. *Is now the time to tell him I want—no, need—him to accept the new job of-fer? Will he think me crazy if I jump into his arms and inform him that he is going to love me forever and put up with me even when I turn as batty and irascible as Great-Aunt Iris? Probably.* She checked her feet, which had stepped into overdrive, sashayed up to him, slid her arms around his waist, and settled her ear over his heart.

"You all right?" He held her at arm's length and tilted her chin up.

Running her finger along the collar of his blue-and-silver-checked dress shirt, she smiled. "Remember when you declared your never-ending love for me?"

His blue eyes twinkled. "And the after-party, yes. Why? Would you like me to declare it again?"

"You just want the reward."

"I plead the fifth as you Americans do on the risk of self-incrimi-nation." He played his thumb over her bottom lip. "That's not what's bothering you, though."

"Nothing's the matter." At his growl of disbelief, she batted away his concern and stared at the checks on his shirt.

"Great-Aunt Iris isn't feeling well, and she won't let anyone do anything for her. She's just sitting there with Great-Uncle William at her side." She fixed her gaze on his. "Do you think love like they have is attainable?"

"Yes. Maybe not for some, but I know one thing." He tipped her chin up with his finger. "I am one of those people who work my bloody arse off for something I believe in, and I very much believe in us." His kiss sealed his promise, and after he released her lips, he cuddled her into his chest.

Her buzzing cell phone interrupted their tête-à-tête. With a growl, she dug out her phone and glanced at the screen. "It's Joy. Time for the preshow, apparently." So much for telling him her plans for them. Perhaps she should take it as a sign that every time she opened her mouth to declare herself, someone or something rudely interrupted her.

"You will be careful?" His brow furrowed.

She smoothed out the lines with her thumb. "I'm with Joy. What could possibly go wrong?"

Not giving him a chance to poke holes in her shaky argument, she pecked him on the lips and dashed off for hair and makeup. It was showtime, the Foxed Hound was the stage, and Timothy Elliot was the audience. Eliza hoped it ended with a standing ovation and not a stage full of rotten tomatoes and resounding boos from the crowd.

ONE layer of foundation, two feathered swipes of blush, two false eyelashes, myriad blended eyeshadow colors, and a spackling of cinnamon-spice-colored lipstick later, Eliza, her black curls bouncing around her face, stepped down onto the tiled floor of the foyer. Joy, equally as stitched together with makeup and hair products, all tottering on two-inch wedges, clunked down the last few steps.

"Where are we off to? Going to visit the king?" Commissioner Cronk, resplendent in an oversized dress the color of green olives, gave them both a once-over. And not a very nice one, if her pinched lips meant anything.

"Amelia, I'm glad to see you looking better than this morning," Eliza said, despite the fact that the woman was still about as green as her dress.

Amelia's gaze darted to Joy then settled coolly on Eliza. "Thank you. I feel much better. You know how that is. When you finally know what's wrong, then you can begin fixing it."

Eliza shuddered at the underlying meaning. "Have you seen Chief Constable Kapoor?"

"No," Amelia said a little too quickly and a little too loudly. Her gaze flicked down the hall toward the library, one of the main meeting rooms for the weekend.

"That's okay. I wanted to ask if there was anything you all might need before I head off for a day of emergency shopping with Joy."

"I don't believe so. Your main staff are so helpful, and everything is going so smoothly. Besides, we have meetings all day. But you will attend the evening soirée, correct?"

Eliza bit her inner cheek. The last thing she wanted was to partake in canapés and conversation with Cronk or Kapoor, but as the mistress of Pemberley, she knew her absence and refusal to rub elbows with her guests would reflect poorly upon her abilities. *Where is Nancy and her political talent of schmoozing and bamboozling people?* Nancy would be able to turn on her fake smile and make everyone in attendance—besides Eliza, of course—feel welcome, all the while wishing them several miles away from Pemberley. In the morning, the police would be gone. She could do one more night. She could paste on a smile and schmooze with the best of them if that meant keeping Kapoor's sniffing nose from discovering her dirty little secret. Two dirty little secrets if she counted Garrison, who was shacked up with Wentworth in Pemberley's attic.

"I wouldn't miss it for the world. I do hope that you have all enjoyed your stay." And from the bill racked up by Commissioner Amelia Cronk and crew, if they hadn't enjoyed their time, that was entirely on them. That morning, Eliza had gone over the weekend's inventory to put the final touches on any additional charges or changes to their bill and had whistled to herself. Derbyshire's constabulary was either rolling in money, which Eliza highly doubted, or taxpayers who caught wind of the final cost of the "conference" would no doubt raise a stink. Eliza wondered who would take the fall for the financial faux pas. *Kapoor? Amelia?* If she were a betting woman, she would put her savings on Chief Constable Kapoor's allowing his boss and overseer, Amelia Cronk, to fall on that sword.

Amelia offered a tight smile. "Yes, we've enjoyed ourselves very much, thank you." She glanced at her watch. "Well, I must be off. Another round of meetings starts soon, and I want to be prepared."

"Of course. And remember, if something is amiss, my staff are willing and able to assist you."

Within five minutes, Joy was behind the steering wheel, taking a curve a little too quickly, and Eliza, hanging on to the oh-crap handle, replayed her run-in with Cronk. "We're not actually late for anything, you know. You can slow down."

Joy slid a glance at Eliza and turned her gaze back out the windshield in time to honk at a lumbering truck and weave around it. "If you're not champing at the bit to question Timothy, then you're losing your touch."

"I can't question him if I'm dead." Eliza's bicep bulged as she grasped for a stronger hold on the handle.

"Fine. Grandma-driving mode activated."

Eliza wasn't sure which grandma Joy was driving like, but that inspiration, apparently, had never driven under seventy miles an hour in a sixty-mile-an-hour zone. Taking what she could get, she relaxed her arm slightly, and as soon as Joy zipped into a parking space on the side of the Foxed Hound, Eliza hopped out and thanked her lucky stars for arriving in one piece with not one hair out of place.

"There. Safe and sound." Joy curved around the front of the Range Rover and nudged Eliza with her hip. "Who's got bad cop? Good cop?"

"No cop. We're simply two young women out for an afternoon of shopping and needed some refreshment." Joy's empty hands reminded Eliza that hers were empty as well. "The bags." With a huff, she traipsed to the back of the SUV, opened the hatch, and grabbed pre-stuffed paper shopping bags emblazoned with names of stores in the area. There was no need to go shopping when Joy's closet was full of brand-new clothes with the tags still attached.

Cover story complete, Eliza studied her cousin. No woman, after hours of shopping, looked unfluffed and unfazed. She reached out and fluffed Joy's hair.

"Hey!" Joy swatted Eliza's hands away. "You'll mess up my hair." She peered in the Range Rover's tinted window at her reflection. "See what you've done. I have flyaways now."

"That's the whole point. I've seen you after hours of trying on clothes." Knowing she needed to look a little fluffy herself, Eliza took her hair to task. "There, now we both look like we've been trying on clothes for hours."

"My dear cousin." Joy grinned. "If anything, it looks like you were doing a little more with your clothing off."

Her face heated, and she pressed the back of her hand to her cheeks. "You should take a break from writing bodice rippers and try a different genre. How about a cozy mystery? Those are fairly innocuous."

Joy sniffed. "Why should I make up mysteries when I get to experience them for real with you?"

"Good point. Now, are we ready?"

"As we'll ever be."

With sashaying hips, wind-blown hair, and shopping bags swaying to the beat of their feet, Eliza and Joy stepped into the pub and found seats on the tall barstools at the bar.

The pub's quiet atmosphere was probably due to the fact that it was two in the afternoon.

Timothy Elliot came through a little door off the side of the bar and stuttered to a stop. From his dilated pupils and his hand combing through his hair, he had seen them. He ambled up, placed his elbows on the wooden surface, and smiled. "Well, look at what the wind blew in. What can I get for you, ladies?"

Joy ordered a gin and tonic, and as Eliza didn't care for Pine-Sol in a glass, she ordered Riesling.

Timothy slid the glasses across the bar and eyed the bags settled like customers on the barstools. "Looks like you ladies have been busy."

"Oh, this is nothing." Eliza smiled in what she hoped was a sultry manner and played with the stem of her wineglass.

Timothy's gaze followed her fingers' undulations. His tongue darted out before he averted his gaze.

Like taking candy from a baby. Eliza's smile broadened, and she leaned toward Joy and whispered loud enough to ensure Timothy "overheard" them, "Are you sure that was Wentworth we saw sneaking back into the woods behind the bakery?"

Timothy choked, coughed to cover his choke, and turned red in the face, then his eyes bulged like a hunted hare's.

"Are you okay?" Eliza reached across the bar and laid her hand on Timothy's arm. She was pretty sure she didn't have clammy hands, which left his sweat as the culprit for his moist arm hair. His muscles quivered under her touch. As much as she wanted to think her beauty was the reason for the reaction, she knew it was Wentworth's name that had caused Timothy's body to vibrate.

He cleared his throat and tugged his arm away. "I'm fine. Something in my throat is all."

After gazing about the nearly empty pub, he straightened, and his face tightened. He apparently had come to some decision, and

Eliza prayed it was the one she had anticipated. She hoped Timothy wasn't the type of man to keep a secret or allow others to take part in one without him having his fingers in the mix.

He eyed Eliza and Joy, leaned forward, and whispered, "Did you say you saw Wentworth?"

Joy cut Eliza a severe glare. "I told you not to mention it. And here you go blabbing it out in the open."

"No, no." Timothy leaned farther over the bar.

Might as well lay on it.

He scooted his elbows so close they nearly touched hers. She forced herself not to move them.

"Don't worry. Your secret is safe with me. I want to make sure that he doesn't come back here to harm any more of my customers. I'd hate if anything happened to, say, you two lovely ladies."

Eliza didn't need to force a blush, as her face was already heated with anger and disgust. She did, however, avert her gaze demurely until she could ensure that her return gaze would be filled with long-ing instead of loathing.

"That's so sweet of you," Eliza crooned, surprised and somewhat dismayed that her fake-sweet voice came off as more Southern belle than Midwest city girl.

"Think nothing of it." He patted her hand long enough for her to be sure he'd left his sweaty fingerprints all over her skin.

Joy, inclining her head as close to his as possible without making contact, murmured, "It's so nice to know that there are such brave men in the world."

Does he actually believe any of this? Eliza kept her internal snort from vocalizing itself. *What man in his right mind would take any of this ooey, gooey garbage seriously?* Based on Timothy's dilated pupils and flushed face, he certainly did. *Good grief. If I were a man, I'd take him out back and beat some sense into him to save my gender from em-barrassment and ignominy.*

She tuned back in to the conversation in time to hear Timothy say, "And I would do anything to protect you from the likes of Finn Wentworth."

"I know all the horrid things you already told me about him, but my cousin here has not. I'm sure you're a better storyteller than I am, and if you're not busy, would you mind? It's so much better to know your enemy well, don't you think?"

His flushed face reddened until Eliza feared his head would release steam. "Yes, of course. I mean, there's not much to tell except that Wentworth is a bloody thief and liar. He refuses to relinquish Kellynch Hall to its rightful owner, me! It should have gone to my ancestor, William Elliot, eons ago, but no. That stupid old senile prat, Sir Walter Elliot, passed it on to his daughter, Anne. Can you imagine? A woman in charge of an estate?"

Afraid of what might come out of her mouth if she opened it, Eliza nodded in commiseration.

"Anyway, she married some bloke named Wentworth, and from then on, Kellynch Hall and the baronetcy are property stolen from my family."

Joy tapped the back of his hand. "Poor William Elliot. Poor you. Imagine having people calling you Sir Timothy Elliot. Has a nice ring, that."

Timothy puffed up his chest. "Wentworth doesn't even use his title. Imagine that!" He shook his head. "I have lawyers working on it, on him, but he's a bullheaded stubborn wanker and won't see reason. But what can one expect when a man comes from a line of thieving liars?"

If anyone came from a line of thieving liars, it was Timothy, but Eliza kept her face one of expectant admiration. "I was always suspicious of him. You should have seen how heavy-handed he was during his investigation at Pemberley back in July. Thought he was all that and a bag of potato chips, that's for sure." She pouted, making sure she put her full bottom lip—her best asset, at least according to Joy—to good use. "But I never took him for a murderer. An arrogant ass, yes. And as you say, a thieving liar, but not a murderer, surely."

"You'd be surprised at what a man can do when cornered. Wouldn't surprise me if Wentworth killed Felix to silence him, to shut him up over some dirty little secret. Rotten cops have to keep their secrets buried deep."

The only rotten one so far was Timothy, but Eliza smiled and circled the edge of a ring of condensation left by Joy's glass. His eyes followed her red-tipped fingernail. "It's too bad for Felix, of course, how awful, but with Wentworth out of the way, dishonored, and when caught, rotting away in prison, your bid for your rightful estate should be reasonably considered, right?"

"It would certainly give me an edge. But really, it would be so much easier if he were de—" A vein in his neck popped, and his Adam's apple bobbed. He blinked a few times and ran his finger along the collar of his black polo. "Sorry, lost my train of thought."

Yeah, right. "We were talking about how awful Wentworth is and how his demise—I mean, his dishonorable actions and an imminent prison sentence—would make your case for your estate easier."

"Yes, much."

How, Eliza wasn't sure, as according to Wentworth, the will, even though written hundreds of years ago, had consistently been ruled a sound and true document. Kellynch Hall would never belong to William Elliot's particular branch of the family. It had forked off from Anne's branch, never again to be within a leaf's grasp of the avaricious Timothy. He was truly delusional and—from the gleam in his eyes and his twitchy fingers ripping apart a bar napkin— unhinged and dangerous.

The pub's door opened, and in walked an attractive middle-aged man. He gazed about the room, gave a cursory nod to Joy, and homed in on an empty table directly behind them.

Joy nudged Eliza with her knee and whispered, "That's the dishy Dr. Hamilton."

"Really?" No wonder Great-Aunt Iris thought him a gentleman and both Monica's mother and Wentworth's wife took extra time preparing for appointments with him. "Care to introduce me?" She hadn't known how to get to Dr. Hamilton to pump him for information on poisons and how he had suspected hemlock, but fate had smiled kindly upon her for once.

Tired of Timothy's rantings against Wentworth but wanting to cast her net for one more clue, Eliza added a hint of condolence to her tone and tapped the back of his hand. "You must have been so shocked the night of Felix's murder. And to add insult to injury, on a Friday night, no less. I'm sure this place was pumping, huh?"

"It was a bloody dumpster fire, that's what it was. That ridiculous excuse for a waitress, Amanda, the one who screamed the pub down when she found Felix's body, was no use, of course, after the fact. Not that she was much use before. We were already short-staffed, and here she was, flirting with customers and not minding her job."

"How unfair. Probably didn't get any breaks, then, during the night." Joy fluttered her eyelashes at him.

He puffed up his chest. "I do take my job seriously, but a man's got to have a break every once in a while, you know. Managed to squeeze in a few smoke breaks. If it weren't for the stupid girl, I could have taken more."

"Yes, as my Great-Aunt Iris says, it's so hard nowadays to find good help." Eliza rested her elbows on the counter, leaned forward to give her cleavage-baring shirt its time in the limelight, and dropped her voice. "We've taken up enough of your valuable time, but it's so good to know that you're on top of things with this whole Wentworth situation. We women like to know there's a powerful man in charge."

"Would you mind if I got your number? You know, to warn you if I hear something about you-know-who."

"Of course. You should get Joy's." Eliza bit her lip as Joy's heel connected with her shin. "International cell plans are so expensive. I try to not use mine at all, if at all possible."

Obviously believing her lie, he eagerly punched in Joy's number as she gritted out the digits.

After several flirtatious attempts at goodbye, Eliza stood beside Joy at Dr. Hamilton's table, and when his smiling face beamed up at her, she forgot every question she wanted to ask him about poison.

Chapter Eleven
Enter Dr. McDishy

I had the dubious honor of conversing with Mrs. Clay tonight at a card party hosted by Sir Walter and his daughters. I had initially suspected her of ingratiating herself into Sir Walter's affections. I have, however, changed my mind (which any woman should be able to do with impunity), for Mr. Elliot was also in attendance, and I cannot say that my first impression of him was incorrect. He is a man not to be trusted, and I fear for my dear friend Anne, especially after witnessing secret looks he shared with Mrs. Clay.

Lizzy Bennet Darcy

Bath 1814

" Dr. Hamilton, I don't think you've met Eliza Darcy yet." Joy fanned out her arms as if showing off valuable wares at an auction house.

He smiled, displaying white teeth marred only by one front tooth slightly overlapping the other. Laugh lines crinkled around his chocolate-brown eyes as he held his hand out. "It's a pleasure to meet you, I'm sure." Motioning to the empty chairs around his table, he invited them and their shopping bags to join him.

Eliza scooted her chair in, and while he exchanged pleasantries with Joy, she studied him. His age, which she'd first pegged as middle age, didn't fit him as it should. There were no speckles of gray in his curly chestnut-brown hair, and his face was unlined by the wrinkles normally associated with a man in his mid to late forties. As a doctor, he probably took his health seriously, and it certainly showed, as Eliza doubted he was younger than forty. Something about his manner, the steady way he held Joy's gaze during conversation, bespoke a mature man comfortable with himself and one who carried a wisdom far older than his outer age suggested. Outlandish flirting would not work on that man. Of course, that said more about Timothy and his weakness for flattery than anything. If man cards were a thing, and if Timothy were a card carrier, he really should take his out back and burn it. No, if Eliza wanted any information from Dr. Hamilton, she would need to change tactics.

His gaze flicked to her, and he caught her staring. Disarming her with another smile, he gestured to her near-empty wineglass. "Can I buy you another one? My treat."

"Why not? Thank you, Dr. Hamilton." Her middle already swarmed with warmth from her first glass of wine, but while having a second might make her more prone to giggling, it at least gave her the chance to sit a little longer with the doctor and glean whatever she could.

Dr. Hamilton raised his arm, and a waitress came over and took their orders. "Please," he said when the waitress left, "call me Malcolm."

"My great-aunt speaks very highly of you." That was certainly an understatement, as the old woman had nearly come to fisticuffs with Wentworth when the DCI had dared to question the dear doctor's talent.

"Ah yes, Mrs. Darcy. She's been a patient of mine for over a year. She is... quite a delight." The twinkling in the doctor's eyes hinted that he had other adjectives in mind.

"Oh, she's something, that's for sure," Joy said.

"She's definitely independent and energetic." Eliza's grin slipped.

"Is something the matter?"

"No... Well, she's not feeling very well. She's not at all like her peppy, mischievous self," Eliza said.

"What are her symptoms?" Malcolm sat up a little straighter.

"Oh, she's lethargic, weak, has a cough. No fever, though. I checked before I left."

"Probably an onset of a cold. You will let me know if she gets worse, won't you? I normally don't make house calls, but I'll make an exception in Mrs. Darcy's case. She really is one of my favorites. Never know what you're going to get with her. And I like people who keep me on my toes." He pulled a business card from his wallet and slid it across the table. "Here. My mobile, as well as my surgery telephone number, is on there. Call night or day."

"Thank you." Eliza tucked the card in the back pocket of her skinny jeans. She would have to tell Wentworth there was a reason Dr. Hamilton was so well-liked. She had known him for only ten minutes and already wanted to get on his roster of patients. Perhaps she could fake a sickness. No, he would see right through that. She got the impression that he was a man who didn't watch the world go by in a blur. He saw people and noticed things. It was no longer a surprise that he'd noticed poisoning on first encountering Felix's body.

Eliza took the interruption of the arriving drinks to nudge Joy and give her an exaggerated get-on-with-it look.

She must have gotten the correct hint because after taking a sip of her second gin and tonic, Joy sighed. "Isn't it horrid what happened to that man? And here. Right above us, too, if I'm not mistaken."

"Yes, death is always a tragedy." Malcolm dipped his head as if in an impromptu moment of silence. Before Eliza could join him, he shook his head. "It's the poor waitress I feel most sorry for. I visited with her on Friday, and she's still reeling from the shock of it. Poor thing."

"A little birdie told me that you were one of the first at the scene," Joy said. "It's a good thing that you were there."

"Nothing good about it. I wasn't much use to poor Felix. By the time I arrived, he was long gone. How horrible to know that I, a doctor, was in the same building with a man dying in my vicinity, and I did nothing."

"But there was nothing you could do. You didn't know."

He waved away Eliza's reassurance. "No. Still, I was able to assist poor Amanda. That is something."

"She certainly had a shock. And I'm sure that a victim of poisoning isn't a pretty sight." Joy shuddered.

Malcolm's cheeks reddened. "Poison? How did you know? Ah yes, I'm afraid that between Amanda's hysteria and my ill-advised slip of the tongue, what the police wanted to keep secret is no longer that. I, of course, don't blame Amanda. She's a child, really. But I should have known better. Did know better."

"I wouldn't worry about it. It was bound to come out sooner or later. Village gossip and all that jazz." Eliza took a sip of her wine. "We heard from Amanda's mom that all her daughter could remember was Felix's black eyes and a mousy smell in the room."

"Keep in mind that I'm not an expert in poisons, but once, early in my career, I had to treat a person for accidental hemlock poisoning. Thankfully, she had ingested very little, and we got to her soon enough that we were able to save her life, but it was touch and go for a while, and without artificial respiration, she would have died. Hemlock is notorious for having no antidote. Usually, exposure to it is a death sentence."

"So you knew right away?" Eliza asked.

"Not necessarily. Many poisons can extremely dilate the eyes. It was the smell that I couldn't put my finger on until later. A musty odor, really. The killer must have crushed the plant in the room, as the smell was stronger than I'd have thought if diluted in whatever he had to drink."

Eliza's brain whirled through what she already knew. The strong odor indicated that the killer must have concocted the poison in the room. Which was not only odd and dangerous to the killer's secrecy, but it also negated the idea that Felix had already been poisoned hours before.

ELIZA itched to write the information swimming through her head on her makeshift crime board with her sleuthing team. But as mistress of Pemberley, she had to rub elbows with her weekend guests. Guests she couldn't wait to see the backs of in the morning.

But first, she needed to check on Great-Aunt Iris. After knocking softly on her great- aunt and -uncle's bedroom door and receiving a "come in" from her great-uncle, she slipped in. Despite it being a sunny late afternoon, heavy drapes cloaked the room in darkness, and the soft light of a bedside lamp barely touched the deep shadows of the room. Great-Aunt Iris, tucked in like a small child, was sleeping, but from her pinched face, it was not a restful sleep.

"How long has she been sleeping?"

Great-Uncle William shuffled to the bed, sank onto the mattress next to his wife, and held her limp hand in his. "For about an hour now. She occasionally mumbles to herself and is restless."

Eliza placed the back of her hand on her great-aunt's forehead. "Still no fever, which is good."

Her great-uncle's forehead creased as he watched his wife sleep.

"She'll be okay. Great-Aunt Iris is too stubborn to be ill. She'll get better simply by her own will. You'll see." Not really emboldened by her own words, she whispered, "But you will let me know if she takes a turn for the worse, right?"

"Of course." His lifeless voice matched his hopeless gaze.

"Why don't you let me sit with her for a while? You look tired. I'd hate for you to get sick too."

As his wife had done to her a thousand times, he waved away her concern. "No. I'll sit with her. She's cared for me almost my entire life. If I can't sit here and watch her sleep, then I don't deserve her."

"I'll have one of the staff bring you some tea."

He nodded his thanks but never took his eyes off his beloved. "Yes, that'll be fine."

After slipping from the room, Eliza gave Willow the task of furnishing Great-Uncle William with tea and an assortment of Mrs. Bankcroft's goodies and headed to her room to change for the evening's festivities.

Alone in her room, without even Caesar to keep her company, Eliza sank to her bed and cradled her head in her hands. She dashed a tear away and reminded herself that Great-Aunt Iris wouldn't approve of such nonsense. Her great-aunt was tough, and if the mental and physical aftereffects of experiencing WWII and losing a child hadn't done her in, a cold wouldn't either.

Repeating that to herself, Eliza ambled to her closet and chose a pair of black slacks, a white V-neck dress shirt, a red blazer, and matching red heels. After finishing her outfit with a rose-gold necklace and dangling earrings, Eliza took a deep breath, held it in, and headed out of her room and down the hallway to a party she most certainly did not want to attend.

Raised voices wafted down the hallway from one of the guest suites. Pivoting from the top of the stairs, she moved along the hallway, the carpet muffling her quick steps.

"You promised you would not say a word."

Eliza skidded to a halt outside one of the closed bedroom doors, the one Amelia Cronk had paid an enormous fee to stay in over the weekend. She was sure Amelia's voice had demanded silence, but she couldn't be sure. Of the few women present at the police conference, not many spoke with what Joy referred to as the Queen's English. *Of course it's her, you dingbat! Who else would be in the room she's staying in?* Eliza shook her head at her own ineptness.

A man's muffled voice spoke, but it was low and husky, and Eliza couldn't make out the words or identify the voice.

"You realize this will ruin not only my professional career but my private life." Panic laced Amelia's perfectly enunciated hoity-toity accent.

Eliza pressed her ear to the keyhole, hoping to catch a clear response.

"Keep your voice down." Chief Constable Jayesh Kapoor's voice sailed right through the keyhole. "If anyone finds out, you'll have more to worry about than your precious career and your love life. Think of your fiancé's broken heart when he realizes the brat you carry isn't his. He'd have to be a feckin' eejit to not notice when the bairn's born. Hard to hide the Asian blood of the father when both of you are as Anglo-Saxon as they come. I'm sure your precious fiancé will have questions."

Eliza screwed her face up at Kapoor's words, and for a few seconds, silence reigned. She imagined Kapoor and Amelia staring at each other like in old Western movies, wondering who would make the first move.

"Don't forget," Amelia hissed, "that I have a few aces up my sleeve, one of them being an alibi-less individual on a certain night in question."

"Don't be an idiot." Kapoor's normal lazy, unaffected voice reverberated with panic. "We both know the consequences of such indiscretion. Now that we have this all settled, we better join the group. We don't want our absence to raise suspicions, do we?"

Eliza didn't wait around for Amelia's response and sprinted away from the door and down the steps. Gaining the foyer, she paused, placed her hand over her heart, and steadied her breathing.

A man's laugh echoed down the staircase, and soon Kapoor, with Amelia smiling at his side, descended the steps. His gaze latched on Eliza's. "Ah, Miss Darcy, just the woman I wanted to see. Commissioner Cronk and I both wanted to thank you for a job well done. Pemberley is fantastic, and your staff? They were wonderful. Top marks to you and your staff."

Eliza dipped her head. "Thank you. I'm afraid I won't be able to attend this evening's festivities for long. My great-aunt is ill, and I feel awful leaving her alone."

"Of course." He let go of Amelia's arm and offered his to Eliza. "Shall we?"

After taking his arm, she followed his lead, and instead of being led to the ballroom for the soiree, he guided her to the doorway of her uncle's study. Amelia ducked into the ballroom, and Eliza followed Kapoor into Uncle Fitzwilliam's study.

She was alone with Kapoor. Goose bumps erupted on Eliza's arm. Forcing a smile, she asked, "Is there something I can help you with?"

"No. Rather, I believe there is something I can help you with."

"Really?"

"Yes, I gather from some of your staff that things have gone missing from the house and that one of your outbuildings has a broken window."

It took every ounce of willpower to keep her surprise and horror confined. Under no circumstances could she show even the slightest weakness to this man, who still had her arm intertwined with his. *Why didn't I check on how Garrison got into a locked building?* Amateur mistake. *And my staff? I hadn't thought they were tattletales.* Perhaps Mrs. Bankcroft was right in her mistrust of Willow. As the new kid on the block, the young woman wouldn't have the same ties or loyalty to Pemberley or its family.

"My staff should have known better than to burden you with such trivialities. I'll speak to them about it."

"On the contrary, they didn't. One hears things, you know. But please don't concern yourself over me. I am happy to extend my services in finding your petty thief. Thieves who start small usually work up to grander things." He leaned in closer and dropped his voice. "And as for the broken window, I suspect Wentworth."

"Really?" Her gut churned.

"I got word that a few hours ago, someone saw Wentworth slip into the woods near Lambton. Wouldn't surprise me if he was surviving off of stolen goods, vandalizing places to get what he needs."

"Did they say who saw him?"

"That worthless chap Timothy Elliot, bartender at the Foxed Hound, claims he saw him ducking into the trees."

At least, Timothy's need for notoriety and importance had saved her and Joy from being linked to asking questions.

"You think he was here, then? On the property?"

"Where else would he be? Your uncle was his friend. Probably thought to seek shelter here, snuck on the estate, broke into one of the outbuildings, but then realized the police presence here and hightailed it back to town."

"Surely, he wouldn't resort to breaking and entering. Besides, he seemed like such a good detective. I still can't believe any of this is happening." She didn't need to put on an act to make her last statement ring true.

Kapoor's eyes sharpened and zeroed in on her. "That is your first mistake. Be careful, Miss Darcy. Wentworth is a dangerous man."

<hr>

IT took thirty minutes for Eliza to extricate herself from the conference shindig and fifteen to make sure Great-Aunt Iris was tucked in and hadn't taken a turn for the worse. Forty-five minutes had passed since Kapoor's warning about Wentworth being a dangerous man, and her ears still rang with the hatred in the chief constable's voice. Although sitting across from Wentworth and being the target of his stony face gave some credence to Kapoor's warning.

"He thinks *I'm* dangerous?" Wentworth's voice cracked.

Eliza exchanged glances with Heath, who sat next to her on the floor, his hand in hers. Joy, who had commandeered the only remotely comfortable chair in the attic, bit at a cuticle. The only unwise one, Garrison, had the gall to begin to vocalize a comment. With a withering look from Wentworth, Eliza's spineless cousin pinched his lips shut until they whitened around the edges.

That rhetorical question finished, Wentworth snatched a marker and stabbed the air with it, punctuating his command to "add to the list."

After disengaging her hand from Heath's, Eliza stood next to Wentworth and read what they had so far. It was clear they had neglected their crime board. The last clue she'd written dealt with Dr. Hamilton unofficially diagnosing poison as the cause of death. She cracked her knuckles. Time to rectify the oversight.

Eliza spun around. "Well, team—" The absence of a white-haired little old lady knitting and harrumphing was palpable. The only one oblivious to Great-Aunt Iris's absence was Garrison, and he didn't count. Swallowing the lump in her throat, Eliza blinked away the burning sensation at the backs of her eyes. Soon, her great-aunt would return. "Let's fill this board up so we can get you off the hook for a crime you didn't commit."

"Who's to say he didn't commit it?" Garrison grunted and hugged his chest. "Bloody good-for-nothing coppers sticking their noses where they don't belong. Although I did hear through the grapevine that it was my cousin, here"—he jerked his head toward Eliza—"who solved the first Pemberley problem and not you, so perhaps you don't actually have the intelligence to pull off a murder. You certainly can't solve them."

Joy hopped from her seat and stuck her face so close to his that their noses touched. With an index finger, she poked his chest. "Shut your bloody mouth, you little weasel. After all you've done, the heartache and destruction you not only caused but seemed to relish, you of all people have no right to say anything. Do. You. Understand. Me?"

Eliza wanted to tag on a "Hear! Hear!" but Garrison's twitching eyes and blotched face proved that Joy had made her point clear. Wentworth tilted his head at Joy, a small smile tipping one corner of his mouth.

Within twenty minutes, Eliza, with the help of Joy's occasional amendments, added to their crime board. She stood back, chewed on the capped end of the marker, and glared at the evidence. "Well, team, can anyone make sense of this mess?"

Heath came to her side, snatched the pencil hanging on a string from the wall, and circled one name that popped up with every piece of evidence. "I think we should take a closer look at Timothy."

Eliza was about to argue but, after adding up the circles, reconsidered. "You might have a point."

Wentworth's eyes gleamed with something akin to joyful vengeance. "Might? I think your man has a point." He held up a finger. "One, Timothy was there the whole night." A second finger popped up. "Two, he was the bartender. No one would question what he was doing to the drinks, and he could, theoretically, do whatever he wanted behind the bar without anyone being the wiser." A third finger joined the other two. "Three, he admitted himself that they were short-staffed that night, so no one would have questioned his bussing the tables. If anything, they would have thought him a hard worker for stepping in in a pinch."

"Fourth," Joy interrupted, "he could have set aside the glasses, and when he went for his 'smoke break' as he claimed, he could have easily set the stage in Felix's room without anyone questioning his absence."

"Do you remember when Felix took his break?" Eliza asked.

Wentworth's eyes narrowed, and he sat silently for a few seconds. "No, sorry. I tried not looking at the man. Makes me sick."

"I wonder if the waitress, Amanda, would remember. That's a line we can investigate tomorrow." Eliza added it to her ever-growing to-do list.

"Don't forget that it was Timothy who took my and Eliza's lie and volunteered the information that he saw Wentworth slinking around in the woods. He couldn't have seen you, right?" Joy slanted a questioning look at Wentworth and received a growl in response. "So, he didn't see you, then. Then why lie? Why bring it up at all?"

"Because in his pea-sized brain, I'm sure he's confident that with me behind bars, he can have Kellynch Hall." Wentworth sagged on his cot.

Something didn't sit right with Eliza. "In his world, that might make sense, but why commit murder? And why Felix Payne? I don't take Timothy as being a cold-blooded murderer."

Wentworth snorted. "You of all people shouldn't be surprised at how a killer can often look like an average everyday citizen."

Silence permeated the room, and Heath grasped Eliza's hand and ran his thumb over the top of it.

Eliza sighed. "You're right, but that still doesn't give us any insight into *why* Timothy would want Felix dead."

Chapter Twelve
Just What the Doctor Didn't Order:
Brandy and Byron

*I have made the acquaintance of Admiral and Mrs. Croft, and Darcy
and I agree (as we always do when he agrees to agree with me) that besides my own dear Uncle and Aunt Gardener and my beloved Jane
and her Charles, that we have not met better, more well-matched people. Their long love and adoration for each other prove that not all
marriages diminish into a mere tolerance of one's life partner, a fate I
witnessed nearly every day at home and one I feared was a natural consequence of living under the same roof with one person. Darcy claims
we will be even more in love in thirty years, and after witnessing the
Crofts, I wholeheartedly believe him.*
Lizzy Bennet Darcy
Bath 1814

Sunday mornings and the family's habitual coffees, scones, and
conversation after church were usually Eliza's favorite. Posted by
the front door and seeing the back ends of police officials leaving
Pemberley, Eliza decided that Sunday might beat all others. Only
two guests were left, and she ground her teeth as Kapoor and Cronk
took their dandy old time descending the staircase. Despite the
smiles on their faces, their rigid body language hinted at a not-so-
friendly conversation seconds before coming down the steps.

"Ah, Miss Darcy." Kapoor took her to the side. "I have good news for you."

Eliza couldn't imagine what good news the man had to offer, so she braced herself for whatever "good" news he was about to gift her with.

"I would be remiss in my job if I didn't offer you or your estate protection with a murderer at large, especially as he had connections with your uncle and this place. It would not surprise me if he attempted to weasel his way into Pemberley."

"While I appreciate the gesture, it is really quite unnecessary, I assure you."

"It is a mere trifle. I have posted two of my officers on the property and have given them direct orders to watch for any suspicious activity. You may rest easy now."

She would never rest easy again. "Thank you. I'm sure I will."

Eliza shook Cronk and Kapoor's proffered hands in farewell and waited until she was sure no peeping eyes in a rearview mirror could clearly see her and wiped her hands on her pants. Whatever was wrong with Kapoor and Cronk was as fuzzy as Great-Aunt Iris's logic, but something didn't feel right. She shook the feeling off and entered a police-free Pemberley—minus the one holed up in her attic and the two somewhere on the property. Her heart sank. Keeping Wentworth safe from Kapoor's vengeance sounded more like a far-off fairy tale, and a future prison sentence for them both felt more like reality than fiction. That meant another thing added to her list. Before checking on Wentworth and his prisoner, she ducked into her great-aunt and -uncle's bedroom to check on her patient.

The heavy curtains kept out the morning sunshine, and the closed space had gained the odor of a sickroom, giving the place a suffocating aura. A Tiffany lamp glowed blue and purple with dripping wisteria, casting a faint light over her great-aunt's pale face. Great-Uncle William snored softly in a chair beside the bed. Not wanting to wake either of them, Eliza gently pressed the back of her hand to Great-Aunt Iris's forehead. Her skin warmed with the heat radiating from her great-aunt's skin.

She hurried to her bedroom, where she'd stowed Malcolm Hamilton's business card.

He picked up on the fourth ring. "Hello. Dr. Hamilton speaking."

"Malcolm, this is Eliza Darcy. I hate calling on a Sunday, and I hope you don't mind me calling, but Great-Aunt Iris is running a fever."

"I don't mind at all. I'm glad you called. I have some things to finish up, but then I'm free to zip out to check on her. Will that work?"

"Thank you so much, Malcolm. I appreciate it."

"You're welcome." He hung up, leaving Eliza gripping her phone until her knuckles whitened.

It's just a cold, it's just a cold, it's just a cold, she repeated as she went hunting for Joy and Heath. She found Joy in the library, deep into her work-in-progress's chapter six, so deep that it took Eliza wiggling her fingers in front of Joy's face to get her cousin's mind back to reality.

"What are you doing?" Joy peered over her blue-light-blocking glasses. "I'm in the middle of creating a super-sexy environment for super-sexy things to take place between—"

"Yes, yes, super-sexy human beings. I get it. But Great-Aunt Iris is running a fever. I called Dr. Hamilton, and he'll be over as soon as he can."

Joy snapped her laptop shut and set her glasses on the closed cover. "How bad is the fever?"

"I don't know. I didn't check, as I didn't want to wake her up."

"We should probably wake her up and prepare her for his visit. She won't be pleased at having the delicious doctor seeing her in dishabille."

"You were using the thesaurus during your setting-the-stage scene, weren't you? Not sure we should use the word in connection with Great-Aunt Iris."

"Point well taken. Well, whatever state she's in, I'll make sure she's presentable."

Eliza followed Joy from the library, but instead of trailing her up the staircase, she turned down the west hallway leading to her office. Heath, when at Pemberley, made it his office space as well, and when she entered the room and saw his salmon-and-white-checked dress shirt stretch across his back as he hunched over his desk, she was reminded why she didn't mind sharing the space one bit.

He must have sensed motion because he swung around and plucked out his earbuds. His delighted smile wilted upon seeing her face. He set his pen down and placed his hands on her shoulders. "What's wrong?"

"It's Great-Aunt Iris. She's developed a fever. I called Dr. Hamilton, and Joy is prepping Great-Aunt Iris for the impending visit."

"Yeah, I don't think your great-aunt will appreciate a surprise visit from 'Dr. Dreamy.'"

Eliza couldn't crack a smile at Heath's crooked one-finger air quotes.

"Hey." He cuddled her into his chest. "If I know one thing, it's that your great-aunt is too stubborn to let a little cold get the best of her."

"But what if it's not a cold?"

Heath didn't answer and simply held her. He kissed the top of her head. "Should we go see how Joy's coming along with her probably less-than-cooperative patient?"

Eliza sighed. "Yes, but I need to make sure Mrs. B has a tea tray ready. I'm hoping to tempt Great-Aunt Iris with some of Cook's delights. She needs to eat something."

After stopping in the kitchens and arranging for tea and sandwiches and dainty desserts to be served as soon as Dr. Hamilton arrived, Eliza and Heath wended their way through the halls and up the staircase.

"Ever thought about installing an elevator?" Heath glared at the steps they'd walked up. "I lose count of how many times I take these a day."

"Consider it exercise." Eliza grabbed his hand and laughed as Caesar scampered up the steps with ease and sat at Heath's feet without breathing heavily.

Heath glared at Caesar and whispered, "Show-off."

"Come on. You'll catch your breath as we walk."

"Seriously, though. I can run for miles without any issue, yet these stairs kick my bloody arse all the time."

"Please don't ask me to go on a run with you. Ever. If you ever see me running, it's because something or someone is trying to eat me or kill me, and then you should run too."

"That's fair."

The door to her great-uncle and -aunt's bedroom was ajar, and a ray of hope burst in Eliza's chest when her great-aunt scolded Joy for picking out the wrong color tracksuit.

"...does not see a doctor while wearing that color. I have seen oatmeal with better tone than that material."

Joy's exasperated voice joined with the clink and clank of hangers banging against each other. "Then why do you have something the color of congealed oatmeal in your closet?"

"Never you mind about my wardrobe. I've seen what you wear."

Joy gasped, and before her cousin could retort with something just as childish, Eliza, followed by Heath and Caesar, stepped into the room.

"Great-Aunt Iris, you look ..." Words failed Eliza, and saying things like "haggard," "ten years older," or "shriveled and pale" would not positively affect the patient. But Great-Aunt Iris looked all those things. Perhaps it was the white Victorian-style nightgown that covered her great-aunt from chin to toes that bleached her of her usual peach complexion. The hundreds-year-old fashion certainly did not scream life and vibrance. Great-Aunt Iris's face was drawn and pinched, and her hair, which she usually painstakingly styled with curlers, hung limply around her face.

"Like death?" Great-Aunt Iris quipped.

"Don't say that." Eliza sank onto the bed next to her great-aunt.

"Why not? It's true."

INSTEAD of beginning an argument she knew she wouldn't win, Eliza ignored her great-aunt's statement and placed her hand against her forehead. "You're still running a fever."

"Of course I am. And how do you think having this... this..." She waved a limp hand in Joy's general direction. "Messenger of impending doom selecting my outfit will help me not have one?"

Heath leaned over and whispered in Eliza's ear, "With her old irascible self coming to life again, I think she's out of the woods."

Great-Aunt Iris cocked her head and narrowed her eyes at him. "What did you say, young man?"

"Nothing, ma'am. I was telling Eliza here that I think you look lovely."

Great-Aunt Iris sniffed, speared him with a second glance, then turned her attention to Eliza. "Was it your idea to call Dr. Hamilton?"

"Yes, but I'm afraid for you. Fevers, especially for people who are..."

"Ancient?" her great-aunt offered.

Eliza snuck a look at her great-uncle, who sat in a chair next to the bed. "Ancient" was probably too young for him, but her great-aunt was only starting to creep into the "old" category. "No. For people who are well into their golden years, fevers are dangerous and should be taken seriously."

"Well, don't sit there gaping at me as if I am going to drop dead right here. I look like a drowned rat, and I will not have Dr. Hamilton see me in such a state. Joy, put away the puce unless you want me to look like a corpse. Grab the emerald green. No, not that green. I said emerald, not shamrock."

Joy looked ready to set fire to Great-Aunt Iris's tracksuits.

"Great-Aunt Iris, why don't you try sitting in this chair so I can do something with your hair?" With Heath's help, Eliza settled Iris in the chair. From the look on Heath's face, he must have noticed how bird-thin she'd felt. To hide her worry from her great-uncle, she busied herself at her great-aunt's toilette table and gathered a brush and hair pins.

"Now don't go making me look a right trollop. I've seen how young girls do their hair nowadays."

Eliza bit her lip to keep her smile in check. "I'll do my best."

Within ten minutes, Great-Aunt Iris, dressed in an emerald-green velour tracksuit and with her snowy white hair pinned neatly back from her face, seemed smaller and frailer than before. She rested her head against the side of her high-back chair, and her eyes flitted closed.

"Poor dear." Eliza covered her great-aunt's lap with a quilt. Great-Uncle William sat alert in a chair next to his wife, and his hand rested on the armrest near hers. "Great-Uncle William, you should get some rest."

He shook his head but didn't speak.

A knock on the door preceded Tash, who announced Dr. Hamilton, who bustled through the door with a black medical bag clunking against his thigh as he walked into the room.

"Sorry it took me longer than anticipated." He reached into his bag, squirted out some hand sanitizer, and after rubbing it in, slipped on gloves and knelt before his patient. "Mrs. Darcy?"

Great-Aunt Iris's eyelids fluttered and opened slowly. She struggled to sit up straight in her chair.

"Now, now, Mrs. Darcy, take it easy. Here, let me." Dr. Hamilton helped her and shared an amused glance with Eliza, Joy, and Heath as the old woman preened her hair.

"I'm sure I look a fright, Doctor, but girls these days don't know how to dress for specific occasions." Even though she had said "girls," her gaze landed on Joy.

"You look a picture, ma'am, and I'm sure these young women did a fine job." He smiled at Joy then turned his attention to his patient. "Now, tell me what's wrong."

Before her great-aunt could begin with the fall of mankind in the garden of Eden, Eliza started her out a little closer to the onset of her symptoms and filled in with her great-aunt's actual symptoms of weakness, loss of appetite, and having a "meh" approach to everything.

After listening intently, Dr. Hamilton dug out a stethoscope from his bag of tricks and listened to Great-Aunt Iris's heart. "And when did the fever start?"

"I don't know when it started, but she didn't have one last night when I checked on her around ten. And I didn't check on her this morning until around nine," Eliza said.

"Mrs. Darcy, take a deep breath, please." After repeating his request several times and placing his stethoscope in different positions on her chest and back, he rocked on his heels and smiled gently at his patient. "Mrs. Darcy, did you get your flu shot?"

Breathing deeply as instructed moments before had apparently taken all of Great-Aunt Iris's lung capacity, as the impudent doctor was saved from a grand harrumph. Instead, she treated him to a regal look of disdain. "I have never gotten my flu shot, and I've never been sick a day in my life."

"Up until now, you mean," Joy pointed out.

Eliza was very happy she had only thought it and not stupidly said it out loud.

Dr. Hamilton wisely stayed out of the fray and waited until Great-Aunt Iris was finished boring a hole into Joy with her gaze. "I believe it a possibility that you have influenza. I would like to start you on Tamiflu right away while we wait for testing."

Great-Aunt Iris shook her head and opened her mouth, but before she could speak, Great- Uncle William reached for her hand. He didn't say anything, but the look they shared sent a tingle of warmth through Eliza's heart. Heath placed his hand on her shoulder, and she tilted her head until her ear touched the back of his hand.

Great-Aunt Iris's sigh broke the moment. "Do as you think best, Doctor."

"Are you sure? I don't want to push you into doing something you don't want to do."

"I'm sure."

Remembering the awful experience of influenza testing, Eliza figured her great-aunt didn't want an audience and ushered Joy and Heath from the room.

Ten minutes later, Dr. Hamilton joined them in the hall. "She's all tucked up in her bed again. Please get as many fluids in her as possible and, if you can, get her to eat something. I'll have the lab at the emergency room run the tests, and hopefully, we'll get the test results by midafternoon. If it is the flu, I'll get a prescription sent to the pharmacy." He winked. "I know the pharmacist, and she owes me a few favors."

"Thank you, Malcolm. Do you think she'll be okay?" Eliza asked.

"I never make promises, but if we get her on Tamiflu and she rests and gets the proper nutrients, I'm certain your great-aunt will be back to her old self soon." He smiled. "Keep an eye on her and call me immediately if she worsens."

Joy offered to walk him out, and as soon as they were gone, Eliza led Heath to her room and burrowed into his chest as soon as the door shut behind them.

"Stop it," he murmured into her hair.

"Stop what?"

"Thinking of worst-case scenarios."

"I can't help it. What if—"

"What-ifs will only drive you crazy, and from your family tree, I don't think you have far to go." He put her at arm's length and grinned.

She rolled her eyes but didn't argue. "You're not wrong. Well, what do you recommend to keep my mind off negative things?"

His eyes darkened, and he dipped his head. "I have a few ideas."

Joy burst through Eliza's bedroom door. "I'm sure Willoughby will be absobloodylutely devastated when he realizes I've replaced him with the dishy doctor."

"Will he, though?" Heath murmured under his breath.

Joy speared him with a glare. "Anyway, I can't wait for Willough-by to come to his senses and propose to me."

"Have you even gone on one official date?" Eliza asked.

"No, but those aren't necessary for true love to run its course."

"You should leave Shakespeare to the experts. Besides, why wait for Willoughby to propose? Why don't you do it?" Eliza asked.

"There are some things I will not stoop to, so for now, I will re-place the bloody idiot with Dr. Malcolm Hamilton. His name's got a nice ring to it, doesn't it? He's a man who takes action when neces-sary."

"Good luck." Heath settled onto the chaise lounge and slung his arm across the back.

"I don't need luck." Joy grinned.

Eliza sat next to Heath and cuddled into his side. "You might not need it, but I need all of it. How am I supposed to juggle the needs of the estate, the you-know-whos in the attic, a sick great-aunt, and a murder investigation? Oh, and two officers gifted to us by Kapoor?"

Heath blew out a breath and massaged the back of her neck. "That's a gift he really shouldn't have given. We'll have to be extra conscientious about our comings and goings."

"Without looking like we're breaking the law," Joy added.

"But I promised Uncle so faithfully to stay out of trouble."

"This time, you didn't go find trouble. It came to you." Joy smiled ruefully and shrugged. "That should count for something in the end."

All three glanced at the ceiling.

"Speaking of trouble, shall we check to make sure they haven't killed each other?" Eliza started for the door. "Any bets on who's still intact?"

AFTER finding Wentworth and Garrison alive and in opposite corners, Eliza arranged the food she'd stolen from the kitchen while Heath had distracted Mrs. Bankcroft. "If you think I'm going to serve you two, you have another think coming. Get off your butts, come to the table, and eat." Although she didn't blame Wentworth, at least, for his sudden lack of appetite. If anyone had a reason to begrudge Kapoor's gift, it was him. Wentworth shook himself as if tossing off the idea of two constables looking specifically for him and gathered up his food.

While Wentworth and Garrison ate, Eliza filled them in on Great-Aunt Iris's possible diagnosis. "So when Dr. Hamilton gets the test results and orders the prescription, if necessary, Joy and I will zip into town. It will be a perfect opportunity to gather more intel from Timothy."

"You still think he's a serious contender?" Wentworth eyed the clues on the crime board.

"His name does pop up quite a bit, and he is the bartender. Considering how easy it would have been for him to poison Felix's drinks and collect the glasses, I think we should keep him at the top of our list." A snippet of conversation between Kapoor and Cronk popped up in her mind. "Speaking of our list, I think we should, um, add Kapoor and possibly Cronk to the board."

Wentworth's eyes nearly bulged from his head. "What? Kapoor is many things, but a murderer?"

Eliza refused to be intimidated by his bark. "Then explain to me why he has you all but locked up and about to throw the key away. I overheard him and Cronk argue, and I don't know what she has over him, but she reminded him that he didn't have an alibi."

Wentworth's frown deepened. "He specifically mentioned not having an alibi for Friday night?"

"Yes—no—" Eliza closed her eyes in an attempt to conjure up the conversation. "I don't think she mentioned Friday, but what other night could have such a hold over him? And as for Cronk, she's apparently carrying another man's baby. A man who isn't her fiancé."

Joy rubbed her hands together. "Oh, this is turning into a delicious soap opera. Do we know who she's having an affair with?"

"No, but from what I overheard, it'll be hard for her to convince her betrothed that the baby is his when it's born."

Wentworth waved away the juicy drama. "I don't give two rats' arses who Amelia Cronk has been having it off with. Kapoor is the main problem, and don't forget that he has his dirty fingers in every crime pie around here. Could be any night where not having an alibi might make him sweat." Wentworth scrubbed his face until Eliza was sure he'd rubbed his skin off. "Kapoor's a bastard, there's no mistake, but he's not a murderous one, but put him up there if you need to."

Eliza huffed and printed Kapoor's name on the board. She added *hates Wentworth, worried about no alibi on ? night, dirty cop?* and *something fishy going on with Cronk.* Then she handed Wentworth the marker. "Care to add anything else?"

Wentworth crossed his arms.

Eliza's phone rang. "It's Malcolm." She cradled her phone to her ear. "Hello, Doctor. Ah, I see... Yes, a very good thing we caught it early. Okay. Joy and I will swing by the pharmacy. Thank you again. At the Foxed Hound?" Eliza raised an eyebrow and grinned at Joy. "Of course. We would love to. Yes, see you then."

"What was that all about?" Heath asked.

"Malcolm is a godsend." Eliza shoved her phone into her back pocket. "Great-Aunt Iris tested positive for influenza, but with the medicine and plenty of TLC, she has a bright prognosis, at least, according to him. I'll go check on our patient, give her and Great-Uncle William the news, and be sure that Mrs. Underhill, Tash, Mrs. B, and Willow are all on board for giving her the best care." *You should be staying behind to help your great-aunt, you ninny, not gallivanting around the country, solving a case you shouldn't have gotten mixed up in in the first place!*

Heath must have sensed her inner conflict. He laced his fingers through hers. "I know for a fact that your great-aunt would be seriously displeased if she caught you nursing her instead of solving a murder. Besides, I'll make a better nurse than you would anyway."

Eliza dashed away a stray tear. "Oh, really?"

"I shall read awful poetry to her, mainly Byron, and will sneak her the occasional brandy when no one is looking."

"Don't you dare." Eliza nudged him with her shoulder.

"You're right. Quoting Byron might do her in." Heath pulled Eliza in for a quick embrace. "Now, off with you."

Joy followed Eliza to the top of the steps. "What about the last part of your conversation with the good doctor?"

Eliza grinned. "Looks like your goal of becoming Mrs. Dr. Dishy might come true. Malcolm would love to meet us at the pub at four. Apparently, the pub is as sacred as church on Sundays. Perfect cover for going to the Foxed Hound... again." She pointed at Garrison before descending the stairs. "You, behave. Especially with Kapoor's hounds sniffing around."

Halfway down the long gallery, she split ways with Joy. "I'll meet you in the foyer in a few minutes." She quietly entered the sickroom. A sliver of light peeked through the heavy curtains, illuminating the sleeping form of her great-aunt and Caesar, curled up at her feet. Great- Uncle William lay asleep beside her, softly snoring. Eliza tiptoed over to the bed and lightly pressed the back of her hand to her great-aunt's forehead.

Her eyelids fluttered open. "Here to deliver the bad news?"

"There is no bad news to deliver, but you do have the flu. I'm running into town with Joy to get your medicine, and in the meantime, you are to behave and to eat and drink whatever Tash or Mrs. Underhill or Willow bring you."

Great-Aunt Iris blinked at Eliza's brusque command then smiled. "Was wondering when you'd get the courage to put me in my place."

"I'm serious." Eliza lightly held her hand, spotted and lined with age. "If anything were to happen to you, I don't know what I'd do."

"Pshh." She swatted away Eliza's worry as if it were an annoying gnat. "Now, go before you wake your great-uncle."

"Are you sure you don't want me to stay?"

"I want this case solved so I can clear Pemberley's attic of riffraff." Iris patted Eliza's hand and closed her eyes, obviously dismissing her niece.

After petting Caesar and giving him strict instructions to look after Great-Aunt Iris, Eliza left the room and went in search of the head staff. Ten minutes later and assured that they would give her great-aunt the best of care, Eliza hurried to the foyer, grabbed her purse and Joy, and drove into Lambton for another stab at Timothy Elliot.

Chapter Thirteen
Bloody To-Do Lists

I accompanied Anne today on a visit with on old school friend of hers, a Mrs. Smith. Poor woman lives in poverty with no family or friends to attend her in her ill health. Anne's devotion to her friend since residing in Bath proves Anne is a woman to admire and treasure as a steady friend. In concern over Mr. Elliot's attentions toward Anne, Mrs. Smith divulged Mr. Elliot's sordid history, his hatred for the Elliots, and his unwavering need to secure the baronetcy at all costs. His quest for Anne is not for love but for worldly gain, a title, and an estate. Mr. Elliot always did remind me of Wickham, and now I know why.

Lizzy Bennet Darcy

Bath 1814

Two Bloody Marys in and Eliza was reminded why she usually stopped at one. Blinking to clear her foggy thoughts, she settled her gaze on Dr. Malcolm Hamilton. His handsome face was turned toward Joy, and every time he smiled, Eliza understood why Joy had set aside the often absent and feckless Willoughby.

"Thank you again, Dr.—"

"Malcolm. Please."

"Sorry." Eliza smiled. "Malcolm, thank you again for taking time out of your Sunday to make a house call."

"It's my pleasure. Your great-aunt is a delight."

Joy snorted but smiled. "She keeps the place lively, that's for sure."

"And you were able to pick up the Tamiflu?" he asked.

"Picked up and delivered. I didn't want her to wait for her first dose." Eliza glanced down the bar, where Timothy was starting a tab for a new arrival. The Foxed Hound was apparently the place to be on a Sunday afternoon, and Eliza thanked her lucky stars there hadn't been a table open. She was saved from having to come up with some half-baked excuse for sitting at the bar to speak with Timothy, but only the sitting part had come to fruition. She'd yet to get a chance to milk Timothy for more information.

The pub's door crashed open, and in stepped Oliver Wright. Despite the cool autumn weather, he dripped with perspiration. He eyed the patrons, raked Eliza with his gaze, snorted, bellied up to the bar, and demanded a whiskey and Coke.

Eliza's shoulder blades touched. Good thing Great-Aunt Iris wasn't there, or she would definitely have given the oaf a good old what-for. Pretending to pay attention to Malcolm and Joy's conversation, Eliza used her peripheral vision to spy on Oliver. She almost felt sorry for Timothy. It was impossible not to, as he was as white as a ghost and seemed to be looking for a quick exit. Even though she was close enough to hear normal conversation, Oliver had dropped his voice to a harsh whisper, and she couldn't catch a word.

Before she could figure out how to infiltrate their conversation without being conspicuous, the pub's door opened again, and in walked Chief Constable Kapoor. He caught sight of her and made a beeline for her. "Good afternoon, Miss Darcy."

"Hello, Chief Constable."

"Figured I'd come to Lambton's lifeline"—he gestured around the crowded pub—"and see if I can catch any wind of Wentworth." He tapped his finger to his nose. "Nothing from my men yet, but I doubt it will be long before something shows up."

Yeah, and probably something you plant on my property as an excuse to search it. She jerked her head. "Timothy Elliot there is your man. He's the man who saw him duck into the woods."

Kapoor glared at Timothy with disdain but claimed a barstool on the opposite side of Oliver. Oliver snapped his mouth shut but didn't move. Kapoor, ignoring Oliver, started questioning Timothy. The bartender's eyes lit up with a fresh audience, and soon, Timothy's arms were gesticulating in all directions.

Already familiar with Timothy's anti-Wentworth ravings, Eliza tuned him out for the most part and cut into Joy and Malcolm's flirty banter. "Who knew the Foxed Hound was such a hopping place on Sundays?"

"For most of these men, this is their church." Malcolm, sitting on the opposite side of Joy, leaned forward and grinned. "And for some, an escape from their families."

From the looks of some of the men, including Oliver, Eliza figured they attended "church" every day. "What's your excuse?" Eliza smiled. "Escaping from God or family?"

"Some would say both, but I'm here enjoying your and Joy's company." He scanned the room. "I think my excuse is more honorable than that of most men in here."

Joy rested a hand on his arm and leaned in. "Don't you think that sometimes, the less-than-honorable excuses are the most fun?"

Eliza rolled her eyes at Joy's come-on and Malcolm's apparent appreciation of it.

Timothy's fist pounding the bar broke off Eliza's retort, and she gaped at him.

Timothy's face was cherry red and contorted in anger. "I saw it for myself, I tell you, and if you go around telling all your witnesses that they're bloody blind, you won't have any." Not waiting for Kapoor's defense, Timothy reached under the bar and plunked a plastic baggie by Kapoor's hand. "Think I don't have anything good?" He nudged the baggie with dried flowers in it until it touched Kapoor's fingers. "What's that, then? Yeah?"

From several feet away, it resembled dried baby's breath. Eliza leaned a little closer, putting herself closer to Oliver's hairy tattooed arm, and squinted at the specimen.

"Why don't you tell me?" Kapoor's voice, though clipped, remained calm.

With shaking hands, Timothy snatched the bag, opened it up, and shook out the dried stem of small white flower clusters. Doubting her initial flower guess, she scooted closer to Joy. "That's not baby's breath, is it?"

Joy craned her neck and peered down the bar. "I can't really tell from here, but it looks a lot like Queen Anne's lace."

"Where did you find it?" Kapoor's question grabbed Eliza's attention, and she tuned back in to their conversation.

There was no use pretending not to eavesdrop. Everyone else had stopped their conversations, the pub had gone quiet, and all eyes watched the standoff.

"Found it in one of the rooms upstairs. Thought it might be important."

"As the room the victim died in has been fully processed, I trust that you did not find it in there?"

"No." Timothy ran a finger along the inside of his shirt collar. "It was in one of the other rooms. A few doors down from the dead bloke's."

"Why would a dried stem of Queen Anne's lace from outside the crime scene be of any interest to me?"

Timothy glared at the bundle of tiny white flowers as if it was its fault he was losing street cred with the chief constable. "But what should I do with this, then?"

"I don't care what you bloody do with it," Kapoor snapped. "Before you think about wasting my time again, make sure you have actual evidence." He stood up, and with one more scathing glare and a reminder to not waste police time, Kapoor stalked out of the pub.

"Bloody idiot," Oliver mumbled under his breath and took a swig of his drink.

Eliza wanted to salute the oaf with her glass, but the reigning silence kept her lips shut and her glass firmly on the bar. Soon enough, though, pub patrons settled into renewed and invigorated conversations. From the snippets Eliza caught, Timothy and Kapoor had earned their fifteen minutes of fame.

"Well." Joy clapped. "That went swimmingly, I'd say."

"Not for Timothy." Eliza frowned. She wanted to get a closer look at the dried flower stem. *Probably from a dead bouquet of flowers.* But something had Eliza's sleuthing antennae quivering. If Timothy had found it with the rest of the remains of a flower bouquet, he wouldn't have thought twice and would have thrown it away. True, he wasn't the sharpest tool in the shed, but Eliza doubted he would sift through dead flowers only to pluck out one accent and declare it a vital clue. She needed to know when and where he had found it. Eliza studied the ceiling and tried to picture the room Felix had died in. So far, she hadn't weaseled her way up there, but somehow, some way, she needed to.

More than ever, Eliza needed to question Timothy, but she couldn't yet. Not with Oliver sharing air space and eyeing the dried plant, and not with an entire pub's attention on the man she needed to interrogate. Timothy's restless movements and darting tongue licking his lips every three seconds spoke of a serious case of nerves, and that meant he knew something—or at least suspected something. His attempts not to look out at the patrons belied his need to look at someone. *Or for someone?* She couldn't get a look at the rooms, and she couldn't question her main informant, but she could get a closer look at the dried stem. With a jerk of her hand, she tipped over her Bloody Mary in Oliver's direction. Red booze slipped past a few olives and a pickle spear and trickled over the bar and into Oliver's lap. He hissed a nasty swear word, jumped to his feet, and glared at Eliza.

"I am so sorry." Eliza clasped a hand to her mouth in what she hoped resembled regret. "I don't know what happened. One moment, my drink was in my hands, and the next, well..." She gestured to his wet jeans.

He clenched his hands, but instead of planting one of them in her face, he spat on the floor, called her a derogatory name dirty enough that the whole pub gasped, gave the dried plant one last glance, and left the pub, slamming the door shut on his way out.

"Bloody hell." Joy grasped Eliza's shoulders. "I thought he was going to kill you." She tilted her head and studied Eliza's face. "You all right?"

Eliza released a pent-up breath. "Yeah."

With Timothy fetching a mop, leaving the dried stem unguarded, she picked up the small stem and twirled it. Something about it seemed familiar, but she couldn't place it. "This isn't baby's breath." She held it out to Joy and Malcolm. "Any idea what it is?"

"I told you. It's Queen Anne's lace."

Malcolm squinted. "Not sure, but you're right, Eliza. It's definitely not baby's breath."

Eliza brought it to her nose and sniffed. "Oof! That smells awful." She held it at arm's length and tilted her head, studying it. Yes, she had seen something like it recently. *But where?* It could be a juicy clue, or it could be what it probably was, a nasty weed the wind had literally blown in. She slipped her phone from her pocket, took a picture of the stem, and shoved her phone back when Timothy returned with a mop.

She bit her tongue against a stream of questions and reminded herself that now was not the time. No, she would have to find a way to talk to Timothy, pick his brain, and try to glean more information about the night of Felix's death and the strange, nasty-smelling clump of dried white flowers.

A young woman in skinny jeans and a black polo emblazoned with the pub's logo came through the back door and nodded a curt hello to Timothy. She froze, and Eliza followed her gaze. The girl was transfixed by the dried flower stem.

"Get on with you." Timothy none-too-gently led her out from behind the bar. "You're not paid to stand around and stare."

The girl glared at him but shoved a notepad and pen into her black apron and began taking orders from pub patrons.

Joy nudged Eliza's arm and whispered, "That's Amanda, the girl who found Felix's body."

From the young woman's pale face and fidgety movements, Eliza guessed she was still suffering from the aftershocks of the discovery even though a week and two days had passed. She looked younger than Eliza had figured, but perhaps it was the twisted mass of brown hair nestled at the top of her head or her makeup-free face except for black-lined eyes. Whatever it was, Eliza guessed Amanda was no older than twenty and, like her friend Monica at the Trusty Teapot, was stuck in limbo between high school—or "college," as the British called it—and university.

Amanda had seen either that same dried flower stem or something similar. Eliza needed to question her but without seeming a snoopy sleuth. Eliza gnawed on her lip. At the rate she was sleuthing, Wentworth and Garrison would be holed up in her attic forever.

"I can sleep when I'm dead." Great-Aunt Iris pointed a gnarled finger at Eliza, who had the audacity to recommend rest over hearing a recap of their adventures. Swamped by the sheer size of her four-poster mahogany bed and decked out in her Victorian night garb, Great-Aunt Iris looked harmless and weak, and her pale skin and the bluish tint around her eyes still worried Eliza, but she knew the old lady's iron backbone and stubborn tenacity. Great-Uncle William had finally taken a much-needed break, but even if he'd been present, his resolve would have toppled to his wife's will.

Joy unsuccessfully hid a smile behind her manicured hand, and Heath, who still sat beside the patient's bed and clutched a poetry book, winked at Eliza.

Eliza tried a different tactic. "If you don't get the proper rest you need now, you might be out of the investigation altogether."

"Pishposh." Great-Aunt Iris sniffed. "If the poetry your young man has been reading to me didn't kill me, nothing will." She plucked feebly at a string on the quilt tucked under her chin.

Heath shrugged but didn't say anything. Feeling slightly sorry for him, Eliza made a mental note to make it up to him later. A flash of heat coursed up her neck. "How about we strike a compromise? For every piece of information I give you, you have to take an hour's rest. So, three pieces of information equals three hours of sleep and so on. Deal?"

Great-Aunt Iris narrowed her eyes at Eliza and sighed. "As you wish." She struggled to sit up straighter and waved away Heath's attempts to help her. "I'm old, not a cripple." Finally settled, she folded her hands over her chest and peered at Eliza, her eyes glittering. "Well, girl, don't keep me waiting."

After Eliza told her great-aunt about the Timothy–Oliver standoff, Kapoor's random appearance, and the nasty-smelling flower clump, Great-Aunt Iris twiddled her thumbs. "What do you think those two were talking about?"

"Beats me." Eliza jerked her head toward her cousin. "Joy here might be useful, but she was too busy flirting with the good doctor."

Before Joy could retort, Great-Aunt Iris harrumphed. "She's liked plenty of stupider people before. The doctor would be an improvement, I'm sure."

"Am I included on the stupider list?" Heath asked, his lips twitching.

"The fact that you have brains enough to love my great-niece keeps you off the list." She tilted her head as if trying to see every angle of Heath's person. "For now." With one final look of warning toward Heath, she turned her attention to Eliza. "Now, where were we? Ah yes, so you didn't catch what they said?"

"No, but whatever was said seemed to scare the color out of Timothy." Eliza stood. "Now, a deal is a deal. I gave you three tidbits of info, and so you must rest quietly for three hours."

Great-Aunt Iris squinted at the marble clock on her bedside table and grunted. "Half six. I'll wake up in time to go to bed."

"I could read you more poetry."

"You will do no such thing." Great-Aunt Iris shooed away Heath and his poetry book. "You have done enough damage today." Her face softened with a smile, and she gestured for him to return. She patted the back of his hand. "Thank you for keeping an irritable old woman company."

Eliza sighed. Never had a day felt more like a week and yet still left her feeling short on time. She needed to report to Wentworth, make sure Garrison was still alive, meet with Mrs. Underhill and Mrs. Bankcroft about the upcoming week's menu and plans, and call her mom for a family emergency update. *And find a way to question Amanda, pick Timothy's brain, find out why Oliver terrifies Timothy, figure out what's up with Kapoor and if Cronk plays a part, identify a stinky dried flower, solve a murder case, and get Wentworth and his nemesis out of my attic, all while keeping Kapoor's watchdogs none the wiser.*

With that list repeating through her mind, she tucked in her great-aunt, kissed her forehead, and followed Joy and Heath from the room.

"I have some writing to do. I have big plans for my lovers, and I can't leave them waiting. Do fill me in on what I miss." Joy sashayed down the hall, turned right at the corner, and disappeared.

"Are you leaving me too?" Eliza hooked her finger between two buttonholes on Heath's dress shirt. "Have a kissing scene to write?"

"I'm more of an action man." His lips captured hers, and for a moment, all her worries evaporated.

She felt weightless in his embrace, and after he released her lips, she snuggled into him and swirled her fingers around the checked pattern of his shirt.

"We haven't talked yet about my new job. We might not find another time." His voice echoed in his chest.

She disentangled from his arms and cupped his cheek. "I have three questions for you."

He quirked an eyebrow. "Are these yes-or-no questions, or do they require long-winded answers?"

Ignoring his question, she held up one finger. "One, is this new job something you want, like, really want?"

"Yes."

"Two." Eliza's middle finger joined her pointer. "If I moved back to the States after you get this job, would you regret taking the job?"

A flicker of panic sparked from his eyes. "You're not trying to tell me something, are you?"

"No." She smoothed her thumb over his crinkled forehead. "And I'm the one asking questions here, mister."

"In that case, I would resign my position and follow you across the pond."

"Three." She turned his hand palm up and placed her palm over his. "The more I'm with you, the more I want to be with you, and the thought of you leaving..." She hung her head, and silence lingered between them. "When you leave, does it make your heart hurt?"

"Like it's splitting in two?"

She nodded.

Heath's finger tilted her face up, and she gazed into his corn-flower-blue eyes. "It's rather concerning how my heart does that, and to save my heart, I only have one choice. Accept this job. Can't risk a heart attack or something, now, can I?" He kissed her hard and fast until she was sure her heart would gallop right out of her chest.

After catching her breath, she leaned against him. "So you're choosing to be closer to Great-Aunt Iris, then?" She grinned. "She'll be so excited. More Byron."

"I'm afraid your great-aunt will be sorely put out when she learns I'm not staying for her."

Judging by his husky tone and the way his hands were roving new paths on her body, Eliza guessed she was the lucky lady. She unwillingly wriggled from his arms. "Well, one world problem solved. Now, on to the next on my ever-growing to-do list. And I think someone has a very important phone call to make."

"You're not overworking yourself, are you, Miss Eliza?" Mrs. Bankcroft planted her fists on her plump hips and gave Eliza a once-over. From the concern on her face, Eliza was sure the cook had already concluded that she had overworked herself. And if anyone was overworking herself, it was Mrs. B. Instead of finding the cook in her room, Eliza had discovered her mixing a concoction that smelled of lime and coconut.

"No, Mrs. B. Just tired is all." *And stressed and worried and—*

"That all comes from not eating good and proper."

Eliza toyed with the button of her skinny jeans that was digging into her belly button. That certainly wasn't the problem, but she smiled, settled onto a kitchen stool, and placed the week's itinerary on the kitchen island's wooden surface. "Luckily, we don't have a lot going on this week. We don't have another group until Friday night.

Can you get a menu together for me by Tuesday, and I can put the order in?"

Mrs. Bankcroft squinted at the schedule listing the upcoming group. "Twitchers?" She huffed and pushed the agenda toward Eliza. "Never understood bird-watching. And what they'll find in the woods this time of year, I don't rightly know."

"As I understand it, it's this group's annual get-together to discuss their findings and such." Eliza grinned at Mrs. Bankcroft's scrunched nose and shrugged. "It takes all kinds."

"There's some kinds this world don't need, and you can take my word on that." Mrs. Bankcroft studied her again. "You do look peaked. Maybe you got the flu, like Mrs. Darcy."

That was the last thing Eliza needed. "No, I'm fine." She tapped the paper. "Does Tuesday work, or do you need a little longer?"

"Yes, yes. You young people are always in such a hurry."

Eliza refrained from reminding Mrs. B that during mealtimes, she was the one demanding the servers quit lollygagging and get to work. "Why are you in the kitchen so late, anyway?"

After giving the mixture one last stir, she stuck the bowl under Eliza's nose. "What do you think? My daughter sent me this recipe, and I couldn't sleep until I'd tried it out. It's supposed to go over shrimp."

It smelled of tropical places, and Eliza was tempted to ask Mrs. Bankcroft to sauté up some shrimp for a bedtime snack. "It smells delicious."

"Good, because that's what I'm serving for lunch tomorrow." Mrs. Bankcroft covered the bowl with plastic wrap and placed it in the restaurant-style fridge. "Now, I'm off to bed. And you should be, too, by the looks of you."

"I will be. I'm going to grab a snack first. Good night, Mrs. B."

Eliza waited until the cook's footsteps faded before pillaging the cupboards and snatching a few goodies from the fridge. With arms full of food, she paused at the kitchen door, scanned left and right, and scampered to one of the servants' hallways for cover. Now that no staff lived on the premises except for Tash, Mrs. Bankcroft, and Mrs. Underhill, whose rooms were in the opposite wing, there was little to no danger of meeting someone in the abandoned halls. Before she peeked out of the first-floor's servants' door, she pressed her ear to the wood and strained to listen for any sound. Hearing nothing, she glanced both ways, speed walked to the secret bookcase, and nearly dropped her hoard when the bookcase swung open. She swallowed a yelp and glared at Garrison.

"What in the heck do you think you're doing?" Eliza hissed. "Get back in there. Now."

"Don't get testy. I was getting hungry. That's all."

Eliza nearly kicked him up the steps but thought better of it, as she might hurt herself. "Move, Garrison, before I move you."

He opened his mouth but snapped it shut and scampered up the steps.

Eliza followed, grinding her teeth and planning her what-were-you-thinking speech for Wentworth. But upon entering the attic, her feet ground to a halt, and her scolds evaporated on her tongue. Wentworth lay motionless on his cot, one arm flung over his face as if he had been protecting himself.

Eliza whirled on Garrison. "What did you do to him?"

"Me?" he squeaked and evaded her pointed index finger. "I didn't do anything." Garrison sidestepped her and kicked the cot. Wentworth snorted and rolled over. "He's not dead, you numpty. He's sleeping."

A rush of air escaped Eliza's tight chest. As much as she never wanted to apologize to Garrison, she forced an "I'm sorry" past her lips and offered him food as a peace treaty. "Here, I grabbed a few slices of ham, too, but I had no room for any condiments. It's harder than you think sneaking food up here."

"Is that why you've been starving us?" Garrison spoke around a mouthful of biscuit.

Eliza ignored him and shook Wentworth's shoulder. "Wakey, wakey, eggs and bakey."

Wentworth sat up and rubbed his eyes. "Did you say bacon?"

"Sorry. No bacon. I have cold ham, though." Eliza sank into a dilapidated chair next to his cot. "Sorry it's been so long between meals. I grabbed quite a few smaller snacks to get you through tomorrow if I can't get up here in the morning."

"No harm done, although my stomach was starting to wonder if my throat had been slit." Wentworth grabbed a few slices of ham and chewed viciously.

"Guess what your roommate was doing while you were napping," Eliza said.

Wentworth shot his "roommate" a look that had Garrison shrinking in his chair. "Trying to find ways of killing me in my sleep?"

Garrison ignored him and shoved another biscuit into his mouth.

"I can't answer for what goes through his head, and I don't want to know what goes through it, but I found him sneaking out from behind the bookcase."

Wentworth got to his feet so quickly that he nearly toppled his cot. "You what?"

Garrison put his hands in front of his face, probably to ward off a potential blow. "I didn't mean any harm. I was..." He peeked at Wentworth through his fingers. "Hungry."

For several seconds, Wentworth's body vibrated with anger, and from the vein bulging in his neck, Eliza feared he would have an aneurysm. "You incompetent git, have you totally lost your mind?"

"I was hungry," Garrison repeated and shrugged.

For his lumbering size, Wentworth moved quickly, and before Garrison could escape, Wentworth's nose nearly touched Garrison's.

"Listen here, you stupid sod, I don't care if you're on the brink of starvation. If you ever do anything to jeopardize Eliza again, especially with two officers posted around the property, I will tie you to this chair. Do I make myself clear?"

Sweat beaded on Garrison's forehead. "Crystal."

Wentworth sank onto his cot and rubbed his neck. "I'm going daft trapped up here. Have you made any new leads?"

Eliza filled him in on the pub events. "So I'm thinking that Timothy and Oliver are in cahoots and that Timothy isn't the one in charge."

"I wouldn't peg him as a leader of anyone. Seems likely Oliver is in charge. Both want me out of the picture. Both want revenge."

"Here." Eliza pulled up the picture of the dried flower. "I know I've seen something like this before. I thought at first it was baby's breath, but it smells nasty. Joy thinks it's Queen Anne's lace." She smacked her forehead. "Of course. I'm such an idiot. I even looked it up, right here, in fact, and listed off its deadly properties. It's poison hemlock." After a few swipes to her phone screen, she shared the images with Wentworth. "See? Even dried, the tiny white flowers look like these." She pointed at a picture of bunches of five-petaled white flowers.

"And where did Timothy say he found it?"

"He didn't say, and Kapoor blew it off as inconsequential." Eliza chewed her lip. "But this muddies the waters even more. Why bring the plant itself? Why not crush it at home or his evil lair? Why was it not found in Felix's room? What room was it found in? Who had that room?" Eliza massaged her temples. "And if Timothy was the killer, why would he bring attention to himself by showing the weapon to the *police*?"

"Looks like you have to tackle Timothy one more time." Wentworth smiled apologetically.

"Great. Just great."

Chapter Fourteen
Things Go All Sixes and Sevens

Darcy and I enjoyed a rare afternoon alone. Since Adelaide's birth, we have scarce had a moment to ourselves. Darcy maintains the splendor of Sydney Gardens has nothing on my fine eyes. I do so enjoy a husband who lies for the sake of my vanity.
Lizzy Bennet Darcy
Bath 1814

Eliza stared at her phone screen. It was only nine o'clock, and she had missed five calls from her mom. The number five was such an awkward number. She hadn't much use for a lucky number, but she sure avoided buying five of anything at the grocery store. After giving herself a pep talk, she called her mom and sighed when her mother picked up on the fifth ring.

"Eliza, where have you been?"

Oh, I don't know. Solving a murder, attempting to keep two grown men a secret and alive in a tiny room, worrying about Great-Aunt Iris's health... "Good question. I don't even know." She chewed her lip. "How are... things?"

"That's why I called. I know how worried you've been, and I didn't want to leave you in the dark. Your father still doesn't feel up to talking to you. He's so ashamed of his past that he's having a hard time processing that his daughter knows it all."

Eliza wasn't sure if she wanted to talk to her father either. The family atomic bomb that had dropped on her days ago still shook her to her core. She squeezed her eyes shut, pinched the bridge of her nose, and reminded herself that her father had been young, dumb, and in love and that she had no right to hold his past mistakes over him. No matter what, he was still her father, and she loved him. She exhaled sharply. "That's understandable, but please tell him I love him and that if you and he are working through it, then I have no right to be angry. Oh, and tell him that a nice start to talking again could be answering my texts."

"Yes, well, we both know your father is a stubborn man, but I'll do my best." Her mom sighed. "We've decided to see a counselor to help facilitate our healing. Having a third party present will probably help your father process his past and help me come to terms with what he did before I even met him. It's odd, really, being hurt by something he didn't even do to me."

"I don't think it's odd at all, Mom. Keep me updated, though, okay? I feel so out of the loop over here. How's Uncle?"

"He and your father have had some pretty late nights, but I think it's more catching up on old times and making up for all the lost time. We're all pretty confused about how Nancy got her sticky fingers all over this situation." Her mom's breathing hitched. "In a way, it's a good thing, though, that this all came to light. This way, we can all be a family." Her mother's voice broke on the word "family," and she softly sobbed.

"Mom." Eliza paused. "It's going to be okay. Between counseling and Dad and Uncle coming to terms with the past and dusting off their relationship, things will be okay. More than okay. They'll be great."

Her mom sniffled. "You're right. I hate her, you know. And I feel awful for feeling that way, especially as I've never met the woman and she technically didn't do anything to me."

"You're not missing much. Trust me." Eliza smiled at her mom's bark of laughter. "She's not worth hating. In fact, it puts all the power back in her grubby little hands. It's better to forgive her. That way, you can forget her and move on with life with Dad. Besides, you got him in the end, anyway."

Her mom chuckled. "Look at you being so wise."

"Can I get that statement in writing?"

"Let's not get too hasty. Oh, I hear your father. I need to go."

"Tell Dad to call me."

"I can't make promises about your father, but I promise to pass on the message. I love you."

"Love you, too, Mom."

Eliza sighed in relief and placed her phone in the back pocket of her skinny jeans.

Joy popped her head around the doorjamb of Eliza's room. "Fancy a cuppa?"

Thirty minutes later, they were seated at the Trusty Teapot. Monica bustled over, and instead of her usual effervescent smile and warm welcome, she frowned. "Oh my goodness, Miss Darcy, Miss Bingley, have you heard the news?" Not waiting for them to answer, she pulled up a chair and plonked into it. "It's about Timothy Elliot. Someone beat him to a bloody pulp."

"What?" Eliza sat straight. "Timothy, the bartender at the Foxed Hound?"

"Yes. Someone found him in the alley behind the pub this morning. Near death he was, too, or so I understand. But you know how gossip goes around here."

"That's awful." Eliza's head whirled with facts, and in her mind's eye, she conjured up her crime board. Timothy's name connected with the crime scene so well that she had placed him at the top of her suspect list until his very un-killer-like behavior of shoving the dried murderous plant under Kapoor's nose. And now his beating threatened to knock him off the murderer pedestal for good. Of course, the beating could be unrelated to the crime. He had proved an annoying pest, a man who involved himself in other people's business a little too much. Anyone could have sent a message to back off.

"Eliza?" Joy tapped Eliza's hand. "All right?"

Eliza blinked. Monica had left, and Joy was cocking her head at Eliza. "Yeah." She squeezed her forehead. "No."

"You don't think Timothy's beating is a random attack, do you?"

"I don't know what to think. But there is something I would very much like to know. Was the beating a warning, or was it attempted murder?"

"This throws a spanner in the works, doesn't it?"

"Yes, I'm afraid it does." Eliza drummed her fingers on the white tablecloth. "We need to revisit our crime board."

They changed their orders to to-go orders, and Eliza clutched the drinks as Joy sped to Pemberley, taking hairpin turns a little too fast for comfort. "How many speeding tickets do you have?"

Joy grinned. "I don't get speeding tickets."

Eliza rolled her eyes, refrained from asking for details, and called the hospital, knowing she would be told the standard rigmarole that updates were available only to family, blah, blah, blah. But a girl had to try. Moments later, she poked the red phone icon and plunked her phone in her lap. She needed to find out the extent of Timothy's injuries, but the hospital receptionist had been less than cooperative. Staring sulkily out the window at the English countryside zipping by, Eliza considered viable scenarios. The crunching gravel of Pemberley's drive drew her from her thoughts.

Back at Pemberley and after checking in with the staff, Eliza and Joy zipped up the steps as fast as their hot drinks would allow and mall-walked past the portraits and down the long gallery and came to a stuttering stop.

Kapoor's officers loitered by the bookshelf, and one was randomly taking books off the shelf, thumbing through them, and putting them back.

Joy's free hand clutched Eliza's forearm, and Eliza flinched when her grasp tightened. "Bloody hell," she hissed, "what are we going to do?"

Eliza blinked, hoping to dispel the apparition before her, but as per usual, fate or the stars or the gods denied her, and after three blinks, the officers still stood by the bookshelf, pawing the literature. The former English teacher in her wanted to praise their reading endeavors, but the sleuthing part of her, the part that feared a jail cell, wanted to smack their grubby hands away. But that would only draw suspicion, not deflect it.

Intent on the books, the officers hadn't noticed the women yet. Eliza formed a hasty plan.

"Ready to do what you do best?" Eliza whispered.

"You mean be my flirty, amazing self?"

"Yes."

"What will you do?"

"Redirect their attention while you dazzle them with your good looks and charm. If they even so much as flick *Romance of the Forest*, we're done for. Flirt like you've never flirted before. Pretend they're Jack Willoughby, okay?" Joy's acting skills would have to be on point, as the officers resembled the duo from the Apple Dumpling Gang instead of the suave and debonair Willoughby.

Joy gave her a mock salute, and together, they walked down the hall, careful not to spill their quickly cooling drinks, chattering about men and shopping and whatever else they assumed men thought they chattered about.

"...and that dress, Joy, looked so amazing on you. I'm surprised you didn't buy it." Eliza saluted her cousin with her to-go cup and stumbled to a halt before the officers. "Oh, hello, Officers."

The Don Knotts-looking character clicked his heels and gave them a head-to-toe assessment. "Ladies." He tilted his head in greeting.

Eliza beamed a saccharine smile at him. "Good afternoon, Officers. Glad to see that no place is left unguarded."

"Safety's no accident, ma'am, and we're under direct orders to scour every nook and cranny." He leaned closer, bringing with him the scent of peppermint. "Kapoor's dedicated to keeping you and your family safe from the likes of Wentworth."

Eliza slid Joy a don't-lose-your-cool look. "Yes, it's so tragic when a good man goes bad."

The other officer, a sturdy fellow, who resembled a young, discount Tim Conway, grunted. "Don't listen to Harris, miss. He's got his nose so far up Kapoor's backside he can't see straight. Wentworth ain't bad. I suspect he ran into a bad lot and paid the price. Always thought he was a good DCI." He slid his partner a contempt-filled look. "Harris here ain't been on the force long enough to know the good from the bad."

Harris grunted and returned his attention to the bookshelf. "Say, here's a book right up your alley, Robinson. *Romance of the Forest*." He chuckled and ran his finger down the spine of the book and back up, hooking his index finger over the crest of the binding. "With how your head is in the clouds over your new girl and all."

As a little girl, Eliza had once fallen out of a tree, and the feeling of slowly crashing to earth, every second a warning of the pain soon to come, had consumed her little body. As she watched the officer's finger crooking farther, that same slow-motion sensation blazed to life as she stood in the grand hall outside the cleverly hidden secret room. A room that would no longer be secret once Harris's finger pulled the book toward him. If that happened, the pain she'd suffered years ago would pale in comparison to the revelation of Wentworth and her part in concealing him. What was worse was that Joy and Heath and even Great-Aunt Iris would be held culpable too.

She flicked Joy, who was standing next to him, a panicked look.

"Harris, is it?" Joy looped her free arm inside his and smiled up at him. "Can I let you in on a little secret about women?"

His attention no longer on the book, Harris stared bug-eyed at Joy, and his tongue darted along his bottom lip. "Secrets about women? Sure. I mean, I don't need the help, but good old Robinson could probably use it. I don't have problems keeping my birds from flying away, if you know what I mean." He winked and nudged Joy with his elbow.

From the flicker of loathing in her cousin's eyes, Eliza was sure Joy would lose her cool, but Joy, ever the true actress, smoothed her hand over the officer's arm. "Of course, some men need more help than others."

Eliza set her drink down and smoothed a finger up and down the book next to the one-that-must-not-be-flicked.

"Ever read Emily Brontë's *Wuthering Heights*?" Eliza asked.

Harris shook his head without looking at her, his eyes tracking the movement of Joy's fingers.

"The male lead, Heathcliff, is quite the romantic lover boy and is a true paragon of gentlemanly behavior, and if you replicate his mannerisms and how he treats women, you—excuse me, I mean, Robinson—will have all the ladies swooning over you."

Eliza snorted a laugh and covered up her faux pas by picking up her cup and taking a sip of her drink. "Allergies. Old houses tend to be a hotbed for dust and that sort of thing."

To save herself from another coughing fit at the idea of the morally gray and at times horrible and abusive Heathcliff being the poster boy for romance and love, Eliza led Robinson down the hall and away from the bookshelf, hoping Joy would herd the gullible Harris after them. "Have you searched the tunnel? I thought I heard noises from it earlier, but that could be mice. It would ease my mind if you two strapping men could check." Eliza led them down the steps and into the library, and after setting her drink down, she grandly gestured to a deep paneled alcove in the bookcases. "Voila!"

When the two officers blinked at her in confusion, she flicked the intricate carving of a lion's head and pressed on the unlocked paneling. "Let's try this again. Voila!"

"Blimey," Robinson whispered and unlatched the flashlight from his police utility belt.

"Say, there ain't any ghosts, are there?" Harris asked, his voice hitching.

Joy grinned. "What? A handsome, strong man such as yourself scared of a few ghosts?"

"Pftt, I was joking. I don't believe in ghosts." Harris's eyes bulged as he took in the dark recess, unclipped his flashlight, and motioned for his partner to go first. "Ladies first and all that."

Robinson grunted. "Ah, put a sock in it, Harris." After a curt nod to Eliza and Joy, he dipped inside the tunnel, Harris whining at his heels, and disappeared, the only flicker of light coming from their flashlights until the beams melted into the darkness.

Eliza blew out a breath and leaned against a bookshelf. "That was a close call. Good job on redirecting what's-his-face's attention."

"You owe me, big time. I actually had to touch that slimeball."

Eliza chuckled, grabbed her drink, looped her arm through Joy's, and meandered out of the library and back up the steps. "Nice revenge, though, on recommending Heathcliff as a romantic role model."

"As long as it gives that wanker at least one black eye, I shall be avenged."

After double-checking that no loiterers lurked in the picture gallery or the hallway and retrieving Joy's abandoned beverage, they squeezed in behind the bookcase and clambered up the steps.

"You two sound like a herd of buffalo." Garrison's smirk evaporated under Joy's glare.

Wentworth eyed Eliza's to-go cup with such desire that she sighed and offered her precious Ethiopian spiced tea to him. He took the cover off and stuck his face in the curling steam for a few seconds before taking a sip. "Thank you."

The dark, dank room would send even the most sparkling personality into a funk. In that case, Wentworth certainly needed a bracing cup of tea to lift his spirits. Her lips twitched in a grin. "You're welcome." Sighing, she sank onto the cot beside him. "There's been a development. Someone beat up Timothy."

Wentworth's mouth was hidden by the coffee cup, but his right eyebrow quirked. "Not surprising. Think it's related to Felix's murder?"

Eliza squeezed the back of her neck and stared at the crime board. "I don't know what to think anymore."

"I do." Garrison leaned his chair back until the front two legs hovered an inch above the floor. Eliza wanted nothing more than for the chair to tip backward, taking its occupant with it, but the clamor would certainly draw attention.

"Didn't know you could think," Joy said.

Eliza rolled her eyes. "Don't sit there pouting, Garrison. If you want to get out of this attic—"

"And into my jail cells," Wentworth cut in.

"Your jail cells?" Garrison chuckled. "Yours? The way things are going, me old mucker, there will only be one cell, and that's yours."

Eliza laid her hand on Wentworth's shoulder, pushing him back down on his cot. "You stay." She whirled around and pointed at Garrison. "You speak. But only about what you know about Timothy."

He studied his cuticles for a few seconds. "Remember when I told you that Oliver killed Felix and by framing Wentworth—"

"DCI Wentworth to you," Wentworth ground out between clenched teeth.

Garrison flicked a glance at the DCI and paled. "And that by framing *DCI* Wentworth, he could kill two birds with one stone?"

"Yes, yes, out with it already," Eliza said.

"Well." Garrison puffed out his cheeks. "Actually, I'm a little skint at the moment."

Joy tsked. "You really are a prat. Eliza here has already agreed to compensate you. Now spill it."

"Why have only one mole when you can have two?"

"Why on earth did you not tell us this earlier?" Eliza's hands clenched, and for a second or five, she imagined driving them into Garrison's smug face.

"You didn't ask." Garrison shrugged as if he hadn't a care in the world.

Eliza waved her hands at the crime board. "You've had access to this. You've listened to our conversations. You knew we had come to a screeching halt in the case. At what point were you going to volunteer the information?"

"He wasn't." Joy descended on him and stuck her face in his and stabbed him in the chest with her finger. "Tell us everything you know. Now. Or..." Joy dropped her voice and whispered in his ear, and while Eliza couldn't hear all of it, she heard "Nancy," and from Garrison's shrinking body and whitening face, Eliza guessed Joy had zeroed in on Garrison's deepest fears. How Nancy still had power over him was anyone's guess, but Eliza knew all too well Nancy's power from prison and the heartbreaking consequences of being on that woman's wrong side. She wouldn't put it past her aunt to have sketchy friends and criminal alliances on the outside.

Whatever had puffed up Garrison evaporated, leaving the same simpering, sycophantic little weasel Eliza had met upon first arriving at Pemberley. His fancy clothes, wrinkled and in need of a good wash, and expensive watch looked ridiculous on him, more like a costume than an outfit.

"Does Oliver know that you know?" Eliza asked.

Garrison shrugged. "I don't know. As soon as the conversation turned more toward violence and less about money, I legged it."

For once, Eliza believed him. Garrison was a weasel and a crook, but he wasn't violent. "So, how do you know Timothy was Oliver's eyes and ears?"

"It's one of the last things I heard running back here."

"That's why you came back, innit?" Joy asked.

Garrison scratched his head. "Didn't have anywhere else to go. And Oliver and Timothy knew my normal hideouts."

"And while you are stupid," Joy continued, "they wouldn't think you stupid enough to seek refuge in the one place you were hiding from."

Eliza bit her tongue. There was no sense in scolding him over the danger he could have brought to Pemberley. What was done was done, and more than likely, he wouldn't have cared anyway.

"So, now that that is all hashed out, please tell us all you know." Eliza pulled a marker cap off with her teeth.

"I've already told you. Oliver wanted to destroy Felix and DCI Wentworth. He recruited Timothy as a spy, and I was along for the ride until talk turned violent. That's all I know."

"You... you ..." Wentworth's eyes narrowed, and a vein in his forehead bulged and pulsed.

Eliza slid from the cot and crouched in front of Wentworth, cutting off his view of Garrison. "We need to concentrate on what matters. He didn't go through with it, so that speaks for something. What that is, I have no clue, but he's where we can keep an eye on him." She dropped her voice. "And when we get this all figured out, I will hold him down while you cuff him, okay?"

"Deal."

"Good. Now, let's get down to business."

All four of them crowded around the crime board, Eliza and Joy separating a glowering Wentworth and a cowering Garrison. Eliza added *found and displayed dried hemlock to police* and *beat up that same evening* under Timothy's name. Her hand stilled. "Wait a minute. Could it be a coincidence that Timothy got beat up the same night he displayed his prize?"

"I don't like coincidences," Wentworth said.

"Me neither." Eliza pursed her lips and studied the board.

"He certainly didn't keep his find a secret, and he and Kapoor had garnered a lot of attention," Joy said.

Eliza snapped her fingers. "Kapoor. There's something fishy about him, and I don't like the fact that I don't know where he fits in all this." Her hand circled toward the board.

"He's dirty all the way through, but murder?" Wentworth left his question hanging in the air and shrugged. "A man capable of what I suspect him of might not find it hard to step over the line and commit murder in order to save his own skin."

"And he knows that you wouldn't think twice about bringing him to justice," Eliza said.

"Which is exactly why he has it out for me. If he can make a solid argument with the damning evidence against me that I killed Felix and put me away for life, he won't have to worry about me and the secrets I know and can sit a little easier on the throne his illegal activities created." He scratched his now-bearded cheeks.

Eliza scowled at the cardboard surface. "We're going to need a bigger board."

"Here." Joy snapped a few pictures of the crime board and carefully tore the cardboard off the wall and flipped it around. "I know we'll have to work around the taped seams, but this should do for now."

"Great idea. This will give us an opportunity to move our clues around. So, what do we have? Do we take any suspects off the list?"

"What about Timothy?" Joy asked.

"His beating doesn't really give us anything solid to go off of. Could be he ticked off the wrong person, could be a warning for him to keep his mouth shut, could be he—"

"Is a prat." Wentworth grunted.

"Yes, that, too, but I think we keep him as a suspect. If he didn't do the actual killing, he played a part, I'm sure." Eliza printed Timothy's name at the top of the board and drew a line under it. "He was at the crime scene, had access to the glasses without drawing any kind of suspicion, 'found' the dried hemlock, and had motive to ruin Wentworth's life."

"But there's no connection between Timothy and Felix," Joy said.

"True." Eliza wrote *connection to Felix?* under Timothy's name. "Minus this little snafu, Timothy would have access to the room keys and, I would guess, be keeping track of who rented the room." She sucked in a breath and closed her eyes. "I'm an idiot."

"What's wrong?" Joy asked.

"How many times have we been at the Foxed Pub and *not* searched for the room registry? There has to be one, right?"

"But why does it matter?" Joy asked.

"Because the hemlock was found in a different room, and if we know who all rented rooms, we will know who else was at the pub that night," Wentworth said.

"Maybe the person who left the hemlock didn't rent a room. Anyone can access the upper level of the pub," Joy said.

"But it's one more puzzle piece. One we can discard because it's useless or one we need to complete the picture." Eliza traced the board with her index finger.

"Whether or not that stupid git committed murder, he sure did a proper job of setting me up to take the fall." Wentworth scowled at Timothy's name.

"If he hadn't been beaten up, he'd be at the top of my list for murder and framing you for it," Eliza said.

"What about Oliver?" Joy picked up another marker and wrote as she spoke. "Known violent criminal, knew Felix, hated him, and wanted revenge on him and Wentworth..." She chewed on the end of the marker. "Does anyone know if he was in the pub that night?"

"No, but he was obviously threatening Timothy last night and was there for the whole hemlock show-and-tell," Eliza said.

"But we're the only ones who know what it is. Oliver might not have known the importance of it," Joy said.

"I need to find a way to talk to Timothy." Eliza massaged her temples. "Maybe I can sneak into the hospital. Can't be too tight of security, right?"

The inner corners of Joy's eyebrows touched. "Leave me out of your little scheme."

"How else do you propose we get to Timothy?"

Joy's phone buzzed. "What now?" Her face paled, and she let out a small gasp.

Eliza's heart sank to her stomach. "What is it?"

"It's Timothy. He's dead."

"What are you doing standing here in the dark?"

Eliza spun around at the sound of Great-Aunt Iris's voice. "What are you doing here, standing at all?"

Great-Aunt Iris tutted and, before Eliza could hustle across her office, stutter-stepped to an embroidered brocade chair and sank into it with a sigh. "It's as gloomy as a tomb in here. Open those curtains and let some light in."

Still stunned at her great-aunt's appearance, Eliza did as commanded and pulled on the rope. The heavy curtains slid back and revealed what she had shuttered two hours ago: a sunny fall day and a garden resplendent with yellow and pink chrysanthemums, lavender asters, black-eyed Susans, and blaze-orange crocosmias. She couldn't enjoy such beauty still alive in an autumn garden when she knew Timothy, a young man, had never gotten the chance to experience his autumn.

"You have yet to answer my question, my dear."

Eliza chuckled. "And you haven't answered mine. Shouldn't you be in bed. *Resting?*"

"I can rest when I'm dead." Great-Aunt Iris preened at the front of her hot-pink velour tracksuit. Her white cloud of hair no longer hung limply around her face but was styled into wispy curls.

Ignoring her great-aunt's latest mantra, Eliza settled into a chair next to her. "And who let you out?"

"I knew I was imprisoned. Besides, all I had to do was give your great-uncle a kiss, and he let me go."

"What about Heath? He was on sentinel duty."

"All I had to do was brandish my knitting needles." Great-Aunt Iris tapped Eliza on the knee with a gnarled finger. "You should pick a man with a backbone next time."

"There won't be a next time." She leaned forward and whispered conspiratorially, "I think he's the one."

Great-Aunt Iris pursed her lips and cocked her head. "Well, his taste in poetry is abysmal."

"I'm not deciding on a future with him based on his poetry."

"Oh, my dear, but you should. Now that I'm off of house arrest, I'm here to help you."

"But you're not off of 'house arrest,' and I have no qualms about tattling on you to Dr. Hamilton."

"My dear, when you hear what I have to tell you, I believe you will change your mind."

Eliza didn't trust Great-Aunt Iris's smile, but she settled further into her chair. "What do you have up your sleeve, then?"

Her great-aunt grinned like a Cheshire cat. "What if I told you that I can get you an interview with the elusive waitress, Amanda, without coming under police suspicion?"

Eliza leaned forward and squinted at her aunt. "How?"

"I am friends with Amanda Fielding's grandmother, and Gemma, Amanda's mother, is hosting a birthday party in honor of Tabitha's eighty-seventhbirthday this evening. I had not accepted the invitation earlier, but as I am no longer unwell, I will go."

"Did Dr. Hamilton give you the 'no longer unwell' diagnosis?"

Great-Aunt Iris speared her with a gaze. "I believe I have lived long enough to know when I am well and when I am unwell." She cleared her throat and tilted her head with regal composure. "Now, where was I? Oh yes, now that I am *well*, I plan on going, but I need a driver." She gave an exaggerated wink and tapped the side of her nose. "Are you up for the job?"

"But how do you know Amanda will even be there?"

"Because her mother said so when I called to let her know I would be attending."

Concern for her great-aunt's health and excitement over finally finding a believable excuse to talk to Amanda warred in Eliza's conscience. As a dutiful niece, she should force her great-aunt to rest. As a desperate amateur sleuth who needed two men on the point of killing each other to get out of her attic, she should accept the offer.

Eliza eyed her great-aunt, who looked suspiciously innocent, sitting primly in her chair with her hands folded in her lap. "You win." She held up a finger. "On one condition. You do not overdo it, and the minute you feel tired or unwell, you let me know, even if I haven't had a chance of speaking with Amanda."

"I promise."

Eliza checked her great-aunt's hands for any signs of crossed fingers. "So, when is this shindig?"

"Cocktails and hors d'oeuvres start at four, and as Gemma is a better cook and baker than she is a hairstylist, we should be there early before they are all gone."

"But isn't she your hairstylist?"

Great-Aunt Iris fluffed her hair. "Yes, so that should give you an idea of her cooking and baking skills. And if we keep dillydallying, there will be no food left."

Taking her great-aunt's warning to heart, Eliza jumped to her feet. "I'll go alert the team of the plans."

"And I will go put on my birthday suit." Great-Aunt Iris shuffled from the room, her left white tennis shoe squeaking with every step.

Eliza shook her head and prayed that her great-aunt really did have a specific suit she wore on birthdays.

Chapter Fifteen
A Replay of Murder and Repressed Memories

Darcy and I made the unfortunate acquaintance of the Elliots' Irish cousins, Lady Dalrymple and her daughter, Miss Carteret. I have never met more insipid people in my life, and Sir Walter's social-climbing machinations are quite obvious, as he courts his wealthy relation's favor in spite of their dull and unclever conversations. I feel quite sorry for Anne, being surrounded by relations who are so below her in personality, morality, and intelligence. I shall speak to Darcy about inviting her to Pemberley.
Lizzy Bennet Darcy
Bath 1814

Over her glass of champagne, Eliza studied her hale-and-hearty-looking great-aunt, decked out in a mint-green tracksuit with a string of pearls encircling her neck, sitting with the birthday girl. Surprisingly, "girl" wasn't too far off, as Tabitha Fielding looked closer to seventy than she did ninety. Perhaps Tabitha had found the fountain of youth, or maybe it was the sunlight pouring through the spotless picture window of the Trusty Teapot that gave the elderly woman a translucent glow. Rubbing at the crinkle etched in her forehead that she had recently dubbed her what-in-the-heck wrinkle, Eliza re-upped her promise to take better care of her skin and to quit scowling at others' stupidity.

"Couldn't keep her under lock and key anymore, I see." Malcolm joined Eliza and studied the pair of octogenarians.

"I've never seen anyone bounce so quickly back to health."

"Or so she thinks." Malcolm frowned. "There's a risk she could overdo things and get sicker as a result. Watch her, please."

"That's easier said than done."

He chuckled. "I don't envy you your position. Well, I must continue the rounds." He tipped his glass in her direction then gestured to Great-Aunt Iris. "May the odds be ever in your favor."

Doubting her ability to keep her great-aunt from overdoing the festivities, Eliza scowled into her champagne flute. So much for her promise not to increase the dent in her forehead. From the corner of her eye, she spotted Amanda Fielding. Despite being family, Amanda kept to herself and, besides the occasional whispers to her mother or grandmother, said nothing. From the furtive looks her mother kept darting in Amanda's direction, Amanda's taciturn nature was a concern and probably stemmed from the discovery of Felix's body.

Amanda moved toward the buffet table laden with sweet and savory goodies, and Eliza made her move, accidentally bumping into Amanda next to a plate of cucumber sandwiches.

"I'm so sorry." Eliza reached out a hand to steady the girl. "I didn't see you there, and these sandwiches look so amazing, they were all I saw, really."

Amanda smiled weakly. "That's okay. No harm done."

"I understand your mom is an excellent cook and that she made all this." Eliza grinned conspiratorially. "I'm afraid the cooking gene skipped me. I can't even make boxed macaroni and cheese."

Amanda's smile lit up her face. With the dour look gone, her face took on an unjaded innocence that Eliza assumed she'd had before the grisly find. She was once again a bright and pretty twentysomething on the cusp of life. Fate, however, had brought the young woman face-to-face with gruesome death. "Same. My mom can't understand how I make a complete dog's dinner of Cheesey Pasta. Always ends up looking like a soup or a congealed glob of gluten."

Eliza's stomach rumbled for a well-made box of Mac & Cheese—or the British equivalent—and made a mental note to ask Mrs. Bankcroft to probably go against her cook's vows and make her some. Might earn her a skewer with either a nasty look or an actual knife, but it was a risk she was willing to take.

"Until we can get someone to make us halfway-decent boxed mac and cheese, we shall have to survive off this." Eliza grinned and plunked an assortment of tiny sandwiches and other delicacies onto her plate.

Amanda followed suit and gestured to a pair of chairs nestled in a corner. "Would you like to sit with me?"

"That's kind of you. Lead the way." After balancing her plate on one knee and arranging her napkin on the other, Eliza scanned the room. "There's got to be fifty people in here." Including Chief Constable Kapoor, who, according to gossip she had heard in the line for canapés, used to be Gemma Fielding's uni sweetheart. Having a hard time imagining that man being sweet or having a heart, Eliza shook that image from her head and continued her gaze around the room and froze. Oliver Wright loomed large and ominous outside the Trusty Teapot's window. His face was pressed against the glass, and he leered at the mingling guests inside.

Amanda must have noticed the direction of her gaze. "Never mind him. Gran gave him an earful when he tried to crash her party. Told him she wouldn't have the likes of him near her and that the Trusty Teapot was closed for the day."

"I can see why your grandma is a popular woman. I like her already."

"She certainly is the focal point of most people's lives." Amanda lowered her voice. "Whether they like it or know it or not." She grinned and popped a tiny sandwich into her mouth. "Come to think of it, her partner in crime is your great-aunt, I think."

As it was next to impossible to keep her great-aunt from nosing around in investigations, especially one so soon after she'd been ill, Eliza didn't doubt the dynamic duo's powers within the community. "Great-Aunt Iris says her power comes from people thinking her simply an old lady, one who is blind and deaf on top of being senile."

"That's what my gran says, too, but don't let her old-lady act fool you. She's one sharp cookie, and nothing gets past her. Trust me." Amanda rolled her eyes. "There have been many a time where I'm gobsmacked with what she tells me. Why, the other day—"

Laughter exploded from the corner of the room where Tabitha and Great-Aunt Iris sat like reigning queens. Malcolm, his smiling face red with laughter, patted Tabitha's proffered hand and bowed.

"I wonder what those two said to put him in stitches?" Eliza met Amanda's blank gaze. "Amanda?" She waved her hand in front of the girl's empty stare and touched her shoulder, then Amanda shivered. "You all right?"

Amanda blinked. "What?"

"You seemed to be in a whole different universe, one that didn't seem particularly inviting."

"Oh, sorry. It was nothing." She shook her head again, that time more vigorously, and the curl on her lips was more painful grimace than smile. "Nothing. Suppose someone walked over my grave."

Lambton's cemetery already had two fresh graves. She didn't want a third, much less one having anything to do with the young woman sitting next to her.

"Sorry." Amanda dipped her head and studied her ringing hands. "That was in poor taste. It's that, well…" She huffed out a breath. "Ever since finding Felix's body and learning of Timothy's death, that's all I've been able to think about."

"That is a normal reaction to traumatizing situations."

"That's what my mum keeps saying, but I can't get it out of my mind." Tears welled in her eyes. "Timothy and I weren't friends by any stretch of the imagination, and he could often be a prat, but still, it doesn't seem right or fair, you know?"

"Whoever killed Felix and Timothy will be brought to justice. You have to believe that." Eliza placed her hand on Amanda's forearm. "What you experienced is devastating, and you should talk to somebody about it."

"But my gran doesn't believe in such hocus-pocus, as she puts it, and would throw a wobbly if she caught wind of me seeing a therapist."

Eliza clamped her mouth shut on what Amanda's gran could do with her advice and offered her services instead. "It might help to talk to an unbiased third party, like me, perhaps." She gestured to the Godmothers of Gossip. "From the looks of things, I'll be here a while." Her little white lie singed her conscience, but if she could help the girl and glean information, that was a win-win for all parties involved.

"But I don't know what to tell you. Except for finding Felix's dead body, everything was normal pub stuff and rather boring, I'm afraid."

"No matter. I've got yummy sandwiches, dainty cakes, a full glass of whatever alcohol that cute waiter in the corner is hawking, and a great-aunt who won't move for the next two hours."

AMANDA studied the room, and while her gaze never locked in on any one person or thing, Eliza had the sense she was looking for something. Whether that something should be there but wasn't or wasn't there but should have been, she didn't know.

"I'm not so sure about this. I don't want to waste your time or anything." Amanda placed her hands on the chair's arms as if to launch herself from it.

Eliza placed her hand on Amanda's arm. "You are certainly not wasting my time, and if you really don't want to talk about it, I understand. Events like what you experienced are hard to talk about."

Amanda's gaze flitted from left to right as if she was searching for the correct decision. She finally eased back in her chair and smiled ruefully. "Sorry for the dramatics. I don't know what's come over me. Have you ever had that sensation where you smell something or hear something, and it reminds you of an event or person, but you can't put your finger on it?"

Eliza tapped her temple. "With this brain of mine, all the time."

"Well"—Amanda's face scrunched—"I can't help but feel that it's vital I remember it. Like, if I don't, I'll regret it."

Fighting a shudder at Amanda's ominous tone and blanched face, Eliza smiled. "Perhaps talking through your day will help jar it loose."

"It's worth a try, I guess." Amanda rested her elbows on her knees, folded her hands, and spoke to her whitened knuckles. "From the moment I walked in the door, things were off. First was the mysterious and oddly menacing note requesting and assigning a specific comped room and service for DCI Wentworth."

Eliza feigned surprise. "Really? Is that something that happens often?"

Amanda shook her head. "Not really. Occasionally, groups will raffle things, and the pub sometimes donates a one-night stay or something like that, but this was different." A shudder wracked her body. "I wanted to double-check with Timothy—" Her voice hitched, and she pressed a hand to her mouth. "Sorry. I really don't know why I'm getting emotional. He could be a right lazy sod most of the time, but he was my lazy sod, if you get my drift. Anyway,

I wanted to ask him about it because if I got it wrong, he'd have chewed my ear off, but the note had me checking behind my back, and Timothy was running around like a chicken with its head cut off. I stashed the note in my apron pocket, was sure the DCI's orders went through me, and went on with my evening."

"Which was off, you said?"

"Yeah. Usually, the pub is a relaxed place to be, friendly patrons and hours filled with idle chitchat. Friday night, there was a definite tension."

"Why?"

"I didn't figure it out at the time, but looking back, it had to have been Felix's presence."

"Did everyone know who he was?"

Amanda shrugged. "I don't know that, but it's not hard for the tension of a few to leach into the rest. Timothy, for one, was as prickly as a cactus. Couldn't say anything to him without him biting my head off. And then there was DCI Wentworth. Even though he had free food, drink, and room, a bear with a sore paw would have been more approachable than him that night."

"Who else was there?"

Amanda stared at her. "The pub on Friday night is packed, and I was nearly run off my feet."

"Good point. Who sticks out to you? Who do you remember?"

Amanda screwed her face up and tapped her lower lip. "Dr. Hamilton was there, but you already know that. Um... That nasty Oliver was there."

"What?" Eliza sat up straight. "That's the first I heard this."

"Oh, he didn't stay long and left after a blazing row with Timothy. That's what I had pegged as the cause of Timothy's surliness. But now, looking back, I'm not so sure." At Eliza's raised eyebrow, Amanda shrugged. "He kept slipping side glances at Felix and Wentworth. All night long. And when Wentworth left, he hardly let Felix out of his sight. Granted, Felix accused us of serving him bad beer, but it didn't take long for him to get absolutely trollied, so it mustn't have been too bad, then. Timothy was livid."

"Understandably. Then what happened?"

"Things went from bad to worse. The pub was packed, I was one of the only waitresses, Timothy had little to no help behind the bar, and Felix's increasingly odd behavior—" Amanda bit her lip. "I feel awful for the things I thought about him that night. I didn't know he was dying. I thought he was an angry, stupid drunk."

"You didn't know. There's no way you could have known. Don't give it another thought, okay?"

Amanda nodded and sighed. "After Felix started drooling and slurring his words, Dr. Hamilton advised that he go up to his room. Felix ignored him, and after several moments of kindly advice and assurances that he'd feel better in the morning, the doctor whispered something to him that spurred Felix into stumbling from the room and up the stairs. After that, the evening passed on as normal... until... I found Felix." Her breathing hitched, and several seconds of silence passed as Amanda composed herself. "The last part of my duties is to do a round of the rooms upstairs, to check for plates or cups left out by guests. Felix and DCI Wentworth were the only guests that night, so I didn't expect to find much, as I hadn't brought anything up to their rooms, but I figured I'd better go check anyway. Didn't need another reason for Timothy to scold me." Amanda pinched the bridge of her nose and shook her head. "He'll never scold me again, will he?"

Eliza laid a hand over the young woman's trembling one but said nothing.

Amanda sucked in a shaky breath. "Anyway, there was nothing outside DCI Wentworth's room, and when I went to Felix's, I found his door ajar, which was odd, so I knocked and called his name. When I didn't get a response, I figured he'd passed out. I didn't want to leave him if he was sick or needed help, so I opened the door and..." She rubbed her eyes as if trying to erase the images seared there. "And then I don't remember anything else except his black, black eyes, the odd odor in the room, and..." She rubbed her eyes. "Everything else is a blur." She dropped her hands to her thighs and clenched them until her knuckles whitened. "But I know I'm missing something. I know that thing niggling at the back of my brain deals with that moment."

Eliza patted her arm. "It'll come to you. I promise. And I really think you should speak to someone about this." She slid her gaze to Tabitha Fielding. "It's worth risking your grandma's wrath."

Amanda snorted. "That's a rookie mistake. But you're right." She smiled. "Thank you for listening to me wax on and on about this."

"No worries." The sound of her name sailed over the crowd. "Looks like I'm being summoned. If you need to talk again, I'm a phone call or text away." Eliza dug a receipt and pen out of her purse and jotted down her phone number.

"Thank you." Amanda folded it and stuck it in her back pocket. "Looks like your great-aunt is about to yodel your name."

Eliza hustled to Great-Aunt Iris's side before Amanda's suspicions became truth. "Ready to go home?" Eliza's conscience struck her. Because of her great-aunt's paled skin and her lackluster gaze, Eliza should have taken her home much earlier.

Great-Aunt Iris brushed at a few stray crumbs on her mint-green tracksuit. "Don't go fussing over me, girl. I'm as right as rain." She whispered, "Did you get what you wanted?"

"Not sure until I get back to my..." Eliza winked.

After tapping the side of her nose, Great-Aunt Iris thanked their kind hostesses, wished her partner in crime a happy birthday, and dragged Eliza from the Trusty Teapot. "I don't want to hear anything until we assemble in the attic."

"But you should rest, and I'm not sure Dr. Hamilton would approve of you not only doing stairs but being in the musty attic anyway."

"What he does not know won't hurt him."

Eliza refrained from stating that her actions had zero potential of hurting the good doctor and instead could be the death of her great-aunt, but she bit her lip and followed the octogenarian's demand to "drive like Joy and get us home."

AFTER striking a deal that Great-Aunt Iris could join the sleuthing team once again only after she had taken an hour's rest, Eliza escaped to her room. She needed a nap, but it was quite clear that the only one getting any shut-eye was Caesar, who lay curled up in a fluffy orange puff in the middle of her bed. At her footsteps, his right eye opened with enough energy to assess she was home and wasn't a threat before the lid closed again and his deep purrs indicated deep sleep.

"Must be nice," Eliza muttered as she slid onto her bed and cuddled next to Caesar. She pulled her phone from her pocket to check the missed texts and phone calls that the buzzing at the party had foretold. Most were from Belle, venting about horrid customers. Two were from her mother, promising a later phone call but saying that things were better. One was from Uncle Fitzwilliam, inquiring about the state of the estate, promising a speedy return, and wondering if she had managed to stay out of trouble. And one was the long-awaited call from her father: *Sorry I have not spoken with you... or texted back. I'm so sorry, Eliza, that I failed you. Knowing I have your support means the world to me. I'm not sorry those letters arrived, as my dirty laundry needed a good airing, but I have no clue who sent them or how they were sent. I love you.*

Eliza squinted past her blurred vision at her father's text. So, Nancy hadn't won. No matter how she had delivered those letters to destroy the Darcy family, she had not counted on the strength of family and the bonds of love that were stronger than the chains of hate. With the cloud of family drama and near tragedy lifted from her, Eliza felt energized and ready to tackle the problem at large.

Heath knocked on her open doorjamb and grinned at the snoring cat. "Is Caesar accepting guests?"

"No, but his owner is." Eliza patted the mattress.

The mattress dipped under his weight, and Caesar glared at him out of one eye, licked his paw, flicked it over an ear, and settled deeper into Eliza.

Heath laughed. "Looks like he doesn't like to share."

"Looks like he doesn't get a vote." Eliza rested her head on Heath's chest and listened to his heartbeat. Her skin tingled where his fingers traced, and she wanted nothing more than to lie in bed with him for the rest of the day. But she knew Great-Aunt Iris would shuffle along any moment with her infamous knitting needles.

"I don't suppose we can stay here all night?" Heath murmured as he curled her hair around his fingers.

"Great-Aunt Iris would not approve."

"Right. She's quite terrifying. Never thought a tracksuit and knitting needles would put the fear of God in me." He smiled ruefully. "As insane as it sounds, I will miss the constant threat of a side jab when I get my own flat in Lambton."

Eliza leaned up on one elbow and traced his jaw. "You know, you don't have to go. I'm sure Uncle wouldn't mind you staying on."

"As tempting as that offer is, I could never mooch off your uncle's generosity. Besides, if I don't get my own place, we'll never escape your great-aunt." He laced his fingers through her hair and gently brought her lips inches from his own. "Think of all the adventures we'll have," he whispered before kissing her.

Blood coursed through Eliza's body, and heat pooled in her core. She broke off the kiss. "You make a compelling argument. When is our first official date night at your new digs?"

He chuckled. "Monday."

"Then we better solve this case so we can really celebrate." She hopped off the bed before he could entice her to stay longer. "Come on. We can't let Great-Aunt Iris beat us to the attic. She may take care of our Garrison problem the same way she claims she took care of the Nazi problem."

"Does anyone else see the problem with her historical math? I mean, unless she was killing all these Nazi soldiers when she was four."

"I wouldn't put it past her." Eliza's smile slipped. "I'm sure it's her way of reconciling a hard childhood. I've heard her talk about older brothers who died in the war, and the repercussions of World War II didn't end with the final shot. Perhaps her claiming to have taken a more active part than she could have helps to alleviate the pain she experienced."

"If this sleuthing mistress of Pemberley doesn't pan out for you, a career as a psychologist could be a solid idea."

"Yeah, well, if I were good at reading people, it wouldn't take me so long to solve this murder." Eliza grabbed his hand, peeked around the doorjamb, and dashed down the hall and to the gallery. After double-checking for any lurkers, including Kapoor's "gifted" constables—who had proven thorough in their job and had scoured the tunnel for hours before giving up on finding anything but cobwebs—Eliza eased the door open and pulled it shut when Heath slid through.

No sound emanated from the attic's hidey-hole, and while that should have been a good thing, the hair on the back of Eliza's neck stood at attention. Heath must have read her mind, as he took the steps two at a time before her and came to a rocking halt at the top.

Eliza stifled a giggle at the sight before her. Great-Aunt Iris stood in front of the crime board as if instructing her class on how to diagram a sentence, and her two pupils, Garrison and Wentworth, sat staring at her, one in confusion, the other in trepidation.

"Is everything okay up here?" Eliza asked.

"These boys are doing their best to make their presence known to all of Pemberley." Great-Aunt Iris thrust a shaky index finger toward the first "boy," Wentworth. "This one needs to learn how to control his anger and not let the childish and ridiculous behavior of this one"—Great-Aunt Iris's finger then trembled at Garrison—"get to him."

"Don't blame me. You haven't been cooped up with this bloody moron for days." Wentworth's face fell at Great-Aunt Iris's glare, and his gaze darted about as if looking for an escape route.

Joy zipped up the stairs, clutching her sides. "Phew, that is quite the trek." Her gaze flitted from Wentworth's bulging eyes to Great-Aunt Iris's deep frown and reddened cheeks and Eliza and Heath's twitching lips. "Who's about to die?"

Eliza clapped Wentworth on the shoulder. "Well, it was nice to know you."

"I, uh, Mrs. Darcy, please accept my apology."

Great-Aunt Iris waved away his apology. After waddling to the chair Garrison sat in, she glared at him until he jumped to his feet and scurried away to a corner of the tiny room.

Taking that as her cue to commandeer the meeting, Eliza grabbed a marker and wrote Amanda's name followed by *waitress at the Foxed Hound* and *found Felix's body*.

"You don't think she's a suspect, do you?" Joy asked.

"No, but the information she gave me deserves board space. First, she described the night Felix died as having a palpable tension."

Wentworth nodded. "She's right. Could almost cut it with a knife."

"She also reported that Timothy was prickly and that DCI Wentworth was grumpy." She cut her gaze to Wentworth and grinned. Her grin slipped, though, and she rubbed her forehead. "Look, I know you and Timothy weren't on good standing, but how are you doing with the news of his death? He was your family, after all."

Heaving a sigh, Wentworth shrugged. "I honestly didn't have much to do with him, and the bits I did, I detested him. I'm not glad he's dead, and I want his killer brought to justice, but I won't be in line to lay flowers on his grave." He leaned forward and rested his elbows on his knees. "As for that Friday night, I can't say I was in the best of moods, but what with Timothy's presence—may he rest in peace—which alone was a thorn in my arse, and Felix's absurd behavior, I'm not sure anyone can blame me for being 'grumpy.'" He hooked air quotes.

Eliza wrote *Timothy had an argument with Oliver* and *Dr. Hamilton persuaded Felix to go to his room* and pointed at the last tidbit. "Wentworth, did you see this exchange?"

He scratched at his locked-in-an-attic-induced beard. "I don't recall seeing those two talk, but while the doc and I were in line for the loo, waiting for Felix to get his business done and get out, Dr. Hamilton made a few offhand comments about the behavior of drunks and how he was worried Felix was in danger of more than a raging hangover the next morning." Smacking his thigh, he growled. "If only I'd known..."

"It's not your fault. The symptoms for hemlock poisoning are oddly reminiscent of someone being severely intoxicated. But concentrate. What happened?"

"I was so angry with Felix that I told him, none too kindly and in front of everybody, when he exited the bog that he was making a right tit of himself and that if he couldn't handle his drink, he'd best go get blinkered elsewhere." Wentworth shoved his fingers through his hair. "He slurred something about someone advising him to go up to his room to sleep it off and stumbled to the door leading to the rooms. I figured I'd check on him when I went up later, but by the time I headed to my room, I knew I needed to leave before I got violently sick. Never did stop and check on him."

Eliza tapped the tip of the closed marker against her lips. "What room were you staying in? Who knew you had the room for the night?"

Wentworth grunted. "Number three. And no bloody clue. Amanda said it was a gift from a grateful citizen of Lambton and that he or she wanted to remain anonymous and that it was to be a secret."

"From what I got from Amanda, it was more than a secret. Threatened by the written request, she had, at numerous times, wanted to tell someone else but then thought better of it. Didn't think there would be any harm in a comped room." She wrote *comped room a secret?* on the cardboard and underlined the question mark twice. "More importantly, though, if you could easily be framed without your overnight presence, as we've witnessed, why the ruse of the room? Why did you need to stay there?" Eliza tapped the marker cap against her bottom lip. "And why in the heck did Timothy need to be removed from the equation?"

Chapter Sixteen

A Blonde and a Brunette Walk Into a Pub...

It is frustrating to see two people so much in love yet so afraid of speaking their minds. Anne's situation reminds me too much of Jane's. Unlike in Jane and Charles's situation, however, I am afraid there are layers of pain and mistrust keeping Anne and Captain Wentworth from expressing their true emotions. Darcy recommends that I allow two adults to make decisions for themselves, and I, thusly, gently remind him that he did not grant that to either Jane or Charles years ago. I believe my matchmaking skills are up to the test, and I shall endeavor to bring two people who are so desperately in love with each other together at last.

Lizzy Bennet Darcy

Bath 1814

Eliza scowled at her scrambled eggs on her breakfast plate. They had once been fluffy and steaming, but her appetite had apparently run away with her cleverness and intelligence. She swirled the cold and rubbery eggs with her fork, much like her mind swirled the congealed facts of the case around, ending up with a massive lump of nothingness. She stuck her fork into the egg pyramid she'd created and watched as it slowly leaned and finally clattered to the china plate.

"What is wrong with you? Ever since you walked in here, you've been doing nothing but huffing and puffing and mumbling under your breath." Joy narrowed her eyes at Eliza. "What's eating you?"

Eliza picked at a piece of toast, cold and slathered with congealed butter. "There is a vital clue we're missing, and it's at the Foxed Hound. I know it is."

"Let's go to the pub, then."

"The pub's not open this early." Eliza flicked her wrist to wake up her Fitbit.

Joy grinned and held up a finger. "Give me two seconds." She whipped out her cell phone and tapped out a message, her French-manicured fingernails clicking on the screen.

"One... two..."

"Shush. Eat your minging eggs and be patient." Joy bit into a tri-angular piece of toast.

The grandfather clock in the corner of the breakfast room ticked the seconds away, and long after the promised two seconds, Joy's phone buzzed, and a devious grin spread over her face. "About the pub not being open at seven a.m. ..."

"Yes?"

"Fancy a trip to town?"

"You're not suggesting breaking and entering, are you?"

"Me? Suggest such a thing? Why, Eliza dear, I'm shocked. I don't plan on *breaking* anything."

Eliza quirked an eyebrow. "What about the entering part?"

Joy waved a dismissive hand. "That? What's wrong with entering an unoccupied building if one has the access code?"

"And how in the world do you have said access code?"

"Oh ye of little faith." Joy waved her phone back and forth. "Let's just say that I have resources, and occasionally, I use them."

"An old ex, I presume?"

"They really are disastrous human beings, but they do come in handy every once in a while."

"You really are—"

"Intelligent? Resourceful? Bloody brilliant?"

"Yeah, those were the exact words I had in mind." Eliza stabbed her eggs with her fork, and the utensil stood straight. "Shall we gather the forces?"

"I'm thinking the fewer people we have... ah... accessing the property, the better."

"Great-Aunt Iris will throw a fit, and Heath will pout." Eliza covered her plate and fork-impaled pile of eggs with a cloth napkin and prayed Mrs. Bankcroft wouldn't know she was the one who had dared not eat anything. "You think of ways to appease Great-Aunt Iris, and I'll think of ways of making Heath unpouty." Eliza's blood warmed at the plans she already had in store for him.

Joy chuckled and nudged Eliza with her shoulder. "Look who's the bodice-ripping author now."

Ignoring her cousin and the heat washing over her face, Eliza tapped her phone against her palm. "Do I let Heath know our plans or...?"

"In my vast experience, it is easier to ask for forgiveness than permission."

"Whenever I take your advice, I usually regret it."

"Carpe diem, dear cousin. Now, let's go before the team comes down for breakfast and catches us abandoning them."

Eliza tapped out a quick text letting Heath know their plans and added a kissy-faced emoji to soften the blow.

Ten minutes later, Joy parked her Range Rover one alley over from the Foxed Hound, behind the fish-and-chip shop notorious for serving less-than-edible fish but fairly decent chips.

"This looks like an opening scene of a horror film." Joy crinkled her nose.

Large metal containers overflowed with garbage, complete with fish skeletons protruding from opened garbage bags, and several cats, uprooted by the appearance of the Range Rover, scooted into hidey-holes and stared at the two unwelcome guests.

"Smells like one too." Eliza pinched her nose shut and hustled down the alley to the back road. After accessing the alley behind the Foxed Hound, she sidled to the pub's back door, which was scratched and rusted with age and cat claws. She motioned to the security panel on the doorjamb. "Quick."

Joy glanced left and right then jabbed the keys. The lock whirled and clicked. "Bob's your uncle." Joy pumped a fist, opened the door, and closed it after Eliza joined her in the darkened back room.

"Is it creepy in here, or is it me?" Eliza peered at the stacks of boxes cluttering the tiny space. Something—someone—could be hiding behind them.

"No, it's definitely creepy in here," Joy whispered and tugged on Eliza's coat sleeve. "Come on. Now is not the time to faff about."

Eliza led the way out of the room and pushed the swinging door leading to the bar area. No lights backlighting the bottles of booze. No people sitting at tables meant for food and conversation. All was quiet. Too quiet. Her stomach rumbled. She really should have tried to eat breakfast. The skin on the back of her neck prickled. "Where do the people staying the night in one of the rooms go for breakfast?"

Joy's face paled. "Bloody hell. I never thought about that."

Eliza opened drawers and cabinets, unearthing cups, plates, and assorted dining room paraphernalia, and swore.

"What's wrong? What are you looking for?" Joy asked.

"The guest registry. One of the many things I've neglected. Help me find it. It has to be here somewhere." Eliza pointed at the bar cabinets she hadn't rifled through. "You look through those, and I'll take a peek in the office."

The pub's office was about as dark and creepy as the back room. Eliza couldn't shake the feeling of eyes watching her. Instead of running as her survival instincts demanded, she plowed through the papers on the scarred wooden desk. Nothing. She opened the top right-hand drawer and exhaled. "Found it," she whispered as loud as she dared. "Joy?" She risked a louder whisper.

Joy's blond head popped around the corner. "Did you find it?"

Eliza waved her over. "We're in luck. There's no one staying here. But I suppose food service people will arrive shortly to prepare for lunch, right?"

"With the luck we're having with the investigation, yes."

Eliza narrowed her gaze at the lines of names and stabbed her finger at Felix's. "Look. According to this, he was the only guest that night. If Wentworth is right about the anonymous gift of a room, you'd think it would at least be in the pub's records."

"What if the room was a ruse? Something to get him here that night. Anyone can gain access to the upstairs rooms. So, if the pub did not officially gift him a room, someone could and, from the looks of it, did use the easy access to trap Wentworth."

"I hate when you're right."

"I know. It's a trial to be right all the time, but it's one I'm willing to bear." Joy grinned.

Eliza rolled her eyes. "So, everything was going well for our miscreant until Wentworth ate some fish from the neighboring restaurant, left his room, and snuck out the back staircase and went home. I bet you more money than I have that the person behind this had the proverbial nail in the coffin nicely arranged to peg Felix's murder on Wentworth." Eliza snapped her fingers. "The dried hemlock! I bet you, again, that the bunch of flowers that was found in a different room than Felix's was found in—"

"Wentworth's 'gifted' room." Joy grinned.

"I think you and I should go to Vegas."

"Before or after we solve the case? Because I could have my bags packed in less than an hour."

"And leave Wentworth to molt away with Garrison?" Eliza cut off Joy's forming yes. "I'd give my left kidney to know if the room Timothy found the dried hemlock in is the same one Wentworth was staying in."

WHEN an engine revved outside the pub, Eliza jumped. "We best hurry up before we're rudely interrupted." After snapping a picture of the registry page, she placed it back in its spot and hustled from the office, Joy hot on her heels. They reached the base of the steps, which had taken on a rather unsavory aura.

"You go first." Eliza made a sweeping gesture.

"Really? You're willing to sacrifice me to whatever ghosts might lurk in the corners?"

"There's no such thing as ghosts."

"Then how do you explain the one right behind you?"

Eliza yelped, wheeled around, and confronted nothing but the time-stained wood-paneled wall. "That's it. You go first."

"That's fair. Besides, I'm really not afraid of ghosts." Joy sauntered past her and paled when the first step creaked.

Eliza chuckled. "Karma, my dear cousin? Not really afraid of ghosts, huh?"

"It's not fear. It's respect." Joy scurried up the steps and tiptoed down the dark hallway. "Something about closed doors gives me the creeps."

"Everything about this place is giving me the creeps." Eliza paused outside the infamous room number six.

No police tape cordoned off the door, but in case the police came back for some reason, Eliza pulled on a pair of gardening gloves she had pilfered from one of Pemberley's sheds and jiggled the doorknob. Before opening the door, she squatted and squinted at the aged brass knob. The police would have dusted it for prints, and from the lack of residue, Eliza guessed housekeeping had already tidied up the place. Somehow, some way, Wentworth's prints had been on the outside and inside knob of the crime scene without him being in Felix's room. Unless Wentworth had indeed committed the crime. Eliza rubbed her eyes with her knuckles. No, there was no way. Someone was trying to frame him and doing a very good job of it.

Eliza chewed on her lip. "Do you... Could it be possible that the rooms got mixed up?"

"How so?"

"Like Wentworth got this room, and Felix had Wentworth's room, and the murderer dragged Felix's dead body here."

"But remember, Felix was here before Wentworth and already had a room. This room. Besides, the registry doesn't look doctored, and Wentworth's room was down the hall."

Eliza squinted harder at the doorknob. "Then how in the world did Wentworth's fingerprints get on this knob?"

"Are we one hundred percent sure he didn't do it?"

Eliza scoffed. "Wentworth would never kill anybody."

"Would you bat an eyelash to find Wentworth standing over Garrison's dead body?"

"No... Yes... I don't know, but it's Garrison, so I wouldn't put it past Great-Aunt Iris to stab him with her knitting needles, either." Eliza jiggled the knob again. "It's pretty loose."

"This pub is as old as the hills. It's surprising this whole place doesn't disintegrate."

"Fair point." Eliza fully turned the doorknob and stepped inside the room.

No boogeyman jumped out from under the bed. No chalk outlined a body's shape on the floor. No remnants of poison had left their ghostly drops on the rough-hewn wood floor. Eliza almost

wished whispers of murder still lingered. Anything to dispel the or-
dinary, innocuous setting from forgetting that a man had died within those four walls.

"I don't like being in here," Joy whispered as she lifted the bed-
covers and peeked under the bed.

"Then let's hurry up."

"What are we looking for anyway?"

"Clues."

"Anything a little more specific?"

Eliza threw her hands in the air. "All I know is that Wentworth
was never in this room, yet his fingerprints were found on the inside
and the outside of this room's doorknob, and a glass with his fingerprints and DNA were found on this table." Eliza leaned her hand
against the edge of the round table topped with a purple vase of fake
daffodils spilling cattywampus from its flared opening.

The table tipped, Eliza caught herself on a nearby chair, and
two of the rounded feet shaped like eagle claws detached from their
moorings and spun before clunking against Joy's high-heeled boots.

Eliza dusted herself off, snatched the clawed orbs from the floor,
and twirled them by their screws. "At least this will be an easy fix. I
really don't want the 'breaking' charge to be added to the 'entering'
charge." She got down on her knees. "Here. You tilt the table toward
you so I can stick these back into the legs."

"How do you know which one goes where?"

"They're identical, so I'm pretty sure they're interchangeable."
Eliza's hand stopped midtwirl. "No, it can't be that simple, can it?"

"What are you talking about?"

Eliza held up her finger and attempted to screw the foot into
each leg. Both fit. No one would ever be the wiser that the table's ea-
gle-clawed footings had been switched. "Just like..." Eliza hopped to
her feet, knelt beside the door, and peered at the doorknob.

"What are you doing? Have you gone barmy?"

"No. Come here." Eliza crooked her finger, and when Joy came up beside her, she pointed at the tiny screws attaching the brass knob to the base connected to the wooden door. "Look. This knob is only screwed onto the base. It's not attached like modern doorknobs. If I had a screwdriver, I could easily switch this knob with any of the ones in this pub, and no one would be the wiser."

"Blimey! Are you saying that someone switched the doorknobs between Wentworth and Felix's rooms?"

"Why get Wentworth a room, then? Why go through the trouble of the whole charade? Wentworth could have easily killed Felix without checking in first. However, in order to get damning evidence, his fingerprints *had* to be on the inside and outside of the doorknob."

"But what about the fingerprints and DNA on the glasses?"

"They would probably not be solid enough on their own. A good lawyer could have spun that in a dozen different directions, but having Wentworth's fingerprints on the door to and from the crime scene was the murderer's pièce de résistance." Eliza kissed the tips of her fingers. "'Fingerprints don't lie, but humans do' is exactly what a jury would have thought."

"Here, hold this." Joy shoved her phone at Eliza, opened the main compartment of her purse, and dug around before giving a victory cry and holding out a bobby pin. "Try this."

Eliza pursed her lips. "I think it's too wide."

"You won't know until you try it."

Eliza attempted to insert it at various angles, but the metal of the bobby pin was too thick for the tiny screws. "Don't suppose you have a screwdriver in there? I bet Great-Aunt Iris would have a screwdriver in her purse."

"She does." Joy plunked the bobby pin back in her purse.

"Really?"

"Oh yes. Asked her about it once, and she told me to mind my own business and that if she wanted to carry a screwdriver in her purse, no one could tell her otherwise."

"Hey, what about a credit card or something? Maybe if I can get the corner in, I could give it a good twist. It's not on very tight, which leads me to believe that whoever changed out the knobs was in a hurry."

After more rummaging, Joy whipped out her wallet and extracted five credit cards.

Eliza quirked an eyebrow but said nothing as she grabbed one and inserted a corner into the tiny wedge of the screw. "Bingo. Now, a little twist and..."

The screw plopped into Eliza's waiting hand. Then the second screw from the other side of the knob joined the first, and Eliza slid the knob out from the base.

"Bloody hell, look at that." Joy peered owlishly at the base, where a metal connecting rod protruded. "So the same can be done on the other side?"

"Yup. I mean, we're essentially trapped in here until I get this on again, but we could repeat the same process for the outside one."

"It didn't take you long at all."

"And I had a credit card that didn't work well. Someone who had everything to risk and had a screwdriver could do this in a few minutes."

"And if the bar was as busy as Timothy—God rest his soul—and Amanda claimed it was, anyone in the pub that night could have killed Felix and exchanged the knobs and planted the glasses, knowing that when Forensics did their thing, Wentworth's fingerprints would be on the glasses and the doorknobs."

"I would bet that if the police dusted for prints on room three's doorknob, there would be either no prints at all, because the murderer wiped it clean, or no Wentworth prints, because he never went into Felix's room that night." Eliza slid the knob back on the metal rod, seated it correctly, and screwed it back on.

"Come to think of it, the murderer's plan was dastardly, that's for sure, but brilliant. The doorknob they tested would have had all the 'correct' prints on it. Wentworth's, Felix's, probably housekeeping's or Timothy's. Nothing wiped, nothing odd."

As much as Eliza wanted to disagree, she couldn't. Whoever had framed Wentworth had done a thorough enough job that if Eliza failed her friend, Wentworth was bound to spend a very long time in prison for another man's crime.

AFTER putting Joy in charge of delivering the large duffel bag containing the provisions they'd bought for Wentworth and Garrison in Lambton and gathering everyone in the attic, Eliza met Tash, Mrs. Bankcroft, Mrs. Underhill, and Willow for their midmorning meeting in the kitchen.

Tash and Willow met her with a smile. Mrs. Bankcroft met her with a scone slathered with clotted cream and raspberry preserves. Mrs. Underhill met her with a pointier-than-usual chin and a more-than-regal haughtiness. Murder and mayhem had taken up so much of Eliza's world that she'd almost forgotten Mrs. Underhill's mutinous vibe. She certainly didn't have the time to deal with a recalcitrant housekeeper, so she added that to her ever-growing to-do list to deal with if—no, when—she solved the murder and got two grown men out of Pemberley's attic.

Eliza bit into her scone and failed to suppress a groan. "Mrs. B, these are the best you've made yet."

The cook beamed with pride and fiddled with her apron. "Ah, go on with you now, Miss Eliza."

After failing to say anything nice to the intimidating housekeeper, Eliza opened her laptop and handed them printed copies listing the upcoming weekend's group and the weekly and weekend menu. "Let me know if anything should be changed or added. We have bird-watchers this weekend, and they won't have separate meetings as the police did last weekend, but they have requested that one of the rooms have round tables and chairs set up for a lecture series from a local bird expert."

Mrs. Bankcroft huffed and mumbled something under her breath that sounded like "bird expert my foot" as she scanned the paper in front of her. "They want white soup, pigeon pie, and negus?" She glared at Eliza as if she'd put the idea in the minds of the upcoming bird enthusiasts. "Don't tell me these twitchers are Regency nuts too?"

Eliza bit her cheek to keep her grin in check, as she wouldn't put it past Mrs. B to never feed her scones again. From the pained look on Tash's face, he seemed to struggle between a laugh and thoughts of future starvation. "I'm sure they are not Regency reenactors, Mrs. B. Pemberley is an estate that evokes that time period, though, so perhaps they want to get the full atmosphere."

"Well, I ain't dressing in any Regency dress, you understand?" Mrs. Bankcroft waved a wooden spoon slathered with some type of batter at Eliza. "And they're not allowed in my kitchen."

"Now, now, Mrs. B. We've never allowed guests in here."

Mrs. Bankcroft swiped the air with the spoon, sending droplets of batter in all directions, including Eliza's shirt, Mrs. Underhill's coiffed red up-do, Tash's perfectly pressed white button-up shirt, and Willow's nose. "You don't know them twitchers."

Feeling the conversation had devolved with no promise of normalcy, Eliza reminded them to let her know by midafternoon if things needed changing. Her genuine smile for Tash, Mrs. Bankcroft, and Willow slipped when she attempted the same for Mrs. Underhill. "Thank you all so much for all your hard work. If it weren't for you, I'm sure Uncle Fitzwilliam would come back to a Pemberley on fire and in chaos."

While Tash and Mrs. Bankcroft pooh-poohed her self-deprecating comment, Mrs. Underhill stared stonily at her. Eliza offered one more thank-you and escaped the kitchen and the housekeeper's obvious disdain.

"Miss Eliza." Willow's hoarse whisper echoed down the long hallway.

Eliza turned and smiled. "It's just Eliza, remember?" She squinted at the young woman's face and motioned at her nose. "I think you've taken a little bit of Mrs. B's cooking with you."

Willow's pale cheeks rosied, and she swiped the tip of her nose. "Did I get it?"

"Yup. Now what can I do for you? Did you need anything?"

Willow darted a furtive look behind her. "Can we talk somewhere more private?"

Eliza ushered her into a little-used sitting room and settled in an armchair covered in embroidered birds of paradise. She motioned for Willow to sit in the matching chair next to her and waited for the young woman to speak.

"It's about those officers. The ones who are here to guard Pemberley."

Eliza's interest piqued to a fevered level, but she leaned back in her chair and feigned indifference. "What about them?"

"Well, they were asking questions, questions about the upper windows, the little round ones, and wanted to know what floor they belonged to."

"Those are the attic windows." Eliza forced a smile. "Nothing up there but dusty old things that I still haven't sorted through." *The Apple Dumpling Gang aren't as stupid as they look.*

Willow chewed on her bottom lip. "Thing is, they asked to go up there, and as you weren't around for me to ask, I let them. I hope that's okay. They weren't too keen on me finding you to ask, and I didn't want to make them suspicious."

"Suspicious?" Eliza hated the squeak in her voice. She cleared her throat. "Why would you worry about making them suspicious? It's just an attic."

Willow quirked an eyebrow, making Eliza feel more like a recalcitrant four-year-old caught with her hand in the cookie jar rather than Pemberley's mistress and Willow's boss. "If you say so, but I thought I'd let you know that the attic was searched, and the officers left covered in dust bunnies but satisfied that there were no ghosts or Wentworths hiding up there."

Eliza forced a smile and stood. "That's good. Thank you for letting me know, Willow. Now, if you'll excuse me, I have to... to... see to business."

Willow stepped in her path. "Please don't concern yourself if I can keep a secret. I can keep a secret better than anyone. I wanted you to know the officers have been sniffing pretty close to your quarry."

"How? When?" Eliza gave up and shook her head.

Again, the young woman's eyebrow flicked upward. "I don't mean any offense, mind you, but no one ever goes to that bookcase at the far end of the gallery more than you and Miss Bingley and Mr. Tilney, and that's just as of late, after Wentworth went missing. It's not too hard to put two and two together."

Eliza's stomach dipped to the tips of her toes. "Does anyone else know? Does Mrs. Underhill suspect something?" *Dear goodness, if that woman suspected anything, she wouldn't hesitate to tattle to Kapoor.*

Willow smiled. "I told Mrs. Underhill that I would take over the duties on the second floor, as I knew she was busy with other things. She didn't think twice giving me more work. Seemed to relish it, actually." She leaned closer and whispered, "I don't know if Wentworth is or isn't holed up somewhere in this grand house, but I do know one thing. Wentworth is an innocent man, so I will do anything I can to help."

"How do you know he's innocent?"

"He was my church youth group leader when I was a teenager, and I was friends with his kids. Nothing about him even whispers to the idea that he could do what everyone says he did." Willow tapped the side of her nose. "Your secret really is safe with me." With that, Willow left the room, leaving Eliza alone and unnerved.

Eliza inhaled and exhaled, closed her eyes, and centered her thoughts. Having Willow as an ally could come in handy, and knowing the officers had already searched the attic and found nothing suspicious boded well for them. However, she would need to remind everyone to be extra vigilant. They had become careless in their comings and goings, and to have anyone else figure out their dirty little secret would be disastrous.

She left the room, closed the door, and rammed into Heath's chest.

"So, this is how it will be in the future, is it? You leaving your sidekick behind to have adventures." Heath grinned as he caught her in an embrace and kissed the top of her head.

"Joy did say it was easier to ask forgiveness than permission."

"Since when do you listen to Joy?"

"Today will be the last time, I swear."

He held her at arm's length and grinned. "That's one heck of a whopper, that is."

Eliza ran her thumb across the dimple in his cheek. "As soon as you get your own place, I won't be under Joy's bad influence so much."

"Maybe you're the bad influence." He dipped his head, but instead of kissing her, he paused. "Hey, what's wrong?" He traced his finger along her forehead. "Your what-in-the-heck wrinkle's very, well, wrinkly."

Eliza batted his hand away. "Willow knows," she whispered. "We've been careless in our movements, and she noticed how often we visited the often-forgotten-about bookshelf."

"Can we trust her to keep quiet?"

"I think so. She seemed genuine in her promise to keep our secret and thought it ridiculous that people could accuse Wentworth of murder." She pulled him along down the hall. "Come on. I have to warn the troops about being more careful, and I made a break-through at the pub."

After double-checking and triple-checking that the gallery was empty and no one was around to see them sneak behind the book-case, Eliza took the steps two at a time and reached the top, huffing and puffing. *I really need to add working out to my list—and saying no to Mrs. B's treats!*

"Are you the Big Bad Wolf come to eat all the little piggies?" Garrison asked around a mouthful of food.

Great-Aunt Iris's knitting needles stilled, Wentworth's eyebrows shot to his receding hairline, Heath growled, and Joy studied her fingernails as if assessing whether they would do the job that needed done.

"Excuse me?" Eliza narrowed her eyes at him.

He gestured at her with a circular flick of his wrist. "With all that huffing and puffing, I thought that's who was coming up the steps."

"What counts for self-defense in this country?" Eliza asked Wentworth.

He jerked his head toward Garrison sitting cross-legged on the floor. "With that, I would count anything as such. The law would probably look the other way."

Garrison smiled smugly. "And how long do you think you'll be the law around here?"

Heath was on him before Eliza could blink. Garrison's toes fought for purchase on the floor as Heath held him up by his shirt collar.

Eliza briefly admired Heath's muscles rippling under his shirt before laying a hand on his shoulder. "It is cruel to punish little children and fools, and as Garrison is both, put him down."

"But this bloody plodder needs his arse kicked." Heath brought Garrison gently to his feet and wiped at the sweat beading on his forehead. When Garrison stood rigidly in front of him, Heath lunged. "Scram back to your corner, you miserable sod."

After Garrison did as directed, with an extra squeak and two rather unnecessary snivels, Eliza patted Heath's shoulder. "I promise that when all this is over and Wentworth is safely back where he belongs, you can give said arse kicking."

"And I promise to look the other way." Wentworth grinned from his usual spot on his cot.

"Would you like one of my knitting needles?" Great-Aunt Iris held out one of the many extras she stored in her oversized purse.

"What, Joy, nothing to offer?" Heath asked.

Joy tapped a French-manicured nail to her ruby-red lips. "I believe that revenge is best served cold." The twisted smile she gave Garrison made even Eliza's neck hairs stand at attention.

"If everyone is done with promises of future violence, can we get back to business? Business that has taken on a rather insidious vibe." Eliza waited until everyone had settled and chatter stopped. "Willow knows about Wentworth being up here."

Silence reigned for a split second before being torn asunder by a crude swear word courtesy of Wentworth.

"She promises to keep our secret and did a good job of keeping the officers' suspicions at bay. She said they wanted to look around the attic and left with only dust bunnies."

Wentworth shrank onto his cot and had never seemed smaller.

Eliza sat next to him and patted his shoulder. "She said you had been her youth group leader and that she was friends with your kids. She's positive you didn't do anything wrong and swears she'll keep our secret. Heck, she even took on the duties of the second floor so Mrs. Underhill didn't have as much of a reason to be bustling about out there."

Wentworth closed his eyes and exhaled. "Yeah, we can trust her. She was a good kid. Solid head on her shoulders, that one." He skewered Garrison with a glare. "But we have to be extra quiet. And I don't feel confident about leaving the attic at night to dump the chamber pot out."

"Remember, the officers aren't in the house at night. You'll still be good for that, I think," Eliza said.

Before Wentworth could give in to the doldrums and give up on her, she jumped to her feet and removed a marker tip with her teeth. "Joy and I found an interesting break in the case at the Foxed Hound." She waited a beat, a smile pulling at her lips.

"Well, what is it?" Heath asked. "The suspense is killing me."

Eliza grinned and wrote *doorknobs of rooms were switched* on the crime board.

Wentworth's jaw dropped. "What the bloody hell?"

Chapter Seventeen
A Spoonful of Honey

It appears my matchmaking skills are not needed, as my dear friend Anne and her beloved Captain Wentworth have renewed their love for one another, and Anne has accepted Captain Wentworth's proposal. I do so wish her a lifetime of happiness, and if she loves her captain as much as I love my Darcy, and if he adores her as much as Darcy adores me, then I have no doubt that they will live happily all their days.
Lizzy Bennet Darcy
Bath 1814

Wednesday morning dawned with ominous winter clouds and an "important" update from the constables that there had been no sighting of Wentworth. As Eliza sat at her usual table at the Trusty Teapot, her hopes of a breakthrough in the investigation—that her big find of the switchable doorknobs would unlock the case and set Wentworth free—turned as black as the weather.

"How can something so big lead to absolutely nothing?" Eliza stirred her usual Ethiopian spiced tea with such vigor that little droplets splattered onto the white linen tablecloth.

Joy snorted. "That's what my heroine thought this morning after a night with—"

Great-Aunt Iris choked on her tea, and after a coughing fit that had Eliza reaching for her phone to call the ambulance, Great-Aunt Iris tutted. "Really, Joy, there's no need to speak of such things. Although now that we're on that subject—"

Heath loudly cleared his throat and mumbled, "Please be poison, please be poison" into his coffee mug.

Eliza held up a staying hand. "I. Don't. Want. To. Hear. It."

Joy's grin slipped, and she patted Eliza's hand. "Sorry. Look, something will turn up. I promise."

"But don't you see, the longer the you-know-whos are stashed in the you-know-where, the likelihood of someone finding them increases. And then I—we—all get charged with aiding and abetting a criminal. I'm surprised we haven't gotten caught yet." She dropped her voice. "If Willow knows, it's only a matter of time before other members of the staff notice. Mrs. B is already suspicious about the plates and such that have gone 'missing.'"

"Hush." Great-Aunt Iris placed a wrinkly hand on Eliza's. "It's the good doctor." She patted her fluffy white cloud of hair and smiled as Dr. Hamilton approached their table.

"May I join you lovely ladies?" Dr. Hamilton grinned at Heath. "And Heath, of course."

Joy pushed out the chair next to her and nearly cooed. "Absolutely."

After Dr. Hamilton got settled and ordered his black coffee, he smiled at Great-Aunt Iris. "And how's my patient this morning?"

Great-Aunt Iris huffed. "I'm as healthy as a horse."

"And stubborn as a mule," Joy mumbled into her teacup.

Great-Aunt Iris gave a grand harrumph but continued, "And as I stated earlier, Dr. Hamilton, I haven't been sick a day in my life."

"Of course, of course." He winked at Eliza when Great-Aunt Iris's attention was distracted by a passerby outside the window. "Now, Mrs. Darcy, I know you've never been ill, but your recent brush with... less than your usual health... leads to some concerns. I would like to see you in my office before the week is out to make sure you are running at optimum strength."

For a second, Eliza feared she would refuse, but the good doctor smiled, and Great-Aunt Iris preened, brushed an imaginary crumb from her mint-green velour tracksuit jacket, and blushed. "I'm sure I can clear my schedule."

Eliza nudged Joy's calf under the table to stem the snort she knew was brewing inside her cousin. "Don't worry, Malcolm. I will get her in this week."

"Call my surgery, and my secretary will get you in."

A tired-looking young mom tugged along two young children, a redheaded boy and a blond girl, who oohed and aahed at all the goodies in the display case. The little boy broke away from his mother's grasp, smacked his grubby little hands on the glass barrier, and swirled his tongue on the glass as he gazed longingly at the tiny cakes.

Joy gagged. "That's gross and exactly why I will never have any children."

Great-Aunt Iris smiled wistfully at the young lad as if reminiscing about her own young child, John, who had died too young, or her young nephews, Fitzwilliam and Andrew, whom she and Great-Uncle William had taken in as their own.

Eliza opened her mouth to admit that she often wanted to do as the young boy was doing, but her words froze at the look on Malcolm's face. While Joy's and Heath's radiated disgust and Great-Aunt Iris's radiated appreciation for past years, Malcolm's radiated nothing. It was as if a memory had wiped away all emotions, leaving the poor man with nothing to hold on to but a sinking black hole.

Goose bumps littered Eliza's skin, and she wanted to touch him to bring him back from the spell that bound him, but she feared he would shatter into pieces. Joy, Heath, and Great-Aunt Iris were all still captivated by the drooling child and the struggling young mom trying to break her sucker fish of a son away from the display case. Someone needed to break Malcolm from the evil spell he was under. She was about to put her hand on his forearm when the young boy squealed in protest as his mother tugged him away from the goodie enclosure. Malcolm started and wiped a hand over his face.

Eliza laid her hand on the back of his. "Are you okay?"

He blinked. "What?" After she gestured to the little family exiting the tearoom, he exhaled. "Oh, that. It's nothing, really."

She quirked an eyebrow.

"Can't get one past you, can I?"

"What can't you get past my niece? She does have a snappy brain. Why, a couple of months ago, she solved a murder." Great-Aunt Iris beamed with pride.

Malcolm smiled indulgently at his elderly patient. "I'm sure she did, Mrs. Darcy."

"But she did. In fact, the murderer was—"

"Aunt Iris, I don't think Dr. Hamilton has time for murder-mystery stories." Eliza bit back a smile at her pouting great-aunt and returned her attention to Malcolm. "Are you sure you're okay? You looked as if you'd seen a ghost."

"Really, it's nothing." He held up a staying hand. "As a doctor, one does not always have happy endings for all one's patients. That little boy reminded me of a patient I lost years ago, one of my first ones, actually, and deaths like those never do leave you."

Great-Aunt Iris laid a papery-skinned hand on his. "I am so sorry. I know how you feel. After my own little John passed away, I thought I would never feel happiness again. If it were not for little Fitz and Andrew, who became mine after their dear parents passed away, I am sure I never would have smiled again."

"Yes, Mrs. Darcy, one must remember the ones we still have and take joy in that." With a pained smile, he got to his feet. "I hate to leave you ladies on such a sad note, but I do have to get back to my surgery. I only came in for a coffee and a scone, but your loveliness distracted me."

Joy and Great-Aunt Iris simpered at the compliment, but Eliza couldn't shake off the feeling of unease and her pity for Malcolm.

HEATH attempted to help Great-Aunt Iris into the back of Joy's Range Rover and was promptly rewarded with a swat.

"I'm not an invalid, young man. Now, leave me be."

Eliza, standing beside Heath, watched in trepidation as her eighty-something aunt hoisted herself into the back of the SUV, and she kept her body near in case she had to catch her falling relative.

Great-Aunt Iris clipped on her seat belt. "See? I told you I was fine."

"You did complain of a 'dodgy hip,' so I was trying to be helpful." Heath shrugged and shook his head ruefully.

Great-Aunt Iris tsked. "When I want you to be helpful, I'll let you know."

Eliza rolled her eyes at Joy, who grinned at her and Heath from the Rover's driver's seat.

Out of the corner of her eye, Eliza spotted Chief Constable Kapoor followed by Police Commissioner Amelia Cronk coming out of the bank. They slinked to a dark-blue BMW and darted looks up and down the sidewalk before Kapoor slipped into the driver's seat and Amelia the passenger seat.

"I wonder what those two are up to," Heath said.

"I was thinking that same thing." Eliza tapped her fingers on the open window of Joy's Range Rover.

"What are you waiting for, girl? Go after them." Great-Aunt Iris unbuckled her seat belt, waved off Heath's assistance again, and slipped out of the SUV. "Joy and I will find another way home." She all but dragged Joy from the driver's seat and pushed Eliza into it, then she pointed her finger at Heath, the tip of her nail close to his sternum. "You go with Eliza and keep her safe."

Heath barely got out "I'll do my best, ma'am" before Great-Aunt Iris tugged Joy down the sidewalk and toward a chemist shop, claiming, "Come along, girl. I need pads for my bunions."

It didn't take long for Eliza to catch up to the BMW, and she made sure to keep a significant distance between her and Kapoor and Amelia. And instead of cursing the cars that zipped in and out of traffic or pulled out in front of her, she welcomed them as camouflage. They passed through several villages, and Eliza nearly lost her quarry in the winding and twisting roads of a larger village.

Eliza squinted at the clock display. "Good grief, we've been driving for over an hour. Where are we?"

"We're in Great Manchester, but I'm not familiar with this county." A village sign loomed on the horizon, and as soon as Heath could make it out, he said, "Looks like we're about to enter Marple."

"As in Miss Marple?"

Heath grinned. "You're the Christie expert."

Eliza added *research origins of Miss Marple's name* to her list, and when the BMW pulled to the curb, she did the same. "They're certainly not in their jurisdiction anymore."

Kapoor and Amelia exited the car, and by the time they reached the front door of a building in the shape of a giant wicker beehive, Kapoor looked as if he would rather slam the door in her face than open it and usher her through.

Eliza grabbed Heath's hand and dragged him down the sidewalk toward the beehive-shaped building.

"What's your plan?" Heath asked as they neared the front door painted a honey yellow and overlaid with painted bees swarming the surface, welcoming all to the Beehive Inn.

Eliza laughed at the sign declaring Open for Bees-ness. "Not thinking we'll have an issue coming up with one on the fly. You make a scene, and I'll look at the guest registry. Also, pretend we're madly in love."

"Pretend?" His face fell, and his hand went limp in hers.

"Oh, you know what I mean. Make it obvious that you can't wait to get me alone."

After Eliza placed one of her rings on her left ring finger, turning it so the gold band showed, she and Heath stumbled through the door, arm in arm and nearly chest to chest. They bumped into the reception desk, and Heath nearly bent Eliza in half and kissed her until her toes curled into her half boots and she figured she would turn into a gooey puddle on the floor. With her wits still about her, Eliza broke off the kiss and rested her elbows on the reception desk's counter, which was painted to look like a honeycomb.

The blushing receptionist blinked at them behind thick-lensed glasses, giving the fifty-something gray-haired lady an owlish appearance. Bedazzled bees decked out with yellow and black rhinestones darted to and fro over the woman's honey-colored button-up shirt as her chest heaved. "Can I, can I... ahem... Can I help you?" She adjusted her name tag engraved with the name Margaret.

Heath nuzzled Eliza's neck, and she squealed and playfully swatted him. "We just got married."

"At the registry office." Heath nibbled Eliza's earlobe and beamed at the receptionist, who blushed crimson and tucked a piece of wayward hair behind her ear.

Eliza thrust her left ring finger so close to the receptionist's face that Margaret tilted her head back to get a good look. "And we're looking for a room." She leaned across the counter and folded her hands as if in prayer. "Please tell us you have a room available for... well..."

Margaret stammered, "Well, now, I don't... um ..." Her gaze darted about in panic and eventually spotted an open ledger on the desk behind her. She cuddled it to her bosom as if it were a shield to ward off any young-lover vibes and plonked it down on a lower shelf on her side of the counter. "I have several rooms available. Let me see." She sent them a wary glance before going back to the ledger.

Eliza elbowed Heath in the ribs.

He howled in pain and crumpled to the floor.

Eliza yelped. "Oh, please, my boyfr—my husband needs help. Please help."

Margaret peeked over the counter, and at the sight of the prostrate and handsome man writhing on the floor, she shot to her feet and knelt beside him. "Are you okay?" she shouted in his ear. "Can you hear me?"

Heath cringed, and Eliza guessed it wasn't an act but was actually pain from the woman's voice piercing his eardrum.

Eliza pawed at the woman's upper arm. "He has these fits often... since childhood. He needs a place to sit while the fit passes."

Heath mouthed, "Fit? Really?" when Margaret's attention was on taking his pulse. He closed his eyes again and allowed a small trail of drool to dribble down his chin.

"Oh dear, this fit's particularly bad. Please help him!" Eliza cried.

"We should call the ambulance," Margaret said while palpating Heath's chest rather unnecessarily.

Eliza patted her skinny jeans and hoped the sound of her hand clunking against her phone in her back pocket went unnoticed. "Drat! I must have forgotten my phone in the registry office."

Margaret pulled her phone from her pocket. "I've got mine right here."

Eliza inwardly cursed the woman and the woman's phone. "No, look, the worst is over now. He needs to sit for a moment." She pointed at Heath, who leaned up on his elbow and gave them a wobbly smile.

The woman quirked an eyebrow.

"Margaret. Maggie. May I call you Maggie? I've always loved how that name rolls off the tongue." Heath's silky voice tempted the receptionist's gaze from Eliza to him.

Margaret blushed and stammered, "Yes, yes, of course."

"Well, then, Maggie, if you could be a dear and help me to my feet and find me a comfortable chair away from prying eyes while I recover, I would forever be in your debt."

Eliza pictured the woman swooning as Joy's fictional heroines did when confronted with handsome and charming maleness.

Heath wrapped an arm around the woman's solid shoulders, winked at Eliza behind Margaret's back, and shuffled to the office. Not wasting a moment, Eliza zipped around the counter and ran her finger down the page of names. Apparently, bees-ness at the Beehive Inn was slow. Out of the ten rooms available, two were booked. Room six was assigned to a Mr. and Mrs. Giovanni from Naples, Italy, and room two was reserved by a Mr. and Mrs. Smith from London.

Eliza rolled her eyes. She hadn't taken Kapoor for a fool, but apparently, she'd been wrong. No one in their right mind would use the stereotypical incognito name if they wanted to, in fact, remain incognito. Eliza shrugged. *Not my circus, not my monkeys.* She had more than enough monkeys wreaking havoc among her circus without taking on two more.

"Oh yes, please tell my lovely wife that she shouldn't alarm my poor mother, as that will send Mummy into an unnecessary tizzy." Heath's voice sailed from the back office.

Eliza zipped around the reception desk, dug out her phone, and placed it to her ear. "Yes, Mrs. Tilney, I will be sure dear Heath gets plenty of rest. Yes, I... just a minute." Eliza held her palm over the receiver end of her cell phone. "How's my dear husband doing?"

"He's on the mend and doing much better and told me to tell you *not* to tell his mum."

Eliza put on her best sheepish look and winced. "What he doesn't know won't kill him, right?"

Margaret tapped her finger to her nose. "Your secret is safe with me."

"While my sweetheart is resting, may I book a room, please?"

"Of course, of course." Margaret dipped her head and examined the ledger. "Let me see..."

"Oh, please tell me you have room number one open. One is my favorite number." She leaned across the counter and dropped her voice. "And as two became one today, I think it would be good luck, don't you think?"

Margaret stammered, blushed, and brushed at the bees dotting her shirt. "Of course, of course."

"This isn't the honeymoon suite, is it?" Heath fingered the white lace curtains embroidered with bees. "And what's with all the bees?"

"It's the Beehive Inn." Eliza exited the tiny bathroom with a glass, sadly not covered in anything bee-ish, and gestured for Heath to join her at the adjoining wall between their room and that of "the Smiths." She placed the glass's opening against the wallpaper swarming with bees and placed her ear to the bottom of it.

"Does that actually work?" Heath eyed the glass.

"It does in books and movies. Now shush." Eliza closed her eyes and concentrated.

For a second, she thought she had failed, but voices from the other side leaked through the walls and into the glass. Eliza's excitement quickly died, however, and she slid the glass off the wall and slouched on the nearby bed. "You want to know what's ironic?"

Heath sat beside her on the bee-spattered bedspread and tucked her into his side. "That we're on our 'honeymoon' in a room that looks like it could produce honey at any moment?" His smile faded.

"Oh no, you don't mean...?" He took the cup from her hand, pressed it to the wall, and after a few seconds, rejoined her. "Bloody hell! What are the odds that Mr. and Mrs. Smith are actually Mr. and Mrs. Smith from London?"

"Well, it sure isn't Kapoor and Cronk." Eliza chewed on her bottom lip and pounded her thigh with a fist.

"Don't worry. I'll be back in a jiffy." Heath kissed the top of her head and left the room, leaving Eliza alone with all the bees.

When Eliza got to two hundred on the bee count, Heath came waltzing through the door with a new key card and a grin. "Who's ready for a room change?"

"How did you manage that?"

"Maggie and I have a right understanding, I think."

"You wooed her into that key card, didn't you?"

"A gentleman never tells."

Eliza collected her purse, mumbling, "Gentleman my foot," and zipped out after him.

After gaining entry to room seven, Eliza collected a glass for herself and a glass for Heath, and they pressed them to the adjoining wall between their room and that of "the Giovannis."

"Bingo," Eliza hissed when Kapoor's Irish accent sailed through the wall.

"...and I wouldn't be too sure that your *precious* fiancé doesn't know your dirty little secret already. I've heard grumblings, you know. As much as he's a feckin eejit for wanting to marry you, he's not as dumb as he looks. I think he's put two and two together." Kapoor's thicker-than-normal Irish brogue was laced with anger, and Eliza imagined spittle flying from his mouth and flecking poor Amelia's ruddy face.

Cronk's resounding curse word, foul enough to make even Heath's eyebrows shoot to his hairline, had Eliza rethinking her piteous description of the police commissioner. Eliza winced at the sound of something slapping a hard surface, but when no outrage or "ow" accompanied the slap, Eliza assumed no physical harm had been done—yet.

"How I deal with my fiancé is my affair, not yours." Amelia's voice cut through the wall. "Besides, me having another man's baby is a far cry more forgivable than a man, an officer of the law no less, up to his neck in criminal activity." Papers rustled.

"Where did you get these?" Kapoor's voice had taken on a quiet quality that made Eliza's skin crawl.

"You made your first mistake when you took me for a fool." Amelia laughed. "Go ahead. Rip them apart. I know where the originals are, and I can prove without a shadow of a doubt where you were the Friday night of Felix Payne's murder."

Kapoor snarled.

"Oh, and if anything happens to me, I have arranged for these pics to be published in every newspaper in the UK."

Eliza's palms stung. She blinked at her whitened knuckles, released her tight fists, and rubbed at the crescent shapes indented in her palms.

"Where was he Friday night?" Heath whispered.

Eliza waved away his question and pressed her ear harder on the glass.

"See here? What would a law-abiding citizen and renowned member of the police force be doing meeting with one of the most dangerous Irish mobsters in the UK? I wonder what would happen if a rather plucky and go-getter reporter got a whiff of this?"

"That's none of your business," Kapoor hissed.

"Oh, that's where you're wrong. It is very much my business and will continue to be my business."

Eliza placed the glass on the bedside table and attacked a cuticle. "If we could somehow get Amelia to work with us, we could ruin

Kapoor, get him fired, and then Wentworth would be out from under his destructive power."

Heath shook his head. "Why don't we concentrate on proving Wentworth's innocence before we go after proving Kapoor's guilt?"

"When did you get so wise?"

"When one spends time with the wise"—he took her hand—"one becomes wise."

Eliza laughed and smacked his chest. "Careful, Maggie will get jealous."

"Maggie, shmaggie. There's only one girl for me." He kissed her.

"Enough of your shenanigans." Eliza sidled off the bed. "We have work to do."

"I wasn't committing any shenanigans. I was trying to have a romantic moment."

Eliza eyed all the bees on every conceivable surface of the room. "Not sure that's possible in this environment. Anyhoo, we must get back to the team. While Kapoor still might have orchestrated Wentworth's entrapment, he didn't kill Felix."

"But he could have paid to have it done. If he's in league with mobsters, I wouldn't put it past him knowing a guy."

Eliza sat for a few moments and tossed about ideas. "It's no use. I need my crime board."

"How about we get some nosh before hitting the road?"

Eliza's stomach rumbled in agreement. She hadn't eaten since breakfast at the Trusty Teapot, and she'd had only one scone and her tea. "Should we see what the Beehive Inn has for lunch options?"

Heath's forehead furrowed. "I bet you honey will be somewhere on the menu."

"I one-up you and bet that honey will be in *everything* on the menu."

An hour later, they left the Beehive Inn with stomachs full of honey-glazed carrots, honey-garlic-glazed salmon, honey-balsamic-glazed brussels sprouts, and baked brie in puff pastry drizzled with a generous dose of honey.

Eliza rested her head against the passenger window and groaned. "I don't think I'll ever be able to eat honey again."

Heath chuckled as he maneuvered out of village traffic and onto the winding country road leading them back to Pemberley. "Or look at it."

Watching the countryside zoom by hypnotized Eliza, and before she knew it, the Range Rover's wheels crunched on Pemberley's graveled driveway. She jerked to attention, wiped the drool from her face, and squinted at Heath. "How'd we get here so quickly?"

"Time flies when you're sleeping for half of the drive." Heath grinned and put the SUV in park. "Come on, Sleeping Beauty. We have a report to give the team."

Chapter Eighteen
Wine 'Em and Dine 'Em

I never thought I'd be sad to say farewell to Bath, but as I write this diary entry, I can hear the servants rushing about carrying trunks and whatnot to the chaise and four. While I shall not miss the Lower Rooms, I shall miss Sydney Gardens and, of course, visiting with Anne. I invited her and Captain Wentworth to Pemberley, and they accepted our invitation. I hear Darcy call me; the carriage is ready for our departure. Bath has been an adventure, and one that I will treasure.
Lizzy Bennet Darcy
Bath 1814

Eliza felt like a butterfly pinned in a display case. All eyes were on her. Some gaped in astonishment while others blinked as if computing what she had told them.

"You mean to say that that blighter Kapoor is in cahoots with the Irish mob?" Wentworth rubbed his face so hard and so long Eliza feared he would rub his features clean off.

Eliza squirmed under Wentworth's gaze. "That's what I heard through a glass and a wall. Perhaps Amelia is mistaken?"

"No, no." Wentworth's hand sliced the air. "Things make some bloody sense now."

"But how does this help Wentworth's case?" Joy asked.

Eliza chewed on a marker tip and glared at the cardboard crime board. Even with Kapoor off the table for murder—at least the getting-his-hands-dirty bit—it didn't disprove the involvement of any-one else.

"What happens if we take Kapoor completely off the suspect list?" Heath interrupted Wentworth's building growl. "Now, now, hear me out. We have too many puzzle pieces on the table, so to speak. If we limit the amount of information we're looking at, we eliminate certain facts quicker."

"So, if we remove Kapoor from the board, who's left?" Eliza asked.

"Oliver Wright," Garrison piped up. "I told you from the begin-ning he was the one, but did anyone believe me? No." He crossed his arms. "You all went on a wild-goose chase, and look where that's got me." He flung his arms about, signifying the tiny, cramped room.

"You?" Great-Aunt Iris laid her knitting on her lap and pinned him with a regal glare. "How, young man, does any of this revolve around you?"

"I—well..." Garrison's mouth opened and closed several times, but the sustained look from Great-Aunt Iris had him shutting his lips, crossing his arms again, and closing himself off from the rest in a sustained and pouty silence.

"As much as it pains me to say, Garrison may have a point." Eliza held up a finger to stem Garrison's victory speech. "Oliver has the strongest motive to kill Felix and frame Wentworth. Really, with Timothy's death, Oliver is our only viable suspect left."

"But no one saw him at the pub at the time in question," Joy said.

"Remember, though, hemlock can take time to take effect. He could have gotten his hands on some hemlock and administered the dose before the events at the pub, and by crushing some and plant-ing the evidence in the rooms, confusing everyone about the time of the administration of the poison. By using poison, he gave himself an alibi." Eliza circled the air around the board with her marker. "Does anyone else get the strange feeling that we're missing a vital piece of evidence on our crime board?"

"Perhaps you're peckish and in need of one of Cook's treats." Great-Aunt Iris's needles clicked along melodically to her dietary advice.

"No," Joy said, "Eliza's right. There's something niggling at the back of my mind too. Something someone said in this room."

The sense of urgency to remember said forgotten thing affected everyone except Garrison, who busied himself with sulking and muttering.

"Cop gut is one thing, but facts are facts." Wentworth groaned as he got to his feet. He'd always been a robust man but an active one, and Eliza suspected that the cramped space and forced silence had taken their toll on Wentworth's body. "If we look at this subjectively, Oliver Wright fits the magical three—means, motive, and opportunity. With his past, we know he's not scared of violence, and in his diseased little mind, he has ample reason to want my career destroyed and me to be behind bars and for poor Felix to die. Sadly, if what Garrison says is true about Timothy being a stooge in Oliver's employ, then it's quite possible that Oliver tired of Timothy or thought him a liability and offed him."

"If that's true, we've caught the murderer of two men, and if we can bring evidence against Kapoor, we can relieve him of his position and job, which would in turn free you from his claws. You're a free man." Eliza pumped her hand.

"As much as I want to celebrate with you, more people than Kapoor want my head on a silver platter, and knowing that he's in cahoots with the Irish mob..." Wentworth shrugged.

"But for this case, this indictment against you, we can clear your name." Eliza placed her hands on his shoulders and shook him. She ignored his raised eyebrows and shirking shoulders. "Don't you see? You're a free man, and you don't have to be his roommate anymore."

She jabbed a finger in Garrison's direction. "And you can arrest him, something you've been itching to do for a while, right?"

"Hey! There was no need to remind him of that," Garrison whined.

"But what if Oliver didn't do it?" Joy asked.

A sliver of unease pierced Eliza's conscience, but she was tired. Tired of hiding Wentworth, tired of dealing with Garrison, tired of worrying about how to decorate a tiny prison cell, and plain old tired. "It's not like we're sending him to the dungeons or to the gallows. Besides, with every one of our suspects either dead or alibied, Oliver is the only one left."

"So, all in favor of declaring Oliver Wright the perpetrator?" Heath raised his hand.

One by one, all except Garrison, who pouted even harder in the corner, raised their hands but slowly and without any zest.

"Okay, then." Eliza rubbed her hands together. "So, Wentworth, now what?"

He narrowed his eyes at a spot on the floor and was quiet so long, Eliza suspected he hadn't heard her.

"Went—"

He cut the air with his hand. "This doesn't feel right."

"Do you always make an arrest on the suspicion that you're right or on the basis of evidence?"

"Evidence."

"We have the evidence." Eliza's fingers ticked off each item on her list as she spoke. "We have Oliver pinned for means. The poison. Opportunity. Poison takes time, giving him an alibi, and motive. You sent him to prison, and Felix screwed him over. Timothy probably overplayed his hand, forgetting he was dealing with a hardened criminal. If you weren't stuck in this hellhole and were the lead investigator in this, would you arrest him?"

"Yes."

"Of course you would, you bloody idiot," Garrison muttered.

A memory clicked in Eliza's brain, and before Wentworth could launch himself on her slimy cousin, Eliza clapped a hand on his shoulder. "Wait." She tapped the marker tip against her lips. "The day in the pub when Timothy showed Kapoor the dried hemlock and was essentially laughed at by Kapoor..."

"What about it?" Heath asked.

"I heard Oliver mumble 'bloody idiot' under his breath as Kapoor left the pub. I had thought he was essentially airing his general beliefs about the man, but he had been eyeing the hemlock... and not in an I-wonder-what-it-is kind of way but more like he knew what it was but was trying to figure out how it ended up in a baggie and on the bar of the Foxed Hound."

"So what are you saying?" Joy asked.

"I'm saying that Oliver called Kapoor an idiot not as simply an insult but due to the fact that Kapoor literally missed a vital clue, the poison, that was foisted on him. Yeah, looking back, Oliver seemed to take an interest in the dried substance, even so far as to give it one last glance before leaving. Would he take such interest in dried baby's breath? I highly doubt it. However, I'd take interest, too, if my murderous ways confronted me from a plastic baggie."

"Could that be why Timothy got beat up?" Joy asked. "It makes sense to think that Oliver wouldn't blink an eye at beating someone to death in order to get information out of him. I'd move heaven and earth, if I were a murderer, of course, to find out how and where someone found evidence of my nefarious deeds."

"And if the victim doesn't talk, then make sure he doesn't ever speak at all." Heath squinted at the crime board. "Poor Timothy had no clue he was signing his death warrant when he was swinging that little baggie around, did he?" He grabbed the marker from Eliza's hand and circled Oliver's name.

"So, we really got our man?" Joy asked.

A smile twitched at Eliza's lips, but dread clenched her heart and melted her growing smile into a frown.

WEDNESDAY morning dawned bright, and hints of light seeped through the curtains. Eliza cracked an eye open and stared into Caesar's yellow-slitted gaze. He yawned, offering her a gaping view of his sharp teeth and pink tongue, which he used to groom her hairline. She shooed him away, rolled onto her stomach, and buried her face in her pillow. Caesar, undeterred, sat on her lower back and kneaded her backside.

While Caesar busied himself with squishing her squishy bits around, Eliza concocted a plan. First, she would make an anonymous phone call to the police station. Second... Eliza's mind blanked. There was no second part of the plan. Wentworth was still a wanted man, and just because Kapoor had a second suspect didn't mean he would remove his talons from Wentworth's throat. And until Kapoor was exposed for the criminal he was, the chief constable had power over Wentworth.

"I need to talk to Amelia." Eliza catapulted from her bed, and Caesar, whose cat reflexes saved him from crashing to the floor, glared at her from the edge of the bed. "Don't pout, buddy."

Caesar went on pouting while Eliza hurriedly dressed and even squeaked through the partially closed en suite bathroom door to pout as Eliza applied blush and mascara and pulled her hair into a messy chignon.

"How about we get Mrs. B to cook up some kippers for you?" Eliza petted his silky fur and twirled one ear gently between her fingers. Mrs. Bankcroft rarely cooked anything special at Eliza's request, but for Caesar, she would whip up a five-course meal with a smile.

Caesar's upright tail twitched, and he followed Eliza out the door, down the hall and steps, and as soon as the kitchen door came into view, he darted around her and zipped into Mrs. Bankcroft's domain.

"Good morning, Master Caesar." Mrs. Bankcroft set the bowl of eggs she'd been whisking on the wooden kitchen counter and scratched between the feline's ears.

"Good morning, Mrs. B." Eliza slid onto a kitchen stool, set her elbows on the counter, and rested her chin in her hands.

"And a good morning to you, Miss Eliza." Mrs. Bankcroft finished massaging Caesar's ears and did a double take at Eliza. "Why, what's wrong, my girl?"

Eliza flicked at a crumb Mrs. B's usually vigorous cleaning had missed. "Nothing."

"Now don't you go lying to Mrs. B, now." She pushed the bowl of eggs toward Eliza. "Here. I find beating things helps with stress. Now talk."

Eliza beat the eggs as instructed, but instead of talking, she glared sulkily into the mixture. At the cook's clearing throat, Eliza huffed. "Fine. Have you ever had to do something that you knew was wrong, but you couldn't find a way out of it?"

"This about the detective chief inspector you're hiding in the attic?"

The whisk hit the edge of the bowl, flipped out, and sent whipped egg flying everywhere. Eliza's jaw dropped. Even Caesar paused in his toe-licking and blinked at Mrs. Bankcroft.

"But... how..." Eliza stared at the cook.

"I might look a fool, and an old one at that, but it wasn't too hard to put two and two together."

Eliza opened her mouth but snapped it shut again. After several seconds, she tried again. "But I still don't understand. How did you... Willow said no one else knew. Does anyone else besides you two know?"

"Of course. Tash. Do you really think you could have kept your secret without Tash and myself?" Mrs. Bankcroft crossed her arms.

"Oh, Mrs. B, I'm sorry." Eliza zipped around the counter and hugged her. "I should have known I could trust you and Tash."

Mrs. Bankcroft unstiffened and patted Eliza's back. "There, there, that's enough of this nonsense." After Eliza let her go, Mrs. Bankcroft fiddled with her apron.

Panic seized Eliza's heart. "Does Mrs. Under—"

Mrs. Bankcroft laid a knobby finger to her lips. "Shush, now, Miss Eliza. No, no one else knows. And now that I know Willow knows, I'll make sure she's doing her part to keep your secret." She must have sensed Eliza gearing up to give her another hug, and she pointed at the kitchen stool. "Quit asking questions, sit, and whisk those eggs."

Too afraid to disobey, Eliza plopped onto the stool and did as told. Mrs. Bankcroft sprinkled flour on the wooden counter, plopped dough from a towel-covered bowl onto it, and started kneading the mixture. After several minutes, Eliza sniffled and swished away a tear. Dear old Mrs. Bankcroft and Tash. Another tear plopped off her cheek and missed the bowl of eggs by a hair's breadth.

Mrs. Bankcroft pushed the bowl away from Eliza and, with a flour-covered thumb, swiped at a hot tear streaming down Eliza's face. "There's no reason to go crying in my eggs. Does this something wrong that you don't want to do have to do with you-know-who?" She pointed at the ceiling.

Eliza nodded.

"And you-know-who is innocent, right?"

Again, Eliza nodded.

"Well, then, Miss Eliza, it seems simple to me. Whatever wrong thing must be done to free the innocent, then you must do the wrong thing."

There was so much to explain, but Mrs. Bankcroft's kitchen help would arrive at any moment. Eliza would have to discuss everything with her later. "Mrs. B, you are a godsend, and if I haven't told you before, you and Tash are lifesavers, and I treasure you."

Mrs. Bankcroft blushed, and she swooshed at Eliza with a towel. "Get along with you now, Miss Eliza, and stay out of trouble." Before Eliza reached the kitchen door, Mrs. Bankcroft loudly whispered, "And the sooner Pemberley gets back to normal the better, don't you think?"

Eliza smiled and left the warmth of Mrs. Bankcroft's kitchen. *How in the world did I ever think I could get away with anything without those two old bloodhounds sniffing out my secret?* So much for Kapoor's bloodhounds sniffing out her dirty little secret. Kapoor would burst a blood vessel knowing two household staff had done something his prized constables could not. All the way to her great-uncle and -aunt's bedroom, she scolded herself for not trusting them. She knocked softly and tapped her toes as she waited for either her great-uncle or Great-Aunt Iris to open the door. Finally, her great-aunt appeared. Resplendent in a tropical-patterned kimono, she looked like she belonged on a beach somewhere, sipping a frothy pink drink complete with pink umbrella.

"You look like you're ready for a day at the beach." Eliza leaned down and kissed her great-aunt's proffered cheek.

"It's your great-uncle's favorite too." Great-Aunt Iris blushed.

Eliza's face warmed, and she cleared her throat. "Good to, ah, know. Anyway, I need your help with something." Eliza darted a look at the ceiling. "Can you be down for breakfast in thirty minutes?"

Great-Aunt Iris tapped her finger to the side of her nose. "Nothing like a bit of spy work in the morning to keep one young, I say."

Eliza was making her way to the breakfast room, tossing around what her next steps would be, when a hand pulled her into a curtained alcove.

Heath stemmed her yelp of surprise with a kiss that left her breathless. She broke off the kiss for air and rested her head on his chest. His heart hammered against her ear, reminding her that with all the chaos and unknown clouding her existence, Heath wouldn't be leaving her. He was staying. For her. For them.

"I love you," she whispered.

He tilted her chin with his finger. "I love you more."

She grinned. "Prove it."

And he did and would have continued to if not for an attack of knitting needles wielded by a five-foot-one-inch white-haired warrior wearing an emerald-green tracksuit.

Eliza scrambled to straighten her top, patted her extra-messy chignon, and stared at her great-aunt swathed with heavy brocade curtains. "How did you know we were in here?"

Great-Aunt Iris gave a grand snort. "Why does the younger generation think they were the first to commit shenanigans?"

Heath shuddered and, when Great-Aunt Iris poked him in the rib with a knitting needle, released Eliza. "And you, young man, have a question to ask my nephew, don't you?"

"Lord Darcy? What question would I have for him, Mrs. Darcy?"

"No. Mr. Tilney, Eliza's father, Andrew."

Heath's red face drained of color then reddened again. "Um, yes, of course, Mrs. Darcy, but don't you think it—"

Great-Aunt Iris tutted. "I don't think, young man. I know." She grabbed Eliza's hand. "Now, my dear, what is it you wanted from me?"

Eliza gave Heath a helpless shrug as her great-aunt towed her away from the alcove and down the hall.

ELIZA paced the floor of the drawing room, rarely used except for important company. Not that Amelia Cronk was important company, but she was someone Eliza needed to impress. If the mint-condition Regency-era furniture, priceless paintings, and vibrant tapestries couldn't impress Amelia, then Eliza was in trouble. Granted, Amelia had seen Pemberley, but she hadn't seen the opulent drawing room. Hopefully, the shock value of seeing the room, learning of Great-Aunt Iris's connections, and partaking of Cook's opulent tea service would woo Amelia into playing her hand with Kapoor quicker than she might have intended. To free Wentworth from Pemberley's attics, Eliza had to ensure that Kapoor, at least for the time being, had no power over the DCI.

"How do I look?" Heath walked into the room and spread his arms.

Eliza swallowed. "You look, ah..."

"Like a right lord of the manor?"

She was used to seeing him in his starched dress shirts, but the sapphire-blue cashmere V-neck sweater partnered with an open-collar white dress shirt and dark-gray chinos gave him an air of relaxed sensuality, of a man who had not a care in the world but to topple back into the sumptuous bed he'd crawled out of. And from the way he'd tousled and gelled his dark hair, Eliza figured that was the impression he wanted to give. And it was working.

He ambled over, kissed her, and rested his cheek on top of her head. "Do you think I'll woo Amelia into spilling all her secrets?"

Eliza played her finger down the V cut of his sweater and back up. If she wasn't careful, he would woo all of Eliza's secrets out of her, including the time she'd written letters to herself from her crush. "I think if you're not careful, you might even make Great-Aunt Iris fall in love with you."

Heath laughed and spun her around. "You look gorgeous."

Eliza fingered her cream-and-gold cable-knit sweater dress, which was cinched at the waist with a gold belt. "It's not too informal, is it?"

"It's perfect." He smiled and pulled her in for a kiss, but at the squeaky footsteps coming down the hallway, he backed away with a wink, sat on a settee, picked up a book lying on the coffee table, and pretended to read.

Great-Aunt Iris, royally wrapped in a black dress and a pearl necklace and with matching earrings, strutted on squeaking black Velcro-strapped shoes into the drawing room. "Where's Joy?"

"She drew the short straw. We're so close to being done with this charade that I would hate if something—or someone—ruined it, so she's babysitting." It was a favor Eliza knew Joy would hold over her for a long time.

"You look a picture, Mrs. Darcy." Heath smiled up at Great-Aunt Iris and was rewarded with a regal nod.

"You as well, Mr. Tilney. Perhaps my great-niece is not so daft after all."

Heath coughed on a laugh and hid his face in his book, and Eliza sighed in relief when the doorbell rang. In a few moments, Amelia Cronk, the one woman who had the power to release Wentworth from Kapoor's hold and Pemberley's attic, would walk through the drawing room door.

"Everybody know your parts?" Eliza whispered as she settled herself into a mahogany chair and picked up a magazine on the British countryside.

"Do you want me to retell the story of how I made a right arse of myself in children's theater?" Heath grinned.

Tash opened the door. "Miss Amelia Cronk, ma'am."

"Thank you, Tash." Great-Aunt Iris struggled to her feet and waved away Heath's helping hand. "Do come in, Miss Cronk. I hope you do not mind that I invited my great-niece, Eliza, and her... intended... Mr. Heath Tilney."

Amelia, dressed in an unflattering outfit of brown tweeds, ignored Eliza and latched her gaze on Heath. Her pupils dilated, and Eliza couldn't blame her. "Hello again, Mr. Tilney and Miss Darcy." Amelia gave Eliza a cursory nod and smiled at Great-Aunt Iris. "It's so kind of you to invite me, Mrs. Darcy."

"Think nothing of it. It is you who is kind enough to humor an old woman." She held up a finger to stem whatever Amelia was going to say. "Eliza dear, will you ring for tea, please?"

Eliza fulfilled the request and, as she did so, took in Amelia's form. Still frumpy, still frazzled. Nothing about the woman screamed "police and crime commissioner," and nothing about her would lead anyone to think she was having romantic liaisons behind her fiancé's back. Perhaps Amelia had blackmailed Kapoor into using his position and illegal connections to rig the election for Amelia, and in return, Amelia would use her position to keep him in his. Eliza shivered. She hated blackmailers, and from what she'd overheard at the Beehive Inn, Amelia was one slick customer.

"So, Amelia. May I call you Amelia? I've always loved how that name rolls off the tongue." A lazy smile curved Heath's lips.

Eliza swallowed a snort. *Good grief!* First with the Beehive Inn lady and now with Amelia. If he had tried that with her months ago on the plane when they first met, she would have punched him. She chewed her lip and watched Heath flirt his way into Amelia's trust. On second thought, she'd have probably done what Amelia was currently doing: staring doe-eyed at the handsome blue-eyed Englishman with enough freckles to make him look harmless but with a smile that promised a less-than-innocent experience. Eliza's body warmed, and she distracted herself by arranging a scone with raspberries and clotted cream and two cucumber sandwiches on a china plate.

Eliza settled herself in a wingback chair and winked at her great-aunt. Time to get the show started. "So, Amelia, I hope you're feeling better than you were when I last saw you."

"Oh yes, thank you." Amelia's hand rested on her distended belly.

"That's good. I hear the first trimester is the roughest."

Amelia blushed. "Yes, I... uh..."

"Eliza, don't you see you've made her uncomfortable?" Heath rested his hand on the back of Amelia's chair and dropped his voice to a stage whisper. "Americans and their brash way of speaking."

Eliza's face warmed, and despite knowing his words were all an act, she clenched and unclenched her hands. "I'm sorry, Amelia. Heath tries to train the American in me right out, but he can't make any headway." She smiled as graciously as possible. "I hope that you and Chief Constable Kapoor—"

Great-Aunt Iris gasped and clinked her teacup on its saucer. "Please do not mention that odious man."

"Aunt, please," Eliza hissed. "Amelia here probably doesn't want to hear your grievances."

"No." Amelia sat forward, and her eyes glinted. "As a commissioner, I realize it is my duty to know of any issues."

Great-Aunt Iris shook her head. "No, my niece is correct. I mustn't air our family's troubles to complete strangers."

"But Amelia isn't a stranger, Mrs. Darcy, and besides, in her capacity as the police and crime commissioner, she has the power to help you and Lord Darcy, of course," Heath said.

"Lord Darcy?" Amelia's eyes sharpened at the name drop. "This affects Lord Darcy as well?"

Great-Aunt Iris dabbed at the corner of her eyes with a daintily embroidered handkerchief. "No, Eliza's correct. I cannot speak. My nephew would not appreciate me airing his private affairs, especially as it concerns money matters."

Amelia's gaze zeroed in on Great-Aunt Iris. Suppressing a grin, Eliza sat beside her great-aunt, leaned over, and whispered loud enough so the hawk-eyed and eagle-eared Amelia wouldn't miss a word. "I think Uncle should be the one discussing the matter that Kapoor's presence is keeping him from making a million-pound donation to the constabulary."

Amelia spluttered, and seemingly remembering that she wasn't supposed to hear a whispered conversation, patted at her throat. "Sorry, I swallowed wrong." She checked her watch. "I, uh, have another appointment." She got to her feet and held out a hand to Great-Aunt Iris. "Mrs. Darcy, thank you so much for inviting me and for the lovely tea. And if you need anything, please do not hesitate to reach out." After writing something on a business card, she handed it to Iris. "My personal mobile number is on the back."

"Thank you, Miss Cronk. It is refreshing to know that a woman of your caliber is in charge of our wonderful constabulary. I will make sure that my dear nephew, Lord Darcy, hears of your kindness."

"You are too kind, Mrs. Darcy." After a blinding smile at Heath and a curt nod toward Eliza, Amelia left the room with a pep in her step.

"Do you think she fell for it?" Great-Aunt Iris asked.

Eliza tried to temper her excitement, but she couldn't stop the grin spreading across her lips. "I bet by the end of the day, we'll hear an announcement of Chief Constable Kapoor's early retirement."

Chapter Nineteen
Past Ghosts Rear Their Ugly Heads

Home at last. While I love traveling and experiencing the world with my family, I do so love my Pemberley. Adelaide Rose was rather fidgety on the journey, and I find myself overly exhausted and more irritated than normal. I shall seek out Cook for one of her soothing teas and then take Adelaide for a walk in the rose garden. After hours in the carriage, both of us need exercise and fresh air.
Lizzy Bennet Darcy
Pemberley 1814

Eliza's Thursday mornings were usually spent scrambling on last-minute arrangements or darting over the county on emergency shopping trips for the upcoming weekend's guests, but instead of opening her laptop to see what sort of scrambling she needed to do, she sank in her office chair, swiveled back and forth, and triple-checked her phone for information regarding Kapoor. The constabulary hadn't made an official announcement, and Eliza didn't want to rely on gossip from Joy's "resources." She worried her bottom lip between her teeth and tapped her fingers on her chair's armrest. Surely by then, Amelia had played her hand. But nothing about the case had gone to plan. Perhaps Amelia had gotten cold feet or her fear of Kapoor was greater than her greed.

The office door burst open, and Joy, followed by Heath and Great-Aunt Iris, towered over Eliza.

"Have you seen the news?" Joy swiveled her phone screen to face Eliza. "Look!"

Cross-eyed at the proximity of Joy's phone, Eliza pushed it back and squinted at the trending update via the Derbyshire Constabulary's social media post: Retirement of Chief Constable Jayesh Kapoor. Eliza didn't read the fine print. She didn't need to know what excuse Kapoor had given for such a sudden life change. Whatever it had been was sure to leave him looking holy and law-abiding instead of like the corrupt law enforcement officer he really was. Eliza sighed. He still had his connections, and Wentworth wasn't entirely out of the woods, but he could be free from Pemberley's attics very soon.

"What's the next step?" Heath asked.

"Tell Wentworth and let him do the talking. I'd really hate to screw something up this late in the game. He'll know who to talk to and what to say." Eliza headed to the door. "Let's all meet in five minutes, okay?"

After Joy and Great-Aunt Iris left, Heath gathered Eliza in an embrace. "What's wrong?"

"I feel like I'm throwing Wentworth from the hot frying pan into the fire. He was—is—a fugitive from the law. There has to be some sort of punishment for that, right?"

"But there are extenuating circumstances."

"And it wasn't only Kapoor who hated Wentworth. They can't be that stupid, to fall for Kapoor's sudden retirement and Wentworth's sudden appearance. They'll find a way to come after him, won't they?"

Heath kissed the top of her head. "Probably, but for the time being, they've lost. With the evidence so strong against Oliver and the clues leading to the obvious conclusion that Wentworth was set up, they'll have no choice but to drop the charges."

"Are you sure?"

Heath puffed out a breath and gave her one last squeeze before releasing her. "No, but he can't live in Pemberley's attics any longer, and you have to move on from this." He swiped his thumb gently across her cheeks. "You've done all you can, and you have to believe that justice will prevail."

Eliza pulled her shoulders back. "You're right. Let's get this over with."

With a churning stomach and tingling nerves, Eliza snuck through Pemberley, reluctant to give up the secret spot, and climbed the secret staircase.

Wentworth met her at the top of the steps. "Is it true?"

Joy and Great-Aunt Iris resembled cats who had gotten into the cream. So much for waiting for her to tell the good news. "That Kapoor has resigned as chief constable?"

Wentworth nodded.

"Yes, he has."

Eliza had expected a handshake, maybe even a thatta-girl slug to the shoulder. What she didn't expect was being squeezed to near unconsciousness in the bear-like arms of Detective Chief Inspector Finn Wentworth. After Eliza's claps on his back in hopes of release, he let her go so fast she stumbled backward, and he stammered, "I, uh, sorry about that." He gestured to all of her and then to all of him.

Eliza hid a smile and swooshed his apology away. "Time to power up your phone. You have calls to make. And I'm sure your wife and kids have been worried sick about you."

His face slackened. "Bloody hell. Who do I call first? My partner or my wife?"

"Who will be the least likely to forgive you if you didn't call them first?" Heath asked.

After a fifteen-minute conversation with his wife, consisting of many "I'm sorries" and dotted with a few "I'll have to fill you in laters," Wentworth took a deep breath. "Wish me luck."

While Heath kept watch over Garrison, who had already tried to sneak down the stairs and into the larger attic via the hidden panel, Eliza, Joy, and Great-Aunt Iris tuned in to Wentworth's conversation and his body language. Eliza had never experienced such a roller-coaster of emotions. One moment, Eliza was chewing her cuticles to the quick. At a frown from Wentworth, goose bumps exploded on her arms. If his voice dropped to a whisper, she squeezed the life out of Joy's hand. As Wentworth hung up after his half-hour conversation with his partner, Eliza wasn't sure if she should laugh or cry.

"Well?" Eliza circled her hands impatiently. "What did she say? Did she believe you? Is there hope?"

Wentworth thumped down on his cot and toyed with his phone. "I'm still under suspicion."

An ugly swear word escaped Eliza's lips. Great-Aunt Iris blinked at her but, instead of scolding, nodded and viciously knitted.

"But all is not bad. I now have a chance at being treated fairly. With Kapoor gone, my other enemies are, for the lack of a better word, neutered for the time being."

Great-Aunt Iris tsked and knitted more furiously than before.

"So, you'll still go to jail?" Eliza's heart sank. She had, despite all her work, failed her friend.

Wentworth shrugged and got to his feet. "I don't know exactly, but from the conversation I had with my partner, Floribeth, I have hope now." He placed his hand on Eliza's shoulder and smiled. "Hope I didn't have before."

A scuffling and stream of swear words startled Eliza, and she spun around and gaped. From the looks of her comrades, she wasn't alone in her surprise at the sight before her.

Garrison, who had been crouched in the corner, was in the middle of the tiny room, cowering before a towering five-foot-one-inch white-haired avenging angel.

With her knitting needles pointed at Garrison's chest, Great-Aunt Iris bared her teeth. "If you think for one moment that I will let you escape after all the pain you've brought upon this family and my nephew, you have another think coming. You will not evade justice a second time."

Garrison's gaze flicked from the blazing eyes of Great-Aunt Iris to the rest of the posse. "Are you going to let her threaten me like that?"

Wentworth snorted and moved a step closer. "I'm rather enjoying this, actually, and I only wish Mrs. Darcy were a few years younger. She'd be a great asset to the force." He winked at Great-Aunt Iris, who blushed but didn't object to such familiarity. "Now, are you going to choose the hard way or the easy way? The easy way won't hurt as much, but I won't object to you choosing the hard way."

For a moment, Eliza feared Garrison would choose the difficult route. With Great-Aunt Iris's knitting needles within striking distance, though, Garrison chose wisely, stood slowly, and put his arms behind his back. "I don't know why I even tried coming back." He skewered Great-Aunt Iris with a glare. "This family was always a bunch of nutters."

Heath stepped in front of Garrison, but before he could grab the man by the shirt collar, Great-Aunt Iris interceded. She placed a knitting needle directly over Garrison's heart and glared up at him. It should have been a ridiculous image, Great-Aunt Iris's nose on point with Garrison's sternum, but the sternness of her pink, flushed face and her avenging-angel halo of white hair caused Eliza's hair to stand on end. Surely, her great-aunt would not commit murder.

"There is one thing I know for a fact, Garrison Wickham. I would rather come from a family of nutters than a family whose bloodline is laced with jealousy, hatred, and the propensity to willfully destroy the lives of others. Your father was a ne'er-do-well, and your father's father was one. If we were to trace the Wickham lineage, you'd find that your sixth-great-grandfather, George Wickham, was the master of manipulation, and while he didn't succeed in destroying the Bennet family altogether, he did manage to ruin the life of at least one woman." She removed the knitting needle from his chest. "You have an opportunity to change your family tree, Garrison, but you will not do it here or anywhere else near Pemberley again."

Great-Aunt Iris did her usual three-point turn, gave Eliza a weak smile, and squeaked her way down the steps, calling after her that she was going to find her husband for a well-deserved nap.

Joy rubbed her eyes and stared at where Great-Aunt Iris used to be. "Did that just happen?"

Heath chuckled and wrapped his arm around Eliza's waist. "Yes. Yes it did."

Wentworth blew out an exaggerated breath. "Remind me to never get on your great-aunt's bad side, Eliza." He grabbed a length of rope he'd asked Eliza to get him earlier and tied Garrison's hands behind his back. "Come on. You've got an appointment you can't be late for."

Minutes later, Pemberley's courtyard was a whirlwind of activity. Constables Harris and Robinson, conveniently present due to their vigilant watchdog duties, led Garrison, cuffed and swearing, to a police car. Another constable's radio squawked out information that Oliver Wright had been apprehended. Wentworth's partner, Floribeth de Vera, a short but scrappy-looking Filipina woman, smiled brusquely at Eliza and ushered Wentworth into her car.

After watching the parade of police cars leave the estate, Eliza excused herself from Joy and Heath and trudged to the attic that had hidden Wentworth safely from the world. She crossed her arms and glared at her makeshift crime board. The elusive clue had not magically appeared. Whatever hope Wentworth had, Eliza wished he would share. For all she knew, she'd sent an innocent man back into the jowls of a corrupt law enforcement system and sent a man who had nothing to do with the murder of Felix Payne back to prison.

"You should be celebrating." Joy clinked her champagne glass against Eliza's. "Come on. Drink up."

Eliza tore her gaze from her mimosa and glared out the drawing room windows at the Friday morning sunshine and curled farther into Heath's one-armed embrace. Since Wentworth's departure, Eliza had paced for hours, and when nighttime had put an end to her erratic movements, she'd slept in fits and starts. It didn't matter whether she paced the drawing room's carpets or traipsed the tiny attic room's wooden floor or stomped on the autumnal garden's dried foliage. Even after the early-morning phone call from Wentworth filling her in on the new developments, her gut told her she was wrong.

When she only shrugged, Joy huffed. "Seriously, Wentworth's essentially on house arrest, which is better than a jail cell, until this all gets figured out, and the person who fits the means, motive, and opportunity formula is safely off the streets of Lambton, and we are enjoying your uncle's finest champagne."

Eliza gave up and sipped her drink. "I suppose you're right."

Joy beamed. "This is absolutely brill. I mean, we can get back to normal, right?" She fanned herself. "Because let me tell you, I have one doozie of a love scene to write." Her smile faded, and she studied Eliza. "You're saying that to make me shut up, aren't you?"

Eliza shook her head. "No. Seriously, everyone needs to get back to normal. I'll quit moping about. Besides, we have twitchers descending upon Pemberley in T minus nine hours, and I have work to do."

Joy checked her watch. "Well, good to know that at six, I need to hide for the remainder of the weekend." She saluted Heath and Eliza with her glass and left.

Eliza slid her hand down Heath's arm and intertwined her fingers through his. "I'm afraid I have to dash. I didn't get to my panic buying yesterday. Care to join me?"

"Wish I could, but I need to finalize some things before my new job starts and settle a few minor points with the moving company." His grin deepened, and his dimple winked at her. "Monday will be here before we know it." He brought her hand to his lips and kissed it. "I'll be back for the arrival of the bird people." He clawed his fingers and mimicked a bird of prey descending on its helpless victim.

Eliza swatted at him. "Don't let Mrs. B see you do that. You'll only give her another reason to dislike them."

After Heath left Pemberley, Eliza sat down at her laptop to print her shopping list and groaned when her phone rang. "What can a girl do around here to get any peace and quiet?" She grinned and stabbed the green phone icon. "Dad?"

"Hey, sweetie."

Tears welled up in Eliza's eyes and threatened to spill down her cheeks. "It's good to hear your voice. How is... How are..."

"Things are going well. Your mom and I, we're better and stronger than before. I, uh, wanted to say sorry, is all. Sorry for my past mistakes, sorry for betraying your and your mother's trust, sorry for being—"

"Dad, I still don't understand why you did what you did, but I forgive you. Not that you need my forgiveness or anything like that. I'm glad that Nancy was foiled again and that she wasn't able to destroy what you and Mom have." Eliza chewed her bottom lip. "Have you ever figured out who sent the letters? She couldn't have gotten her grubby little hands on them in prison, could she?" An image of Mrs. Underhill flashed through Eliza's mind, but she put it on the back burner. Maybe Uncle Fitzwilliam would have some advice for her whenever he decided to come home. "Say, when is Uncle coming back?"

"Saturday."

Eliza squeaked.

"Is something the matter?"

Eliza pursed her lips.

"Eliza? Are you in trouble?"

"No." Her voice went up at the end of the *o*. She tried again. "No." But that time, her voice was too low to be natural.

"You are in trouble, aren't you? After your last run-in with murder and mayhem, I thought you'd learned your lesson."

"I did... but... trouble found me this time." Which wasn't a lie. It was Wentworth who'd shown up sopping wet on her doorstep.

Silence reigned for several moments, and Eliza imagined her dad pinching the bridge of his nose and taking a few cleansing breaths. "I hope so, and please, Eliza, do be careful. I don't think you understand how truly devastating it would be if something were to happen to you." His voice cracked, and he cleared his throat. "Your mother and I wouldn't be able to cope, and it would probably send me—"

"Dad, I get it. You'd probably spiral into a deep, dark—"

"Now is not the time to be flippant. I'm serious."

The missing clue niggling at the back of Eliza's mind burst into clarity. "Oh my gosh. Oh my gosh."

"Eliza? What's wrong?" Her father's voice was laced with panic.

"Dad, I love you. I gotta go, though. Give my love to Mom and Uncle."

"Don't you dare hang up on me."

"Sorry, Dad," Eliza muttered as she swiped the red phone icon. That would probably earn her an impromptu visit from her parents, but if it got them back over the pond, then it was well worth it.

Her phone buzzed with a text, but she ignored what was surely a scolding from her father and tapped the phone icon next to Wentworth's name. It rang and rang and rang. "Come on. You're on house arrest. What else do you have to do but stare at your phone and wait for news?" Eliza hung up, waited three seconds, and called again. The same never-ending ringing. She considered calling the police, but she was still too raw over how they'd thrown Wentworth under the proverbial bus, driven over him, then backed up several times. *Besides, what would I even say? That a man no one has even put on their radar is responsible for Felix Payne's murder?*

She called Heath, and after a few rings, his voice messaging told her to leave her name and number after the beep. She ignored the notification that she had one unread text message. Her father would have to wait. She needed to bounce her idea off of someone. After trying to call Wentworth and Heath again, she stuffed her phone in her back pocket. She had to see Wentworth.

Fifteen minutes later, Wentworth, wrapped in a plush dark-blue robe, peered owlishly at her from his open front door. He shook his head, and beads of water clinging to his curly hair scattered in every direction, including Eliza's eyelid. "What in the bloody hell are you doing here?"

Eliza swiped at her eye, smiled brightly, and handed him a tray of Cook's biscuits. "I brought you a welcome-home present." She tried to peer inside his house, but his frame blocked her view. "You alone?"

His eyebrow quirked, and he tightened his robe belt. "Last time I checked."

She used the cookie tin as a battering ram to push him inside his house and slammed the door.

"Are you barmy? What's wrong with you?" He stared at her as if she'd grown ten heads. "I always thought you were a nutter, but now you've convinced me of it." Gesturing for her to follow him, he led her into a tidy and cozy living room.

"That's probably true, but I certainly wouldn't be here with you dressed as you are if you had answered your phone." She gestured at his robe, paced to a leaded-glass picture window facing the empty street, and peeked through the edge of the lace curtain. "I didn't know you lived on the edge of town."

"I like my seclusion. Now, sit down and tell me what's gotten you in a dither."

Eliza, still clutching the cookie tin, sat on a dark-brown leather chair. "Remember that elusive clue we couldn't remember?" When Wentworth nodded, Eliza continued. "Do you also remember telling us about the child that Felix was accused of killing but your testimony cleared him of charges?"

"Of course I remember. It was my bloody story."

"Then you remember the father who swore revenge?"

Wentworth's growl caught in his throat. "What are you getting at? Do you really think Teddy Price's father, after all this time, is out for revenge?"

"I don't think he had a choice. He couldn't touch Felix while Felix was in prison, and his plan would only work if you could then be framed for the murder."

"But who do you think this man is? Don't you think I would have recognized him? I sat in a courtroom across from the man for weeks."

"But someone could change their looks. Plastic surgery. Even changing hairstyle and facial hair. Besides, it's been years." Eliza's phone rang. She blinked at the unknown number, but as her thumb hovered over the hang up button, her gut told her to answer. "Hello?"

"Oh, Miss Darcy, it's me, Amanda. Amanda Fielding. I'm so glad you answered. I tried texting you, but when I got no response, I thought I'd ring you instead. I, ah, remembered that thing I couldn't put my finger on at Nana's party."

"And what was it?" Eliza's skin prickled.

"It was a laugh. His laugh."

The doorbell rang. "Who is it now? Another housewarming present?" Wentworth grumbled and waved Eliza back down after she rose to her feet. "Sit. At least give me the impression that I'm still in charge in my own home." Wentworth stalked from the room, his robe billowing behind him.

Eliza ignored the prima donna inspector. "Amanda, I don't understand. Whose laugh and why—"

Amanda's words spewed out so fast, Eliza barely caught them all. "The timing. It was all off. I mean, how could he have been in the pub area when he said he was when I heard his laugh from the hallway?"

"Whose laugh?" Eliza wished she could smash her hand through the phone and shake the girl into speaking.

Seconds later, Wentworth returned, Dr. Malcolm Hamilton's left arm tucked up and around Wentworth's left shoulder and his right hand holding a gun to Wentworth's temple.

"Hello, Eliza. Looks like you're in the wrong place at the wrong time." He stared at the phone pressed to her ear. "Another word, even a whispered whisper, and I will put a bullet in this man's brain. Do you understand?"

Eliza's heart slid to her toes, and an oily sensation swirled in her gut. She pretended to hit the hang up button and slipped her phone onto the coffee table. "Hello, Mr. Price."

MALCOLM Hamilton nudged Wentworth forward. "Looks like our American friend here is not as dumb as she looks."

Eliza bit back a retort when Wentworth narrowed his eyes at her, and she sat for a few seconds, trying to formulate words that wouldn't come out as a scream or a string of nonsense. She gave up and concentrated on keeping her shaking to a bare minimum.

"Sit." Malcolm pushed Wentworth into a matching leather chair next to Eliza, and instead of training his gun on Wentworth, he pointed it at Eliza's chest.

Her body went cold, and stupid hot tears pricked the backs of her eyes. She bit her inner cheek until she tasted blood. There was no way she would let Malcolm—or whatever his real name was—see her cry.

Wentworth's fingers made small divots in his chair's armrest, but his voice was smooth and silky. "You're Teddy Price's father?"

"Don't." Spittle flew from Malcolm's mouth, and he jerked his gun at Wentworth. "Don't let my precious boy's name ever cross your lips again."

Wentworth slowly put his hands in the air. "I'm sorry about your boy. I really am. As a father myself, I can imagine your pain, and I want nothing to do with it."

"You know nothing of pain. What do you know about it?" Malcolm's voice cracked, but the gun trained on Wentworth didn't so much as vibrate. "You. You let a murderer, a child murderer, the man who slaughtered my boy go free."

Wentworth's shoulders drooped. "When your son was killed, Felix Payne and I were too busy trying not to drown in a car that we had stolen."

Malcolm's gun twitched. "That's not what you said twenty-five years ago."

"You're right." Wentworth dipped his head and studied the floor. "I was too afraid of losing my job, so I didn't tell the whole story."

"If you were lying then, how do I know you're not lying now?"

Wentworth opened his mouth but snapped it shut again.

"Malcolm?" Eliza tried not to jerk when he turned his gaze and gun on her. "What's your name?"

"What's it to you? You're not going to need to know it here in a few minutes anyway."

Another wave of icy sensation overtook her, and she involuntarily shivered. "You'll never get away with it. You know that, right? If you shoot us—"

"Shoot you?" Malcolm's mirthless laugh activated Eliza's goose bumps. He waved his gun at Wentworth. "No, he's going to kill you, and then he will sadly take his own life." His left hand slipped into his pocket, and he took out a syringe. "I only brought enough for one man, but as this dose is enough to kill a large horse, I think you two can share, don't you think?"

For the first time, Eliza noticed Malcolm's latex-gloved hands and wondered how long it would take for Amanda to know that something was wrong. But even if the girl could overhear the conversation, she had no idea where Eliza was. Nausea roiled in her stomach, and she swallowed against the rising bile. "People will have seen you drive up."

"Will they?" He trained his gun on her chest again when she opened her mouth. "Now, shut up." Keeping his eye on her, he laid the syringe on the floor and nudged it gently with the toe of his boot. "Pick it up, Wentworth."

When Wentworth hesitated, Malcolm squeezed the trigger.

"No!" Wentworth roared.

Malcolm sneered. "Lucky for you and Miss America here, double-action triggers have some wiggle room for errors in judgment." He glanced at the syringe on the floor. "Pick it up. There's a good man. Now, put it to her neck, under her ear."

Wentworth hissed a swear word and with a shaking hand brought the needle close to Eliza's skin.

"Put the needle to her skin." When Wentworth failed to follow his directions, Malcolm snarled. "That needle touches her skin, or I'll put a bullet through her forehead. Do you understand me?"

"I'm so sorry, Eliza," Wentworth whispered.

She flinched as the needle pricked her skin. Waves of gray shimmered in her peripheral vision. *Do not pass out, Eliza. I forbid you to pass out.* "May I ask what's in it?" Eliza croaked.

"Does it matter?"

"Yes, actually, it does." But it didn't, really. All that mattered was buying time. Faces flashed through her mind. Her parents, Uncle Fitzwilliam, Heath, Joy, Great-Aunt Iris, Great- Uncle William, Belle. Anger flashed through her, and she squeezed her hands, but instead of squeezing against her own flesh, they squeezed the tin of Mrs. Bankcroft's cookies. Clearing her throat, she tried to catch Wentworth's gaze. The second their eyes met, she flicked her gaze to her lap and then concentrated on Malcolm. "I want to know if it will be painful."

"I don't believe death by hemlock is as noble as Socrates's biographer wanted us to believe."

Eliza fought the shiver building inside her. She certainly did not need to invite the needle pressing on her skin into her jugular vein. "It's sad that I won't have a chance to sample Mrs. Bankcroft's cookies."

Malcolm blinked. "What?"

"Oh, I'm sorry. Did I say cookies? I meant to say biscuits." She whipped the tin like a Frisbee at Malcolm's face.

He flung his hands up, and his grip on his gun loosened. Wentworth, with a growl of rage, launched himself off the chair, tackled Malcolm to the ground, flipped him on his stomach, and trained Malcolm's gun at his back. "Don't move." Without looking at Eliza, Wentworth asked, "Eliza, in the pantry off the kitchen is my toolbox. Inside my toolbox are zip ties. Can you bring them here?" The calmness in his voice soothed her frayed nerves, and her shaky legs took her successfully to the kitchen and back with the zip ties.

"Now, here. Take this." He planted his left hand firmly in the middle of Malcolm's back and handed her the gun. "And if he moves, shoot him."

Malcolm snarled. "You think she would actually shoot me? Probably doesn't even know how to hold one." He twisted his head to sneer at her.

Memories of her grandparents' farm and target practicing with her grandfather calmed Eliza's racing mind. The weight of the handgun grounded her, and she placed her right index finger along the trigger guard and supported her right hand with her left. She smiled at Malcolm's widening eyes. "Not used to seeing a girl with a handgun, I see. Might I remind you that I'm not just an American girl. I'm a Midwest, South Dakota girl who has, once or twice, shot a handgun. Now, shut up and don't move."

Malcolm's face drained of color, and he plopped his head on the floor and sobbed uncontrollably, repeating his son's name over and over. Within seconds, Wentworth had zip-tied Malcolm's hands and ankles, slipped the gun from Eliza's grasp, and set it on the coffee table far from Malcolm.

Wentworth's living room shimmered around Eliza, and her vision sparkled. Pointing a gun at tin cans and targets with her grandfather had been one thing. Pointing it at a human being was totally different. "I think I'm going to be sick," Eliza hissed through clenched teeth.

"Here." Wentworth guided her to a chair as far from Malcolm as possible. "Sit and put your head between your knees until it passes."

Through the buzzing in her ears, she heard the deep rumble of Wentworth's voice calling the police and Malcolm's low-pitched keening for his long-dead son.

Chapter Twenty
To Be or Not to Be Mistress of Pemberley

The tear drops wetting the pages as I write are tears of happiness. There was a reason for my exhaustion and irritability. I am with child, and I quiver with anticipation as I wait for Darcy to return. It appears that Bath does have health benefits far beyond the "miraculous" waters. Perhaps Darcy and I should return every year. My heart is near bursting with happiness, and I never thought I could feel this content. My uncle Gardener once said before making Darcy's acquaintance that the mistress of Pemberley would have to put up with a great deal, and I with my misplaced pride and prejudice had agreed with him. Little did I know then that to be mistress of Pemberley is an honor and being Darcy's wife is a joy incomprehensible, and one I truly do not deserve. Oh, I hear his footsteps. I must go.

Lizzy Bennet Darcy

Pemberley 1814

Eliza screened herself behind sheer curtains embroidered with tulips and looked out her bedroom window at the bird-watchers, twittering about something in the flower garden. What they noticed that had their arms flailing and their mouths moving excitedly, she couldn't tell. Mrs. Bankcroft's predictions of mayhem with the incoming "twitchers" had yet to come to pass, and other than being overly excited about birds, they seemed a normal bunch. Although, with the pandemonium of the past two weeks all culminating the day before with the arrest of Oliver Wright for the murder of Timothy and the arrest of Stephen Price for the murder of Felix Payne, Eliza welcomed the somewhat odd but harmless bird lovers.

Eliza's phone pinged, and after reading the text from Belle, she grinned until her cheeks hurt. Her best friend was actually coming to Pemberley over the upcoming New Year. Plans tripped through her mind, and she grabbed Caesar from the tulip-bespattered bedspread and danced about her room.

"Can you believe it, Caesar? Belle's coming here."

Caesar peered at her with his slitted gaze and growled.

"That's right. You hate her. Well, you can spend the entire time in the kitchen with Mrs. B, then."

At the mention of the cook's name, Caesar wrestled himself from her arms and sashayed from the room as Heath entered it.

"Why, you look cheerful." Heath pulled her in for a kiss.

Eliza shoved her phone in his face. "See?"

He pushed the screen away so he wasn't cross-eyed. "Ah, I get to meet the infamous Belle." His face crumpled. "With her and Joy under one roof, I might take a vacation. Care to join me?" He cuddled her to his chest and swirled curlicues up and down her spine. "Just imagine Tahiti, white sands, our bare toes... and other bits... dipping in the warm aquamarine waters."

Before he could woo her into abandoning her friend to only Joy, Eliza broke free and smacked him lightly on his chest. "You are incorrigible."

"Some would say that's what they like most about me."

Eliza toyed with the V-cut of his new mint-green cashmere sweater. "I like your new sweaters."

He snatched her hand and kept it from more exploratory measures. "You drive me insane, do you know that?"

She bit her lip and smiled wickedly at him. "Do I?"

He crushed her lips in a kiss that left her feeling weightless, and after he ended with a nibble to her bottom lip, he cupped her cheek. "After I heard about your... adventure... I couldn't breathe. The thought of losing you nearly sent me to my knees." He rested his forehead against hers and closed his eyes. "You have bewitched me, Eliza Jane Darcy, body and soul, and I don't know what to do with that emotion."

Eliza swallowed around the lump in her throat. Her chest tightened, and she struggled to gain a breath. "Looks like we're in the same boat." She whispered a kiss across his cheek. "I love you."

"I love you more." He dipped his head to her neck.

Eliza squealed and sprinted from the room before Heath could catch her in another embrace and arrived breathless and panting in the drawing room doorway.

"Well, well." Great-Aunt Iris tutted. "Look who's decided to join us." Her eyes twinkled, and she smiled at Eliza with a cat-that-got-in-the-cream grin.

Eliza cleared her throat, went to the sideboard for Mrs. Bankcroft's promised negus, and slid a glance at Heath, who sat as innocent as could be on a couch made for two. He patted the cushion next to him, and she settled into his side.

Firelight from the drawing room's fireplace flickered off the faces of everyone Eliza held near and dear, including Uncle Fitzwilliam, who had arrived not long after dinner. She sipped at the negus Mrs. Bankcroft had made for the bird-watchers, who had finally trekked from her garden and off into the darkness on the hunt to spot long-eared owls. The hot mulled wine warmed her from the inside out, and she whipped off the blanket she'd cocooned herself in.

Uncle Fitzwilliam's muttonchops quivered with suppressed laughter. "So, Eliza, when were you going to tell me about you sticking your nose in police business... again?"

Eliza jabbed her elbow into Heath's ribs when he snickered. "How did you find out?"

"A little birdie told me."

Eliza pinned said little birdie with a glare.

Wentworth, looking rather dapper in a baby-blue cable-knit sweater and khakis, saluted her with his glass of brandy. "Don't look at me." He cut his gaze to the fluffy-white-haired old lady placidly knitting in the corner next to her snoring husband.

"I thought you said you could keep a secret," Eliza scolded.

"Oops, did I let one slip again?" Her smile was anything but innocent.

"I thought you told me once that your entire sleuthing gang could be trusted." Wentworth grinned.

"There's always *that* one, though," Heath whispered.

"Young man, is there something you would like to say out loud?" Great-Aunt Iris pointed a knitting needle at him.

"No, ma'am, I was saying to your lovely niece here how—"

"Yes, yes, I'm sure you'll have something poetic to wax on about, but really, Eliza, do make your young man behave and tell us all about the shoot-out at DCI Wentworth's house."

"It wasn't a shoot-out, Aunt."

"Well, that's what I told Tabitha Fielding. She will be so disappointed."

"And so will the whole village." Joy grinned. "Come on, you two." She gestured with her glass of negus to Wentworth and Eliza. "Do tell of this 'shoot-out.'"

After several minutes of dramatic retelling, peppered with corrections and redirections from Wentworth, Eliza folded her hands in her lap. "And that, my friends, is how it all went down."

"So, Dr. Malcolm Hamilton is really Stephen Price, a heartbroken father, who spent nearly three decades nursing his hatred for you and Felix?" Joy perched on the edge of a chaise lounge and clasped her glass.

"So it would seem." Wentworth heaved a sigh. "I had forgotten that Stephen was a medical student at the time of his son's death. The rest, changing one's name and identity and looks, especially after twenty-five years, isn't too difficult if you know the right people. Add to that the fact that no one from Lambton knew him or about the death of Teddy Price twenty-five years ago."

"And he orchestrated it all by himself? Oliver and Timothy were never involved?" Heath asked.

"Not as far as we can tell. Oliver and Timothy had their own agenda, but that was thwarted by Stephen's plans." Wentworth scrubbed his face. "Stephen orchestrated my 'free' room, grabbed the DNA-riddled glasses, poisoned Felix, and after Felix was dead, set up the room, switched out the door handles, planted hemlock in my room, and then proceeded to act shocked when he was alerted to Felix's death by that poor waitress."

"Who remembered his laugh echoing down the hallway before she found Felix dead."

"A little too late." Wentworth's lips twitched.

"Yes, but her testimony that he didn't go up to the rooms until she started screaming will certainly not help his case."

"Wow." Joy nestled in the chaise. "That takes some planning and dedication."

"And he had the time to ensure that every i was dotted and t was crossed," Eliza said.

"It was nearly the perfect crime. If it weren't for Eliza here finding out Kapoor's dirty little secret and making Cronk play her hand earlier than she probably would have, and making the connection to Teddy Price's father, I'd be under arrest for murder, and the real murderer would be walking free."

Uncle Fitzwilliam beamed at her. "Perhaps, Eliza, you have missed your calling."

Eliza took in the scene around her, grateful for everything from Great-Aunt Iris's incessant knitting to her great-uncle's constant snoring to Joy's adventurous spirit to Uncle Fitzwilliam's heartwarming smile and—her heart stuttered in her chest when her gaze locked with her beloved's—Heath's intoxicating passion and dedication to her. She knew where she belonged. Like Elizabeth Darcy, who had fought for her family and her people, Eliza planned to do the same for as long as she had breath.

"No, Uncle Fitzwilliam. I know my calling." She saluted the room. "To be mistress of Pemberley, of course."

Author Notes

While I strive to keep the original storylines of Jane Austen's beloved characters and their stories as authentic as possible, I had to work some author magic integrating Austen's plot for *Persuasion* into my modern retelling. While we as modern-day readers would expect—nay, demand—Sir Walter Elliot show his love and appreciation for Anne by transferring the baronetcy and Kellynch Hall to her, thusly making Anne a baronetess, this does not happen. (Baronetcies are hereditary titles, not peerage titles, and females could be holders of this title in their own right.) I'm afraid that as Austen left it—spoiler alert—the dastardly William Elliot eventually becomes the next baronet with the scheming Mrs. Clay as the next Lady Elliot. However, in my Austen universe and to make my storyline fit Miss Austen's, I had to take certain liberties. And quite honestly, I'm not even a bit sorry for granting Anne Elliot the recognition her father should have given her and stripping the rakish William Elliot of what he never deserved in the first place.

Acknowledgments

To Jane Austen: I formally apologize for messing with your beautifully drawn-out plot for *Persuasion*, but I hope you understand that I had to make changes so my plot could plot!

To my family: Thank you for feeding my Austen addiction and just a quick reminder: any and all Austen paraphernalia is appropriate for all birthdays, Christmases, Groundhog Days (if you're ever inclined to give a gift to celebrate a rodent seeing its shadow), Valentine's Days (to show me you really love me), and all other bank holidays.

To my editors: Rashida B. and Angela M., thank you for making my manuscript shine like a brand-new penny!

To my publisher: Thank you for your continued support of my writing dream.

About the Author

Jessica Berg, a child of the Dakotas and the prairie, grew up amongst hard-working men and women and learned at an early age to "put some effort into it." Following that wise adage, she has put effort into teaching high school English for over a decade, being a mother to four children (she finds herself surprised at this number, too), basking in the love of her husband of more than fifteen years and losing herself in the imaginary worlds she creates.

Read more at https://www.jessicabergbooks.com.

About the Publisher

Dear Reader,

We hope you enjoyed this book. Please consider leaving a review on your favorite book site.

Visit https://RedAdeptPublishing.com to see our entire catalogue.

Check out our app for short stories, articles, and interviews. You'll also be notified of future releases and special sales.